MOTHER
faker

Playlist

Sparks Fly (Taylor's Version) - Taylor Swift
Good As Hell - Lizzo
Every Little Thing She Does is Magic- Sleeping At Last
R U Mine? - Arctic Monkeys
Nobody Gets Me - SZA
2 Be Loved (Am I Ready) - Lizzo
Solid Ground - Vance Joy
Firework - Katy Perry
Fearless (Taylor's Version) - Taylor Swift
Into You - Ariana Grande
Electric Love - BØRNS
*What Makes You Beautiful - (One Direction)
*Beckett would sing this every day for Liv

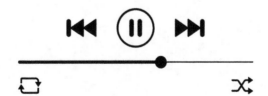

Dedication

To every woman who ever said, wouldn't it be fun to live together and raise our kids without a man. This ducking book is for you.

P.S. There were no ducks hurt in the writing of this book. The same can not be said about broody billionaires.

CONTENTS

1. Liv	1
2. Liv	5
3. Beckett	13
4. Liv	20
5. Liv	32
6. Beckett	42
7. Liv	46
8. Beckett	53
9. Liv	64
10. Beckett	69
11. Liv	78
12. Liv	83
13. Beckett	94
14. Liv	104
15. Beckett	116
16. Liv	121
17. Liv	130
18. Beckett	136
19. Liv	142
20. Beckett	148
21. Liv	155
22. Beckett	161
23. Liv	166
24. Beckett	171
25. Liv	179
26. Beckett	187
27. Liv	194
28. Beckett	203
29. Liv	211
30. Liv	219
31. Beckett	232
32. Beckett	241
33. Liv	249
34. Liv	257

35. Beckett   266
36. Liv   277
37. Beckett   288
38. Liv   297
    Epilogue   307

    Mother Maker Sneak Peek   319
    Acknowledgments   327
    Also by Brittanee Nicole   329

Liv

1

"You ou want me to open the stadium up to a bunch of preschoolers?" my boss grits out, his forehead wrinkling and his green eyes boring into me. "They'll probably piss on the field."

God. The man could be so dense.

I place my hands on my knee and stare down Beckett Langfield. "First of all, they aren't dogs. And statements like that are exactly why the media says you don't like kids."

"I like kids," he says matter-of-factly, like the sky is blue and the grass is green.

Internally, I roll my eyes at my clueless boss. Beckett Langfield likes three things: his steaks rare, his women bare, and the billions he's got in the bank earning interest. Beckett wouldn't know what to do around a child, let alone convince anyone he likes them.

Laughing in his face wouldn't be my best tactic here. Not with a man like Beckett. So I placate him and spin it, as the head of PR for the Boston Revs so often has to do.

"This isn't about what you do or don't like," I start, lying through my teeth. "This is about giving the appearance of what you like. And right now, it *appears* that you don't like kids. We need to change that."

"All because I said no to *one* charity," he grumbles, gripping the edge of his seat on either side of his legs so tight his knuckles are white.

"It was *St. Jude*, and it was the *way* you said it that caused the problem."

"The stadium is booked that night."

This time I can't stop my eye roll. "Yes, for a swimsuit edition event. You picked pinup models over preschoolers."

"I never used those words. That's what the media ran with," he defends, his frown turning into a scowl. "I didn't even know St. Jude was the organization reaching out to book the event. All I told Wendy was to let them know we were booked."

With a shrug, I lean forward. "Wendy ran her mouth, so now the story is that you don't like kids."

"But I *do* like kids," he growls as the limo we're traveling in jolts and the tires screech to a stop. Without a seat belt to hold me in place, I go tumbling forward, straight into my boss's lap.

"Fuck," he groans above me.

Lifting my head, I peruse the length of him, realizing then that I literally headbutted him in the crotch. As in, my head is currently touching my boss's dick.

"Oh my God," I cry, trying to right myself. Of course, in my attempts to do that, my hands land on his thighs, and then the car jolts forward again, this time causing me to punch him in the balls.

"What the hell, Liv?" he howls, pulling his knees together to protect his junk.

But I'm still too close, so as he squeezes his legs together, my head ends up trapped between his thighs, causing me to lose my balance and fall forward again.

The door to the limo swings open, and Charlie, our driver, leans in. "Mr. Langfield, I'm so sorry—"

I try to turn my head, but I'm literally stuck in a death grip between Beckett's thighs. Above me, he's still groaning in pain, unaware that we have company.

"Oh, shit!" Charlie shouts. His eyes bulge when he catches sight of me. "Um, we hit a dog, um... I'm sorry to interrupt, but..."

I elbow my way out from between my boss's legs and grab for a seat belt to right myself. "For God's sake, Charlie, you aren't interrupting anything. I just fell down when you hit the brakes."

Charlie's red face sags in relief, but we both turn when Beckett cries out again in pain.

"I need to go to a hospital."

With a huff, I scoot down the seat and slide out of the car. "You do not," I call back to him. "Men are such babies." Standing straight on the sidewalk, I pull my skirt down and adjust my top. I'm sure my hair—which is normally in a bun on the top of my head—has been destroyed by Beckett's thigh burn. Is that a thing? I think it just might be. I rub my neck where he had me in his vise grip and wait for the big baby to get out of the car.

"You killed my dog!" a little boy shouts at Charlie.

My stomach drops, and I can't help but groan at how bad this is.

I love kids. And dogs. I'm not trying to be insensitive, but why couldn't this have happened to someone else? I close my eyes and breathe in for four, then out for four, preparing myself to approach the bereaved child and his mother.

The little boy can't be older than eight. He's about the same size as my Winnie. She's dramatic, and I expect this kid will be too.

"I'm so sorry," I say, striding over to the mother.

Her lower lip is trembling and her face is streaked with tears.

She looks like she's absolutely beside herself. "Were either of you hurt?"

The kid points at Charlie, who's still standing by the back passenger door. "He killed my dog!"

Poor Charlie looks gutted, his face ashen like he might collapse at any second. Beckett, of course, is still MIA. I swear, if that man comes out here howling about his broken penis, I'm going to scream.

"Someone call the cops!" the kid wails. "He killed my dog!"

I hold up my phone, indicating to his mother that I'll make the call. A report will have to be filed, but hopefully I can talk her into accepting a nice settlement so we can keep this out of the press. Offering that kind of incentive right now, though, won't calm her child.

As I turn around to make the phone call, Beckett finally appears. I motion for him to smooth things over—something he's surprisingly good at when it comes to women. He can use his absurdly good looks to win the mother over, and then she can calm her child down.

As I talk to the dispatcher, though, the voices behind me get louder. Spinning on the sidewalk to assess the situation, I find the kid pointing an accusatory finger at Beckett. "Aren't you the kid hater?"

Oh no.

Without hesitation, he winds up and kicks Beckett in the shin. At that exact moment, the dog springs to life, scaring the living hell out of all of us and causing Beckett to fall forward. Naturally, he lands on top of the kid, and half a second later, I hear the click of a camera.

Oh, hell, I really hate my job.

Liv

2

"Hunnys, I'm home," I shout as I open the door to our brownstone. I'm still shaking my head at the sight that greets me every time I make my way up the front walk. An Easter Bunny, a reindeer, and a few overgrown plants decorate the lawn. Christmas lights surround the front window, and the sign in the window wishes all who pass a Happy *Valen* Day. The *tine's* has fallen off, and none of us has bothered to tape it back up. The place is a bit of a disaster, but it's home.

I toe off my shoes and peek past the dark foyer. It's eerily silent. "Dylan?" I sing, nerves fluttering in my belly.

Dylan doesn't know how to be quiet, so clearly, something is wrong. Did the kids tie her up? Is she gagged and bound somewhere? I wouldn't put it past the twins.

Since we moved in together two months ago, Dylan has taken over after-school care for all the children and full-time care for Adeline and Finn. She's been a godsend since my ex-husband moved on from the nanny. Kendall, although having a propensity to sleep with Drake, was really good with children. Now that the affair is over, though, she's no longer around to help with the kids.

While on vacation a few months ago, I admitted to my best friends that my life wasn't nearly as perfect as I led everyone to believe, and Shayla and Delia responded by admitting that they were also drowning. Dylan came to the rescue with a genius idea. She suggested we move into the brownstone Delia's great aunt had left to her and raise our kids together *Fuller House–*style. There are seven kids between us, so it's been quite the learning curve.

As I pad across the raw plywood floor down the hall toward the kitchen, where I usually find Dylan this time of day, I have to duck a little to dodge the particles falling from the ceiling. *The house is settling*, Delia tells us almost nightly. Yeah, settling right into our soup bowls.

She downplayed just how much work the brownstone would require. Don't get me wrong, I'm grateful to be living with my besties, but this house has significant issues, and I'm not sure any of us has the funds to deal with it properly.

That's a problem for another day, though. Right now, I need to find my kids.

And Dylan.

Where the hell is she?

"Dylan? Finn? Winnie?" I shout.

My youngest daughter's faint babbling drifts downstairs. Is she just waking up from a nap? I check the clock on the ancient white stove. It's so old, it actually flips over to show the time, and it makes a ticking noise that some would find aggravating. At this point, we're all used to it.

It's 6:05 p.m. Adeline is in her crib, and everyone else is missing. What the hell is going on in here?

Heaving out a breath, I trudge up the narrow staircase, being sure to step on the far left side of the second to last step. If hit just right, the loose board will tip up and smack your ankle. Hurts like hell, but apparently, not enough for Delia to agree to temporarily replacing it with a piece of plywood.

We need to preserve the house's character and integrity, she says.

Deep breath in, two, three, four. Out, two, three, four.

It'll all be fine.

After successfully avoiding the step, I reach the landing and hustle to the end of the hall. Since Adeline sleeps in my room, the girls insisted I take the master. Attached to one side of my room is a second, smaller room. It's a bit of a disaster, but eventually, I intend to turn it into a nursery.

One day.

If I ever have time.

The only access point to the nursey is through the closet, unfortunately, but it does have a pretty circular window that lets in the perfect amount of light.

Finn and Winnie each have their own rooms near mine. Though Finn idolizes Dylan's fifteen-year-old son, Liam, and begged to bunk with him, his room is two floors below mine, so that was a no. I'd prefer to keep my four-year-old close, despite what a big boy he claims to be.

Pretty sure Liam approved that decision. He shows little interest in anyone in the house, which is why I'm surprised when I peek into my room and find him leaning over the railing of her crib.

"And then he told me if I didn't give him the five bucks, he'd beat the—"

I clear my throat loudly, thankfully cutting him off before his story gets too mature for my toddler.

Liam spins, his face turning red. I'm not sure if it's because I caught him about to say a bad word to my two-year-old or because I caught him talking to her, period.

"Hi, Aunt Liv," he says quietly, his attention darting everywhere but at me.

Smiling at my baby girl, I shuffle into the room. At the sight of me, she holds her arms up, scrunching her hands open and closed. She's getting so big. Despite the exhaustion I feel in every inch of my body, I can't help but scoop her into my arms and take a second to soak in her goodness. One hit can hold me over for hours most days.

That's all we really get as mothers. Moments. We spend the vast majority of our waking hours running or yelling or scrambling or failing. But these few seconds of quiet after work, when it's just Adeline and me, make me feel like maybe I'm not doing such a terrible job after all.

Over Addie's head, I stare down Liam, who's backed up from the crib. "Where's your mom?"

He gives me one of his devilish smirks, and immediately, I know my best friend is up to one of her crazy schemes.

"Phil didn't see his shadow," he says with a shrug.

"Phil who?"

"Come on, Liv, get with it. Punxsutawney Phil," Liam goads.

Squinting, I clarify. "Punxsutawney Phil didn't see his shadow almost two months ago, and somehow that means your mother is missing today?"

Liam's goal in life these days is getting one over on us. I'm not 100 percent sure he doesn't have Dylan and all the kids tied up in the basement right now.

Liam smirks again, stuffing his hands into the pockets of his jeans. "She's worried about the vegetables."

"What vegetables?" I set Adeline on her feet and heave out a sigh. "We don't even *have* vegetables."

"Right. Because Phil didn't see his shadow." His tone is so serious. Like he thinks that explanation makes perfect sense.

Squeezing my eyes shut, I breathe in for four and out for four. When I look at Liam again, he's studying me with that aloof expression he wears so often. Mouth pressed in a flat line, eyes dull and uninterested. I swear, the kid is constantly taunting all of us, and none of us are smart enough to keep up.

Still at a loss, I try again. "To be clear, the groundhog, who normally crawls out of a hole in Philadelphia in February, didn't see his shadow? And because of that, almost two months later, your mother and my children are missing? Because she's worried about *vegetables*?"

Liam shrugs. "Now you've got it." He pets the top of Adeline's head and winks at her. Then he saunters out of the room, pulling the headphones he constantly wears around his neck over his ears and tuning the rest of the world out.

"Guess he's done with us," I mutter to my daughter. "Come on, Addie. Let's go see if we can find our family." I hoist her up on my hip and continue my search.

WITH NO LUCK in the rest of the house, I head to the backyard—if we can even call it that. Although this home sits on one of the largest lots in the neighborhood, this is Boston we're talking about. The yard is nothing more than a patch of grass bordered by a wooden fence that's missing more slats than it has.

Groaning—because our list of projects is at least a mile long, yet Delia has repeatedly rejected our suggestions for each and every one—I step through the back door. It creaks on its hinges as I step over the threshold, sending a shudder working through me at the sound. Once I'm outside, I finally spot several tiny bodies crowded in a circle. Each child is kneeling with their head down, swaying back and forth.

What in the hell?

Dylan's auburn hair falls in a curtain around her face, blocking my view of her expression. But she, too, is swaying. She's also chanting words I can't quite decipher. She rolls her body as if she's coming up from child's pose, and her green eyes lock on mine. A bright smile crosses her face, and she jumps up and dusts off her jeans. The action does little good, because the mess coating the fabric isn't dirt. It's mud. And she's covered in it.

Frowning, I look from her to the ground, then back again. "What are you guys doing?"

Dylan dips her chin, looking at the kids, who are all still swaying and humming, then slumps a bit. "The universe is mad at us."

"The universe is what?"

I don't know why I'm even asking the question. Dylan has a thing about the universe. She's been going on about it since she got knocked up in college. Most people would blame a lack of contraceptives for her predicament, but not Dylan. She said the universe sent Liam to her, and she barely batted an eye at the dramatic change in her life.

Okay, I'm probably rewriting history a bit. The first year or two after Liam was born were a challenge for her, to say the least, but in general, Dylan doesn't let much bother her.

I envy that ability more than I'd ever put into words.

Dylan wanders over, tickling Adeline when she reaches us. "The universe is mad."

"Probably because of all the meat we're eating," Shayla calls as the door creaks open again. She's dressed in workout gear, which means she probably just finished up a session with a client. Shayla is a physical therapist and as fit as they come. Where Dylan is naturally thin, Shayla is toned and drop-dead gorgeous.

What I'd do to have her body.

As long as it didn't include giving up Diet Coke or working out for hours a day. I suppose that means that, in reality, I wouldn't do a whole heck of a lot to have her body.

Dylan shakes her head and tugs her rose quartz pendant back and forth along its chain. "No, that's not it."

Shayla beelines it for her son, Kai, ignoring us completely.

"What are you doing outside without a coat? You'll catch a cold."

"The fresh air is good for him, Shay," Dylan says softly.

We try not to step on each other's toes, and obviously, we all have different parenting styles, but Shayla lives with a heightened sense of anxiety. Though it's not without good reason. She lost her husband to cancer a few years ago, and Kai is all she has left. I can't imagine the thoughts that must run through her head at night. I'd never sleep.

Shayla turns to Dylan with a frown, probably preparing to lecture her about why Kai needs a jacket, but she lets her shoulders sag and blows out a breath instead when she takes in Dylan's soft expression.

"I suppose you're right." She turns to her son. "Let's go in, though. It's getting dark now, so the chill really is going to hit you soon."

Kai shoots Dylan an appreciative nod and takes off for the back door.

"And don't run!" Shayla shouts after him.

I squeeze her arm as she approaches, and she leans her head against my shoulder. Still propped on my hip, Adeline pats Shayla's dark hair with her pudgy hand. In response, Shayla leans in subtly and inhales that baby scent.

I'm telling ya, it's like a drug.

"Oh my gosh, I'm starving. Please tell me dinner will be ready soon," Delia says, peeking into the backyard without batting an eye at the scene before her. She's wearing a suit, and her blond hair is done up in her signature ponytail. She looks like a runway model for office wear.

"If you mean will dinner be delivered soon, then yes, dinner is soon," Dylan says with a smile.

Pretty sure Dylan will tell us that this is also the universe's doing. Apparently, the universe wants us to eat pizza at least once a week.

"Perfect," Delia says as she pulls the tie from her hair and shakes her head. "Book club after dinner?"

I try to hide my groan, but it slips out. Delia doesn't notice, but Shayla and Dylan shoot me commiserating smiles. This week's book was an autobiography. Though last week's wasn't fiction either, at least it was about how to be one with our bad-ass selves. Not that I had time to read either of them.

Shayla loops her arm around me and leads me inside the house. "Life may not be perfect, but at least we're all together."

Beckett

3

Across the table, my father scowls at one article after another as they pop up on his phone.

"You screamed, 'I hate kids'?"

Pressing my tongue to the roof of my mouth, I pull in a breath and force myself to remain cool. "I said I *don't* hate kids; *he* said I hate kids."

"The seven-year-old you then tackled to the ground?" he snaps.

"He kicked me—"

"So you tackled him?" My father glares at me over his phone screen. "What the hell? He's a child, Beckett!"

"Dad, I—"

He doesn't let me get a word in, though. With a shake of his head, he stands, slips his phone into his pocket, and points at me. "Fix this. The grumbles about your dislike of children were bad enough. Now we've got season ticket holders boycotting and sponsors threatening to pull their accounts."

Disappointment radiates off him as he glowers down at me. I don't dare argue that it's all fucking bullshit. That I never said a word about disliking kids. That I didn't tackle the seven-year-old brat. I actually do like kids... when they aren't assholes, at least. And for the record, I'm pretty sure that one was.

Sighing, I accept my father's anger. "I'll fix it." Even at forty-two, I hate disappointing the man. What I hate more, though, is that he still has so much control over my life. Every time I turn around, he's dangling the baseball team over my head like a damn carrot I'll never actually get to eat.

Baseball has been my life for as long as I can remember. As the firstborn, I had my pick of sports since our family dabbles in almost all of them, but my mother swears I came out of her womb swinging a bat.

"Call that matchmaker, Grace Kensington. She's the one your brother used, isn't she? Have her set you up with a couple of single mothers. Show the media that you don't mind them. Maybe get engaged to one and really prove them wrong."

Stomach dropping, I gape at my father. "Get engaged?" He must be joking.

Of course my father doesn't actually want me to go and live out a damn happily ever after. His only concern is our family image. Fuck.

"Boston Children's Hospital has already called. They're threatening to cancel our partnership. If we're not careful, the Hansons will pull their whiskey from the stadiums and cancel their advertising. That's millions of dollars, Beckett. If you have to date a fucking mother to fix this, you'll do it."

"Fine," I grumble.

"Call Grace Kensington. She'll help you fix this. And get Liv on it. She'll know what to do."

Rubbing my head to ease the headache this entire situation has created, I resign myself to his ridiculous plan.

HOURS LATER, I groan as I study my hand. "Fold." I slam my cards onto the poker table.

My brother Gavin smirks and tosses in four black chips. Our younger brother, Brooks, inspects his cards for another minute before he matches Gavin's bet. Aiden, the youngest of us boys, throws his cards down too, and after one more round, Gavin is scooping up his winnings with a big smile on his face.

"The only one who ever stands a chance is Sienna." Gavin grins, referring to our sister. "Although Beckett normally gives me a run for my money."

Hiding the scowl that wants to creep onto my face, I bring my whiskey to my lips. After a long sip and a deep breath, I pick up a cigar.

When Aiden reaches for one, Gavin growls, "My star center is not going to fucking smoke during the season."

Brooks chuckles in the way only a goalie can. He's double the size of the rest of us. I'm not actually sure where his size comes from. Hours in the gym? Protein shakes? Figure skating? Who the fuck knows.

I slice the head off the cigar and stick it in my mouth. Then I grab the lighter and finally relax as my finger coasts against the switch.

"Those things will kill you," Gavin grumbles as I suck in a breath.

Blatantly ignoring him, I tip my head back and blow out the smoke.

"You're in an even worse mood than normal." Gavin's goading me. He knows precisely why I'm in a fucking mood. "Your dick still sore?" he teases.

Across the table, Brooks snickers and Aiden chokes on his drink. "I thought the kid kicked you in the shin."

I grit my teeth and glare at Gavin. "He did."

"Then what's wrong with your dick?"

Gavin smirks. "Liv headbutted him there."

"Olivia Maxwell," Aiden croons. "She is one hot mom."

Annoyance bubbling up inside me, I glower at him. Fuck, if my brothers are good at one thing, it's pushing buttons.

"Liv really headbutted you in the dick?" Brooks asks, his eyes dancing with amusement.

"That's not why his dick hurts, though," Gavin continues. "His problem is that Liv finally got close to his dick, and now he has blue balls."

I grind my molars and shoot figurative daggers at my asshole brother. "Don't you have anything better to do with your life than worry about my dick?"

Gavin unleashes his signature easy smile. It's annoying as hell. He's a happy guy, always has been. Me? Not so much.

"Someone's gotta worry about it. Little guy isn't getting the action he wants."

Brooks smacks the poker table, sending the cards and chips flying as he chortles. Fucking *chortles*.

Aiden laughs so hard he snorts.

Pushing my chair back with a screech that's barely audible over the ruckus my brothers are making, I stand. "Well, this has been fun."

Gavin reaches for me, gasping for breath between fits of laughter. "No, don't go—I'm sorry." He cups a hand over his mouth like he's trying to rein himself in. It doesn't help. "I won't refer to your dick as 'little guy' again."

"You think I give a fuck what you say?" I run my hand through my hair, then slump back in my chair, my gut churning with not only anger at the circle of idiots around the table, but with genuine fear. "I'm stressed," I grit out. "Dad is threatening to take the team from me if I don't fix this PR disaster."

Gavin tosses his hands up like it's no big deal. "Liv will fix it."

"I don't think she can this time. He wants me to talk to the woman who set up those dates for you."

"Grace James?"

"Ah, I forgot she married Cash," I mutter.

Cash James owns a whiskey company, and his sister married our best friend, Jay Hanson.

Shaking his head, Gavin waves a hand. "Grace is great at what she does, sure. But what does dating have to do with the 'Beckett Langfield hates kids' shit?"

"He doesn't want me to just date." My chest tightens at the thought, and I hang my head. "He wants me to date a woman with kids. Show the world how much I like them. He wants me to get fucking married."

Brooks bellows this time, and Aiden giggles like a fucking schoolgirl. Gavin is oddly silent as he studies me. It makes me nervous. He's never quiet; I'm the quiet one—the moody one, the one people have to wait on to make a comment.

"Well, say something," I demand.

Gavin lets out a low chuckle as he rubs his thumb across his whiskey glass. "I think Dad just might be onto something."

My chest constricts, making it hard to breathe. "Not you too. I don't hate kids. I don't need to change my image. This will all blow over soon."

Humming, Gavin drops his elbows to the table. "Suit yourself. I just figured if you could find a way to help Liv out and also wind up dating her, you'd be game."

My heart lurches at his suggestion. "Liv's married."

"Liv's recently divorced," he replies evenly, his fingers steepled in front of him.

"She's *what*?" My jaw falls slack, and I gape like a goddamn fish.

How come he knows that? And why?

"I never liked that guy," Brooks grumbles.

"How do you even know her husband?" I cock one brow and huff.

All three of my brothers stare me down in response.

"Ex-husband. She's been working for us for over ten years, Beck," Gavin replies.

Waving a hand between Aiden and Brooks, I retort, "These two don't even work in the office."

Brooks arches an unimpressed brow. "For now. But you keep fucking up, and Dad'll hand me your job when I'm ready to retire."

I roll my eyes even as my gut twists. He's not entirely off. If I don't fix this PR nightmare, my father won't hesitate to hand the baseball team over to one of my brothers. The boys can only play hockey for so long. Eventually they'll be ready for desk jobs too.

Aiden holds up his arms. "Don't look at me. I don't want your job. They'll be burying me in my skates."

Gavin holds out a fist for a bump, and Brooks laughs. It's always been like this. We all grew up wearing skates, but baseball was my first love. Though it made me the odd man out with my brothers, it meant one-on-one time with my father, who loves the game as much as I do. So I've always assumed the team would be mine someday. If only he'd let go of the reins. Though with my string of screw-ups lately, that's looking less and less likely.

"Liv's really divorced?" I'm still dumbstruck over this information. The woman spends nearly 70 percent of her time in the office next to mine. We share meals and we travel together. We make one hell of a team when it comes to recruiting players, yet I had no fucking idea her marriage had fallen apart.

Gavin nods. "Yeah, and the ex isn't making it easy. He fought her on the house and won. Last time I spoke with Liv, she was worried about child support and custody. I bet she'd agree to fake date you if you'd connect her with a good family law attorney and help her piss off her ex." He cocks a brow in challenge.

I don't give it a moment's thought. Snuffing my cigar out, I stand and shoot each of my brothers a pointed glare. "I'll get her the best damn attorney money can buy. Her ex-husband will wish he never met her."

Brooks smiles. "That mean you're going to ask her to be your fake girlfriend?"

I don't even hesitate. "No."

Liv

4

Friday morning, I'm late getting to the plane for my trip to Las Vegas with the Boston Revs because Shayla made us all join her for a morning stretch and then Dylan forced us to chant our thanks to the universe. She says it will help with the vegetables. I don't have the bandwidth to even attempt to work out the connection there.

Delia made up for it, though, with a double espresso that could knock the pants off the Pope.

Though I've been in a mad scramble all morning, I can't help but feel just a little lighter than usual because I'm getting a weekend away without the kids.

Even if Beckett is more of a pain in my ass than all seven kids.

"Welcome, Liv. How are you today?" Lindsay, the regular flight attendant, asks as I step onto the private plane.

Smiling at her, I search the plane to see whether Beckett has already arrived. When I catch sight of him, my smile quickly turns into a frown. He's glaring as he slips his suit jacket off his broad shoulders.

I jump and swallow a gasp when Lindsay slaps my back.

Apparently, we're hugging friends now. I lean in, because why not.

With an awkward chuckle, she says, "There's a dryer sheet stuck to your back."

When she pulls it off and holds it up, I swipe it from her hands and slide it into my pocket with a groan. "I swear, I haven't always been this much of a hot mess."

Lindsay gives me a genuine smile. "Momming is hard."

"Amen," I mutter under my breath.

"Can I bring you a coffee?"

Closing my eyes, I nod. "Bless you."

"Want me to add a shot of whiskey?"

I side-eye my boss and consider it. "No, but if you put some in his, then maybe he'll tone his glare down a notch."

She gives me a knowing smirk and sashays into the galley while I head toward Beckett, hiding what a hot mess I really am. Squaring my shoulders, I lift my chin and channel the Liv who has it all together. The one who puts him in his place daily. It's the only way the two of us work.

"Morning, sir," I say as I set my purse on the seat opposite him.

"You're late," he grumps. No *good morning*. No *hi, how are you?*

We're off to a roaring start.

When I don't respond, Beckett takes me in from head to toe. When he gets to my feet, his eyes narrow. "And your shoes don't match."

Dropping my chin, I examine them, and sure enough, one of my black pumps has a pointed toe and the other is rounded.

Shit. This divorce is killing me.

Living with twenty-five kids is killing me.

Okay, seven, but Dylan can sometimes make it feel like there are far more. Her free spirit and easy-going demeanor are a breath of fresh air, but there is absolutely no semblance of order in our house. At all.

"Shit," I mutter. What else can I say? I'm standing across from one of the most eligible bachelors in Boston after delaying our flight to Las Vegas, and I'm not even wearing matching shoes. "I'll get a matching pair out of my luggage when we land, Mr. Langfield." I close my eyes so I don't have to witness his exasperated expression. It'll only amplify my humiliation.

Day in and day out, I maintain the façade of a woman who is completely put together—hair always in a bun and heels sky-high to give me a little height. Always dressed in my signature black to cover my curves. Basically, I'm a walking fraud when I enter the building. Outside the office, I'm nowhere near that put together, but my goal for the last decade has been to never let the man in front of me know that.

I slide into the seat next to him, ignoring the smell that assaults me. Fresh leather and a hint of spearmint. He always smells clean, and it takes every ounce of my willpower not to inhale deeply every time we're in close proximity.

Beckett cranes his neck and glares. "We've worked together for over ten years. Why do you still call me that?"

I peer up at him as I buckle myself in. "Huh?"

"You call Gavin by his first name. You even call my father Preston." He frowns at me for a long moment, as if he's diving deep into his memories.

"You don't pay attention to half the things I say to you, yet you've picked up on my conversations with other people?" The words slip out before I can stop them.

Beckett's lips twitch as if he wants to smile, but his eyes remain hard.

"Sorry, sir. That was rude. Can we start over? I've had a bad morning."

If I didn't know any better, I'd swear Beckett's face softens, and he nods. "Yeah, neither of us has had a great day, it seems."

Beside us, Lindsay appears with a cup of coffee. "Can I get you anything else?"

I shake my head and Beckett does the same.

"We should be airborne in a few minutes. If you need anything, just let me know." She disappears, leaving me with my coffee and swirling thoughts about what could be so bad about Beckett's day.

But when I turn back to ask him, his attention is already fixed on his computer screen, so I let it go.

Hours later, the man is still wearing the same damn scowl, only I have no idea why. We made the trade he was shooting for, and the Revs won their first game of the series. The team didn't just win, they killed it—nine to one. We missed a no-hitter by one run. It was an incredible game, so the man's attitude is unwarranted.

"Liv," Beckett says, studying me as I approach him. His voice raises an octave, as if he's actually happy to see me. Or maybe surprised, like he conjured me himself.

Oh God, he must need something.

"Mr. Langfield." I tip my chin and settle on the stool next to him at the bar. "Great game."

The bartender places a napkin in front of me, and I order a glass of pinot noir. I don't drink much, but I'm hoping the alcohol will help me relax so I can get a good night's rest. We have another game tomorrow, then a late flight home, where I'll be back on child duty—otherwise known as motherhood.

Tonight's my one night of freedom. Only I can't help the giggle that sneaks out, because I've traded in babysitting one set of kids for another. This one just happens to be a needy grown man.

As the bartender sets the wine in front of me, I turn to Beckett, feeling his steely gaze on me. I can only ignore his death stare for so long. "Cheers," I offer, holding up my glass.

His eyes narrow when I tap my glass against his, which is dangling rather precariously from his fingers.

Bloodshot eyes meet mine. It's obvious he's had quite a bit more than that one whiskey.

"What are we toasting?" he slurs.

Is he drunk?

I twist my lips. "A great game?" When his expression remains sour, I add, "Are you okay, Mr. Langfield?" I motion to the bartender and request a water.

Beckett drops his head and groans. "It's gotten worse, Liv."

While I still call him Mr. Langfield, he's always used my nickname.

"What happened now?"

"Sabrina spoke to the press."

"Your ex?" I arrange my expression into one of neutrality, but I've never liked the woman. For some reason, he puts up with her pretty regularly. Their mothers are friends, and they grew up together—there's always a reason for why awful people spend time with one another.

"Who else would I be talking about?" he grumps.

"Okay, how did she make it worse?"

He blinks at me and drags a hand down his face. "She said she doesn't know why it's news that I don't like kids. I've never liked kids. It's why we broke up."

I suck in a breath. "That bitch."

His eyes widen at my response, and he straightens on his barstool. I don't normally curse in front of the people I work for, but honestly, I'm too tired after last night's book club, and I'm frustrated after the shit show that was my morning. I don't have it in me to censor myself.

Delia made us talk about the autobiography until eleven p.m. Full discussions about the woman and whether we thought her childhood affected how she lived her life. It took every ounce of restraint I possessed not to scream that I had no idea why she did what she did, because I hadn't read the damn book. Throw in the long day with travel and the game and add in this glass of wine and my drunk boss, and basically, my filter is slipping big time.

"She didn't mean to throw me under the bus," he explains, bringing me back to our present problem.

I arch a brow and huff under my breath. He's far too trusting if he truly believes that.

"But none of it matters. The point is, we've entered DEFCON 1. I didn't want to do this, but I'm going to have to do what my father suggested."

"Which is?"

"Marry a woman with kids."

I eke out a sound that resembles a laugh and shrug. "As much as I appreciate that you thought to ask me first, I'm not interested, Mr. Langfield."

Beckett's only response is a narrowing of his eyes.

"I'm joking," I say, pasting on a smile. "I know you aren't asking me. But seriously, this is a bit of a stretch. Tomorrow I'll get to work on a way to spin everything."

"Why would you think I *wasn't* asking you?"

A breathy laugh escapes my lips. "Please. I'm so not your type." He frowns, but it's not his usual asshole frown. This one is more confusion than anything else, so I quickly add, "Not that you're mine."

He rears back and grunts. "I'm everyone's type. Now tell me why I'm not yours."

"Everyone's type?" I laugh. I mean, he is. If you like that whole tall, dark, handsome, and broody thing. And also, he has nice eyes. Even if he spends most of his time glaring. The contrast between his green irises and his dark hair takes me by surprise every time I look at him. Like I somehow expect them to be brown, and then he goes and surprises me when he blinks.

He doesn't answer my question. No, he just continues assessing me.

I sigh. "I've seen the women you date."

Beckett's eyes grow wide, making my heart lodge itself in my throat.

"I mean… Forget it. What are we going on about, anyway? We have to come up with a plan."

He smiles at that, and now my stupid heart is tripping over itself. "I have."

Pressing a palm to my chest, I blow out a relieved breath. Finally, we're getting somewhere. "Excellent. So what's the plan?"

"We're getting married."

Eyes going wide, I cough out a loud, unladylike laugh at the absurd suggestion.

Beckett merely keeps that damn smile fixed on me. Has he lost his mind?

"You're drunk."

On the bar in front of me, my phone buzzes. I squeeze the side twice so it goes to the lock screen. It's a picture of the kids and me. A rare one, where the kids' faces are clean, no one's hair is too out of control, and their clothes aren't covered in food or dirt.

Beckett peeks over at the image, and his face softens. He picks up the device and holds it next to his face. "Don't you think we'd make a great-looking family?"

Is this guy delusional?

"Mr. Langfield—"

"You really should call me Beckett now that we're engaged."

"We aren't engaged," I huff.

"You want a ring?" he asks, his brows raised. "Of course you do. Do you prefer gold or platinum? You never wear anything but those diamond studs." He angles in until he's so close to my face I can't breathe.

Is he going to kiss me? The thought sends a shiver down my spine. Whether it's a good shiver or a bad one is yet to be determined.

"Gold it is," he murmurs, and then I swear to God, he sniffs me.

Do I smell?

Possibly like the pancakes I fed Addie this morning. Or maybe coffee. God, I hope I put on deodorant. Being a mom means constantly asking yourself these questions and never truly knowing the answer.

He backs up, but only slightly, and looms over me. "What do you say? I'll give you a healthy raise." He tilts his head and looks off to one side like he's formulating a plan. "We'll attend events together, *which we already do,* share some meals, *which we already do,* and make sure we're photographed together, *which we already are.* The only thing that will change is that you'll have to bring the kids around a bit more. But I swear I'll be good to them."

"Mr. Langfield—" I stop myself when he glowers. "Er, Beckett, while I appreciate the offer, and I'm sure you would be fine with my kids, you must have better options. Maybe you can hire actors to pretend to be your wife and kids?" Granted, the idea is just as ridiculous, but it doesn't involve me or my kids, and that's all that really matters.

"My father will find out," he mutters.

"So?"

"He doesn't want me to fake marry someone. He wants me to grow up. He wants me to *real* marry someone."

I blanch. "But we wouldn't be getting real married."

He shrugs like this is everyday conversation. "Why not, though? I can sell a real relationship between us. We spend 90 percent of our time together as it is, Liv. No one will find it hard to believe that after your divorce, I asked you out and we became something more. We went to Vegas, and I couldn't help myself. I had to make you mine immediately."

"Hard to believe?" I rear back. "It's *impossible* to believe, Beckett. Until this second, I was pretty sure you didn't even know about my divorce."

He throws back the last of his whiskey and motions to the bartender for another. "Gavin told me." He lowers his voice an octave, and it comes out smoother, kinder, almost. "How come you didn't tell me? I would have helped you find a divorce attorney."

What is happening? Did I bump my head on my way in to work? Maybe our plane crashed and I'm trapped in an alternate reality. Beckett Langfield has never cared about the personal lives of his employees, let alone wanted to sit down and discuss them.

I fold my hands on the bar top and pull in a calming breath. It's time to take control of this conversation. "I don't need your help. I've handled my divorce just fine on my own."

He nods. "I'm here if you need help, Liv."

The tone of his voice warms me, and though I try to fight it, a soft smile spreads across my face. I bring my wineglass to my lips to hide it. "Thank you, Mr.—" I take a deep breath. "Thank you, Beckett. I appreciate it. We'll figure out your situation. You're a good person. You don't need to get married to save your reputation." I laugh slightly. "And definitely not to a single mom whose life is a disaster."

Dropping one elbow to the bar, he turns so he's facing me full-on. "Your life is a disaster?"

With a scoff, I shake my head. "I don't really want to talk about it." Ready to move on from this conversation, I bring my glass to my lips again, only to discover it's empty.

Beckett waves at the bartender again, and when he refills my glass, Beckett instructs him to leave the bottle and bring over a second glass. Then he pours himself one and clinks it against mine. "To not talking about it," he says with a lift of his lips that could almost be considered a smile.

He takes a slow sip, and as he places his glass down and licks across his bottom lip, a flush creeps up my chest.

Beckett Langfield has a nice tongue.

A long one too.

Do people normally have nice tongues? Probably not. But of course he does. Beckett has a nice *everything*. Like those damn hands. When he flexes the one resting on his thigh, a whimper escapes my throat.

Shit. I peek up, hoping like hell he didn't hear me, but naturally, his eyes are locked on my mouth, as if he's studying where the sound came from. His gaze alone ignites a flame inside me. And suddenly, it's an inferno in here. I pull on my top, hoping the movement will cool me, but all it does is garner his attention. And now those eyes flash with fire as he stares at my breasts.

Oh shit, I'm pretty sure I'm drunk now too.

And if there's one thing you shouldn't do, it's get drunk with your hot boss in Vegas. You never know what'll happen next…

A WARM PALM slides up my back, and I groan. "Not now, Winnie."

She's always sneaking into my bed, and her body temperature at night rivals the fires of hell.

Tossing off the sheet, I relish the hit of cool air, then peek one eye open. That's all I can handle, because my head feels like a thousand-pound elephant is sitting on top of it. My stomach rolls as the sun blares in my face, and I smack my eyes shut.

"Why?" I whine. Why is it so bright in here? We have the tiniest windows in this house. How is light that bright even getting in? "Turn off the light." Winnie must have turned it on in the middle of the night when she snuck in.

At the deep growl near my ear, I snap my eyes open and scurry to the edge of the mattress, heart pounding and fight-or-flight mode activated…and that's when I see it.

Beside me, in all its naked glory, is an ass. Okay, not just an ass. There's a body attached to the ass, obviously, but all I can see is the very plump, very round, *very naked* ass. My eyes can't actually look at anything else.

It's also surprisingly shiny for an ass. No hair to speak of. It must be an expensive ass.

Stop looking at this stranger's ass, I instruct my eyes, which fail to follow commands.

I grab for the sheet and wrap it around my also very naked body, and then I count.

Deep breath in, two, three, four. Out, two, three, four.

In, two… Holy fuck, I'm naked in bed with a stranger.

In, two, three—

He groans and shifts, squeezing the pillow beneath his head, and that's when I discover precisely who that ass belongs to.

Beckett Langfield.

As in Beckett Langfield is lying in bed next to me naked.

And I'm naked.

We're both naked. In bed.

Oh my God.

Still wrapped in the bedsheet, I leap off the mattress, my stomach rolling. Scanning the floor for clothes, I snag the first thing I find, then dart to the bathroom.

Shutting the door as quietly as possible, I collapse against it, panting, "Oh my God. I think I had sex with my boss."

I slump to the floor, squeezing my eyes shut and slap a hand to my face. Dammit. What happened last night? How did I end up in his hotel room? And naked?

Why are we both naked?

"Think, Liv!" I hiss.

I scrape my hands down my face, startling when cool metal

runs across my cheek. What the…? Holding my left hand out, I stare down at the largest diamond I've ever seen. My lungs constrict violently, making it almost impossible to breathe as horror fills me.

"Oh my God. I think I married my boss."

Liv

5

"So you just left him there? Butt-ass naked? Did you even check to see if he was wearing a ring too?" Dylan asks, a hand slapped to her face, no doubt covering a wide smile.

"I'm glad you find my marital status amusing," I mutter as I slink further under the covers.

Sneaking out of the hotel room undetected was a bit of a challenge. So was hopping on a commercial flight when I was supposed to be at the game. I sent Beckett's assistant an email, informing her that I'd woken up with a stomach bug and asked that she call him to let him know I'd left.

I'm a coward.

"We don't even know if you're legally married," she says, far too jovially, her auburn curls bouncing around her face.

"Could you at least pretend to be upset about this?" I hiss.

Dylan folds her lips over themselves. She's sitting cross-legged on top of my comforter, fiddling with her rose quartz pendant, while I'm doing everything I can to disappear under the covers. God. How am I going to face my boss tomorrow?

"Has he called?"

Once. He called once and left a message. "*Liv*," he said, his voice tight and desperate. He took several deep breaths, then he was silent for a long moment before he finally choked out, "Please call me when you get this. I hope you aren't really sick. But if you are, I hope you feel better."

It was probably the most he'd ever said to me in a voicemail. Normally, he barks instructions and hangs up without a goodbye.

His voice this time, though? It sounded like he actually cared.

I pull the covers over my head and groan. "I can't talk to him."

Above me, Dylan giggles.

I peek out from under the sheets to glare at her.

She holds up her hands. "Calm down. Even if you really married your boss, it's not like it's the end of the world. Hell, you just finalized one divorce; what's one more?"

"Do you hear yourself? The ink isn't even dry on my divorce decree. I cannot be married! How am I going to face Beckett tomorrow?"

Dylan raises her eyebrows, her expression still so goddamn giddy. "Is it because you saw his ass? He's got a nice one, doesn't he? There's obviously a stick lodged up there, but I bet it's round and juicy. Kinda makes you want to take a bite out of it."

My mouth falls open, and the headache I've been nursing since the moment I woke up naked beside my boss returns. "Are you insane?"

She lifts a shoulder and tilts her head. "It's debatable. But I'm not the one who married my boss."

I throw a pillow at her, and she tips over sideways, dissolving into laughter.

"You can't tell anyone."

Dylan's face falls and she rights herself. "Oh no, we aren't doing this again. Remember what happened the last time you all made me keep a secret?"

"You tormented my boss with voices, got us all drunk, and made us strip around a fire pit?"

She rolls her eyes. "No. I had a meltdown and came up with the ridiculous idea that we should all move into a dilapidated house."

We both peer up at the water stains on the ceiling directly above my bed. We need a new roof. And new stairs. Hell, we need a new house.

"Don't lie. You're happy to be living with me," I prod, smiling for what might be the first time since I woke up yesterday morning.

She shrugs. "You're all right."

A giggle escapes me, but I sober quickly when I remember what I'm up against. "Dyl, seriously, what am I going to do?"

"You're going to get dressed, and we're going out for brunch. Then we'll pick up your kids from your no-good ex and spend the day having fun. The universe obviously has a plan. Trying to figure it out is a waste of time."

"That's your suggestion, then? Leave it to the universe?"

She smiles, and I swear, her eyes sparkle. "The universe brought the four of us together all those years ago, right? She's got a plan."

CONFIDENT THAT THIS weekend was all some sort of misunderstanding, I walk into the Langfield corporate offices with my head held high and the diamond ring tucked safely in my purse.

"Liv!" Gavin's secretary hollers, her glasses sliding down her nose as she chases me down the hall.

I smile, and genuine affection tugs at my heart. She is a

disaster, like always, and I'm nicely dressed, with my hair in a bun. Dylan was right; the universe is righting the world again. Everything is back to normal.

"Hey, Stace, how was your weekend?" I ask over my shoulder as I slow my pace so she can catch up.

She launches into a story about a disaster of a date, but halfway through, she slaps a hand to her chest. "Oh no! I'm late. Can I finish this over lunch?"

"You got it," I offer.

She smiles, and with a wave, she scurries back down the hall. Unlike Stacey, I'm no one's assistant—even if Beckett has never gotten that memo.

He has a secretary and a personal assistant. He also has a driver, a butler, a chef, and an ex-girlfriend, who, like clockwork, shows up once a month to vie for his attention.

I have no doubt he pays for plenty of other services—not that I want to think about them—and yet, despite all that luxury, all the people fawning over him at all times, the man never smiles.

I'm instantly on edge when I open my office door and find him propped up against my desk. For what might be the first time in his life, he's actually wearing a genuine smile, and he's holding a picture of me and my kids.

I clear my throat, and he jumps a bit, his smile disappearing as he slips off my desk and stands. "You're late."

Before I reply, I slowly count in my head, reining in my anger and annoyance. "By five minutes. And I didn't know we had an appointment. What can I do for you, Mr. Langfield?"

He glowers at me, and his shoulders sag. "We got married, Liv. Could you please, *please*, try to call me by my first name?"

My spine goes ramrod straight, and a squeak escapes me. I was *not* prepared for such a blunt conversation so early on Monday morning.

He smiles, and I swear my heart stops. It's breathtaking.

"You thought I'd forget that little fact?" He holds up his left hand and wiggles his fingers, drawing my attention to the black wedding band circling his fourth finger.

Holy fuck. We really got married.

I mean, I definitely thought we did. I kind of sort of remember a man who looked like Elvis—if you squinted and were obscenely drunk, which we were—pronouncing us husband and wife. If my boss's bare ass is any indication, then I can safely assume we consummated the marriage too. And I have a ring on my left hand, or I did until I hid it in my purse, ready to return to my... *husband?*

I open my mouth, but no words come out, so I close it again and swallow past the lump in my throat.

"What are you thinking?" he asks, scrutinizing me with a small frown.

The way he's staring is uncomfortable because he seems far too comfortable, like he's seen me naked. In all likelihood, he has.

I highly doubt I waited until after he was asleep to get undressed. We probably had sex.

God, I can't believe I had sex with Beckett Langfield and don't remember a single second of it. I'd smack myself if I didn't have company.

"Liv?" he says softer. When I don't reply, he hangs his head and sighs. "It's not the end of the world."

"We got married!" I hiss. Clenching my fists and shooting daggers his way, I round my desk, shove my purse into the drawer, and slam the damn thing shut.

Beckett sticks his hands in his pockets and rocks back on his heels. "Yes, I suppose we did."

"Why aren't you freaking out? Oh, you have a plan, don't you? Of course you have a plan. You're Beckett Langfield. Everything always works out for you." I huff and drop into my chair.

Rationally, I know it'll all be fine. Beckett doesn't want to be married to me. We'll fill out some paperwork, and it will be like it never happened. He's got the resources to keep things quiet, which means the news won't get back to Drake. For the first time in forty-eight hours, a tiny wave of relief hits me.

Beckett settles into the chair on the other side of my desk. "I do have a plan."

"Great. Just tell me what you need me to sign, and we can forget this entire mess."

Beckett frowns and scoots forward in his seat. "Well, no, that's not my plan at all. Actually, to be fair, this is Gavin's plan."

"*Gavin*? You told Gavin that we got *married*?"

The creases in Beckett's frown deepen. He almost looks hurt. "No, I haven't told anyone."

I lean back against my chair and blow out a breath. "Thank God."

"Is being married to me really that awful?"

"Oh, please. Of course it is."

"Why?" His nostrils flare, and his cheeks are a little pink, like maybe I've offended him.

"Not because of you. You're... you." I wave a hand up and down, gesturing to him. "You're great. It's me. I'm a mess."

With his lips pressed together, he scrutinizes me for a long minute, his frown one of concern more than offense or annoyance now. "You really don't think very highly of yourself, do you?"

Shaking my head, I grumble, "Trust me, you don't want to be married to me. This was a mistake."

"Or maybe the universe intervened," he offers.

Gritting my teeth, I bite back a shriek. "Have you been talking to Dylan?"

"Your hippie of a friend?" He laughs and sits back. "No. Why? Is that what she said? Maybe she's not so bad after all," he mutters softly, his eyes still holding mine. It's unnerving the way he's looking at me. Like he sees past the professional mask and the pressed clothing. As if, even after he's seen me with a dryer sheet stuck to my back and mismatched shoes, after I drunkenly married him, then ran out without a word, he still likes what he sees.

In all my years married to Drake, I never felt this seen.

"You can't possibly want to be married to a single mom with three kids."

Beckett shrugs. "It's for the media, just like we discussed."

My heart sinks just a little, but I clear my throat and sit up straight. Right. The media. The bad publicity. That's why we got married.

But then why did we end up naked in bed together?

I swallow and push that question out of my mind. "What else did we discuss again?"

"You mentioned that your house needs work, so we agreed that I'd pay you $100,000 to stay married to me until the end of the season."

Thank God I'm sitting down, because my knees wobble and my lungs seize.

"Think about it, Liv. I'm giving you $100,000, and all you have to do is take a few pictures with me and your kids. Nothing else changes."

"Nothing else changes," I murmur. Could it really be that easy?

One hundred thousand dollars would go a long way in fixing broken steps, and the leaky roof, and well… we could take care of a good chunk of the projects we need to complete, and I could set some of the money aside for the kids' extracurriculars without having to ask Drake for help. Hell, we could hire a babysitter every once in a while so the girls and I can all take a break.

I must still be drunk to even be considering this. "Nothing else changes?"

"Just the balance of your bank account and the diamond on your left hand."

Taking a deep breath, I hold out my right hand. "Okay, Mr. Langfield, I'll be your fake wife."

"YOU AGREED TO *WHAT* NOW?" Delia demands, holding the bottle of wine hostage above my empty glass.

"Oh, fake marriage! That's one of my favorite tropes," Dylan says, bringing her own glass—full of wine, I might add—to her lips.

"Tropes?" Shayla asks, cutting the broccoli on Kai's plate into small pieces. The kid is nine. It's unlikely he'll choke on mushy broccoli, but if Shayla can fathom the possibility, then she finds a solution.

"Yes, like Mafia romance. Or cowboy. God," Dylan gushes. "Those men and their hats. Although sports romance has always been my favorite. Men in tighty-whities? Sign me up!"

Liam groans beside her. I grab the bottle from Delia's hand and pour until my glass is completely full.

Swiping the bottle back, she gives me the stink eye and pours herself a more reasonable portion. "I thought we agreed we were swearing off men."

I take a healthy gulp and shake my head. "I'm not *really* marrying him."

Dylan smiles, looking far too enamored with my situation. "Until you're forced to share a bed. 'Cause we all know what happens next. He'll take a shower, and when he walks out of the bathroom in nothing but a white towel that accentuates his abs, it'll slip just enough that you'll get a peek at the trail of hair—"

"Trail of hair?" Shayla makes a face. "*Gross.*"

Delia and I laugh, but Dylan just smiles like *we're* the crazy ones. "You'll see. He's a broody one, so it'll probably hit her the first time she sees him smile at her kids. Our days are numbered, ladies; Liv is a taken woman."

"I'm not a taken woman." I drop my chin and shoot her a look. "The last man I would ever get involved with is Beckett Langfield."

"You need a contract," Delia says, transitioning from friend to attorney in seconds. She recently left her job at a big law firm to work as a prosecutor. She hops up and hustles to the kitchen. A minute later, she comes back with a yellow legal pad and pen.

When she settles beside me and writes *Rules for Fake Marrying your Billionaire Boss*, I groan.

"He and I have already come up with rules."

Delia stares me down. "Did you discuss PDA?"

"PD-what?" Shay asks as she spears another vegetable.

"Public displays of affection," Dylan advises, her chin tilted high. "Yes, that's a good one to start with."

"Mr. Langfield does not like to be touched," I interject.

"Well, *Mr. Langfield* is going to have to get over that," Dylan croons.

Delia bites the end of her pen and tilts her head back for a moment. "No, this is good. If he doesn't like to be touched, then people won't expect any PDA."

Dylan laughs so hard her wine sloshes onto the folding table. "No. She's going to be the only woman he *likes* touching him."

The way she says it, like she knows precisely how this will go, is slightly concerning. It's not that I think Dylan can see into the future or anything. It's just… she sounds so sure of herself.

Delia scrawls *limited PDA* next to number one, then drops down a line. "What next?"

"Oh, what about laundry? Ajay always helped with the laundry," Shay says with a soft smile.

I squeeze her hand. "That's sweet. Drake never did. This isn't a real marriage, though, so I don't think we need to add chores to the list."

"Compensation?" Delia questions.

I take in a deep breath. "He's going to pay me enough to fix the steps—"

Shay whoops and Dylan cheers before I even finish.

"And the roof," I add. "We might even be able to splurge on a hot tub," I mouth so the kids don't get their hopes up.

"Shut up." Delia's pen clatters to the table. "Just how much is this man giving you?"

I grab the pen and scribble *$100,000* next to compensation.

All three women scream so loudly I clap my hands over my ears.

"Seriously?" Delia asks, her eyes already swimming with possibilities and calculations.

We could check off so many items on our to-do list. Now we just need to find a contractor that she'll actually agree to hire. She's rejected half a dozen already, but there's got to be someone out there who can live up to her expectations.

Yes, moving in with my three best friends and all our kids was a whacky move, but as I look around the table, where Liam is feeding Adeline and Finn is watching him like he hung the moon—and hopefully learning to be just as helpful one day—I can't help but think it was the best crazy idea Dylan's ever had. And just maybe this crazy fake marriage will turn out the same way.

Beckett

6

Since my siblings and I moved out of our parents' home, our family has only one rule: when everyone is in town, we have Sunday dinner together. It's a rare feat since baseball and hockey seasons are long and overlap. Even if every one of us had a game today though, our mother still would have summoned us, because her pride and joy is home from Paris.

As the only girl in the family, my sister Sienna has always been the center of attention. Unlike the rest of us, sports don't interest her, but she still shocked the hell out of us all when she chose to go into fashion design instead of stepping into a role with the family business. She's worked her way through the fashion world, and now she's the face of a brand-new television series filming in Paris.

"Oh, my favorite! Someone must have missed me," my sister teases when I enter the kitchen carrying a bottle of red wine.

She and my mother are picking on the appetizers they've yet to bring out into the living room. I lean down and kiss my sister on the cheek. Her espresso locks which are cut into a bob bounce when she turns and offers me her other cheek and I can't help but chuckle. "So French now."

She beams and her green eyes dance. "It's literally my favorite place in the world."

I scowl. "There's no better place than Boston." Moving past her, I offer my mother a kiss on the cheek as well, then dig out the corkscrew and pour a glass of wine for each of us.

"What's new with you, brother? Harass any more of the youth in your favorite city?"

Laughter echoes off the walls as Brooks and Aiden enter the kitchen. Brooks's long hair is pulled back in a man bun, and his green eyes light up when he spots my sister. In two quick steps, he's got her off her feet and spinning in the air. The cacophony gets louder when Gavin and my father appear as well.

"So this is where the appetizers are hiding?" Gavin grumbles, spearing one of my mother's famous meatballs with a fork.

Clearing my throat, I step into the center of the space. "Since Sienna so kindly asked what was new with me, and since everyone's here, I might as well break the news to you all at the same time."

With my heart beating against my sternum, I pull in a deep breath and scan the faces of my suddenly silent family members. I didn't intend to announce it this way, but I didn't have the balls to do it in the office this week. I kind of expected Liv would change her mind. But it's been six days and she hasn't called it off so here goes nothing.

I clear my throat, even as it tightens further. "I got married."

Gavin chokes on his meatball, and Aiden slaps him on the back.

"Don't you have to be dating someone to get married?" Gavin gasps, his eyes watering.

I hand him a glass of wine, and he gulps it down fast.

"We've kept it a secret."

"You were just saying Dad wanted you to settle down," Aiden pipes in. "Why didn't you say something then?"

Stuffing my hands into my pockets, I lean against the counter and dig deep for the ability to sell this to the people who know me best. "Because I didn't want any of you to think I did it to fix this PR nightmare."

"Who is it?" Sienna asks.

I meet Gavin's eyes and then look to my father. "Olivia."

"Olivia who?" my mother asks, her face a mix of confusion and elation.

Brooks barks out a laugh. "*Beckett's* Olivia."

A smirk spreads on Gavin's cocky face. "You married *Liv*?"

Heart squeezing so hard I'm worried it'll explode, I narrow my eyes on him. "Yes."

My father rubs his forehead, then drops his hand to his side. "Isn't Liv already married?"

"Divorced," Gavin says, though his attention remains on me. "Beckett and I were *just* discussing it."

"You weren't seeing her while she was still married, right?" My mother wrings her hands, all the joy flushed out by fear. "You think what they're saying about you now is bad? If they get wind that there was an affair..."

I sigh. "I did not have an affair. Liv and I are in love. We're moving in together, and that's that."

Gavin presses closer to me. "You're moving her kids into your penthouse?"

It's no secret that I like things a certain way. Always have. No one touches my things, and I prefer it that way.

The thought of kids running around my immaculate penthouse has me reaching for the bottle of Hanson whiskey on the counter and pouring two fingers.

Fuck.

Liv and I haven't worked out these kinds of details yet, but every eye in the room is locked on me, waiting for my response.

"We, uh, plan to stay at her place while we look for a house that'll work for all of us. Don't want to take them from the home they're comfortable with just to stay somewhere temporarily."

"Naturally." Gavin nods. "Hey, Mom, aren't you and Dad looking for a place to stay while the renovations are being done here?"

What the hell?

"Oh, yes. But I haven't found anything that'll work for us and has enough security. Beckett, you wouldn't mind if we stayed at your place, would you?"

I gulp the last of my whiskey, my blood heating and sweat prickling at my hairline. *Shit.*

"Of course he wouldn't mind," Gavin says, throwing an arm over my shoulders. "He's moving in with the love of his life, Olivia, and her three kids."

My stomach drops. Dammit. Liv is going to kill me.

Liv
7

"Where is my black shoe?" I whine, sweeping an arm under the bed in a fruitless search. It's no wonder I got on the plane with mismatched shoes last weekend; not a single one I've found this morning matches another.

Could be the twins. They love pulling tricks, then acting innocent. Though it's just as likely I'm losing my mind.

"Collette, Phoebe," Delia calls, her voice stern. "If you took Liv's shoes, now is the time to fess up."

In unison, with matching sugary-sweet voices, they reply, "We swear we didn't."

Dylan crawls up next to me, smiling as usual. "Don't worry, I'll slip a little whiskey into their apple juice tonight; we'll get the truth out of 'em."

"Dylan," I gasp, my stomach plummeting, but I follow it up with a laugh, because obviously, she's joking.

When I look at her, though, her face is completely serious.

"No whiskey." I point at her in warning.

She shrugs. "I added a little to Finn's and Liam's ice cream last night. They were out before *Real Housewives* started."

I giggle and shake my head. She's a nut. "What about Kai?"

She cranes her neck and shoots me a look. "Even I'm not crazy enough to dose Shay's kid with whiskey."

Flopping over, I fall back against the bed and pull my knees to my chest. "We're a disaster."

She scoots up beside me and rests her head on my shoulder. "But a beautiful one."

My stomach twists for what has to be the twentieth time today. "Do you think I'm making a mistake?"

Sitting back, Dylan eyes me, her head tilted to one side. "How?"

"By agreeing to this fake marriage nonsense. Am I setting a bad example for the kids? They're going to have to go along with it too."

She sighs and gives me a sympathetic smile. "Finn can't keep a secret to save his life, and Winnie? Well... I think it's okay to tell a white lie when it's in the best interest of your kids. And this is, Liv. You're doing this for them."

"And for us." I drop my head back and inspect the water marks on the ceiling. One more good rain, and they'll be dripping down on us. "We *have* to get the roof fixed."

"Maybe he'll give you half the money now," she suggests.

I bite my lip and ignore the now regular ache in the pit of my stomach. We haven't discussed the length of this sham or the timeline for getting paid. I suppose Delia is right; we need a detailed contract.

THIS IS the Monday-est Monday I've had in a long, *long* time. I was forced to wear flats to the office because I couldn't find a single pair of matching heels, then Winnie had a meltdown. Apparently, it's red shirt day at school, and her red shirt was nowhere to be found this morning. To top it all off, Drake called while I was on my way to work, ranting about how one of his friends called to tell him that he saw Finn wearing a dress that matched Adeline's when we were out a few days ago. I hung up on him.

As I slide my feet into the black heels I hide under my desk, I feel a modicum of my usual sanity. A sip of coffee is the next step in slipping into my professional persona—Liv Maxwell, PR extraordinaire.

That sends me into a fit of giggles. God, I'm ready for some semblance of peace around here.

"Good morning, Liv," Gavin says as he breezes into my office wearing a big smile. Unlike his brother, Gavin is always smiling and always joking around. It's like they aren't actually related. Come to think of it, all of his brothers sport grins regularly. Maybe it's hockey? They do get all that aggression out on the ice.

"Morning, boss. How was your weekend?"

Gavin slides into the chair on the other side of my desk, his leg bouncing and his eyes dancing with mischief. Damn, he's even more chipper than usual. "It was great. Though not as good as the weekend before was for you, from what I hear."

Confused, I frown at him. "Hmm?"

"Olivia, I've never been so happy," Preston Langfield practically chirps as he enters my office.

Two Langfields at once? Now this is a surprise.

I rise to greet him, smoothing down my black skirt. "Hi, Preston. I'm glad you're so happy, but I'm not quite sure why."

Behind him, Beckett appears, and *surprise, surprise,* he is *not* smiling. He nods and cocks a brow like he's trying to send a silent message, only I have no idea what it is.

"Well, because I heard you've joined our family! I don't know how the two of you hid your relationship so well, but Monroe and I couldn't be happier."

My lungs constrict so tightly I can't breathe for several seconds, but I garner all the strength and patience I have and rein in the desire to murder the man standing in the doorway, before plastering a smile on my face. "Well, yes. Thank you. Um, I didn't realize we were telling people so soon." I peer at Beckett, hoping he can feel the daggers I wish I could shoot his way right now.

He drops his chin, and his shoulders slump. At least he has the decency to look remorseful. "Figured I'd share the news at dinner last night. It was late by the time I got home, so I didn't have the opportunity to tell you. Didn't want to wake you or the kids," he says, as if we speak nightly. Which would be normal if we were *actually* married.

"I'm just shocked you got my brother to agree to move in with you," Gavin interjects, his smile too gleeful for this early in the morning. "Never thought I'd see the day Beckett would give up his penthouse."

Heart lurching, I drag my attention back to Beckett, whose shoulders are sagging so much he'll be one with the floor soon.

I feign another smile. "Our house is certainly cozy. Not quite as glamorous as the penthouse, though."

Preston nods. "We appreciate it. Monroe is thrilled that we won't have to stay in a hotel during our home renovations."

My stomach drops. What now?

"Anyway, we wanted to congratulate you. You'll come to family dinner this week, right? Bring the kids. Monroe is excited to meet her new grandbabies, though she wasn't thrilled to find out the two of you eloped. First family wedding and all." He shrugs. "But with it being so soon after your divorce was finalized, we understand why you'd want to keep it under wraps. Let's plan a big party and really celebrate it in a couple of months, okay?"

Oh God.

Beckett rounds the desk and stands beside me. "Let's let Liv get back to work. I'll talk to you and Mom about dinner later in the week, and we'll see what we can do about a party."

I swallow and nod, too stunned to do anything but ensure my legs don't give out on me.

"Of course. I'll see you two later." With that, Preston disappears.

I turn to my new husband, eyes wide, waiting for an explanation, but it's Gavin who speaks first. "You two ready to admit that this is fake?"

Beckett bristles beside me, his eyes narrowing on his brother. "Don't you have a hockey team to run?"

Gavin chuckles and stands. "Fine. Have fun with the move. Let me know if you need help." He winks at his brother, then turns to me with a grin. "Can't wait to hear how his first night goes."

As soon as he's out of earshot, I turn to Beckett and hiss, "You said nothing changes!"

Cringing, he takes a step back. "I know. Things got a little out of hand at family dinner."

"You think?" Pinching the bridge of my nose, I squeeze my eyes shut and will the rage bubbling inside me to calm. "You can't move in with me."

"It's not the end of the world." The jackass shrugs like he really believes the bullshit he's spewing. "I make an excellent roommate."

A bark of a laugh escapes me. "When was the last time you lived with someone?"

When he doesn't answer, I let out a loud *ha*. "That's what I thought."

"You're right. I've lived alone for a long time, but I can be a good roommate. Don't you have a spare bedroom I could crash in until we figure this out?"

"Beckett," I whine, clenching my fists at my sides.

His only response is a smile. *Bastard.* The man who only ever frowns chooses *now* to smile?

Crossing my arms over my chest, I grit my teeth. "Why are you smiling?"

"You finally called me by my first name."

I groan. He's seriously insane.

Beckett grasps my wrist and tugs until I drop my arms. "Listen," he says, capturing one hand and squeezing, "I know this is more than you bargained for, but I'll make it up to you. I'll increase the payout. How much do you want?"

I drop my chin and focus on our hands. His are warm and soft, and I'm momentarily struck stupid by the way his thumb smooths across the back of mine. This might be the first time he's purposefully touched me—that I can remember, at least. I really need to get my memories back, because there's a damn good chance I had *sex* with this man.

I pull my hand from his grasp. "We need rules."

A tiny smile forms on his lips. "Rules?"

"Yes. No touching. It's in the contract."

With a laugh, he pulls himself up straighter. "Contract?"

"Yes, my attorney drew up a contract for us."

Tilting his head and frowning, he assesses me for a long moment, like he's trying to figure me out. Yeah, me too buddy.

"Okay, that's a good idea. Why don't I have my attorney look over it, and we can iron out any other important details?"

Right. His attorney. My attorney. See? This is a business relationship. No room for silly feelings or thoughts of how those warm hands would feel on other parts of my body.

"Great. But you can't seriously want to move in with me while we do this."

Beckett drags one of those warm hands along his chin and contemplates the skyline on the other side of the window. Finally, he sighs and turns back to me. "I don't see any way around it.

There's no way my family will buy this unless we really sell it to them. I know it's not ideal, but I swear, I'll be a perfect gentleman. With all the travel I do, I'll barely be around as it is."

"I need one more thing," I counter, fighting back a smile. This will have him changing his tune in a heartbeat.

Beckett nods. "Anything."

"You agree to babysit all the kids once a week." I press my lips together, knowing this will have him running for the hills. There's no way he'll go through with the sham of a marriage if he has to babysit.

Beckett may say he likes kids, but that's a damn lie. He never wanted them, like he said before. That's why he's not married to the woman he was clearly destined for.

He picks up the photograph on my desk, the one he was holding when I found him here last week, and inspects it.

Silently, I count in my head, waiting for the refusal I can guarantee is coming.

When he turns back to me, his green eyes light up. "You drive a hard bargain, Liv."

"I understand." I smile, holding back a snarky *aha!* "We'll find another wife for you."

Beckett frowns. "You think I can't handle taking care of a few kids one night a week?"

My stomach knots. *Dammit.* "Seriously?"

Squaring his shoulders, he looks me in the eye. "I can do this, Liv."

I shrug. "Fine. It's your funeral." He has no idea what he's in for. "I'll email you the address. But don't say I didn't warn you."

Beckett

8

I check the address three times, then turn back to my driver. "Are you sure this is the right place?"

Liv's got to be playing a joke on me. It'd serve me right, forcing her to play along with this stupid plan. I'm not even sure why I'm doing it. She's right. I could have hired a woman and kids to do this and paid a lot less than I've promised her. Or I could have told my father to fuck off and figured out another PR strategy.

Actually, I do know why I'm doing this. Not that I'll ever admit the truth.

"Charlie, do you really see Liv living here?"

His eyes bounce from me to the house situated at the end of the street.

The house beside it? Sure, I'd believe it. But this one? It's just... *No.*

"Does seem suspicious," Charlie agrees, frowning. "But it's the address she sent you. I confirmed the details you texted."

Right. I nod at the house as if I'm making an agreement with it. I won't judge it if it doesn't suck me inside and never lets me out. Sounds dramatic, I know. But here's the thing. There are ghosts on the front porch, and a sign stuck to the window that says *Happy len Day*. There's an Easter bunny stuck to the peeling front door. And *so* many dead plants. A sign that reads *Be Thankful* is propped up on one side of the door, and on the other side is a lopsided bush decorated with lights. It looks like the Mad Hatter's house... or perhaps an insane asylum.

I just can't quite put my finger on what's going on here.

Liv must be pranking me.

That's the only explanation.

With one last glance at Charlie, I march up the steps, and that's when I hear the shrieking. Followed by screams. Dropping my head back, I look up to where the sounds are coming from. Before I have the opportunity to react, a projectile pelts me in the face, and a sound leaves my throat that I'm not proud to say sounds an awful lot like a high-pitched scream.

Throwing my arms over my head, I drop to the sidewalk and heave in a breath. "You okay?" I ask Charlie, though I don't dare look up.

The sound of squeaky doors opening and closing and a riot of giggles have me lifting my head. All I can see from my vantage point is a pair of shiny black shoes.

Above me, Charlie taps my shoulder. "You're okay, boss. It was a Nerf gun."

Craning my neck, I spot Liv on the front steps of the demon house. A boy about her height with red hair and freckles stands beside her, openly laughing at me. On her other side is a little boy holding a Nerf gun. He's wearing a pink tutu over army fatigues and a scowl.

Liv grabs the Nerf gun from his hands and squeezes her lips shut like she's trying hard not to laugh. "Finn!" she finally scolds. "We don't shoot guests."

The red-haired kid holds out a fist to the little guy for a bump. "Nice job."

Behind them, Liv's crazy friend Dylan appears. I met her

when Liv brought her and a couple other friends to my house in the Keys this past fall. I nicknamed this one *Hippy Dippy* because she's a total nut job. She does some ventriloquist shit and creeped me the fuck out the whole time they were there, pretending to be the spirit of my dead grandmother when I thought I was alone.

Both of my grandmothers are alive, so it made no goddamn sense.

Her blond lawyer friend came too. She obviously hates men and threatened me every time I so much as looked at Liv. The only semi-normal one was her short friend with dark hair. Shayla, maybe. She was quiet, at least.

"What's everybody doing out here?" Dylan asks. When she spots me on all fours on the sidewalk a breathy laugh leaves her throat. "Oh! It's the moment he meets the kids! Come, help me set the table, Liam." She squeezes the red-haired boy's shoulder, and that's when I see the resemblance.

"Ah, he's the demon's spawn. Makes sense."

Liv rushes down the steps and grasps my arm, but before I'm humiliated further, I climb to my knees. Dammit, do I feel my age in this moment. I may workout, but when a forty-two-year-old man drops to the concrete, getting up ain't easy.

When Charlie offers me his hand, I shake him off, haul myself to my feet, and wipe at the dirt covering my jacket and pants. So much for making a good impression on her kids.

"You okay?" Liv asks, though the smile hasn't left her face. It's a nice smile and one she rarely gives to me. Although I have to remind myself that she's not smiling *at me*, she's holding back a laugh at my expense.

Brushing at my elbows, I grunt. "What the hell is this place?"

"Home sweet home," she sings, drawing her hand toward the house as if it's a prize.

The little guy in the tutu runs up behind her and latches himself to her hip, his eyes wary as he takes me in. I recognize him immediately from the photo on Liv's desk. His silky brown hair is long enough that it flops over his forehead, almost hiding his eyes, and the tutu he's wearing blows in the breeze. I take a deep breath and crouch down so we're eye to eye. "You got a nice shot."

He blinks at me for a beat, his expression blank, before his grin breaks free. "I'm Finn."

When he holds his hand out to me to shake, I smile. "I think I'll call you Huckleberry."

"Cool," he whispers, his eyes lighting up. *Finally* I got something right.

I peer up at Liv, and she looks down at me, her brow creased, and for a couple of heartbeats, we stay like that.

She tilts her head toward the door. "Come on in. But remember: I warned you." She looks up at Charlie. "You're more than welcome to stay for dinner too."

"No, thank you, Ms. Maxwell," he says from behind me, obviously holding back a laugh. "I'll be back when Beckett calls."

"It's Langfield." I surprise even myself by correcting him. There's a sharp edge to my voice I don't think I've ever used with him.

Charlie doesn't flinch, though. He only smiles at Liv. "Right. Mrs. Langfield, call me if you need me." Then with a wink he's gone.

I turn back to Liv, who's already looking at me, eyes wide.
Mrs. Langfield.

A possessive streak runs through me as I finally get a good look at her—hair in a bun, black sweater and a black skirt that hugs those curves she's always hiding, perfectly professional in the chaos of this moment—and the name runs on repeat in my head.

Fuck, that's hot.

"Mrs. Langfield?" she mouths. I don't miss how her eyes dance as she says the words.

"Oh, but it's okay for you to call me Mr. Langfield?" I tease.

She licks her lips. "You told me I couldn't."

I place my hand on her back and angle in so my mouth is next to her ear. "I may have misjudged just how good it sounds, *Mrs. Langfield.*"

A shudder runs through her body, forcing me to grip her waist to steady us both, and my pinky slides beneath her shirt on accident. The feel of her soft, warm skin makes my dick hard in an instant.

"Mommy!" Finn says, yanking on her hand and pulling her toward the door.

The word *Mommy* alone is all it takes for me to release her. Damn it if there's ever been a more effective cockblock. I drop my hand, realizing just how utterly stupid it is to touch my wife.

My wife.

Holy shit, she's my goddamn wife.

Olivia Langfield. The name sounds too fucking good.

I grin, following her into the house, hypnotized by the sway of her hips.

I may have never wanted a wife, but I'll enjoy the hell out of the time I get to call Olivia Langfield my one and only.

I DON'T MAKE it two steps into the house before I'm assaulted by an ear-piercing screech.

"It's the kid hater!"

The accusation is followed by a swift kick to my shin.

"Motherfucker!" I yell, hopping on one leg.

"Beckett!" Liv hisses, whipping around and glowering.

I grimace and turn to the perpetrator. Before me in the some-what dark foyer is a tiny blonde with her hands on her hips and a smirk on her face, like she's daring me to react. Beside her is her carbon copy. The second tiny blonde holds out her hand expec-tantly. "That'll be one thousand dollars for the swear jar."

"Excuse me?" I balk, crouching to rub my shin.

"Collette, Phoebe, please go play until dinner," Liv says to the Shining Twins. They're evil, I can feel it.

The one who demanded the money holds up a jar. Sure enough, there's a label stuck to it with the words *Swear Jar* scribbled on it. Below it is a big number one, and then three much smaller zeros. "It's the rules, Auntie Liv. We don't make them, but we have to abide by them."

Liv presses her lips together and looks at me. "You wanted to live here," she says, her tone teasing.

Damn. The tone itself makes my cock twitch. Which is insane, because there are two little demonic people leering at us and my shin still hurts. That's what this woman does to me. That's how dangerous she is. Best I keep my distance, otherwise I'll be handing over my fortune just to see her smile.

With a groan, I tug my wallet from my back pocket. "Do you take Amex?"

The twins simultaneously tilt their heads and give me matching bored expressions.

I take in a deep breath and pray for patience. "Can I write you a check?"

"Do we look like we're fools? You could cancel it before we have a chance to take it to the bank," the one who kicked me says. "*Cash only.*"

Blowing out a breath, I pull out one crisp one-hundred-dollar bill after another.

Eyeing my wad of cash, Liv scoffs. "That really is absurd, Beckett."

I shrug and shoot her a grin. "Good thing I have it. Pretty

sure one of them woulda tied me up if I didn't."

Her responding laugh is worth every single dollar I'm giving up. The sound is melodic and happy. When was the last time I saw Liv truly happy? I'd let the girls kick me in the shins over and over again if it meant seeing her like this.

When I hand the cash over to the Shining Twins, they run off screaming, "Look, Mom! We got a thousand dollars off the jackass!"

"Hey! That's a thousand dollars!" I yell. "You can't curse."

The one who kicked me turns around with a smirk. "It's not a curse when it's your name, right, Mom?"

Behind her, Liv's blond friend saunters up.

"Ha." I let out a loud laugh. "Figures Medusa is your mom."

"*Beckett*," Liv hisses, elbowing me in the arm.

"That one kicked me." I point. "And that one scammed me out of a thousand dollars. Then they called me a name. How come you're hissing at me?"

She sighs and rolls her eyes. "You said you would be okay with kids."

"Yeah, *your* kids. Surely they're better behaved than the Shining Twins over there." I thumb over my shoulder in the direction of the trio of blond she-devils.

Liv stares at me, her lip twitching and her eyes brighter than I think I've ever seen them. It only takes a second for her to give up the fight and let the laughter bubble loudly from her lips.

Her friend glowers at us, hands on her hips and her minis flanking her, wearing matching looks of disdain. "*Olivia.*"

Liv covers her mouth with one hand and waves the other. "I'm sorry, really. I'm trying not to laugh."

"Try harder," her friend reprimands. I can't remember her name, but I know I don't like her. I don't like anyone who takes that tone with Liv.

Throwing her attitude back at her, I straighten to my full height and glare. She doesn't back down, though, only shoots figurative daggers so sharp I swear I feel them puncturing my lungs. Then, without a word, she turns on her heel, ushering her two demons along with her.

A little boy in the corner catches my eye. He's so quiet I don't know how long he's been watching. This isn't Huckleberry, and if I remember correctly, Liv only has one son. So who's this kid? Every time I turn around, I swear a new one pops up. I offer him a wave, but he doesn't respond. He only watches me warily. I've already been kicked by one kid, so I squat low so I can introduce myself, hoping to avoid a repeat. "Hello, I'm Beckett Langfield."

His eyes grow wide, and I swear a hint of a smile crosses his face. "Your family owns the Boston Bolts."

I chuckle. I've never been so happy to be associated with the hockey team. I swear this is the first time in weeks I've been referred to by anything other than a kid hater. "Yes, we do."

He squints, scrutinizing me with an intensity far too great for such a little guy. The kid is really sizing me up. "Do you really hate kids?" he asks in a quiet voice.

A soft chuckle escapes me and I shake my head. "No."

"But Collette said—"

I hold up my hand. Collette must be one of the Shining Twins. "She's wrong. I happen to love kids." I cringe and take in a breath, racking my brain for a way to rephrase the statement. I don't like to lie. "Well, I don't hate them, and you seem like an okay kid. Am I right about that?"

He nods quickly.

"Can you tell me your name?"

He looks past me, and I peer over my shoulder, following his gaze, noting that we have an audience.

Beside Liv, her dark-haired friend is watching me. I'm almost positive her name is Shayla.

The expression on Liv's face is unreadable. She's not smiling, but she doesn't look pissed off, which is rare when her attention's set on me. No, she looks thoughtful, like maybe she's trying to figure me out.

Good luck, wife. I'm trying to figure myself out too.

I never go out of my way for anyone, yet I find myself desperate to impress the people who matter to her.

Other than the Shining Twins and their mom. I recognize a hopeless case when I see it.

Shayla nods at him, and I turn back to face my new friend.

"I'm Kai," he says softly.

"Well, Kai, it's nice to meet you. Should we go help with dinner?"

When he nods in response, I haul myself back up and blow out a long breath in relief. There are a lot of people in this house, and I have yet to even meet two of Liv's kids.

Shayla intercepts her son and grasps him gently by the shoulders. "Let's go wash your hands first."

Once they're gone, I turn toward Liv. She's studying me again, wearing that unreadable expression.

"Who's next?" I ask.

Her brows knit together, her dark eyes clouded with confusion. "Huh?"

I try to hold back my heavy sigh, but it breaks free anyway. Running my hand through my hair, I assess her, then scan the dark entry, where we're still standing. Fuck, I'm never nervous, but the need to impress her is screwing with my brain.

You're not my type. Her words echo in my brain, taunting me, consuming me until I can think of nothing else but how to become her type.

"You didn't have to rope all your friends into being here. I don't bite." I go for teasing to mask the hurt. She's known me for over a decade, yet she doesn't trust me to have dinner with her family without having her entourage here as backup. Yes, our predicament is an awkward one, but I'm not a monster—

although I don't blame her for not seeing that when all she's seen is that man at work.

I've truly never cared what people thought of me at the office. I have a job to do, and I do it. I'm trying to turn the Revs into one of the best baseball teams in the country. If I coddled all my employees, shit would never get done.

She watches me, her lips twisting to one side. She opens her mouth like she's ready to respond, but before she can, two more children appear. These two I recognize. Two little girls. Her oldest and her youngest. Finally, I'm going to meet all of her kids.

"You must be Bear," I say, holding out my hand to her older daughter.

She darts a look at her mom but doesn't respond.

Beside me, Liv laughs, and I swear it's the most incredible sound I've ever heard. "It's Winnie."

I smile at her, then at her daughter. "Bear it is."

Liv huffs, but there's no heat behind it. "You can't just change all their names."

Turning back to her, I mutter, "But mine are better," and grin at her youngest daughter. "And what's your name, Little One?"

The toddler with pudgy thighs and a big smile throws her arms around my legs.

Damn, that one little move makes my heart soar. "I think she likes my name choice," I tease Liv.

She snorts and waves toward an open doorway. "Winnie, go help Aunt Dylan with dinner."

Winnie doesn't move at first. She just lifts her chin and takes me in for a long moment. "I like Bear."

The wide grin I direct at Liv has her rolling her eyes. "That's Adeline. Although, at the rate we're going, I'm guessing you'll be renaming her as well?"

I actually quite like Adeline, but teasing Liv is fun. I never get to be like this with her, so I roll with it. "Yeah, Little One it is." At my feet, the girl has her arms outstretched and she's giving me grabby hands, so I scoop her up. As soon as she's settled against my chest, she snuggles into me and lets out a soft little sigh.

"Wow," Liv whispers.

"What?" I keep my eyes on the little girl with the pigtails. One's higher than the other, so they look lopsided, which makes me like Liv even more. At work, she's always perfectly put together, but this house and her children are making it clear that she's anything but. It makes her more real, like I can almost hold her in my grasp. The aloof Olivia, the one above the fray, has always been attractive to me, but this woman is hypnotic. I could easily get lost in her if I don't keep reminding myself that she only agreed to stay married to me because I'm paying her.

"The only other person she's like that with is Liam."

I rack my brain for an image of Liam, but I've got nothing. "Who?"

She folds her lips over to hold back her smile. "The one you called demon's spawn."

I chuckle. "See? You like my nicknames."

She turns on her heels. "No, actually, I don't. But I learned long ago that it's your way or the highway. So we'll roll with it. Come on, Mr. Langfield, meet the rest of your roommates."

My way or the highway? That's not—

Wait, did she say roommates?

Liv

Beckett's expression is pure gold. Horrified confusion flits across his face as we settle at the tables we pushed together in the dining room. We don't yet have a dining table that will fit eleven people, but we found two card tables in the basement and a whole slew of folding chairs. It's not the most glamorous setup, but it works.

I considered putting Beckett at the end designated for the kids to really let him get a taste of what he's in for, but after Finn shot him with a Nerf gun and the man dropped to the ground screaming like he was really under fire and then Collette kicked him in the shin and Phoebe swindled him out of a thousand dollars, I figure we'll ease him into the rest of the news. I still need my job, after all.

Easing the kids into it is a different story. There's no easing into telling them a man is moving in. I never imagined introducing my kids to a partner—real or fake.

I honestly thought that part of my life was over, and while in reality, that is probably true, that doesn't change the fact that I'm now introducing them to Beckett.

I spent the day worrying they'd be upset that their mom was

moving on. Then again, they did fine when Drake moved on... although he moved on with our nanny, so there were no introductions to be made.

What the hell is wrong with me? Am I seriously justifying my husband's infidelity with the nanny because it was easier for the kids?

"Can I get you a drink?" I ask Beckett, realizing we only have wine and juice at the table.

That thought spirals into memories of what happened the last time we had wine, and suddenly, I'm picturing his bare ass. Then there's a flash of him cupping my face as he leaned close after Elvis pronounced us husband and wife, right before murmuring, *"Fuck, I can't tell you how long I've wanted to do this."*

With my heart suddenly pounding in my chest, I study the man across from me, searching for a hint of the guy who said those words. But he's just staring at me like normal—with cold eyes and the hint of a frown.

"Sure, you have any whiskey?"

Delia's chair screeches across the original hardwood floor as she pushes back and folds her arms across her chest. "What, do you think she's going to serve you now that she agreed to fa—"

"*Delia,*" I admonish.

She turns her glare on me. "What happened to the freaking contract, *Olivia*?" She drags out my name to hammer home her point.

My face feels like it's one thousand degrees. I'm going to kill her.

"Mom, this tofu tastes funny," Kai interrupts.

Every head turns toward the kid who barely says more than two words at a time.

"That's not tofu," Shayla screeches. "That's processed meat!" Jumping to her feet, she smacks the food out of her son's hand before he can take another bite and I watch in horror as the chunk of processed meat flies across the table and smacks Beckett in the forehead.

"Food fight!" Liam yells, and within seconds, my fake husband—and my very real boss—is covered in our dinner. Across the table, Delia's still pushed back, wearing a smug smile.

"I'M sorry about your clothes; I'll have them dry cleaned," I offer as I walk Beckett to the door.

We ordered pizza after the food fight, and I gave Beckett one of my white T-shirts since his was covered in food. Sadly, my shirt fit him—it was tight, but it fit. Which means that, for the last hour, I've had to stare at his stupid pecs through the thin layer of cotton. I've never both hated and loved a piece of fabric so much.

It was only made worse when Finn asked him to stay for a tea party. Beckett sat cross-legged on the floor next to my son, who was still wearing a skirt over his fatigues, with Adeline in his lap. Winnie served the tea, and Beckett toasted *Huck* and *Bear* and *Little One*. Then he clinked his teacup with Finn's, holding his pinky out and everything.

Even the twins were intrigued by the entire ordeal—usually, they opt to watch *Jeopardy!* with Delia rather than join us for tea parties after dinner. Delia says it's good for their brains. Honestly, those kids don't need any more smarts; they freak me out with their scheming as it is.

Beckett may be onto something when he called them the Shining Twins.

Of course I love them; they're my best friend's daughters. But still, gotta call a spade a spade.

"Don't worry about it," Beckett replies, giving me what I could swear is an appreciative once-over. "Honestly, though, I didn't expect such a crowd for dinner. I figured it would just be us. You know, a meet-the-family kind of night. So I could get to know the kids and make them comfortable."

He's watching me closely, as if he's trying to figure me out. I don't know what he thinks he'll find. He's already peered behind the curtain and lifted the mask. My life is an utter disaster. For years, I've played the put-together professional around this man, but today, the façade came tumbling down, and there is no unringing that bell.

"This was meeting the family," I tell him, my heart rate picking up a little, because it's just dawned on me that he doesn't get it yet. I'm going to have to spell it out. "The girls, Shay, Delia, and Dylan... they all live here."

His eyes bulge and he chokes on air. "All of them?"

Biting my bottom lip, I nod.

His Adam's apple bobs, and he blinks at me a couple of times, like he's still trying to comprehend my words. "And their kids?"

I can't help but smile. "Yup."

"Even the Shining Twins and Medusa?"

A laugh escapes me at that question. "Yes, even them."

"Fuck," he whispers, dragging a hand down his face. A second later, he goes ramrod straight, his eyes darting one direction, then the other. "I'm going to have to keep a lot more cash on me, huh?"

"Beckett, we don't have to do this. You don't have to move in. Just tell your family the truth."

"No." His green eyes dance, and a smile spreads across his face again.

I swear I've seen this man smile more today than in the previous decade. I'm not sure why he looks so happy; I just told him he'll be subjected to complete insanity if we go through with this.

"You like cruel and unusual punishment?" I ask with a laugh.

Beckett leans in close, and I stop breathing. The scruff on his jaw scrapes deliciously against my cheek as his warm breath hits my neck. "No, but I do like calling you my wife a bit too much."

Before the words even register, he presses his lips against the sensitive spot just below my ear. A soft sound—a blend of a whimper and a moan—escapes me.

"And that sound you make, Mrs. Langfield... Oh, I *really* like that sound."

He pulls back a few inches and holds my gaze. My heart practically leaps into my throat at the spark of desire in his eyes. Without another word, he winks and heads toward the waiting car.

Delia appears out of nowhere and shouts, "Don't forget you're babysitting tomorrow, asshole!"

"That's a thousand dollars, Medusa! I'll make sure the twins add it to the tab!" he hollers with a wave. Then he's gone, ducking into the car and heading down the street.

Dylan laughs from the porch. "Oh, this is going to be so much fun."

Beckett

10

"Y ou really aren't coming to poker night?" Gavin whines into the phone.

"Tell him I'm only in town this weekend," our best friend, Jay, hollers in the background.

Fuck, I've missed that guy. He moved to Paris a year ago, and he and his wife are filming a show about my sister's fashion line. No one deserves happiness more than Jay. Even though he's laying the guilt trip on thick, it's all in good fun. The grin he's no doubt sporting is obvious in the tone of his voice. The man got everything he wanted when he won back his first and only love and discovered he had a daughter. He's a lucky bastard.

"Sorry, guys. I'm on babysitting duty." I chuckle.

When we pull up to the house of horrors, I don't get out right away. I'm gonna need a minute to mentally prepare myself first.

"We should head there," my brother teases. "I'd pay to see you babysitting Liv's kids."

"Yeah, I'd pay if it was just me and them too," I mutter under my breath.

I still can't quite wrap my head around the fact that Liv moved in with her three friends and didn't tell me this is what I signed up for. I wasn't lying when I said I wouldn't back out, but fuck, what I wouldn't give to live with just her and her kids. Her youngest is fucking adorable, her oldest is quiet and well behaved, and then there's Huckleberry. That kid is going to be my buddy. He's four, yet he already owns who he is—rocking the tutu over his fatigues. Most adults could take lessons in self-confidence from him. Fuck, he's awesome.

The Shining Twins and Demon Spawn, on the other hand? Let's just say I know I have my work cut out for me.

"I'm an excellent babysitter." With a deep breath in, I open the door and climb out of the car.

I gave Charlie the night off. I don't need anyone else witnessing my humiliation. There's no way I'll make it through the night without winding up on my ass or holding it because one of the Shining Twins kicked it.

"You're the adult; they can't treat you like that," I remind myself.

"Is he talking to himself?" Brooks asks with a laugh.

Dammit. I stare down at the phone I forgot I was still holding.

"Give him a break." Jay's words are followed by a scuffle, then his voice is louder on the other end of the line. "Hey, Beck, don't let the guys get to you. I was the same way when I was trying to win over Chloe."

Chloe is the daughter he didn't know existed until she was twelve. It was a shock to say the least, but he handled it well, and now they're closer than any father-daughter duo I know.

"Yeah, how'd you win her over, anyway?" I ask, heading for the door.

Jay chuckles. "My brother gave me the worst advice, but in the end, I took it and it worked."

"What was the advice?"

"To be myself."

I can't help but bark out a laugh. "Yeah, cocky son of a bitch. How'd that work out for you?"

"I had to tone it down to her level, of course, but kids are far more perceptive than most people give them credit for. They're like mini adults, so just treat them like you would any new business acquaintance. Find something you have in common with each of them and use that to bond. You've got this."

I nod, even though he can't see me. I constantly have to do that for business. I got this. "Thanks, Jay. We getting a skate in this weekend?"

"Saturday morning work for you?"

"I'll be there." After a quick round of goodbyes, I pocket my phone and jog up the steps.

I raise my hand, ready to knock, but the door swings open before I can.

Dylan pops out onto the doorstep and shuts the door behind her. The smile on her face is as bright as ever.

"Um, hi," I say, unsure why she's blocking me from going in.

Dylan's smile only grows. It's big and kind, but also kind of freaking me out. What is on the other side of that door? "Hi, Becks!"

"It's Beckett," I grump.

Tilting her head to one side, she eyes me and sighs. "We've been over this. I call you Becks, you call me Dippy Do. It's our thing."

"We don't have a thing."

She perks up, practically bouncing in place. "We most certainly do. And you're going to be so happy about that because I'm about to help you out."

Narrowing my eyes, I assess her, trying to get a read on her angle. "You are?"

"Yup." She pops the *p* like she's proud of herself.

Okay, I'll bite. It's hard not to be intrigued when she's this excited about her scheme. "Okay, tell me, Dippy Do."

The way she grins at my use of the shortened nickname makes me drop my head and huff. It's meant to be an insult.

"What is this plan?"

"Well," she says, taking a step closer like she's ready to fill me in on her secrets, "it's two-fold."

"Two-fold?"

"Yeah, two-fold."

"Just don't tell me it involves my dead grandmother. My grandmother is very much alive, by the way."

She snorts. "Whatever you say. I swear she was speaking to me."

"She was speaking *through* you, Dippy."

Her megawatt smile hits me like the midday sun. "Oh my God! Look at us and our shortened nicknames. We really do have a thing."

"Talk," I grunt.

"Okay, so here's the plan…"

THE WOMEN DISAPPEARED WEARING SMILES—WELL, all but Medusa. I've yet to see even a mildly friendly expression on her face. She glared in my direction, then whispered something to the Shining Twins. Then, in a louder voice, she added, "The topic is the pros and cons of capitalism. I'll expect the three best ones to be briefed at breakfast tomorrow."

My brows furrowed. *The fuck?*

As the women head downstairs to camp out in Shayla's office, Liam smirks beside me, as if he can hear my thoughts. "Every night at dinner, Aunt Delia gives the girls a topic to debate between themselves."

"How old are they?"

"Th-they just turned eight," Kai says on my other side.

I hold out my hand to fist bump him and smile, surprised he spoke up at all. "Thanks, Iceman."

His eyes light up. "Iceman?"

I smile. "Yeah, you help me navigate this crew, and I'll take you in to meet some of the guys on the hockey team. Deal?"

Liam scoffs and rolls his eyes. "Aunt Shayla will never allow it." Then he disappears without realizing the damage he's done, pulling his headphones over his ears.

I wink at a deflated Kai. "You just leave that to me."

"He's right." He shrugs. "But I'll help anyway. Just don't sit next to the twins. Aunt Delia told them to kick you if you get too close."

I laugh loudly at the kid's humor. I didn't know he had it in him. But when he just blinks up at me, I snap my mouth shut. Damn, he's serious.

Fucking Medusa. I've yet to figure out how I'm supposed to live with all these kids, let alone deal with her day in and day out.

Shaking off the worry, I take a deep breath and point to the kitchen. "Okay, Iceman, let's eat."

Going from rarely spending any time around children to having dinner with seven of them is the epitome of a culture shock. First, there's the strange food on our plates, which was apparently made by Shayla. Kai told me what everything was, but I'm not quite sure I recognized what he said, and not because his voice is barely more than a whisper. I'm too scared to ask for more details. Bear, Huckleberry, and Demon Spawn all poke at their food, as if agreeing with my assessment.

Little One is lucky. According to Liv, she's picky, so she's got a plate of chicken nuggets in front of her.

The Shining Twins are too busy arguing with one another over capitalism to even notice what they're eating. It's impossible to look away, kind of like a train crash. One takes a bite of food and listens intently as the other one calmly lays out their argument. Then the first carefully takes apart everything the second one just said.

It's equally freaky and impressive. In all honesty, they could probably teach the board of Langfield Corp a few things.

Though most of our plates are still full, one by one, the kids ask to be dismissed. Bear and Iceman—clearly my favorites at this moment—offer to do the dishes. With Little One in tow, I head to the living room, where Huckleberry has asked to have a tea party.

When the doorbell rings a half hour later and the man at the door holds up two large cheese pizzas, I act surprised but make sure all the kids who didn't eat Shayla's monstrosity don't go hungry.

It costs me an extra hundred—Demon Spawn doesn't buy my surprise—but it's worth it when Huckleberry, Iceman, and Bear smile.

Also, I'm starving. Couple the hangry with the lack of order in this house, and I was starting to itch.

My brothers tease that I like things a certain way, but it's not something I like—it's what I need. I need order. When things are a mess, my brain gets fuzzy, my legs get restless, and my heart races. Medication could help, and it has in the past, but I spent several years of my childhood overmedicated and since have found I do best when I manage my surroundings myself.

Shockingly, Demon Spawn offers to put Little One to bed. She's snuggled against him, wearing a sleepy smile, so I agree. To my utter delight, Iceman asks if we can put on the hockey game. Once it's cued up, I sit on the floor with Huckleberry and sip from a teacup with nothing in it while Bear draws on a pad in the corner. The twins ditch us pretty quickly to work on math problems in their bedroom.

When my phone buzzes repeatedly in my pocket, I know it's the group chat before I fish the thing out.

Gavin: How's babysitting going?

Aiden: Hey, that's not nice. We aren't even hanging out.

Brooks: LOL. Only you would assume he's talking about you.

Gavin: He's watching Liv's kids, you dumbass.

Aiden: Oh.

Aiden: Can I come over? I like kids.

Gavin: That's because you are a kid.

Brooks: Don't get him started.

Aiden has removed Gavin from the chat.

Brooks has added Gavin to the chat.

Gavin: You realize I'm your boss, right?

I groan and type a quick response.

Fed kids. No one choked. Now we're watching hockey. I basically rock this babysitting thing.

Gavin: It's only been a few hours. You'll be begging for mercy soon. Don't worry, I won't say I told you so.

Gavin: Too often.

Brooks: LOL. Good job, Beckett. I believe in you.

Aiden: Happy to help next time.

I press the button on the side of my phone to dim the screen and take in the room filled with content kids. *Nah, I got this covered.*

Eventually, Bear and Iceman turn in, leaving me and Huckleberry. At some point, I must fall asleep, because I'm woken by an amused Liv nudging my foot and looming over me.

"How were they?"

The little guy next to me shifts, nuzzling his face against me. Damn, he looks so sweet like this.

"It was exhausting," I admit around a yawn.

She smiles at her son. "They're a lot, I know."

I shift the little boy gently so I don't wake him and stretch to a stand. "It was fun, to be honest. A bit different from my normal Thursday nights."

Her eyes dance, and a whisper of a laugh escapes her. "Different woman every week?"

Groaning, I run my hand over my face. "Is that really what you think of me?"

She shrugs and lifts her brows. "I don't think of you much, to be honest."

"Ouch." I press a hand to my heart in mock hurt.

"You know what I mean." She laughs. "You're my boss, so it's none of my business."

With a low growl, I take a step in her direction. "I'm your husband. Of course it's your business."

Though it's subtle, I don't miss the way she sucks in a little breath. Or how she bites her lip as if she's holding back a sound. Fuck, would I like to learn all her sounds.

"On paper only," she whispers.

"Have dinner with me tomorrow night." It's not a question. I'm not giving her room to say no.

Liv bites that plump lip of hers harder. "Um." She scans the room, looking everywhere but at me, like she's searching for an excuse to decline.

When she opens her mouth to speak, I press my finger against her lips, quieting her protest. "We have dinner with my family on Sunday. If we have any shot at selling this, we need to get our stories straight. We need to make this look real."

She sighs against my finger, her warm breath giving my dick ideas I don't think she'd appreciate. "Right. Make it *look* real."

I lick my lips and pull away, sliding my hands into my pockets to keep from reaching for her. "So dinner. I'll pick you up at seven."

"Why don't we just go straight from work? It'll be easier."

Rocking on my heels, I shake my head. "My wife deserves a good first date. You'll get dolled up. I'll pick you up." From my pocket, I pull out a credit card and hold it up between two fingers. I had my assistant order it when Liv agreed to stay married.

She takes it and examines it, her brows furrowing. "Olivia Langfield."

I can't help the smile that takes over my face or the way my chest gets tight. It's the fucking hottest name I've ever heard. "Use it for anything you need. *Please*," I add, sure she'll object.

She surprises me when she looks back up, expression serious, and nods. "Okay, thank you, Beckett."

As I leave her house, jogging down the steps and toward my car with a lightness I didn't enter with, I can't help but think how tonight was one of the greatest nights I've had in a long time. Every minute of it. Even the kids. *Especially* the kids. That's the thing that's throwing me for a loop, though. Every day since I accidentally married Liv has been better than the last.

Liv

11

Once Beckett arrived, we left the kids with him and convened in Shayla's office with a couple of bottles of wine to discuss this week's selection for book club. I tried to focus on the conversation, but my mind wasn't there. Leaving him in charge of our kids made me nervous—for him and for them.

And for me.

My kids can be a challenge, and I really need this job. Beckett is known for hating kids—it's literally how we got into this mess—and I can't afford to lose my job if he can't handle them.

All evening, Dylan tried to distract me by making ridiculous comments to every one of Delia's book questions. Delia was annoyed—what's new?—and told her that if she wanted to be difficult, then she could pick the next book.

The grin that spread across Dylan's face when she pulled four identical books out of her tote finally perked me up a little.

"What are those?" Delia asked, scrutinizing the bright covers that gave off major romance vibes. By the way her face was scrunched up, she was already regretting her words.

Dylan smirked and picked up her glass of wine. "You said I could pick the book."

Shayla sighed. "I really prefer to read on my Kindle. Purchasing four copies of a book is wasteful."

Dylan rolled her eyes. "It's a book trophy. Live a little, Shay. Take a walk on the wild side and give it a good sniff."

"A good sniff?" I teased.

Dylan brought the book close to her nose and ran the edge back and forth like she was sniffing a good cigar. "Nothing better than the smell of a new book."

Delia then lauded her and told us the benefits of going to a library once a week, but at that point, I'd totally tuned her out because the book title had finally caught my attention. *Marrying Mr. Wrong.*

I turned it over to read what it was about. When I got to the last sentence, I gasped. "You want us to read a book about a woman who accidentally marries a man in Vegas?"

Dylan wiggled a little in her seat, her auburn curls bouncing around her face. "It was between that and *Faking Ms. Right*, where she gets fake engaged to her billionaire boss. Claire Kingsley can do no wrong. Normally, I'd suggest starting with book one, but this book felt so on the nose, I couldn't pass up the opportunity."

"I'm not reading out of order," Delia said, pulling out her phone and tapping the screen. "There, four copies of the first book will be here tomorrow."

Shayla gasped. "What? How?"

"Amazon Prime is a beautiful thing, ladies," Delia said, forgetting her opposition to corporate greed for the moment.

Though the comment was shocking, it wasn't the biggest surprise of the night. After we'd polished off two bottles of wine and wrapped up our conversation—the kind of book club conversation that veers off course at least twenty times—I headed upstairs, expecting to step into utter chaos.

But all I found was a clean kitchen, a basket full of folded laundry, and my son tucked into a sleeping Beckett's side.

Then he called me his wife again. And gave me a credit card. And asked me on a date.

A fake date, I remind myself. Yes, he watched the kids without complaint and apparently cleaned my house, but everything else we're doing is fake.

"Did someone Lysol in here?" Shay asks, inspecting the windows that line one wall like she'll find a cleaning elf has broken into our home.

"I think it was Beckett. He likes things a certain way." In the office, he ensures his coffee cup is sitting in a precise spot on his desk and angled just right. And he's grumpy if anyone so much as slides a paper into the wrong spot.

"Oh," Delia sneers. "I suppose we didn't have the house to his standards."

"I like it." Dylan smiles. "A man who cleans. Now we're talking."

My stomach does a little flip-flop, and my heart flutters in rhythm with it. I bite my bottom lip. "He asked me to go to dinner tomorrow night."

Delia throws herself onto the couch. "You can't go to dinner with him."

Dylan waves a hand at her. "Oh, shush you. She absolutely can, and she will."

My phone buzzes in my hand.

> Mr. Langfield: Take the day off tomorrow and go shopping. Bring the girls. You deserve a break.

Without thinking, I blurt out, "He just told me to take the day off and go shopping. And to bring you along."

Dylan's gold eyes sparkle in the dim light. "Oh, this'll be so fun. Let me see if I can get the neighbor to watch Finn and Addie for a few hours. Liam can handle homeschool with Kai."

Delia folds her arms across her chest. "We can't do that."

Dylan won't take no for an answer, though. "Why? Because you can't take a day off work? Isn't this why you left the big firm? So you could take more time for yourself?"

Shayla worries her bottom lip. "I don't know how Kai will handle being here with just Liam. He's never been home without one of us moms."

I shrug. "Kids are resilient, Shay. He's settling in so well here, and he was fine with Beckett tonight."

Dylan grins. "It's settled. We all need this. Let's go shopping, get lunch, and help Liv get hot for her 'husband.'"

Delia rolls her eyes. "Fine. But we're all getting new clothes, and lunch is on Beckett."

An hour later, I'm staring at the water spots on the ceiling above my bed, still anxious about tomorrow night. I haven't replied to Beckett's text yet, so I type out a quick one and hit send.

> Delia says if she's going shopping then lunch is on you.

The phone lights up almost immediately.

> Mr. Langfield: The credit card is yours, Liv, and there is no limit. Take the girls to the spa, pamper the hell out of yourselves. You all deserve it. And buy something that will make you smile.

In a move at complete odds with the buttoned-up person I've become over the years, I type out a flirtatious response.

> You mean something that will make you smile.

Mr. Langfield: You make me smile, Liv. Doesn't matter what you're wearing. Enjoy your day tomorrow.

I blink at the phone, dumbfounded. Who is this man, and how the hell did he become my husband?

Liv 12

"Oh my God, this man's hands are heaven," Delia says from her pedicure chair beside me.

I can't help but agree as the woman in front of me digs into my heel, making me practically purr.

"Ha! I think this is the first time you've been excited about a man touching you since college," Dylan quips.

On her far side, Shayla practically spits out the green juice she's always trying to force on the rest of us.

"That's mean," I say, though I cover my mouth to hold back my smile.

Delia rolls her eyes and sinks into her chair. "Speaking of men I don't want touching me, we need to put locks on all our bedroom doors and install cameras so we can see what the bastard is up to."

Tilting forward, I gape at her. "Beckett can be a grump, but he's not dangerous, you lunatic!"

"A camera to see what the twins are up to, though…?" Dylan murmurs without moving her lips.

Shayla laughs over the top of her smoothie, but Delia's glare has all of us quieting.

"My girls have high IQs. They need to be challenged. They'd never actually hurt anyone."

"That's what all the white-collar jailbirds say when they're charged." Dylan snorts.

"We're not spying on anyone in the house. Not your kids," I shift my attention to Delia, "and not my boss."

"Husband," Dylan corrects.

"The devil," Delia grumbles.

Shayla shrugs, tucking a lock of her short dark hair behind her ear. "I kind of like him."

"Yeah, well, you like that green juice too," Delia snipes, "so I wouldn't be too excited about your blessing."

"I CAN'T BELIEVE you convinced me to buy this." Standing in front of the mirror in the corner of my room, I flatten my hands along my sides, smoothing the wrinkles in my dress. It's an impossible task, considering the wrinkles are caused by my flabby skin beneath the fabric. The girls had tried to convince me to buy a red dress, but I knew I'd look like a tomato in red. Then they rallied around a blue number, but the last thing I wanted was to look like the inside of a blueberry coming out from the tops and the sides. I grabbed a black dress, but Dylan pushed this green one in my hands and told me I couldn't possibly come up with a food to compare myself to in this color. It's evergreen and absolutely gorgeous. Though she might be right on the food comparison front, I could absolutely compare it to a Christmas tree if I really wanted to be an asshole right now.

"You look beautiful," Shayla says from her spot on my bed. She's sipping a glass of organic wine, looking more relaxed than I've seen her since she moved across the country to live with us.

"You look like I want to fuck you." The crude comment comes from a voice that sounds eerily similar to Beckett's.

I spin around and give Dylan a pointed look. She's got her head on my pillow and her legs crossed in the air.

"That is so freaky," Delia chides. "If you do that damn mime shit when Beckett moves in, I'll kill you."

Shay giggles. "It's ventriloquism, not mime shit."

Dylan jackknifes up and hops to her feet. Her dexterity is almost as impressive as her vocal skills. "No idea what you're talking about. However, I agree with Beckett; I'd fuck you. Emerald green is totally your color."

Toddling over, Adeline holds her arms up and makes grabby hands at me. Dylan jumps in before I can scoop her up, simultaneously stepping between me and a Nerf bullet as Finn runs past our room, screaming, "Captured!"

Winnie lets out a responding screech and ducks into our room, followed quickly by Liam, who holds out his hands to take Adeline. Dylan passes her off, then helps Winnie off the floor.

"Enjoy your date," Dylan sings as she disappears with both of my girls. "I've got home base covered."

BECKETT BLINKS, and a deep grunt emanates from his throat as I open the front door.

Behind me, that Beckett voice from earlier pipes in. "What I meant to say was, you look gorgeous."

Standing in the dim entryway—the light in here is on our to-do list; currently, there's nothing but wires hanging from the ceiling—I whirl around, ready to lay into Dylan and her damn impersonations in Beckett's voice, but I can't find her. She must be hiding. *Asshole.*

Beckett clears his throat. "You do."

He ushers me out the door and is practically mute the entire ride to the restaurant. Unsurprisingly, he has chosen Prime, the hottest restaurant in Boston. For today, at least. It's a well-known fact that wherever the Langfields decide to have dinner today is where everyone else will want to be tomorrow. So it's safe to say this place is good for another day at least.

"Welcome, Mr. Langfield. It's good to see you," the hostess says as she leads us to our table. She's flirty, batting her lashes and swinging her hips as she glides through the restaurant.

Beckett rests his palm at the base of my spine. The heat radiating from him sends a flush straight to my cheeks.

"Regular table?" she asks, pointing at a corner table set up to garner the attention of everyone in the place. The lighting is adjusted just right to give it an air of superiority. Seen but untouchable.

So Beckett.

"I called ahead and asked for a booth," he replies, all business.

She spins, her eyes wide and her mouth ajar. "I assumed that was a joke."

My throat clogs with insecurity and my stomach twists itself into a knot. Of course he doesn't want to be seen at his regular table with me. All of Boston knows that Beckett's dinner companions consist of models or his brothers and that's about it. I'm surprised he brought me to this restaurant at all. The courage I gained from my friends' commentary and from getting dolled up deflates in an instant.

I choke back my absurd feelings and remind myself that this is all fake. We're on a date because we need to sell this, not because he actually *wants* to be seen with me. His team has probably already strategically leaked our location. He doesn't need photos of him next to his frumpy wife circulating. *That* would ruin the story.

"No. When I'm here with my wife, please make sure we have a booth."

Her mouth practically falls open, but she schools her expression. "Of course, Mr. Langfield. Congratulations." Her eyes drift over me quickly, and without another word, she turns and shows us to a much more private booth in the corner.

"Is this spot okay?" he asks as we sit. "I should have asked rather than assuming you'd like a steakhouse."

"As long as no one throws food at me, it's perfect."

He chuckles and leans forward. "I have to know how you ended up living there."

I shrug, clasping my hands in my lap. "It actually happened the weekend you forced me to go to the Keys instead of on my girls' trip."

A server appears at the end of our booth, and Beckett orders a bottle of pinot noir. Something about the way he looks at me as he orders it sends a flutter in my belly.

When the server nods and leaves us, he responds. "You mean when I hosted your girlfriends for the weekend on my private island." He's got one brow hitched, like he's daring me to correct him.

"I was supposed to go to wine country," I pout. "I've never been to wine country. I was really looking forward to it."

Sliding his hand across the table, he grasps mine and squeezes. "Want to go for our honeymoon?" Then the cocky bastard breaks into a smile.

With a huff, I throw my cloth napkin at him. He catches it, laughing, and folds it up perfectly like the good Mr. Langfield, and hands it back to me. Maybe that's why he asked for a booth in the corner. Throwing napkins is certainly not appropriate etiquette for a Langfield.

Ducking my head, I lay it on my lap. "It probably sounds ridiculous, but moving in with the girls saved me."

"And why did you need saving, Olivia Langfield?" The way

he says it, earnestly but also with heat... Damn. Every time he says my fake name, my heart skips. It's utterly stupid and juvenile, but God, it's almost like he's possessive over that damn name.

"You saw my kids." I lift a shoulder and peek up at him. "They're a lot."

"Your kids are incredible. Your friends' kids, though..."

Shaking my head and fighting a smile, I fidget with the silverware on the table. "Parenting is hard. But even more than that, I work long hours."

He winces at my words, but I continue on.

"It's fine. I love my job, but I leave the house while Winnie is getting ready for school. I can't be around when she gets off the bus. Can't help her with her homework. Without a nanny, I'd have to get Finn and Adeline up early and haul them to and from daycare every day. Doing it on my own?" Sighing, I admit the cold hard truth. "I was drowning."

I snap my mouth shut when the server returns with a bottle of wine and give him an appreciative smile.

Once we're alone again, Beckett tips his glass to mine. "To us, Mrs. Langfield."

My lip turns up as I take a sip. I hum at the burst of flavors on my tongue.

Beckett's green eyes brighten as he watches me, still holding his glass aloft. "You recognize the bottle?"

Bringing the wine to my lips again, I shake my head subtly.

"It's what we drank at the bar the night we got married."

I laugh. "Now you're going to get all sentimental about a night neither of us remembers?"

For a long moment, he studies me. There's more tenderness in his expression than I thought he was capable of. "I remember..."

My mind goes blank as I try to think of a quippy retort, but I've got nothing. Fortunately, the waiter returns to go over the specials. Beckett pulls his attention from me, giving me a reprieve from the intensity of his focus, and listens, unsmiling, to the man. He nods along and asks pointed questions—all business in everything he does.

Except for when he's looking at me like he just did. Dammit, my mind is taunting me just like Dylan would if she were here. Like she's perched on my shoulder, chirping her silly little thoughts.

Stupid brain, you're drunk.

"So, you went on vacation with your friends and ended up moving in with them. Then you went out of town with me, only to wind up married. Can I assume that when we go on our honeymoon, you're going to get pregnant?" he teases.

Eyes bugging out, I practically spit out my wine.

Grumpy Beckett I can handle, even riled up Beckett is fine. But flirty Beckett? Flirty Beckett is going to steal my panties, and he may not be too far off with his prediction. If he keeps showing me this side of himself, I may just end up knocked up. This is so not good. "R-rules. We need *rules*," I stutter.

"We're married, and we're going to be living together. Let down your hair and let go of the rules a little."

I run my hand over my perfectly coiffed bun and grimace. "It's important."

"Fine. Tell me your rules," he says in an almost patronizing tone.

"We can't tell the kids that we're married. If you need a few photos with them for the media, that's fine. We can figure that out. But they've lost so much already. I don't want them to get attached to you just to lose someone else."

He sobers, his face taking on the stony appearance I'm used to. "Done."

I swallow. "And PDA. I'm okay with limited PDA in front of your family if necessary, but at home, we're roommates. At work, we're colleagues. Nothing changes there."

He swallows, then runs his tongue along his teeth like he's tasted something bad. "You don't want people at work to know we're married?" Slumping a little, he drops his focus to my hand. His eyes warm slightly at the sight of the ring on my finger.

I slid it back on before I left tonight. I don't want the kids seeing it. That will lead to too many questions I don't want to answer, and I don't want to lie to them if I can help it. But it's important I'm seen wearing it when I leave the house.

"No, people at work are going to find out, if they haven't already. I just don't want it to change how they think of me or how they treat me."

"You're a Langfield now; of course they'll treat you differently."

"Beckett," I warn. "I've worked hard to get where I am, and I did it on my own merit. I don't want to be given any special attention or accommodations because my last name has changed."

He lets out an annoyed sigh. "Fine, but I want to add a rule to this list."

My chest tightens. God, what could this man want now?

"Okay," I hedge, "what is your rule?"

"Date nights. Every Friday."

I stare at him, dumbfounded. "What?"

"My parents have had the same rule since we were kids. Come to think of it, that's probably why there are so many of us."

The chuckle he lets out is like a hit of the most potent drug. Now I get why the man doesn't laugh. If he did, women every-where would be tripping over themselves just to get him to do it again. It's so light and airy, and it scrapes at the space between my clavicles. When his green eyes meet mine, I swear he knows precisely how stupid that sound has rendered me, and he has the audacity to smirk. Holy hell, a smirking Beckett Langfield is dangerous. He's like poison-under-the-sink dangerous, and for a mom, there's nothing worse.

Someone call poison control. I think my heart may have stopped.

"You want to take me out on Friday nights because that's the secret to your parents' happy marriage?" I ask, dubious.

He takes another sip of his drink, cool, calm, and collected—the exact opposite of me—and gives me a nod.

Our marriage is fake. Why does my fake husband care more about our fake marriage than my real husband ever cared about the genuine thing?

He'd make a good real husband. To someone he actually meant to marry, I mean. Not to me, obviously.

"Why did you never get married before?"

His easy demeanor shifts to his default seriousness, and he leans back in his chair. "I told you. I never wanted to."

"But why?" I press. Why did this seemingly perfect man not get snatched up long ago?

"Exactly as Sabrina said; I don't want kids, and most women do."

And that, ladies and gentlemen, is the bucket of cold water thrown on my head I needed. Only I'm a glutton for punishment just begging for a little ice to add to that cocktail, so I push a little further. "Why don't you want kids?"

"I don't have some sad story that will explain this and make you like me more, Liv."

"I don't like you much at all, so don't get too worried."

That comment earns me a signature Beckett glower. His eyes go hard and his jaw practically turns to stone.

"I'm teasing. You're fine." I wave my hand dismissively.

That expression morphs in an instant. His eyes dance in amusement now, his irises almost emerald in the light hanging above the table. "I'm fine? Stop the presses. We need to get that down. My gorgeous wife thinks I'm *fine*."

We're staring at one another, stupid smiles on our faces, and I can't breathe. Beckett Langfield just called me gorgeous. I can't even let myself think about the whole *wife* thing he keeps doing.

"You don't like kids, so obviously this marriage is destined to fail," I tease, only partly joking.

"I don't dislike kids; I just don't want my own. Those are two very different things."

"True." I'll give him that. "So why don't you want kids of your own?"

Our food arrives, and we're quiet for a moment while we cut into our steaks.

"I don't have a lot of free time. You know that already. When I was a kid, my father ran both teams, so time with his kids was almost nonexistent. I'm fortunate enough to share the load with Gavin, though we're looking into acquiring a basketball team, so that'll add more to both our plates."

This isn't a surprise; I've been working on preparations with both Beckett and Preston.

"Growing up, the only time I spent with my father was at sporting events or family vacations. He was never around, and I don't say that lightly. Every night, he was at an event, and at least half those nights, my mother would go with him."

I bite into my steak, a little crestfallen. I see exactly where this is going.

"Don't get me wrong, he loves us. I've never doubted that. And he was a great father, but I spent half my childhood raising my younger siblings. Sure, we had nannies, but actual attention? The kind you get from a loved one—Gavin and I had to step up and be the ones to give it. If I had kids?" He shakes his head and studies his plate for a long moment. "I don't want to do that to them. I love my job, and I'm afraid I'd be no good at balance, so…" He shrugs and takes a sip of his wine.

My heart aches for little boy Beckett. "I get it."

He lifts his head, his brows raised in surprise. "You do? But you have three kids and a full-time job."

I smile. "And sometimes I feel like I'm drowning." Clearly, I've had too much wine. This is the second time I've admitted that to my boss tonight. "I can handle work," I add, suddenly feeling the slightest bit defensive about my abilities in the office.

His Adam's apple bobs, and his jaw clenches. "Liv, you're excellent at your job, and you're a great mom."

"And somehow, I manage to do both," I tease.

He smiles. "No one's ever claimed that you're not exceptional, Olivia Langfield."

But not exceptional enough to keep that name for real. It's a good reminder. Because while this stupid smile won't leave my face, the man sitting across from me has just told me exactly why fake is all we'll ever be.

Beckett

13

"I cannot believe you brought him," I grumble to Brooks, stomping up the steps of the brownstone I'll be calling home sweet home for the next few months.

Gavin hops up onto the porch and smirks. "Wouldn't miss this for the world."

Brooks runs his hands through his long brown hair. It has a little curl to it at the ends that women go nuts over. At games, he keeps it tied back in the tiniest fucking bun. I'd make fun of him endlessly if I wasn't worried I'd jinx myself and my hair would start thinning. So far, I've been blessed. I'm over forty, and it's still dark and thick.

"You're thinking about your hair right now, aren't you?" Gavin jokes. God, it's annoying how well he knows me.

Brooks sighs when I glare in his direction. "Technically, he's my boss. What was I supposed to do?"

"What are you doing?" a woman asks from inside the house. I can't quite make out whose voice it is.

"Just watching the men argue over Bossman's hair."

I smirk at the nickname and the voice. It's Huckleberry. Kid is awesome.

"He just call you Bossman?" Gavin mouths.

The door swings open to reveal a very pissed off Medusa standing in the dark entry. Why the hell don't they ever turn that light on when they answer the door?

"There are more of you. Fantastic."

Now, I'm not saying my brothers and I are the hottest men to ever grace this earth, but we're definitely in the top ten in the city of Boston. We've taken turns being the most sought-after Langfield brother over the years, and currently, that title belongs to Brooks.

Even at thirty, he's still got that baby face that makes it impossible to hate him. His mug is on billboards all over the city because he's the good boy of hockey. Never curses, never does anything wrong, always smiles at reporters and answers their questions politely. Anyone can be an asshole to me, but Brooks... it's like his DNA alters others around him and forces their politeness. Except when it comes to Delia, it seems. If she's not impressed by *him*, there's no hope for the rest of us.

What the hell is wrong with this woman?

"Medusa," I growl, "these are my brothers, Gavin and Brooks. They're here to help me move in."

The responding twitch of her eye calms me. We're in a battle of wills, and if she's not going to like me, then I might as well enjoy pissing her off.

"Bossman, you have brothers?" Huckleberry's awe-filled voice has both the guys beside me chuckling.

"He sure does. I'm Gavin, and this is Brooks."

Huckleberry points at Brooks. "I've seen you in your underwears."

In unison, the three of us burst into laughter. Yes, Brooks is on quite a few billboards wearing nothing but underwear. And I have the unfortunate luck of knowing that they don't stuff them to make him look like he does.

Brooks kneels to Huckleberry's level and fist bumps him.

"Nice to meet you, little man. What's your name?"

Huckleberry throws a thumb in my direction. "Bossman calls me Hucklebewy, but the name's Finn."

"It's Huckle*berry*. We gotta work on those *R*s, kid." I chuckle.

"Giving her kids names already?" Gavin gives me a knowing smirk.

I return the look with a glare.

All my siblings had nicknames growing up too. I no longer use them, but it's my thing. I only did it with Liv's kids to keep me from having to remember their real names and to remain unattached. It doesn't *mean* anything.

"You going to let us in?" I ask Medusa, who's still blocking the doorway with her hands on her hips. Her blond hair is pulled back in a ponytail so tight even it looks angry.

"Them, maybe," she says, pointing at my brothers. "*You*? Definitely not."

"Oh, more hot men!" Dylan cheers as she stands in the dim entryway behind Medusa.

Two down. Where are the others?

Her curly red hair bounces, and the bracelets on both wrists jangle as she waves us in. "Oh, I like the colors on this one," she whispers to Medusa as Brooks steps over the threshold onto the plywood floor. "Becks, you didn't tell me your brothers were moving in too."

Gavin eyes me and mouths, "Becks?"

"It's Beckett," I growl.

She bites her lip like she's fighting back a smile. "We're not doing this again. Hi, boys. I'm Dylan, but to my bestie Becks over there, I'm Dippy Do. We have a thing."

"We do not have a thing," I grumble.

She merely shoots me a disapproving look.

"Fine." I sigh. "We have a thing."

"What kind of thing?" Shayla asks.

"Okay, seriously, how many people can fit in this foyer, and where the hell is my Liv?"

Beside me, Brooks slaps me in the gut and chokes on his laugh.

Gavin mutters, "*My Liv*. You owe me fifty bucks, Brooks. Told you he already broke."

I clear my throat. "*Liv*. Where is Liv?"

"Coming," she calls from somewhere in the house.

My face must respond in some inappropriate way, because Gavin shoves an elbow into Brooks's ribs, and my little brother doubles over, laughing. When Liv appears with Adeline on her hip, my heart spasms. She's wearing yoga pants and an oversized black shirt that falls off her shoulder. Her hair is up in a messy topknot, her face fresh of makeup. Just the sight of her has my insides rearranging themselves. I don't like messes or lots of people, but any time she's near, a wave of relief washes over me and I feel strangely at ease.

"Oh, hi, guys," she says, her face flushing. She brings her free hand to her cheek, as if she's self-conscious about not being done up in her normal skirt suit, perfect makeup, and bun. Dropping her hand, she gives me a stern look that I interpret as a threat to my life. "I didn't know you were all coming."

Shayla reaches for Adeline as Dylan singsongs, "It's moving day. He brought movers!"

Liv bites her lip. "Right. Come in."

I step up to Medusa and eye her until she moves out of our way, then I close in on Liv. It's not like I have much of an option —I have to walk past her to get inside anyway—but I'd be lying if I said I didn't want to touch her. Besides, we're supposed to be happily married in front of my family, right?

But right as I head toward her, ready to pull her close, even if only to run my hand against that bare skin on her shoulder— maybe press my lips there, too—Huckleberry tugs on my pant leg.

"You're movin' in with us?"

Looking down at him, I'm hit with a reminder of Liv's rules. The kids can't know.

"Sorry," Liv says, her voice soft. "I wanted to sit everyone down before you got here, but Adeline thought I'd look good wearing her breakfast so..." She lifts a shoulder sheepishly. "It's crazy here sometimes."

"All the time," Medusa mutters. "You should run. Far."

Ignoring her theatrics, I crouch so I'm eye to eye with my pal who's still waiting for my attention. "Can you get all the kids and the moms into the living room for a team meeting?"

"Team meeting." Medusa snorts.

Beside me, Brooks rubs his hands together. "Oh, I miss Beckett's team meetings."

Gavin bounces on the toes of his Gucci sneakers. "Haven't seen him like this in years."

Hauling myself back up, I snort to hold back my laughter.

My brothers both shoot me looks of amusement and surprise. It's rare that I laugh or smile, especially in front of this many people. Poker nights with Jay Hanson? Yeah. It's impossible not to laugh at that asshole. But just being in this house makes me feel lighter.

Which makes zero sense since its complete chaos—the antithesis of what typically comforts me.

But when Liv's brown eyes meet mine, my body warms, and the constant buzzing in my ears, the unease, melts away.

I probably should see someone about that. Not today, and certainly not anytime soon, but once she's not in my everyday life—

No. I lock those thoughts down quick. I can't think about what will happen when this arrangement is over. Besides, she'll still work for me, even when she's not my wife. It'll be fine. It's all going to be fine.

Or you could just keep her.

"Thought you said team meeting?" Gavin grins at me. The fucker knows precisely what I'm looking at and what I'm thinking.

Dropping to my knees, I look Huckleberry in the eye. "What's the best way to get everyone's attention?"

He smiles. "Living room."

I throw a thumb over my back in invitation, and without needing any explanation, he gets my drift. He hops on and bounces a bit until he's situated. Hauling myself up, I wink in Liv's direction.

She's been watching our exchange closely. I don't miss the way her bottom lip practically dips in surprise. I consider pulling her chin up as we pass her, but I'm following the rules. No touching Liv when we're in this house.

It's for the best anyway. If I touch her, I'll want to keep touching her. It's why I chose a booth over my usual table last night. If we were on display for the world to see, I'd have taken the PDA up a notch, because that's what we were supposed to do. But touching Liv, even in the most innocent ways, will only leave me wanting to touch her in other places.

And maybe I wanted her undivided attention for a bit. To not be bothered every five minutes by a child or a colleague. Two hours at dinner in a corner booth with Liv? It was like hitting the jackpot. Thank fuck she agreed to the Friday date night stipulation. It means last night wasn't a one-time thing.

Idiot. I really shouldn't be so desperate for her.

"Ova there." Huckleberry points to the corner once we've made our way to the living room.

"Here?" I question, spinning to take in the empty space.

He tugs on the collar of my shirt, guiding me closer to the wall, and knocks on the chipped plaster. "If you yell into the vent, everyone can hear ya."

The kid has yet to let me down, so I press closer to the corner and shout, "Team meeting. Everyone in the living room. Now."

In an instant, it sounds like a herd of elephants is loose in the house.

My brothers both eye me nervously. "Exactly how many people live here?" Brooks asks.

"Let's see..." Huckleberry starts counting out names and holding up his fingers. "Mommy, me, Win—"

"Bear," I tease.

Liv lets out a scoff, and Gavin's eyes dance.

"Baby Addie, Auntie Shay, Kai, the twins." He forgets to hold up two fingers here, but I'm pretty sure he's lost count by now anyway. "Auntie Delia, Auntie Dylan." That name brings a sweet smile to his face. "And Liam. So that's... Wait, I rans out of fingers."

I snort. "It's eleven. Add me, and that makes twelve."

Without a sound, the Shining Twins appear in the doorway, wearing matching blue dresses. I swear to God they do this shit to fuck with me.

Brooks follows my line of sight, then does a double take and lets out a shrill scream. "The fuck!"

"That's going to cost you," I mutter under my breath.

One of them—I can't tell which since they're dressed identically—turns to Medusa and holds out her palm. "Mom, we need your phone."

"Why?" she asks.

"Judging by that"—she points at Brooks, who's backed up a few steps but hasn't taken his eyes off the girls—"I doubt they brought enough cash to pay all the fines they're going to rack up. I'm going to give him the QR codes before we start." With her mom's phone in hand, she takes a step toward Brooks. "Do you prefer using Venmo or Zelle?"

"Is she for real?" Gavin asks, leaning in close but keeping his attention fixed on the creepy kids.

"Unfortunately," I mutter.

"How much are we talking here? Dollar bill for every

curse?"

I bark out a laugh. "Thousand dollars a pop. They got ten out of me in an hour at dinner the first time. I've learned to use *ducking* since they got fifteen out of me when I babysat on Thursday night."

"Fifteen thousand dollars?" Brooks asks, his eyes bugging out.

"We've already turned that into forty-five thousand. It's all about the right investments," one of the twins explains.

Gavin is still staring at me, his face etched with real concern now.

"It's fine," I reassure him. "I can handle them."

Medusa laughs her man-hating laugh. "No, you absolutely cannot. But it will be fun watching you try."

"As entertaining as this is," Liv says as Liam and Kai, the last of the kids, find their way into the living room, "we have things to discuss."

The lot of them squeeze together on the couches and chairs situated in the living room. Once again, this should make me anxious. The crowd and the noise. The couches don't match the chairs. There's a bin filled with toys in the middle of the room. The lid is missing, so the brightly colored objects spill onto the floor around it. Magazines, books, and what looks like random game pieces are strewn about on the coffee table, and the fireplace is filled with candles of varying sizes—which is, for sure, a fire hazard.

But I'm not anxious. Not in the least. All because I'm seated beside Liv.

What the hell is wrong with me?

When I warned my brothers that we weren't letting the kids know about our marriage, Gavin grumbled "because it's fake" under his breath, while Brooks nodded and added "we'll do whatever you want, man." Because that's how Brooks is, the good guy, unlike the pain in the ass he brought with him.

In mere seconds, Liv blossoms into the businesswoman I've always been in awe of. "A few months ago, we all moved into this house because we needed the help, right?"

She shoots an appreciative smile in Dylan's direction, and when the redhead smiles back, I grow to like her even more. I like that Liv has people. Though I could do without Medusa, who is still glaring at me from her spot on the couch.

"Well," Liv continues, "Mr. Langfield—"

"Bossman!" Huckleberry shouts from his spot on the floor.

She laughs and rolls her eyes in my direction. "Yes, Finn. As it turns out, Bossman," she says in an adorable, exaggerated tone, "needs help too."

"He does?" Kai asks from his mother's lap, his big, dark eyes assessing me.

She shushes him, but I give him a nod.

"I do."

"He doesn't have anywhere to stay for a few months, so he's going to live with us," Liv says, wearing a big, fake smile and scanning the crowd.

"I'll allow it," one of the Shining Twins mutters, lifting her chin high and scrutinizing me. "He's good for our bank account."

"So that's how you're selling this?" Liam snarks from where he's leaning against the wall. Unlike the rest of them, he's perched about five feet away, arms crossed like he'd rather be anywhere else.

From the other couch, Dylan gives him a look over her shoulder. "We're not selling anything. Beckett needed a place to stay, and the universe provided him with this opportunity. Who are we to say no to the universe?"

In a turn of events I didn't expect, he grumbles, "We aren't."

Gavin's grinning, and Brooks is still watching the Shining Twins like if he looks away, they'll curse him with some witch spell.

Beside me, Liv nudges my arm and widens her eyes in a silent *help me* expression.

I push my sleeves up to my elbows and scoot forward on the cushion. "Listen," I say, making a point to lock eyes with each kid in the room—except Liam, who's got his head tipped back against the wall and his eyes closed. "I'll be an excellent roommate. You'll barely know I'm here because I travel with the team so much. Except on Thursday nights, when, apparently, I'm in charge of you kids."

"Because that's what the universe wants," Dylan sings cheerily.

"No, that's what we need," Medusa grumps.

"Exactly," Liv says. "We'll all benefit. Since Beckett is moving in, he's going to help us out with some of the repairs. Just consider him another... er—" She trips over what to call me, and I know it's because she doesn't want to say parent.

Dammit. I made it abundantly clear last night that I didn't want kids, and now she's stuck.

"He's Bossman, Mommy," Huckleberry says, smacking his forehead like he doesn't understand what's so hard about the concept.

"Right. Consider him another boss. Like the moms."

Gavin snorts. "Always thought he looked good wearing a skirt."

Huckleberry bounces on his knees, his whole face lighting up. "I love tutus! You wanna wear tutus with me, Bossman?"

"Not sure they make them in my size, Huck, but we'll see what we can find."

"Yes!" He pumps one arm and grins so big it almost hurts to look at him.

Liv eyes me, her expression full of a combination of hope and trepidation. As conflicted as the look makes me feel, I like her eyes on me. I like her family. And if I'm not careful, I'm going to like this entire temporary situation a bit too much.

Liv
14

Brooks slips his phone into his pocket and claps. "The moving van is here."

From where she's perched on the edge of the armchair, Delia hisses, "Moving van? If he thinks he's going to move all my aunt's stuff out because it's not good enough for him, then he's got another thing coming."

I throw my arm out in front of Beckett in typical mom fashion, bracing him for the crash, but he doesn't take the hint.

"As lovely as your aunt's furniture is, mine *is* nicer. But since this is a temporary situation, no, I don't intend to replace all your furniture with my own."

If looks could kill, Beckett would be incinerated on the spot, but Delia keeps her mouth shut. Probably because what she'd like to say would cost her a few grand in the presence of her daughters.

"I'm going to take Beckett upstairs to show him his room," I say, shooting Shayla a look that she'll hopefully understand means *rein Delia in before there's any bloodshed.* "Dylan, can you come with me?"

As it is, I'm having a hard time breathing because of the way

Beckett keeps calling me his wife when my kids aren't around. The last thing I need is to be alone in a bedroom with him. Even the presence of his brothers isn't enough of a buffer—the man has made that abundantly clear with all his growls and heady stares.

I can't figure out if it's all an act or not. He makes half the confusing comments when it's just the two of us. When there's no one around who needs to be convinced. I don't get it, nor do I have time to consider it. Currently, seven children are staring at me, wondering what the hell is going on. One friend is on the verge of killing my boss before this temporary situation is over, and another is convinced this is my freaking happily ever after—or maybe she's just trying to get me laid.

Now *that* is something she could work on. With someone other than Beckett, obviously, and not until the marriage is over.

Oh God. What have I gotten myself into?

As Beckett promised, there isn't much in the moving van, so I lead him upstairs while his brothers grab what they can. Dylan is in front of me, smiling over her shoulder every few seconds. It's one of those devilish ones where I don't even want to know what she's thinking, but I also kind of do. I could see the humor in this situation if I weren't the butt of the joke.

"This is our stair. We call him Trippy," Dylan says as we skip the broken step.

"Trippy," Beckett mutters. He's so close that I can practically feel the words against my neck.

"Shayla and I have rooms downstairs. Don't come knocking if the doors are rocking." She laughs. At the top of the stairs, she turns around, wearing a sober expression that looks foreign on her typically cheery face. "But seriously, if you see a sock on the door, don't come in."

"How in God's name could anyone get laid in this house with all the kids running around?" he grumbles.

Gasping, I dart a look at Dylan in a *holy shit, did my boss just say 'get laid'?* kind of way.

"You've got to be creative, but it's possible." With a wink in his direction, she spins on her heel and heads down the hall.

I'm barely able to look at him when he hits the landing beside me, but in my periphery, his cheeks are tinged pink.

"Sorry, that was… Fuck," he mutters.

"I heard that!" one of the twins shouts.

"I'll Venmo you," Beckett replies, already taking out his phone. "Ducking kids everywhere. Definitely no ducking happening in this house."

I burst out laughing. "Good thing it's against the rules, then, huh?" I tease.

He studies me for a second too long, the smile still on his face and a warmth in his eyes. "Yeah."

"Hey, where we putting this? It's fucking heavy," Gavin yells from downstairs.

"We're gonna be rich," Collette sings.

"Beckett!" Gavin yells.

"Shayla!" I holler.

"Girls, why don't we go get some fresh air?" she suggests.

"Can we go to the park, Auntie?" This question is from Finn. "Please? And can I brings my Nerf gun?"

A chorus of "No!" echoes from every corner of the house. I startle when I realize Beckett joined in.

He's still watching me with his lips tipped up in a way that's becoming more and more common. The look makes me feel all melty. He can't keep smiling at me. Or getting along so perfectly with my kids. He's only been here for thirty minutes, and it's already obvious this has disaster written all over it.

My life is one big disaster already. No need to add to the mess.

"This is Liv's room," Dylan says from the end of the hall.

At the sound of her voice, I blink away my thoughts and

shuffle in behind her. I ignore the way my belly tightens when Beckett steps through the doorway into my little sanctuary. With his hands in his pockets, he surveys the space, his lips pressed together thoughtfully.

I try to look at it from his perspective. A full-size bed with a simple white duvet cover and lots of pillows in several shades of light pink. In reality, taking the pillows off the bed every night is annoying, so more often than not, I move them to one side. By morning, at least one of my kids will be in bed with me, so the pillows wind up on the floor.

It's dumb how attached to them I am, but it was something Drake never let me have. Like, who gets upset over decorative pillows?

So when we separated, I rebelled. Not by sleeping with other men or going on shopping sprees. No, I covered my bed with so many pillows it's almost impossible to see the top half of the mattress. Really living on the wild side over here.

Beckett has moved farther into the room as he inspects the layout, and suddenly, I break out into a cold sweat, terrified he's going to open the drawer of the small bedside table he's standing in front of. Why? I have no earthly idea. It's empty. Can't hide anything from my kids, so it's not like there are adult toys hiding in there.

Gosh, when was the last time I used an adult toy? Or had an orgasm?

That thought leads to another that makes my cheeks flame. It's a memory of waking up naked. Beside my very, *very* naked boss.

Naked. And married. Can't forget that part.

As if he can hear my thoughts, Beckett turns and studies me, his green eyes blazing with an intensity that sends the heat from my cheeks coursing through the rest of my body.

Did we consummate our marriage? And if so, why the hell can't I remember it? It's only fair that I should have those memories to flash back on when I eventually do have a room with privacy and some toys.

Who am I kidding? If I could remember that night, there's no way I'd need a toy—one minute and my hand with the images of Beckett thrusting inside me would get me there, no problem.

"It's cozy," he murmurs, stopping in front of Adeline's crib. Shay helped me move it into the corner, since her nursery will now be Beckett's bedroom.

As I turn to the walk-in closet that leads to his space, my stomach flips.

I'm getting all hot and bothered standing in here with this man, even while my asshole best friend silently watches us from the doorway like she knows precisely what's happening.

"Your room is through there. Sorry, it doesn't have a separate entrance... or a door."

He licks his lower lip and hits me with one of those damn smiles, his eyes dancing. "You're putting me in the closet?"

Dylan laughs. "No, silly. It's where Aunt Louise used to sleep. The bed is made up with her sheets and everything," she whispers, like she's filling him in on some big secret. "Delia gets very sentimental about anything related to her aunt, so don't change them."

Beckett's face falls, and I press my lips together to keep from grinning.

"Don't worry," she adds, "we washed them after she passed."

A snort slips out of me, and I disguise it with a cough into my arm. Meanwhile, Dylan keeps that serious expression and Beckett looks utterly stricken.

"Where are we putting this?" Brooks asks from the hall, patting the oversized mattress that he and Gavin must have maneuvered up the stairs.

"Um..." My heart lurches in my chest. There's no way that is fitting in Beckett's new room, if it can even be categorized as that. "Maybe just lean it against the wall for now?"

Gavin shuffles into the room, taking in the space. "This house is gorgeous. I love all the little details."

"Thanks. We were just showing Beckett his room."

Gavin cocks a questioning brow, rubbing his hands together.

"Which is obviously *this* room. Since Liv and I are *married*," Beckett rushes out, looping an arm around my hip awkwardly and pulling me close.

Throwing his head back, Gavin laughs. "Right. And I'm the Dalai Lama. What do you think, Dyl?" he asks, turning to my friend. "I give it the weekend before my brother cracks and shows up at my doorstep, begging me to let him move in."

With a scowl so at odds with her permanently cheerful demeanor, Dylan folds her arms across her chest. "I think they'll be perfectly happy because your brother is madly in love with my best friend." She looks Beckett square in the eye. "And I think he always has been."

Beckett's fingers dig into my hip, and I have to wiggle myself out of his grasp so I don't let Dylan's insanity sit in this space for too long. I don't believe she has magical powers or anything, but the woman is always going on about how, if we put things out into the universe, the universe provides. The last thing I want the universe to think is that I'm begging for Beckett to love me.

That would be insane.

"Why don't I make lunch for everyone?" I offer, scrambling to find something to say.

Beckett checks his watch, then considers me with a concerned frown, as if he knows I'm squirming. As if he can read my mind and is aware that his presence in my room is making me think things I shouldn't. He smirks. "It's only ten, Liv. Besides, we need to get this bed set up."

I want to groan, but I manage to hold back the sound. Looks like Beckett has decided that I'll be sleeping in the attached room with Adeline, and he'll be taking the master with the big bed.

My eyes drift to my pillows, all fifteen of them, and I sigh. I suppose I can bag them up and store them in the attic until this charade is over. There isn't space for them in the closet or what would have been Beckett's room—the twin bed barely fits in there.

Lost in my thoughts, I simply sidestep my way to the door while the men switch out the mattresses. Beckett places my pillows in the corner, along with the sheets and comforter. I leave them to it so I don't have to watch my tiny bit of rebellion disappear and head to the roof for some much-needed air.

There aren't many places to hide in the brownstone. Even with four floors, twelve people in a house is a lot. For so long, it was just the kids and me. Sure, I was married to Drake, and he was around, but barely.

And growing up, it was only my brother, Declan, and me. Declan still lives in the town where we grew up—Bristol, Rhode Island. He's the fire chief now, and unlike me, he's always been single and doesn't have kids.

Maybe I'll take the kids to visit him next weekend. I could use a break from all the insanity.

I press through the door leading to the roof and take a deep breath, inhaling the cool spring air. The sky is gray, which suits my sudden melancholy mood perfectly. In my mind, I envision space heaters up here so we can use it year-round. Dylan would fill pots with plants that she'd struggle to keep alive and that Shay would probably feed green juice. Some sort of play area filled with "toys" Delia would purchase that would make the girls use their brains. Cozy outdoor couches with an ottoman covered in comfy, colorful pillows and blankets for the cool nights beneath the stars. And a hot tub. I want a hot tub so damn bad. Like the pillows, it would be another act of rebellion. Something I always wanted but Drake told me made little sense when we were so busy raising three kids.

Mind you, screwing the nanny also makes little sense, but who am I to point out the obvious?

Pulling my lip between my teeth, I worry at the flesh and let my shoulders fall. I don't want to be bitter, but really, I am. I slump against the cement wall and contemplate the blank canvas. Everything seems to be gray out here.

And then I grimace at the obvious worn spots on the roof that need fixing. A hot tub would probably fall through the damn thing, anyway.

Forcing my attention away from that thought—so much needs fixing, and if I'm not careful, it'll all consume me—I stare out at the park across the street that drew me to this spot on the roof in the first place. I always wanted to live in this area of Boston. If not for Delia's aunt, I'd never have been able to afford it, though.

The door creaks open, but I don't bother turning around. In this house, there is no such thing as being truly alone. Doesn't matter who it is, they'll make themselves known when they want to.

The last person I expect to find me is my boss, but it's obvious he's the one approaching as his rich scent envelops me. Once I get a hit of it, I can't help but take another deep breath and hold it.

God, he smells good.

Beckett leans against the wall beside me, and I work hard to remain indifferent to his presence. In the past, I truly was. I'm not sure when Beckett began seeping into my brain. He makes me feel awkward in my own skin, and suddenly, I've begun worrying about how to impress a man who could never be impressed. So instead, I act the way I used to act, or at least, how I *think* I used to act, and keep myself rigid beside him.

"All moved in?" I try keeping my voice light and airy.

His gaze bores into the side of my face, lighting me up from the inside out. "Yeah, it wasn't too much. Like I said before, I'll barely be here."

"Right." I swallow, keeping my focus trained on the rustling leaves of the trees in the park, reminding myself of exactly what the deal is. Pretend to be his wife in public, barely acknowledge one another in private. Perfect. It's exactly what I need.

What I don't need is for this man to tuck a strand of hair behind my ear, nor do I need him to beckon my attention with a thumb on my chin. "You okay?"

"Of course, Mr. Langfield. Just getting some fresh air." I step back and motion to the door. "It gets crazy in there sometimes."

The growl that emanates from him sends a shiver coursing down my spine. "We're back to the Mr. Langfield business?"

I shake my head gently, trying to knock myself out of the stupor I fell into when he touched me. "Sorry. Beckett, right." I stumble over my words. "I'm going to make that lunch now. You joining us?"

He drops his chin and shakes his head. "Nah, I'm going to take my brothers out to thank them for helping with the move. You sure you're okay?"

I nod. "Perfectly. If you need anything, just let me know."

Then I hustle for the door, leaving my boss and all my damn jumbled thoughts outside.

Hours later, I'm still not okay. Beckett returned from lunch loaded down with shopping bags he whisked up the stairs, then joined us for family dinner. Humoring Kai and Finn, he settled between them at the table and spent the whole meal chatting with the kids.

Since the day we moved in together, the girls and I have tried to catch up with one another while the kids interrupt every five seconds, each needing a refill or a napkin or asking a question we'd answered seventeen times already.

Not tonight, though. Tonight, every time one of the kids asks for something, Beckett is already reaching for it or standing to get it. And each time, his eyes find mine when I begin to rise from the table, telling me with just a look to relax, that he has this.

I'm not used to having a man in our space. I'm not used to having the help of a man, period.

When we're finished, Delia and Shay volunteer to do the dishes, and I head upstairs to start baths. As I wander by the door to my room, I stumble, and for once, it isn't because of a loose board.

The massive bed that sits where my full-size used to is covered with a white comforter, and piled across the top half of it are all my pillows.

Beside the bed, Adeline's crib remains.

I storm straight through the closet and into the alcove where the twin-size bed is set up. The comforter hasn't changed, but the pillow has been replaced. The black travel bag Beckett has taken on every work trip for years sits on top of the mattress.

I suck in a breath. My heart doesn't know whether to leap into my throat or sink into my stomach at what I'm staring at.

"Everything okay?" His deep voice fills the small space and sends goose bumps rippling up my arms.

I spin at the sound, finding him standing dangerously close to me.

He's angled in, with his green eyes fixed on my face, as if he's trying to figure me out.

Good luck, buddy. I'm at a complete loss as to what the hell is wrong with me.

His five o'clock shadow is new. Beckett is always clean shaven and dressed in suits or pressed sweaters with jeans.

Right now, though, he's in a white T-shirt spattered with water, like he just helped with the dishes or maybe checked the temperature of the bath. His wavy brown hair has fallen over his forehead in such a perfectly imperfect way it makes my chest ache. It takes all my willpower not to reach out and push it back. To touch him like I've never touched him before.

I step back and fist my hands at my sides. Touching him would be stupid.

"Not okay." I lean against the edge of the mattress and blink up at him. "Why is your stuff in here?"

He inspects the small space. "Isn't this my room? Or did you want to put me somewhere else?" He folds his arms across his chest and props himself against the doorjamb.

I swallow past the lump in my throat. "Your bed is in the other room." I point behind him and swallow again. My throat has suddenly gone dry.

"Couldn't let my brothers believe we weren't really married." He smirks. "I had them put your bed in storage. I'll make sure you get it back. Although once you sleep on this mattress, you'll never want to go back to the old one."

God, how the sentence could not be more true. Just having Beckett like he is now... I don't know how I'll adjust when he's just my boss again.

Even if that's what he truly is. *Just your boss, Liv.*

"But the bedding..." I stumble, tilting to one side so I can see past him into my room.

"Yours wouldn't fit my bed, and I didn't think you'd like mine. It's dark gray. I probably didn't put the pillows back on the way you like them, but I picked up a few more since yours didn't fill up the king-size bed like it did your full. Not sure they match perfectly. If you don't like them, I'm happy to order more of yours. Just tell me where you got them."

I blink a few times, struck stupid.

"Liv, you're making me nervous," he says softly, his brow creasing. "I'm sorry. I shouldn't have touched your stuff. I won't do it again."

Sucking in air, I stand and finally get my tongue untied.

"Sorry. I'm just..." I pause, searching my brain for the proper words. "Thank you."

His face scrunches in confusion. "Thank you?"

I force a smile. My lips tip up the way I want them to, but my face is tight as I fight back my emotions. "Yes, thank you. My husband—er, ex—he, well... He never liked the pillows. And I just assumed you'd take that bedroom since it's your bed, and it's bigger and—"

Beckett pushes himself off the doorframe and crowds my space, immediately stealing all thoughts from my head. "Your ex was an ass. *I* am your husband now. Don't thank me for treating you the way you deserve to be treated."

My attention falls to his lips. Every time he refers to himself as my husband, butterflies erupt in my belly. This is so bad.

He presses closer.

"*Mom*, the bathtub is overflowing!" Winnie hollers.

Startling, I jump back, then rush past Beckett, not sure whether I'm happy she interrupted or not.

Beckett

15

I t's been almost a full day, and I still can't get the image of Liv on my bed out of my mind. I laid awake in that damn twin bed last night, focused on every sound she made, straining to hear her. Just the image of her lying on my mattress had me so turned on I almost had to take care of that little problem.

And I might have if there had been a door between my room and hers. Maybe I even would have risked it if she didn't have a child sleeping in her room. Or if Dylan wasn't talking like she was Medusa's damn dead aunt through the vents.

Just as I went to circle my fingers around my dick—look, I'm not proud, but I just needed a little relief—the hauntingly annoying voice started.

"*Beckettttt*… I hope you enjoy my sheets."

I stared at the ceiling, willing it to stop, but she was clearly having too much fun.

"And don't forget, I'm watching you. Be good to Liv and the girls."

Scrubbing at my face now, I push away the exhaustion. I have to be on my A-game tonight. Liv is meeting the family.

She's met them all before, of course. She's worked for us for over a decade. But today, she's meeting them as my wife.

Fuck, I love calling her that. It's like I'm a damn caveman, possessive over the word. Over her.

Yet in reality, the woman barely tolerates me.

From my room, if you can call it that, I holler, "You decent?"

She laughs. "I got dressed in the bathroom. Of course I'm decent."

I clench my fists as my heart skips over just the sound of her laugh. It's light and carefree, something usually reserved for people who aren't me. To have her aim that sound at me—even if she's teasing me—fuck, I like it. Too much, if I'm being honest.

Walking through our now shared closet space, I find Liv standing in front of her mirror, fixing her earring and have to bite back a groan at the way her black dress hugs the curve of her ass. Her curves are fucking spectacular.

Once her earrings are in place, she gathers her hair behind her like she's going to put it up in her typical bun. "Leave it down." The words slip out without my permission and her eyes meet mine in the mirror, questioning. I clear my throat and pull my shoulders back. "If you want, that is. You look more relaxed with it down. We've got to convince my family that this is real. Maybe looking more relaxed will help."

Liv worries her lip, but eventually, she nods. "Okay."

The zipper at her back is snagged near her neck, so I step in close to zip it and am immediately assaulted by her sweet scent. She stiffens beneath my touch, her eyes going round as she watches me in the mirror.

With one hand on her shoulder, I brush her hair to the side so it doesn't get caught and angle in close to her ear as I meet her eyes in the mirror. "My family will never buy that we're married if you flinch every time I touch you."

Pinching her lips to the side, she drops her chin, avoiding my gaze. "I'm sorry."

Without letting her go, I study the way she's folding in on herself, as if trying to take up less space with every second that passes. Believing that if she makes herself smaller, she'll somehow blend. She hasn't realized that she's the only one who takes up any space in my head. *Her.* Not some made-up version of her, but the very real woman who's currently shrinking beneath my touch.

We might as well call it all off if she's going to continue to act like this. I won't make her uncomfortable; I'd rather my father bemoan my bad choices and punish me for marrying Liv in what will be another PR mess she'll have to clean up.

"If you don't want to do this, we don't have to. I'll tell my father the truth. Trust me, the fuckup won't surprise him."

Her dark eyes find mine and soften, and then her next words steal my breath. "I think I need to get used to being touched by someone other than my children. Could you maybe…" She bites her lip and searches my face in the mirror. "Could you maybe touch me again?"

It doesn't matter that my hand is only touching her shoulder. Her words have me burning from within. Need snakes through me, and instantly, my cock is impossibly hard.

"Fuck, Liv." The sound is one of pure torture. I settle my hand on her shoulder once again, then gently slide my fingers down her bare arm, watching as goose bumps skitter across her soft, pale skin.

Her body hitches, and she pulls in a gasp. With her focus still fixed on me, she licks those damn plump lips again. I want to see them swollen. I want to see her face flushed because I've worked those lips over for hours.

Fuck, I want her.

I step back and clear my throat. "We should go."

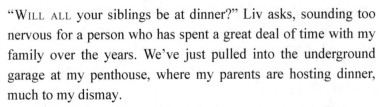

"WILL ALL your siblings be at dinner?" Liv asks, sounding too nervous for a person who has spent a great deal of time with my family over the years. We've just pulled into the underground garage at my penthouse, where my parents are hosting dinner, much to my dismay.

"Pretty sure Gavin and Brooks will be there. Aiden is probably bringing his girlfriend, Jill." I can't help the way my lip curls when I say her name. She's entitled and materialistic and, in my opinion, only sees my brother as her ticket to the high life.

Being used for what we can buy a person or what sort of connections we can make isn't new for any of us, but Aiden has always had this almost doe-like take on love. Like our parents didn't love him enough when he was a kid, and he's just looking for that one relationship to change everything.

His high school girlfriend was different. I've never seen Aiden be more himself around anyone than he was with her. Probably because they were best friends before they fell in love.

"No Sienna?" Liv asks as I open her door and offer my hand to help her out of my silver Bentley Mulliner Batur. It has black and red interior, and although the signature *B*s on the tires and seats don't stand for Beckett *or* Boston, I like to pretend they do. Only eighteen of these cars exist. With 710 horsepower from its twin-turbocharged engine, it's the most powerful Bentley ever made.

It's impractical, but I love it. My penthouse, my Bentley, my vacation home in the Keys... What can I say? I like nice things.

Speaking of which... Before I help her out, I pull the diamond Liv keeps leaving in all the wrong places—namely, not on her finger—from my pocket.

"You forgot this." I slide my hand gingerly under hers, running it beneath that fourth finger.

Her inhale makes me wish we weren't going to dinner with my family. If she reacts this way to such a simple touch, I can only imagine the response I could conjure if I was allowed to get just a little closer. Her eyes widen when she catches sight of the diamond I slipped onto her finger. My band never leaves mine.

"Pretty sure she was heading back to Paris for filming, but I could be wrong."

Liv blinks a few times, then gives her head a slight shake and lifts her chin, taking my proffered hand and stepping from the car. "That's right. I forgot she was working on a show with *Jolie* magazine. When does it premiere?"

"May, I think. They're throwing a big party to celebrate in Paris. It'll be good to see Jay." My best friend was once again back in Paris, and I hated not having him around.

Liv's eyes light up, and she lets out a dreamy sigh. "Paris in May. God, what a dream."

"You should come," I say without any thought as I press the button for the elevator.

"What?" she asks, her mouth dropping open.

Feeling more sure of my plan, I usher her into the elevator. "You're my wife, Liv. People will expect you to be there." I nod once, like it's settled, far too excited about a trip to the city of love with my fake wife.

Liv
16

"You want me to come to Paris with you?" I repeat, suddenly dizzy.

"It would be odd if my wife didn't attend my sister's premiere, wouldn't it?"

With my heart thumping against my ribcage, I worry my lip. I am so in over my head. Sienna is a fashion designer. Beautiful, petite, and running her own empire at twenty-eight. We are eons apart.

The women the Langfield men date can all wear her designs. They all fit. Not just in size—though that's a detail I can't ignore —but in lifestyle too. Why Beckett thought his family would believe he'd marry me is ridiculous.

I appreciate my curves, and I'm happy with who I am, but I'm not naïve. When news of our marriage breaks, the entire world is going to question what he sees in me.

My body isn't just curvy; I have rolls and dimples and more than my fair share of stretch marks. Things that will never change, no matter how many smoothies I drink or how many hours I spend on Delia's Peloton. My body is built differently. It took me a long time, but I'm finally in a place where I accept that.

But others aren't as accepting, and I worry this is all going to blow up in Beckett's face.

"I'll have to talk to the girls about it." That should buy me some time to figure this out. "Not sure if they can watch the kids for that long, but let me know the date."

Beckett shrugs and leans against the elevator door. The view behind him is almost as gorgeous as the man in front of me. The elevator is all glass, and the sun setting over the harbor nearly steals my attention. The oranges and reds swirl together like sherbet, highlighting his navy-blue sweater and jeans perfectly. "We'll bring the kids. Jay's daughter is thirteen, and she's great around the shows."

I snort. Jay Hanson and his wife, Catherine, are Boston royalty. From two of the city's wealthiest families, they could do nothing but produce a perfect, well-behaved child. I'm sure she's never shot glitter all over the ceiling or started a food fight by flinging meat at one of their guest's heads.

"I doubt your sister or the Hansons want three young kids around for that. Winnie would be in her glory, yes, but Finn would probably take out one of the models with a Nerf gun he smuggled in. And Adeline? Diapers, sticky fingers, and models don't mix well. Besides," I sigh, holding his gaze, "you don't like kids. It's best if we keep them out of our little sham of a marriage."

He swallows audibly, his jaw locked tight, but he doesn't respond. The tense silence is only broken when the elevator dings.

The door opens into the penthouse, taking me by surprise, and a moment later, Beckett's family materializes before us.

A warm palm presses against my lower back and Beckett warns in a low, smooth whisper, "Try to keep your jaw from hitting the floor. You're supposed to have been here before."

Gavin saunters over with a beer in his hand and a smirk on his face. "Only she hasn't, has she?" He kisses my cheek and grins. "You gonna call bullshit on this yet?"

I snap my mouth shut and put on my game face. Work Liv is back—the put-together, take-no-shit, confident woman—prepared to woo all my bosses, who just so happen to be my husband's family.

"No idea what you're talking about, Gavin," I say with a big smile. "Happily married to this hottie."

Beckett coughs and pats his chest as if he's surprised. Doesn't he know me well enough to understand that when it comes to protecting any of the Langfields, I'm a pro?

And apparently, I'm a Langfield now too. I swallow that insane tidbit down, concentrating on my surroundings.

Floor-to-ceiling windows leave the room bathed in a red hue from the sunset. The living room is furnished with rich, over-sized mahogany couches. Behind them, the long dining table surrounded by twelve chairs is already set for dinner.

The kitchen is all dark wood and fancy appliances—a far cry from the green Formica countertop and ancient stove in the brownstone. The time is easy to read on this oven. It's already seven o'clock. We're right on time.

Beckett's mother smiles widely and strides toward us. "Oh, Liv, we're so happy for you both!"

Beckett's palm hasn't left my back. In fact, he slides closer and squeezes my hip gently as he settles it there. "Thanks, Mom. How's the penthouse treating you?"

Monroe Langfield gathers me in for a hug, forcing me out of her son's grip. When she pulls back, she holds my upper arms and takes me in.

She's much smaller than me. Her brown hair—which is still dark and rich—falls in loose waves on her shoulders, coordinating perfectly with her camel-colored sweater. Her ears are adorned with what have to be three-carat diamond studs. The rock that glitters on her ring finger is only slightly larger than the one Beckett slipped back onto mine in the parking garage.

"Oh, the penthouse is fine." She waves off his question. "I want to hear about the two of you. How this happened and how my Beckett proposed. Tell me about my new grandbabies. When can I meet them?"

Swallowing past the lump that's suddenly lodged in my throat, I turn to Beckett. Shit, she's really into this. Like we baited her, hook, line, and sinker. It dawns on me then: we're flat out conning his family.

Beckett pulls me back from his mother's grip. "Ma, let my wife get a drink before the inquisition."

Monroe smiles. "You hear that, Preston? He called her his *wife*." She turns back to me, beaming. "Never thought I'd see the day my baby got everything he's ever wanted. We all should have known he was waiting for you. Man's been smitten for years."

I cough out an uncomfortable laugh, even as my stomach does a little flip. That couldn't be farther from the truth, but it's sweet for her to say.

Beckett presses a kiss to my forehead like he does it all the time. "She's always been the one," he says to his mother. "What do you want to drink?"

He looks at me, but I've been rendered speechless. His green eyes are bright as he watches, wearing a smirk like he knows exactly what he's just done. *Asshole.*

"I'll have whatever red wine is open."

"The Jackson pinot noir. I'll have the same," he says, his voice light and full of joy.

"So specific," his mother teases. "I've never had it. Any good?"

"It's the best." Beckett's attention is still on me, and I can already feel he's about to say something that will have my head swimming again. "It's what Liv and I had the night we got married."

"Oh, don't waste it on me, then," his mother says.

Beckett finally steps away and wanders toward the bar, but over his shoulder, he replies, "We've got plenty. I ordered six cases."

What the...?

Even my mind is stuttering at this point. The man is giving me whiplash. The wine wasn't anything special. His family typically drinks bottles that cost the equivalent of my daily salary. Why would he buy cases of the cheap one we had in Vegas?

"Hey, Liv." Brooks ambles up to me and pulls me into a hug. He looks so much like his oldest brother, but with longer hair—each has an uncanny resemblance to Henry Cavill.

Yeah, I'm surrounded by beautiful people.

Brooks is thicker than Beckett. His muscles strain under his black T-shirt, and his jeans hug his strong thighs. When he lets go of me, Sara, my assistant, is standing behind him.

"Sara!" In my excitement to see her, I give her a too-loud greeting that echoes off the high ceiling.

"Hey, Liv. Congrats on the marriage." She moves closer, her blond hair swaying, and wraps me in a hug.

Sara has been a great addition to the team since she moved to Boston a year ago, and since Beckett requires more of my attention than his brother or his father, I've given Sara more responsibility with the hockey team. Is she dating Brooks, though? I can't talk, I suppose; I married one of the owners—stupid freaking alcohol and Vegas decisions—but this is surprising.

As if Brooks can read my thoughts, he explains, "Sara's still finding her way around the City and making connections, but when she discovered my love for Lake Paige and she had no one to go to the concert with," he says, leaning in close, his voice just above a whisper now, "we went together. Don't tell the guys."

Lake is probably the most popular pop star there is, and she married one of Beckett's friends, Ford Hall. It was a bit scandalous when it happened, seeing as she was dating his son just this past Christmas. But Ford is happy, and Lake seems lovely, so to each their own, right?

Sara smirks. "Best friends ever since." She puts her arm around him and squeezes.

What she misses, though, is the grimace on Brooks's face at the word *friends*.

Hmm... seems like our goalie doesn't like being in the friend zone. Interesting.

"Your secret is safe with me, Brooks."

Aiden and Jill appear at my side next. "What secret? You keeping secrets from me now?" he grumbles. "I'm a great secret keeper."

Jill nods in agreement and holds out a manicured hand. "It's true. I told him the name of the color I wear on my nails, since everyone is *always* asking," she says to Sara, as if they're members of some secret society.

Maybe I'm as much of an ass as Beckett, but nail polish? Really?

Sara blinks at Jill's nails and tilts her head. "Isn't that bunny white?"

Jill's face falls. "Um, no one has ever guessed it. How'd you do that?"

Sara shrugs. "My bestie wore that color in college."

Beckett reappears at my side with my glass of wine in hand. As I murmur a thank-you, he lifts my chin and stares at me before he moves in close and brushes his lips against mine. "Anything for my bride."

I melt. Into a puddle. On the floor. Call it now: Liv died from Beckett's kind, sweet, swoony attitude. Dead.

He pulls back, and that damn cocky smile resuscitates me.

"Now that Liv has a drink in her hand, tell us everything," Monroe demands, taking the glass Beckett offers her.

He wanders back to the bar to grab his drink. "I'll let Liv tell it. She's a much better storyteller."

Shit. What story does he want me to tell? I can't go with the truth. *Oh, your son and I got so drunk I don't remember a thing but waking up naked next to him with a ring on my finger.*

That reminds me: I really need to find out whether we had sex.

"Yeah, Liv, tell us everything," Gavin teases.

With a huff, I smack his chest with the back of my hand.

"Not sure what you want to know." My lungs are constricting, making it difficult to get the words out.

Beckett swaggers back, wine in hand and a smirk on his face. "They want to know when everything changed between us. You know, the moment you stopped calling me *Mr. Langfield.*"

I bite my lip and go with something resembling the truth. "Well, everything really changed when he forced me to accompany him to his home in the Keys rather than going to San Fran with friends like I'd planned."

"Your annual girls' trip?" Gavin cocks a brow and turns from me to my husband. "Dude, you interrupted her annual girls' trip?"

Beckett frowns. "I was working on the Emerson trade. I needed Liv there."

Gavin scoffs. "We don't pay you enough."

"Boys," Monroe chides. "Tell us, Liv, what happened on the trip?"

"Well, my friend Dylan is a ventriloquist."

"An annoyingly good one." Beckett's studying me, like he's not sure where I'm going with this. He walked right into it, though, giving me control of the narrative.

"She was having fun screwing with Beckett since he usurped our trip."

"Ass," Gavin grumbles.

Brooks chuckles, and Sara leans into him, and when their eyes meet, I can feel the electricity spark between them.

"Anyway." I shake off the image and the tiniest hit of envy that strikes at the sight of such pure adoration. "She would walk through the house pretending to be Beckett's dead grandmother." I mimic Dylan's voice. "*Becketttt, you need to be nicer to Liv. Becketttt, don't be so grumpy. Becketttt...*"

The man himself groans. "We get it."

Monroe frowns. "Both of our mothers are alive."

"Dylan doesn't concern herself with facts," my fake husband grumbles.

I can't hold back my giggle at his expense. "It only made it funnier."

Beckett's eyes dance as he watches me, clearly saying, *Where the hell are you going with this?*

The smile that splits my face makes my cheeks ache. "She kept doing it at night, and it really did freak the big guy out."

His lips twitch, his full attention locked on me. "She was stupidly good at it."

I hold his gaze, pulled into the depths of his emerald irises. "He came into my room. He was terrified, and he asked if he could sleep there."

Gavin nudges Beckett. "Bro, that's hysterical."

I lick my lips. I'm on a roll now.

"Said he couldn't sleep when his grandmother wouldn't stop talking to him, and since he'd forgotten his favorite stuffed animal—"

With a sound somewhere between a laugh and a curse, Gavin claps. "You still sleep with Blue?"

I snort. Definitely didn't see that one coming. "Oh yes, he can't sleep without it."

Beckett's jaw flexes as he stares me down. "I can now that I have you."

I roll my eyes, but the intensity he's directing at me makes my skin prickle and my heart rate pick up. "He just brings it into bed at night."

"That thing must be falling apart," Monroe says. "I had to stitch it up more times than I can count when he was a boy. He never let it go."

I nod. "We've had to perform surgery on it a few times too. The arms don't want to stay attached. Must be from how tightly he squeezes it. Or because of the way he runs it against his lip to soothe himself to sleep."

Beckett shakes his head, but a hint of a smile slips through his stoic exterior.

Brooks, Aiden, and Sara are laughing so hard they're shaking.

Jill just gapes. "Wait, so you were afraid of someone who obviously wasn't there, and you seriously asked to sleep in your assistant's room? She could have sued you."

Feeling lighter than I have in days, I smirk. "Nah, he looked so scared and weak and he was missing his stuffie…"

"And you were in those blue pajamas," Beckett teases.

I shrug. "Meant to be."

He shakes his head and turns away quickly, but not before I catch sight of a full-fledged smile. He peeks over at me again, but quickly averts his attention so I can't make out his expression. For some reason, I get the feeling he has to look away, like if he doesn't, he might just walk up and kiss me again.

The scariest thing? I really wish he would.

Liv

17

On Monday, Beckett leaves for Arizona. I'd be lying if I said it wasn't a good thing. Dinner with his family was too comfortable, too fun, too picture-perfect for a relationship with an expiration date.

I tell myself that the ease I felt is natural. I've known his family for years. Gavin and I have been friends for so long. And though Sara is newer to the area and to the team, she and I hit it off immediately. Beckett's parents are lovely, of course, and Brooks and Aiden are a blast.

But my stomach aches every time my mind drifts to our eventual divorce. Will this ruse destroy all those relationships for me? I didn't think nearly hard enough about the consequences of our little arrangement before I committed to it, and now I'm being hit with it all full force.

It's not just my kids who could get attached. The Langfields are all invested in our fake marriage, as well as my friends—well, everyone except Delia, who is thrilled that Beckett is out of town for three whole days.

On Thursday, I wake up anxious, unable to pinpoint exactly what has my stomach in a knot. Is it because Beckett's returning today? Or maybe it's because of my annual OB-GYN appointment.

I hate going to the doctor. Not because I'm worried about health issues. Nope, it's because I hate stepping on the scale. The moment when the nurse asks me to take off my shoes always sends me into a panic. *I'd rather leave them on because then I could blame those extra fifteen pounds on my clothes and the flats that are practically weightless.*

It's stupid, this anxiety that needles at me for hours leading up to the one-minute portion of every appointment. But it's impossible to control. Because that one minute then leads to a stern look from the doctor and a lecture about how I am technically obese and should consider exercising and eating right. He'll remind me that I need to watch these things now that I'm getting older.

The thing is, the doctor isn't telling me something I don't already know. The whole experience just makes me feel shitty.

As I'm getting ready, I'm in a tizzy, searching for a single pair of matching heels. "Not one matches," I grumble. "Delia!"

With heels on and blond hair slicked back in a ponytail, my friend appears. She looks perfect, like always. "What's up?"

"Any chance you've found any of my heels in the girls' room?"

"Huh?" she asks, putting the back on the earring in her left ear. "Your shoes are missing again?"

I point at my closet. On the floor lies one black pump, a second black shoe with a smaller heel, and a single brown shoe.

"I'll ask again, but they swore it wasn't them."

Shoulders sagging, I sigh because I so don't have time for this and now I'll have to wear flats. "It's fine. This weekend I'm going to search the whole house. It has to be one of the kids. My shoes didn't just walk off on their own."

"It is odd," she says, following me down the stairs.

Hours later, I'm trudging into the office, feeling like crap. As expected, I left the doctor with instructions to watch what I'm eating, walk more, and "consider a group fitness class like Zumba."

I've got three kids, a sixty-hour work week, and a boss who thinks I'm his personal secretary, when am I going to find time to go to Zumba?

Already defeated and drained before my workday has begun, the last thing I want to see is Sabrina, Beckett's ex-girlfriend.

See? So not my day.

"Olivia!" she coos in her fake friendly tone, pushing dark hair curled in soft waves behind her ear. "Just the person I wanted to see!"

With every ounce of energy left in me, I summon a smile. "Good to see you. Can I help you with something?" I don't stop, hoping it'll be a quick question, but unfortunately, she follows me.

"No, I'm meeting Beckett for lunch. But I have to compliment you on the PR magic you're working. That was quick thinking, giving Beckett the wife and kids cover."

My steps falter along with my heart as I reach my office door. "Huh?"

She stops beside me and places her hand on my shoulder in what I imagine she believes is a comforting gesture. "Don't worry. Beckett and I will be discreet. Obviously can't have him seen out with his girlfriend when he's just announced his marriage." She laughs lightly, like we're in on a joke.

Before I can unravel her words, Beckett rounds the corner. His steps falter when he spots the two of us together.

"Oh, hi," he says, surveying Sabrina, then me, his expression unreadable.

It's almost impossible not to lash out and make a scene.

He told Sabrina about our agreement? He's still seeing her? And here I was, letting myself believe there could be a deeper meaning behind his little touches and kind words.

"Liv, can we go over this problem with Peters?" Sara asks, walking into my office from the other side, where we share a door.

Saved by the assistant.

With far too much enthusiasm, I nod, because let's be honest, I need a minute.

"Y-yes." I clear my throat. "Can you walk and talk?" I need to get the hell away from these people before I give myself away. The key to managing PR is buying time and planning. So that's what I'll do. Buy myself some time to curb my natural reaction before I claw Sabrina's eyes out. Or cry. It could go either way at this point.

I give Beckett a quick nod over my shoulder but keep my eyes averted. "Welcome back, Mr. Langfield. I'll talk to you later. Enjoy lunch, Sabrina."

Beckett doesn't respond, but Sabrina gives me an exuberant wave.

With a tight-lipped smile, Sara leads me out of my office. "What the hell was that about?" she hisses once we're out of earshot.

I told myself I was going to have a juice cleanse shake for lunch, but suddenly, I'm craving real food.

"Can we get lunch somewhere? And not talk about it?" I beg.

With a sympathetic smile and a nod, Sara leads the way.

Because my day hasn't been terrible enough, I get a call from Winnie's school during lunch. I excuse myself and take my food back to my office so I can return the call.

It's the school nurse. Winnie is claiming to have a stomachache, but the nurse mentions that Drake was scheduled to read to the class today but was a no-show.

When I end the call with the nurse, I immediately dial Dylan. Two minutes later, she's set to pick Winnie up. I hate that I can't do it myself, but the Peters issue isn't going to solve itself. This is the exact reason the four of us moved in together. When one of us can't be there, the others step up. In the end, Dylan will probably do a better job of coaxing Winnie's feelings out of her than I ever could. I have no doubt that by the time I get home tonight, my girl will be smiling. Dylan has special powers like that.

Then, because I can't help myself, I call my ex-husband to give him a piece of my mind.

"Hey," he answers after three rings.

"What are you doing right now?"

"Just leaving lunch with a client. What's wrong?"

"Did you forget you were supposed to read to Winnie's class today?"

Silently, I will him to say that it slipped his mind. That he thought it was tomorrow. Really anything that doesn't involve him not caring enough to bother showing up.

Drake sighs, the sound of it crackling down the line. "No, but I couldn't get out of this lunch."

I set the phone down on my desk and breathe in for four, then out for four. I will not cry. I will not scream.

Then I put the call on speaker because the idea of his voice so close to my ear makes me shudder.

"Why didn't you call me? One of the moms would have covered."

He laughs. "Or maybe that new husband of yours?"

Oh shit.

"It's funny, you know? How mad you were when I started dating Kendall. You didn't even have the decency to tell me when you got fucking married."

"Because you started dating Kendall when you were still *married to me*, you idiot. Now that we're divorced, my personal life is none of your business."

"No, but who my kids are living with is my business."

My stomach plummets. Dammit, he's not wrong.

"I'm sorry." I heave a sigh, hating to even speak the words. "I should have told you."

"He's your fucking boss, Liv. What the hell?"

The growl that rumbles from the doorway is so fierce it sends shivers racing through me.

"Talk to my wife like that again, and we're going to have a major problem, *Drake*."

Fury radiates off my husband, the power of it so strong I feel I could reach out and touch it.

"Mr. Langfield," Drake stutters. I think he's actually at a loss for words. Drake works for a marketing firm, and he's been trying to get this company's business for years. It pleases me immensely to know that will never happen now.

"We're done here," Beckett growls before hanging up on my ex, leaving me gaping up at him. Beckett towers over me, his jaw clenched and his chest heaving. "He doesn't get to talk to you like that."

"Like what?"

With a shake of his head, he pulls in a deep breath and clenches his fists at his sides. "The way he spoke to you, how he said your name. *Liv*," he spits. He's mimicking Drake, but in all honesty, it sounds no different from Beckett's normal tone.

I cough out an uncomfortable laugh, trying hard to hold back a sob. "You say my name the same way."

His only response is to stare at me, unblinking.

I don't have time for this—his mood swings or his mixed signals.

His girlfriend was bad enough, and now I have to deal with the Peters situation. God, I can't wait to go home to my kids. I'm so done with this day.

Beckett
18

Red. I was seeing nothing but red.

This day had gone nothing like I hoped. To my complete and utter surprise, I woke up in Arizona, excited to fly home. In a king-size bed, surrounded by silence, *by myself,* I practically jumped out of bed, looking forward to returning to the chaos that exists in the brownstone. I found myself counting down the minutes until my evening with the kids—followed by another restless night in the twin-size bed from hell—all because it would mean Liv would be snuggled up just a few feet away, in my bed.

Complete insanity.

And when I heard her voice in the hall outside my office, I couldn't stop myself from rushing out to greet her, only to find her chatting with Sabrina.

Liv disappeared before I could get a word in, and Sabrina tried to sweet talk me into taking her to lunch, even though I ended things with her months ago. She swore it was okay, that Liv had informed her that our marriage was fake and said she was fine so long as Sabrina and I were discreet. And I saw red.

Fucking red.

Is that what Liv really thinks? That I'd touch another woman? That I would want to see another woman? That she can allow another man to touch her while she's married to me?

In no uncertain terms, I told Sabrina that she was mistaken, and that Liv is the love of my fucking life. *Again*, I reminded her that she and I were through and emphasized the part where there was no way we'd ever have a future together.

Regardless of whether Liv believes what's happening between us is real, I would never cheat on her like her husband did.

And then to be told that I speak to her the way that dipshit of an ex does?

Red. The whole goddamn world is nothing but red.

My brothers have been bugging me all day about going out tonight. I could use a few shots, but more than anything, I need my wife, her kids, and that damn twin-size bed. What the fuck is wrong with me?

I stumble into the house feeling uneasy and surprised my things haven't already been thrown on the front walk.

"Hey, Beckett. How was your trip?" Shayla asks from the kitchen, all bright and cheery.

There's no way she knows about what happened today. If she did, she'd ignore me.

"Liv home?"

"She went straight up to her room when she got home." Shayla scrutinizes me under the fringe of her dark hair. It's cut asymmetrically, so one side always falls over one eye. "Did something happen at work today?"

Sighing, I run my hand over my face. "I think we both had a bad day." I consider leaving it at that, but Shay's genuinely concerned expression has me opening up. From the beginning, she's been nothing but kind to me. She's quiet, but obviously observant. "Can I ask you something?"

Shayla stops cutting the vegetables on the cutting board and sets her knife down. "Sure, what's up? I'm making a smoothie. Want one?"

I hold back my grimace. Dylan warned me about the smoothies. She called them swamp sludge. "Nah, I'm okay. I know tonight is girls' night, but is there any chance I can do something for Liv first? Something that will relax her before you ladies head out?"

Shayla presses her lips together and raises her brows.

"Not like that." I laugh, holding up my hand as my face heats. "Just... what does Liv enjoy?"

Shayla's expression goes soft. "All Liv ever talks about is wanting a hot tub. So maybe a bath?"

A bath. I can do that. "Thanks, Shay."

She watches me for a minute longer, her gaze locking me in place where I stand in the doorway of the kitchen.

I can practically see her brain at work. "Something wrong?"

She shakes her head, her dark hair swaying. "No, it's nothing."

Swallowing past the lump of trepidation in my throat, I step closer. "I have a sister. I know that look."

"It's just..." She licks her lips and averts her gaze. "You have a nickname for everyone else."

"Huh?"

"Kai is Iceman, Finn is Huck, Dylan is Dippy Do. Even Delia has a name."

I let out a light scoff. "Medusa?"

She huffs a laugh, her eyes downcast now. "I just... kinda feel left out."

"Pipsqueak." I gave her the name in my head the first time I met her. I guess I've never spoken it aloud.

"Huh?" She's frowning when she looks at me again.

"Cause you're tiny."

She laughs. "That works, Becks."

My grimace is immediate. Damn Dippy Do and her

nickname.

Shay giggles. "That's what Dylan calls you!"

"She says it's our thing." I shake my head and slip my hands into my pockets. "It's *not*."

"It so is!" Dylan sings as she sashays her way into the kitchen. "But I'm good at sharing, Shay, so you can use it too."

I don't have time for this. "Whatever makes ya happy, Pip. Can I go take care of my girl now?"

Dylan's grin brightens the whole hideous kitchen. "Ya hear that? He called her his girl. I told you."

I laugh. "Yeah, Dippy Do, you told us. But seriously, I need to see Liv. Am I excused?"

She shrugs, all giddy. "I suppose."

I take the stairs two at a time—making sure to skip the loose step—eager as shit to see her. In the bathroom, I start her bath and add floral-scented bubbles I find under the sink. Then I go in search of her. When I'm met with an empty room, I turn off the water and head up the last set of stairs, knowing precisely where to find my wife.

Liv's standing on the roof, looking out over the park. Her shoulders are slumped and her dark hair is down and blowing with the wind. My entire being relaxes now that I'm in her proximity. This feeling is absurd, but I'm done questioning it.

In three strides, I'm behind her with a hand on her shoulder.

Before I can open my mouth to speak, she shakes her head. "Go away, Beckett."

The words don't bother me nearly as much as the sound of her voice. Is she crying?

"What's wrong?" I don't back up, and I don't remove my hand from her arm.

"Why are you here?" She spins out of my grasp. When she turns to me, her face is red and splotchy. "Shouldn't you be with your girlfriend?"

My damn lungs seize at the pain in her voice. "I don't have a girlfriend."

"Ha," she jeers. "Right. You don't commit to anyone."

"I committed to you. I'm committed to our *marriage*."

Her only response is a roll of her eyes.

"Wait. Were you jealous?" I don't know why, but that idea excites me. See? I'm clearly an ass. But if she's jealous, then that means she cares, right?

"No, but we're married. For show anyway. How do you think it looks for you to be out with your gorgeous ex while your wife is getting a lecture from her doctor about being fat?"

And now I'm back to seeing red. "*What?*"

Liv slaps a hand over her mouth and her wide eyes well with tears. "Oh my God. I have no idea why I said that."

"Livy," I say softly, peeling her hand from her face.

"What?" The tears break free and my heart fucking cracks.

Cupping her cheeks, I swipe the tears with the pads of my thumbs, wishing it was as easy to erase every hurtful word ever spoken to her.

"Never again," I whisper.

"Never again what?" She hiccups.

"I'll never have lunch with her again."

Shaking her head, she tries to pull back. "No, I was being ridiculous."

Instead of releasing her, I pull her closer and give her the softest smile I can manage. "No, you were jealous. Just like I was jealous when I found you talking to your ex on the phone. Though that jealousy pretty quickly turned to rage. He can't talk to you like that, Livy."

She closes her eyes and pulls in a deep breath. "Why do you keep calling me that?"

"Calling you what?"

"*Livy.* You've never called me that. I've always been *Liv.*" She mimics the same damn tone her ex used earlier and my teeth nearly crack.

"Because you're my *wife*." I emphasize the last word, hoping she'll hear the meaning behind my words, praying she'll feel the power in them like I do. "I'll be damned if I talk to my wife like I used to talk to you. I'm so sorry, Livy. God, I hate the idea that I ever sounded like him."

With a little shake of her head, she licks her lush lips. The way I want to dip my head closer and possess those lips is a problem. "Now tell me about this damn doctor."

She rolls her eyes, and this time, she does manage to pull out of my grasp. As if she's trying to hide from me, she crosses her arms over her chest and hunches her shoulders, making herself smaller again. "It's nothing I haven't heard before. I gained weight during each of my pregnancies, but I've never been small, and—" She sighs and drops her attention to the top button of my shirt. "It's nothing. I like my curves. It was just one of those days, ya know? And yes, maybe I was a little jealous of Sabrina, but who wouldn't be? She's perfect."

I drop my head back and groan at the sky. Damn, this woman can be so blind sometimes. Edging in closer, I cage her in against the banister.

"Why are you looking at me like that?" she grumbles, lifting her chin as if she's donning armor in preparation for my response.

"I was always looking, Livy. When you were married to someone else. When you were pregnant. When you were a different size after giving birth... I was never *not* looking, and I always liked what I saw." I lean down, my nose brushing against her neck, and inhale her. "You've always had my attention," I whisper against her. "This is just the first time you've noticed, because you're finally looking back."

Pulling back, Liv studies me, her lip caught between her teeth. Let her stare. Let her look for the lie. She won't find it. I've been looking at her like this for years, and I'm tired of pretending I'm anything but obsessed with my wife.

Liv
19

"He drew me a freaking bath."

"Hmm," Shay hums, sipping her wine. "Wonder where he got that genius idea from."

"Let's not give the man a medal just yet," Delia says, kicking back on the couch in Shay's office. "All he did was pour water in a porcelain shell. Water that, mind you, we pay for."

I roll my eyes. "I'm not giving him a medal. And Beckett has offered to pay rent, but I said no. He's living in a closet and he's giving us the money to put toward the house projects."

"Money you're earning because of this whole marriage farce. You're basically an actress. You had to spend time with his family on Sunday, and now, when you travel for work, you'll have to fake it," Delia says, holding her glass of wine aloft. "He's paying you for a service, Liv. Don't confuse all of that with the absurd notion that the man cares."

Her words leave me biting my lip in embarrassment. She's not wrong. This isn't a real marriage; he's paying me to help clean up his image.

"Didn't seem like he didn't care when I ran into him downstairs," Dylan sings. "Calling her 'his girl,' rushing around the house looking for her, drawing her a bath. Real relationships take effort, Delia, and he's making it. *For her.* Because she's worth it."

My head swims and my stomach flips. I don't know what to think of it all. Why is this so confusing?

Tears burn the back of my eyes as I swallow down my emotions, but Shay doesn't miss it. She squeezes my leg and tilts closer. "What's going on for real, Liv? You came into the house looking defeated. Is this all because Drake forgot about Winnie?"

I came home to find my daughter shut away in her bedroom with a drawing pad and pencils. She eyed me and quietly told me she didn't want to talk about it, so I sat on the floor beside her and colored for a bit before Dylan and all her sunshiny brightness swooped in and asked if Winnie wanted to help her paint the studs in her room.

Half the sheetrock in Dylan's room had to be removed because of water damage—we really do need Delia to agree to a contractor—and she swore the exposed studs were screwing with her auras. Okay, she didn't say screwing, because she doesn't have a thousand dollars to pay the twins for cursing, but you get my drift.

"That obviously upset me. And he didn't forget her; he willfully chose to not show up."

"Ass," Delia grumbles.

"He is quite the disappointment," Dylan agrees.

I sigh. "And then, to top it all off, I went to the doctor today. It's just—" I press my lips together, suddenly rethinking my need to open up. I don't want their sympathy over my size. "Never mind."

"No, tell us. We don't keep secrets." Shay squeezes my leg again, ducking forward and locking eyes with me.

"Fine. It's just that, every time I go to the doctor, I dread the moment I have to get on the scale…" I sigh.

Delia nods. "Tell me about it. I legit don't eat for, like, the entire day before."

"What?" I rear back. "You're gorgeous."

Delia frowns. "So are you."

Stomach sinking, I drop my focus to my lap and pick at an invisible speck of dust on my leggings. "Right."

Dylan scoots closer. "Liv, we all have insecurities."

"Right. Mine's just blatantly obvious because it's in your face," I grumble. A second later, I suck in a breath, wishing I could pull the words back in with it. That was mean.

Dylan shakes her head, the auburn curls piled on top of her head swaying. "No, because you're the most honest about it. I hide my insecurities by acting like I don't care about what people think of me. Like being quirky is charming, even though it hurts when people talk to me as if I'm stupid or naïve or ridiculous."

"You always seem so unaffected. That really bothers you?" Honestly, I didn't think Dylan gave two shits what people thought of her.

Her golden eyes are warm when she squeezes my hand. "Of course."

"And I'm psychotic." Shay giggles. "That's what most people think. I'm thankful you understand my concerns after Ajay's death and give me grace, but seriously, I'm unhinged. Sometimes the thoughts of what could go wrong keep me up all night. None of us are perfect, Liv."

"He said I was obese," I whisper, holding the tears back. I'm so freaking embarrassed.

"I will skin him alive," Delia growls, leaping to her feet. "Where is that no-good fake husband of yours?"

Snagging her wrist, I tug until she looks at me. "Not Beckett." I stagger a breath, still shocked by the way he acted earlier. "He said, and I quote, I was always looking, Livy. When you were married to someone else. When you were pregnant. When you were a different size after giving birth… I was never *not* looking, and I always liked what I saw."

"Holy shit," Shay whispers, bringing the tips of her fingers to her mouth.

"Told you." Dylan smiles, flopping back against the cushions. "She's his person. The one who softens him."

"Oh, I don't think she *softens* him." Shayla winks, and we all laugh, even me, through my dumb tears.

I truly don't know what I'd do without these women.

Delia straightens up first, smoothing the fabric of her dress pants. In a heartbeat, she goes from laughing alongside us to red with rage. The glower she's wearing can only mean one thing— she's going on a rampage against the evil in this world.

"And fuck that doctor. You're beautiful, and he's an ass. Also, the BMI scale was created by men using men's bodies. It doesn't account for the fact that we birth children and then have the lives sucked out of us by our spawn. Who the hell has time to monitor their food intake, work out, and be a perfect parent?" She sips from her glass, but the fire in her eyes is still raging, so we wait silently for her to continue. "Fuck the patriarchy and the way it's made us all question our self-worth. If we're being honest here, then I'll admit that the two-parent household image we're inundated with leaves me constantly wondering if I'm enough."

Both Shay and Dylan nod in agreement.

"Even with a man in the picture, I'm failing. Winnie's father chose not to show up today. Who does that to their kid?"

With a *humph*, Delia says, "It looks like your fake husband will live to see another day. I'll save my stabby hands for Drake."

"I don't love how my eye droops when I smile." Dylan holds up one arm and waves. "And don't get me started on the skin under my arm."

"I don't like our weekly books," Shay says quickly, her voice barely audible, like it's confession time and she can't *not* say it.

Delia sucks in a breath and presses a hand to her chest.

I bite my lip and go for it. "I don't either. I never read them."

Laughing, Dylan swipes her Kindle from the table and waves it. "I read smut and then google the books you force us to talk about so I can have insightful commentary."

"Wait. None of you read this week's book?" Delia asks, clasping her hands in her lap. "Dylan picked it out."

Shay smiles. "Oh, I did. It was great, but Delia, the ones you pick? I'm sorry. Not a chance."

Dylan shrugs. "Listen, I need smut. I don't have a man."

"What the heck is smut?" I didn't get to reading the book Dylan gave us, though maybe I should have.

She shoots me a Cheshire grin, her golden eyes dancing. "Welcome to the dark side, girls." She pushes her Kindle into my hand. "Some call it one-handed reading."

"Oh, something to aid my toys. I'm game." Shayla grabs the device out of my hand and skims the words on the screen.

"Toys?" I snort. "The only toys I play with are made for children." Resigned to never having another orgasm, I sigh.

"When was the last time you got off?" Delia's brows sit low over her eyes as she studies me.

My face flames. "I'm not telling you that."

"I had one at lunchtime," Dylan says matter-of-factly. "While Adeline went down for a nap and before I picked up Winnie, obviously."

I laugh. "Thanks for that qualifier."

"I plan to use one of my new toys tonight." Shay waves at a row of packages lined up by the door.

"Wait, so you all…" I cover my mouth and lower my voice to a whisper. "You all take care of yourselves?"

"Masturbate?" Delia cocks a brow. "Yes, it's completely

natural. Men probably do it three times a day, and no one bats an eye."

"*Shh*," I hiss, my whole body heating.

Shay shrugs. "There's nothing to be embarrassed about."

Dylan's devious smile has me nervous. "Shay, you just bought a new stash. Think you have anything Liv might like?"

To my horror, Shay bounces from her spot and moves lithely to the row of boxes.

"That one will be perfect." She drops an Amazon box into my lap. God, that company really has everything.

"I just emailed a link to you. Download that book. Adeline can sleep in the Pack 'n Play in my room tonight," Dylan insists. "Take the rest of the wine upstairs and have fun with your new toy."

The other two bob their heads in agreement. *They're insane.*

"Guys, are you forgetting that Beckett will be sleeping in the closet next to my room?"

"Oh, you're a loud one?" Dylan teases. "I could see it. Makes sense with your aura."

"I am not loud," I hiss.

"Then what's the harm?" Shay prods. "Go on now."

Beckett
20

Pretty sure I have the restraint of a saint. Last night, I overheard Liv and Dylan's muffled conversation when Dylan took Adeline to sleep in her room so Liv could "play."

My cock grew so fucking hard at the thought of Liv tiptoeing into my room. If she wanted to play with me, I was game.

But from where I lay on the twin-size bed, it sounded as though she went through her typical nightly routine before climbing into bed. After a solid twenty minutes of silence, a giggle floated in on the air, followed by a sound that made it clear what type of play she was engaging in.

The buzzing was quickly muted. Fuck. Probably because she'd stuck it inside and fucked herself. I've never been so jealous of a damn piece of plastic in my life.

A moment later, a moan slipped past her perfect lips, and I couldn't breathe for fear that I would miss a single sound.

In no time, the sounds stopped, and her light went out. In the ensuing silence, I had no doubt she was asleep, sated and at peace. I, on the other hand, stayed awake, hard as a rock, and replayed her sounds all fucking night.

Which is why I'm now hiding in Dylan's shower instead of the one I share with Liv. I need to get away from her scent, her sounds, *her*. Otherwise, I'm going to lose my damn mind and drag her into the bedroom so I can show her how much more satisfied she'll be with my tongue between her thighs.

"Fuck," I groan, fisting my cock as I replay every sound she made last night.

Do I feel bad for jacking off in Dylan's bathroom? Only a little. Dylan's the one who put me in this position when she gave Liv a toy and encouraged her to "play," forcing me to listen like a damn creep to my wife pleasing herself in the next room.

Picturing Liv's breasts and the way her nipples would pebble beneath my tongue, I work myself harder.

When the door swings open, I grip my dick tight and hold my breath.

"Oh my God, Dylan," Liv starts. "You were totally right. Last night was amazing."

I stand stock still, the hot water beating down on my back, my hard cock still in hand, trying to hold back a groan.

"Although the words weren't quite enough to do it for me. I ended up picturing Beckett doing what the bossy grump did. Is that bad? That I pictured having sex with my boss?"

Fuck. Someone save me. Knowing I need to do something, I reply in a high-pitched voice, making sure to keep it muffled. "No, he's your husband."

Her responding laughter instantly relaxes me.

"True. But it was so good. I wonder if it would be that good with him. Do you think he'd actually go down on me like that guy did? Drake never liked that."

"Douche," I murmur without thinking.

Liv laughs. "Yeah. God, Dylan, I want him. This is crazy.

I'm, like, sex starved after one measly orgasm. Is this how it is? The more you have it, the more you want it?"

Fuck. Now I can't do anything but picture going down on Liv. Spreading her wide on her bed, holding her down while I make her suffer through one orgasm after another. I close my eyes and pump myself to the image. I need this damn release.

"Did you hear me?" Liv asks.

An instant later, the curtain rings scrape against the rod and I open my eyes, only to be met with Liv's stunned face. I'm unable to control what happens next because the moment her eyes meet mine, my orgasm hits, and I explode all over the wall while Liv stares, frozen in place, her lip between her teeth.

With a grunt, I slap a palm to the wall, completely spent, heaving in one breath, then another. I have no fucking idea what to do now. What do I say to her?

Before I can come up with a coherent string of words, Liv finally shrieks, "Oh my God. I'm so sorry!" and drops the curtain. A second later, the door slams, and I listen as she runs through the house, likely looking for Dylan or a rock to hide under.

Too bad I'm not hiding anymore. Tonight is date night, and I intend to let Liv know precisely what I would do if she would allow it. I'll answer every question she asks. And then, hopefully, my wife will let me show her exactly what I want to eat, and it's definitely not steak.

AWARE THAT LIV needed some time to freak out, I left for work early. But when Gavin wanders in and asks why Liv called in sick, I regret that decision immensely.

"What do you mean she called in sick?"

I pull my phone from my pocket, but I have no new notifications. Not that she'd actually reach out, since she's obviously hiding.

"Oh, weird. Your wife didn't tell you she wasn't coming to work?" The asshole smirks.

Ignoring him and unsure of what else to do, I call Dylan. She seems to be the Liv whisperer. Hopefully she can help.

"Hey, Becks. Miss me already?"

With a groan, I drop my head back against my leather office chair.

Across the room, Gavin laughs. I swear, these two will be the death of me.

"What's going on with Liv?"

"You mean because she grabbed the kids and ran this morning?"

"She did what?" I rasp, my blood heating in my veins.

"Don't worry. It wasn't only because of your little shower encounter." Her chill demeanor only makes me want to pull my hair out.

I close my eyes and dig deep for some semblance of calm. "Was she… Is she upset about that?"

Fuck. I should have told her right away it was me in the shower. I shouldn't have fucking jacked off while she told me how she got off to thoughts of me last night. What the fuck is wrong with me?

Dylan's light laugh filters across the line. "No. She's embarrassed, and she probably thinks you're upset about it."

That knocks the air from my lungs. "Why the hell would I be upset about it?"

Gavin wears an amused smirk on his face as he watches me. I'm so glad he can only hear one side of this conversation.

"Because she's Liv. She worries. And, well, you're *you*."

"What the hell does that mean?"

She laughs again, completely unbothered by my indignation.

"See, Becks? You're proving my point. You have anger issues. We all know it's because you've deprived yourself of what you really want for so long that you can't help it."

"What?" We've gone completely off topic. How does this woman do this to me?

"Liv. You growl because of Liv. She's always believed you growl *at* her, but I saw it for what it was from the moment I met you—you were growling because you didn't have her."

"What the hell are you going on about?"

"See? You did it again. Growling. Roar." She laughs and mimics a damn lion.

Fuck, this woman makes me want to pull my hair out. "I don't growl."

Gavin, who's dropped into a chair on the other side of my desk and has an ankle propped up on a knee, laughs loudly. "You so growl."

"Oh, hey, Gavin," Dylan says into my ear.

Ready to lose my shit, I throw the phone down.

Gavin puts it on speaker. "Hey, Dylan. What's going on with Liv?"

"Like I've been trying to explain, she left, but not only because she was embarrassed about what happened with Beckett."

"What happened with Beckett?" His brows raise and his tone drips with concern.

"Do not answer that question," I growl.

Oh fuck. I totally growl. I'm a damn caveman when it comes to Liv.

"Masturbation is nothing to be ashamed of, Beckett; we told Liv the same thing last night, and by morning, she was singing its praises."

I groan, covering my face. "Please do not say that word."

My asshole brother snorts. "Aw, Beckett, she's right. It's

natural. Although, if I had a *wife*, she wouldn't need her hand to pleasure herself."

I drop my forehead to my desk and sigh. This is absurd. "Dylan," I say, sitting straight again and smoothing out my tie, "can we get to the part where you tell me where the hell my wife went and why?"

"Right. She went to her brother's house. He's always been good with the kids, and she needed some backup after Winnie's rough day."

I immediately sit up in my seat, glaring at the phone. "Why did Winnie have a rough day?"

"Because her father chose not to show up to read to her class after he'd signed up to be there. And yes, you heard me right, *chose*, not *forgot*. He chose not to show up."

"Douche," Gavin grumbles.

Potent rage courses through me, shrouding the world around me in red like it did when the fucker got shitty with her yesterday. "I'll kill him."

Dylan sighs. "Liv's brother will help. Her kids deserve to know they have people in their lives who will put them first. Liv can only do so much since *someone* always has her traveling."

My head throbs and my gut clenches. Fuck. I'm fucking up her entire life.

"I'll make sure her schedule is more flexible," I promise.

Dylan hums. "Honestly, I think what she really needs, if you care like I think you do..." She lets the words linger like that between us.

"Anything," I say without hesitation. I'm all in. "Tell me what to do. I'll do it."

"Show up. Get in the car and go to Bristol and show up. Not just for Liv, but for her kids. If you care about her like I think you do, that's what she needs. Someone to choose her family. To just freaking show up."

I slump in my chair and drop my head into my hands. For

years, I watched my father pick his job over us, and it hurt. But am I really the person she needs to show up? I'm no different from my father; I'm just as busy, just as dedicated. The last thing I want to do is disappoint Liv or her kids.

But I also can't not show up.

I pick my head up and lock eyes with Gavin. "Can you text me the address?"

"Already done," Dylan chirps.

"Thanks, Dippy Do."

When I've ended the call, I brace myself for Gavin to tease me. To ask about the damn shower debacle. *Anything.* But across from me, all he does is study me, his gaze far too knowing.

"Tell Liv I said hi." He pulls himself to standing and buttons his suit jacket. "I hope she feels better."

"That's it? No insults or jabs? No teasing or mocking?"

"Nah. You're giving yourself enough shit in that head of yours." He strides to the door, but as he reaches it, he turns back. "Dad and Mom may not have been there, but you always were. We were lucky to have you. Liv is too."

Then he leaves before I can reply, which is good, because right now, I have no fucking clue what to say.

Liv
21

Calling out of work, pulling Winnie from school, and packing up my kids to hightail it to my brother's house might have been dramatic, but I'm pretty sure I can never face Beckett Langfield again.

At the moment, hiding out in my brother's bachelor pad for the foreseeable future sounds like my best option. He shouldn't mind, right? Three kids and his sister totally won't cramp his lifestyle.

Who am I kidding? Outside of my kids and me, the only people my brother spends time with are the guys at the fire station. And since he's the chief, I'm pretty sure he doesn't even spend that much time with them—he just grunts and commands.

No wonder I've become secretly obsessed with my husband —he reminds me of home.

Declan is one of my favorite people, even if he is a grouch. There's just something about a man who softens for only the people he cares about.

See? I'm delusional. Why the hell would anyone think that kind of behavior is sweet?

"Ahh," I groan, leaning back against the driver's seat.

Finn inspects me through the rearview mirror. "Why so mad, Mommy?"

"Not mad, Finny. Just tired."

On the passenger side of the back seat, Winnie is silently watching the scenery outside the window. Even Dylan didn't have any luck pulling her out of her funk. I'm at a loss for how to make her feel better, and that only makes me feel like more of a failure.

How do I teach my girl that it's okay to be upset when people let her down? How do I show her that I'll spend my life fighting like hell not to be one of those people, but I can't promise that her father will do the same?

A father should protect his child. Put her first. Or at least that's how I always imagined a father would be. Declan and I never had a father, so maybe the image I've created in my mind isn't all that accurate. Our mother worked even longer hours than I do to provide for us, and then Declan joined the fire department and helped put me through college.

To me, family means putting each other first. Once I finished college and landed my job with the Langfields, Dec and I worked to pay off our mom's mortgage so she could work a little less. To this day, my brother helps her around the house and with her bills. For a long time, I treated her to special things periodically, like spa days, but now that I'm divorced, neither she nor my brother will let me help. They'd rather I put any extra cash away for the kids.

That's how families take care of one another. We show up, and we're there when we're needed. That's why I'm heading home with my tail between my thighs—or whatever the saying is—because while my friends are always there for my kids, I can't possibly stick around the house and face Beckett this weekend and I know my brother will help Winnie out of this funk.

"Win, you okay?"

She sighs and nods, but she doesn't turn from the window. "Yup."

"Who wants to stop for ice cream before we get to Uncle Dec's?"

Finn throws his hands in the air. "Me!"

Winnie only shrugs, and Adeline babbles, shooting me a toothy grin from her car seat.

I'll take that as a win.

ALL THREE OF my kids are sticky, happy messes when we pull into my brother's driveway. I texted this morning to tell him we were coming, then again when we left the ice cream shop, so he's outside waiting for us. He scoops my sticky kids up one by one and takes them straight to the hose before they enter his house.

Looks like my husband and my brother have another similar trait—they're both neat freaks.

"Did you guys have breakfast before Mommy loaded you with sugar?"

I hold my phone up to check the time. "It's almost lunch."

Declan laughs and shakes his head. "A real meal it is. Come inside. Tell me what it's like living with all those people."

We make it twenty minutes before Finn brings up Beckett.

"Then there's Bossman. He's the bestest. He lives in Mommy's closet."

"Who the hell is Bossman?" Declan growls.

Dammit. Did I really marry a man just like my brother? I'm beginning to think there's something wrong with me.

"Oh no, Mommy. Uncle Declan owes a thousand dollars."

"A thousand dollars?" my brother croaks.

With a grimace, I nod. "That's the fine for cursing in our house."

"Who the he—eck," he says, glancing at Finn, who nods, silently acknowledging that heck is an okay word, "can afford to pay a grand every time they curse?"

"Bossman," Finn says. "And his brothers."

"Okay, we're going in circles here." Declan's still grumbling when the doorbell rings. He holds up his finger. "We aren't done with this conversation." He disappears then, but a second later, he calls for me. "Liv, could you come here for a minute?"

I check on the kids, but they're all happily entranced by the cartoon playing in the living room. Might as well face the music and tell Declan all about Bossman and the latest debacle I somehow got myself into.

When I step into the entryway, my brother is standing at the closed front door, his jaw locked and his eyes hard. "What the hell is your asshole boss doing at my front door?"

My stomach plummets. "Beckett's here?"

Shit. Shit. Shit. I can't face him. Why is he here? Shit! He's probably going to fire me for watching him do what he did. Of course he is. Who does that? And why the hell can't I get the image out of my head? The groan that rumbled out of him, followed by the growl that sent shivers down my spine. The way his hand moved over his cock, and how he fell against the wall as he came so freaking powerfully, all while he looked at me.

My cheeks are on fire, and my tongue is too thick to speak.

"Since when do you call him Beckett? It's always been *Mr. Langfield this,* and *Mr. Langfield that.*"

Said man knocks on the other side of the door, more loudly this time.

"I can hear you talking about me. The least you could do is say it to my face."

"Oh God," I groan, dropping my chin to my chest and squeezing my eyes shut.

Declan huffs, but he steps away from the door. Resigned and defeated, I pull it open and hold my hand out, signaling to the sexy as hell man on the other side to come in. "Hi, Beckett."

"Why the hell are you inviting him into my house? Can't she take a sick day without being hounded? Did you show up here just to drag her into work? Un-fucking-believable. Grow a back-bone, Liv, and tell this guy to go fly a kite."

"Declan," I hiss.

"Watch your tone when you're talking to my wife," Beckett growls.

My brother's eyes go wide and wild and he sputters nonsen-sical noises. Before he can regain his composure and lose it on me or on Beckett, Finn appears.

"Bossman! You came to play with me here too!"

Without hesitation, Beckett smiles and drops to his knees, prepared for the next moment, when Finn hurls himself into his arms. Then he hoists him up as he stands. "Couldn't let you guys have all the fun without me. What are we doing today?"

"Bossman?" Declan mutters, watching me.

Looks like the cat is out of the bag.

"Dec, I'll explain everything in a few." I sigh, already exhausted, and it's barely midafternoon. "Can you entertain the kids while I talk to Beckett?"

"Actually, I'm good. I brought this bracelet kit. I thought Bear and Huck could help me make some," Beckett says, holding up a pink case filled to the brim with beads and string.

"Yes! Please, Mommy? Can I play with Bossman?" Finn pleads.

I close my eyes and count to four, taking deep breaths as I do. I have no idea what this man is up to, but I'm not opposed to avoiding the inevitable conversation a little longer. I still have no freaking idea what to say to him, anyway.

"Fine," I say, resigned.

"What the hell is going on?" Declan grits out. "Who are Bear and Huck? And why is your boss holding your son like that?" He waves an arm at the most adorable sight.

"Uncle Dec, that's another thousand," Finn warns.

Beckett backs him up with a nod. "I find the word *duck* is an excellent replacement. Really gets the point across. Say it with me. What the *duck* is going on?"

The vein in Declan's forehead is pulsing, and his jaw is locked so tight it looks like he might break a tooth.

I push Beckett and Finn toward the dining room. "Winnie's watching TV. Make yourself comfortable." Then I grab my brother and drag him out the front door. I'm not sure what to tell him, but I better start talking soon.

Beckett

22

I wouldn't say I had much of a plan. All I knew was that I wanted to show up for Liv and her kids, just like Dylan told me to. On the way to her hometown, I racked my brain for ideas, but mostly came up empty. It was early evening in Paris, so I made a call to my best friend. He has experience winning over his wife as well as his own daughter. And when I called, he was on set, so he put my sister on.

"You want to cheer up her daughter?" I could practically see the hearts in Sienna's eyes.

Jay laughed. "I did the Taylor Swift tickets, but Chlo was older."

"I want to stick with simple," I replied. "I don't want to be another man who flashes money at a problem. I want her to know I care… about her."

Because I really do. Throwing money at problems is easy, and our parents did a lot of that, but when Sienna was a little girl, a little quality time went a long way. We had all the money in the world, but what she always craved was time with our parents.

I want to give Winnie that—my time, my attention. I want

Liv to know she can rely on me the way I rely on her daily, like her brother so aptly pointed out.

I'm not even mad about what he said. Since Liv pointed out the similarities between the way I spoke to her and the way her ex did, I've wanted nothing more than to go back in time to pummel my ass.

Not that I've changed, per se, but for Liv and her kids, I can try.

I'm beginning to think there isn't anything I wouldn't do for Liv.

"My uncle Dec is not happy with you, Bossman," Huck says.

"No, Huck, he certainly isn't." I do my best to hold back my laughter. "That's okay, though. We'll get him to like me, right?"

"I don't know... Aunt Delia says you're a man, so not to expect too much."

I frown. Fucking Medusa. "Plenty of men let people down, but not you and me, right, Huck? It's important to be dependable, to take care of the girls around the house. Just like you do with your Nerf gun."

Huck beams. "You gets me, Bossman. No one gets me but you."

My heart tugs in a way it never has before. This kid is one of a kind.

I hold out my fist, but instead of bumping it, he tilts his head and studies it like he's confused. With a smile, I grasp his hand, curl it into a fist, and push it against mine.

He grins wide. Tutus and Nerf guns; what's not to get?

"So, who wants to make bracelets?"

Adeline is napping in a Pack 'n Play that looks strangely like it was already here. As in, Liv's brother keeps it here. Does he have kids? I don't remember Liv ever mentioning a niece or nephew, but I'm beginning to realize that I haven't been quite as attentive to what's going on in her life as I imagined.

Truth is, I've always liked Liv, a bit too much if I'm honest, so I purposely kept my distance. The more I knew about her, the more drawn to her I was, which is odd because her life is full of all the things I've always thought I didn't want.

Complete and utter chaos 90 percent of the time. How the hell does she do it all?

Huck holds up a pink string. "Can we make matching bracelets, Bossman?"

I turn to Winnie, who is doing an excellent job of ignoring us while she watches television. "That's up to Bear. She's the artist. Think you can help us?"

Winnie glances in our direction tentatively, and a little flicker of light ignites in her dark eyes when she spots the pink box of supplies. "Um, sure."

I have zero idea how to make bracelets, so I'm not even sucking up when I ask her to show me what to do. For the next twenty minutes, she walks us through how to string the beads and then how to tie it off.

"How do you spell Bossman?" Huck asks as he picks up another bead.

My lip twitches, and I can't help but smile. "You making a bracelet for me?"

Winnie grins and holds one up. The word *Duck* is spelled out between pink and green beads. I laugh so hard tears fill my eyes. "Thanks, Bear," I say, holding out my arm so she can slide it on.

She rolls her eyes, looking so much like her mother. "It's no big deal."

I lower my head and look her in the eye. "Is to me. Thanks for helping us make bracelets. We woulda been lost without you."

Her freckled cheeks lift in a soft smile.

"How's school going?"

Huck reaches for another bead, his tongue in his cheek. "Don't goes to school. But if ya want, I'm a good worker, Bossman. I could works with you."

Patting his shoulder, I nod, holding back another laugh. "I'm sure Langfield Corp would be lucky to have you. But I was talking to your sister."

She eyes me from under her dark lashes as she strings another bead. "It's okay."

"What would you change if you could?"

She tilts her head and pulls her bottom lip between her teeth like she's really putting thought into her answer. "We don't have a lot of supplies for art class." In a grumble, she adds, "And math. I don't like math."

I laugh. "Neither do I, kid."

From the corner of my eye, I catch sight of Declan standing in the doorway. He's got his arms folded across his chest and a scowl aimed in my direction. Beside him, Liv studies me, eyes wide.

"Everything okay?" I mouth.

She glances at her brother, then shakes her head, as if she's clearing her mind or maybe talking herself out of something.

"Yeah. What are you guys doing?" She shuffles closer and stands over the table, watching Huck string another bracelet.

"Duh, Mom. We're making bracelets." He holds his up by one end and waves it back and forth.

Lifting my chin and shooting her a wink, I hold my arm out.

Her surprised laugh makes my chest tight. "Duck! Who made that?"

I nod to Winnie, noticing a slight blush on her downturned face. "The artist over there."

Liv's brown eyes caramelize as she looks warmly toward her daughter. She turns back to me and mouths, "Thank you."

My chest tightens and I'm forced to look away.

"Want to make bracelets with us, Uncle Dec?" Huck asks.

Liv's brother saunters closer, his hands in his pockets, but his hard gaze doesn't stray from me. The man is pissed. Then again,

I wouldn't be thrilled with any man who drunkenly married my sister in Vegas.

"Yeah, I can take over from here. I'm sure Mr. Langfield has to get back to Boston." His tone says he wants me gone.

I grin up at my wife. "Actually, I reserved a room at the Bristol Harbor Inn. Never been here before. Think you can show me around town tonight, Livy?"

Declan grinds his teeth so hard I can hear it from here, but he doesn't speak.

Liv sighs, and her shoulders sink a little. "Yeah, I'm sure my mom would love some time with the kids. Do we need to go over something for work?"

"Nah, but you and I have an agreement when it comes to Friday nights."

Declan's eyes narrow, and he takes a step closer, like he's ready to put himself between Liv and me. "What kind of agreement?"

She elbows him in the ribs. "Mind your business."

"You got any Diet Coke?" I ask her brother.

He glares at me but tips his chin toward the kitchen. "Yes, in the fridge. Help yourself."

With a ruffle of Huck's hair, I stand and hand the green and pink bracelet I've been working on to Winnie. It says *Bear*.

"This for me?" she asks.

"Yeah, now we match," I say, twisting my wrist so the little beads clack.

"Thanks, Bossman," she says quietly.

As I make my way toward the kitchen, I'm practically floating. Putting a smile on Winnie's face feels like a win to me.

Liv

23

M y brother continues throwing figurative daggers at me as we bead bracelets alongside my kids.

"You married the jackass!" he'd howled when we went for a walk and I finally admitted that I did, indeed, marry Beckett in Vegas.

Even after I assured him it was temporary and only for show, he was pissed.

"He took advantage of you while you were drunk?"

I stuck to the idea that Beckett has been nothing but a perfect gentleman, even if I can't remember the events of that night— during the ceremony *or* after. Never mind our encounter this morning. My brother did *not* need to know about my shower snooping.

"Want me to make you one, too, Mommy?" Finn asks, holding up a multicolor bracelet that says *bossma*.

"I'm the bossma?"

Beside me, Winnie giggles.

God, that's a good sound. Her mood has lifted so much in the last hour.

"No, he's making it for Bossman," Winnie explains.

"Bossma has a good ring to it," Beckett says, wandering back into the living room with a Diet Coke in hand.

He slides into the seat beside me and pushes the soda in my direction.

"You don't want it?"

With a smile, he shakes his head. "Nah, got it for you."

"What? Why?"

"You have one every day at three." His brow furrows as he assesses the can. "Do you not want it?"

I'm too surprised to not speak the truth. "You noticed that?"

His green eyes hold mine. "I notice everything when it comes to you."

Oh.

Butterflies take flight at the tenderness in his expression.

He takes the can back, pops the top, and pushes it toward me again. All the while, I can feel my brother's attention focused on us, like he's trying to figure out what's going on. *You and me both, Declan.*

Addie's cry jars me from the haze I got lost in, but before I can get up, Beckett squeezes my shoulder and stands. "Relax, I got her. Hang out with your brother."

And then he's pushing off toward her Pack 'n Play and lifting her up. "Hey, Little One," he coos. "You feeling left out?" His smooth tone settles my girl immediately.

She snuggles into Beckett's sweater-clad chest as he heads back to the table and situates himself beside me.

"Beads are a choking hazard," Declan grunts.

Beckett smiles. "That's why I won't let her near them. We're just gonna watch, right, Little One?"

Finn holds up his finished bracelet with a big smile on his face. "Look, Bossman. It's finished!"

Beckett holds out his fist, and without instruction, Finn bumps his against it like he's done it before. "Awesome. Slide it on me, Huck."

My little guy pushes it over Beckett's hand and settles it against the one that Winnie gave him. The way the green and pink beads complement his olive skin turns me on in a way that is wholly inappropriate. Why is this so hot? My boss wearing bracelets made by my kids?

Your husband, my wicked mind taunts.

I lick my lips and dip my chin. While I have no idea what's going on with this man today, I can't hide that I like it.

"You sure this is okay?" We're sitting across from one another in a booth, the fire in the oversized hearth blazing nearby.

Beckett grins. "Why wouldn't it be?"

I shrug. "They don't have steak, or your regular wine list."

Though he shakes his head, his smile remains. His posture is more relaxed, his mood more breezy than ever. I'm not sure what to make of it.

"Don't need anything but time with you, Livy. That's all that was in the rules."

The freaking butterflies from earlier erupt in a flurry inside my chest. I have to make a conscious effort to remember the other rules. Licking my lips, I quip, "No PDA. That was another one."

He frowns. "Not really a fan of that one."

The flutter turns to unease in an instant. "Beckett, what are you doing here? Really? If it's about this morning—"

He slides his hand over mine on the tabletop and squeezes. "Can we just focus on tonight? On our date."

"You don't date," I whisper, trying to remember all the reasons I can't fall for my husband.

His green eyes dance. "Well, I didn't before you."

"Sabrina," I start.

"*Was not you.*"

With a gulp, I lower my chin. Looking at him full-on like this is dangerous. But from this vantage point, I'm met with the bracelets he's still wearing. *Bossman* and *Duck* are spelled out in black letters against pink string, accentuated with pink and green beads.

Closing my eyes and trying to ignore the pull this man has on me, I count to ten while I breathe. Four isn't going to cut it.

When I look up again, he's moving around the table.

"Then why did you keep seeing her?"

Beckett slides in beside me and turns so he's facing me. He rests one arm along the back of the booth. The other arm—the one with my kids' bracelets—is resting on the table. The man is practically caging me into the space between him and the wall. "I like companionship. I like dependability. To know precisely how things will go. It's why I'm so hard on my employees. If things don't go as planned, my mind spirals. I *need* control." He flexes his hand like he's uncomfortable with that thought. "Dating? The anxiety that comes with the unknown—what a person is looking for, what their expectations of me are—is too much. Sabrina knew me, knew what I needed and gave it. And I knew how to keep her happy. Until it wasn't enough anymore."

He talks about her in the past tense, but is it really over between them, or just on pause while we're muddling through this thing?

"And now?"

"Life with you is complete chaos." He flattens his palm against the table, like somehow admitting that calms him.

I lower my gaze to the wood grain and nod. "Right."

With that relaxed hand, he nudges my chin up until I'm forced to look at him. Stroking his thumb back and forth, he hovers a breath away. "And I'm having a ducking blast."

My heart stutters, and my eyes find his.

He chuckles as he presses closer. "I should have tried for the chaos earlier." Then his lips brush against mine. "Because I ducking love it."

His tongue swipes against my lips, seeking entrance, and there's no fighting my natural response. I moan into his mouth as electricity zaps through me and heat blooms in my belly. Strong arms snake around me, pulling me close, causing a whimper to escape my throat. I can't stop kissing him.

I don't ever *want* to stop kissing him.

This need, this thirst for him, I have no idea where it came from, but God, I don't know if it can ever be quenched.

I pull back, because I need to see him, need to know this is real.

The desire swimming in his eyes leaves me breathless. He presses his thumb against my bottom lip and dips back in to lick at it.

"What are we doing?" I ask, delirious. My brain caught in a fog of lust, my limbs heavy.

His lips brush against mine as he smiles. "Doing what I should have done years ago. Kissing you, Livy. I'm kissing you, and I don't plan to stop."

Breathless, I edge back and study him. "Why?"

The warmth in his expression steals my last breath. "Because so long as you're my wife, you're mine."

Beckett

24

Sneaking around with my wife might be my new favorite pastime.

Fuck baseball. Kissing Liv and finding places to kiss Liv while inside the house of horrors has become my sport of choice.

For the moment, I've agreed to keep what's going on between us under wraps. The last thing I want to do is let her kids down, and since Liv is currently under the impression that our marriage has an expiration date, I've got my work cut out for me—namely, making my wife fall for me—before we tell her kids that we're together.

But while at dinner on Friday night, and every stolen moment thereafter, I enjoyed the hell out of her. Kissing her in corners, flirting, fucking smiling.

Even work is more fun now.

"Smoothie?" Shayla offers from across the kitchen.

She's in charge of breakfast, and I'm quickly learning to pick something up on the way into the office like Liv does. I now understand why she's always walking in with a store-bought item in hand. The green juice tastes like shit, and that's being kind.

While I generally try not to curse, even internally when I'm in this house, I won't insult ducks by using that word to describe how horrendous the concoctions are.

I shake my head, but she forces a glass into my hand anyway. "You've been glowing since you moved in with us. Don't stop drinking the shakes now."

Dylan lets out a huff of a laugh, sending a lock of her red hair floating. "That's def Livy-induced, right, Becks?"

I glare at her, but when Liv walks into the kitchen, I can't help the way my cheeks lift. Maybe it is Livy-induced.

"Sleep okay?" I murmur when she gets close enough for me to see puffy red eyes with half-moons under them.

She yawns. "Adeline had me up half the night."

I hold back a groan. Addie should be in her own room. Even the slightest sounds wake her up.

"Beckett doesn't want his shake," Shayla says, pointing to the thick green goo in a glass she forced on me. "But you could use it."

Liv grimaces, but only for a moment before she schools her expression into a serene smile.

Brushing her hair out of her face, I murmur, "I'll pick up your favorite espresso on the way in." Then, louder, I say, "No, you're right. I need my greens. No time for you to make one for Livy, though; we'll grab stuff at the office. Go say bye to the kids. We leave in ten."

She bites her lip, the teeniest of smiles peeking through. "Okay, Bossman."

My dick strains at that term. Living in this house is a mind-fuck, for sure.

Pulling in a deep breath, I brace myself. Then I toss back a gulp of the juice and set the glass on the counter. "Thanks, Shay. Gotta run. Have a good day."

Before I can make myself scarce, Dylan calls out, "Wait! I have a to-go cup."

Shay's back is turned again as she adds more leafy shit to the blender, so I glare at Dylan. "Oh, thank God. Wouldn't want to waste a single drop."

As I head for the door, I clock four kids. Each one of them is wearing some version of a light pink shirt. Now, I have no issue with the color or who wears it, but the dye is splotchy and uneven, like these shirts aren't intentionally pink.

"What the hell?" I grumble.

"That'll be a thousand dollars."

Practically jumping out of my skin, I whip around.

One of the Shining Twins is staring me down, holding up a phone with a QR code. Without a word, I pull my own phone from my pocket, scan the code, and transfer the cash.

Her face breaks out in a sinister smile. "Pleasure doing business with you."

She turns on her heel and bounces down the hall.

"Hey," I call. "Why's your shirt white and everyone else's is pink?"

She laughs over her shoulder. "You think I'm dumb enough to let Aunt Dylan do my laundry?"

Delia materializes like a dark angel.

"Medusa," I grumble in greeting.

"Man," she replies in a tone indicating the entire gender is an insult to society.

When Dylan's son Liam appears in the doorway, ready to help get the rest of the kids off to school, I bite back my laugh at his obviously pink-dyed shirt.

If looks could kill, I'd be six feet below. "Have something to say about Ma?"

Like a light to her son's darkness, Dylan appears next to him with a pink piece of fabric in hand.

"Did I miss a memo about house uniform day?" I tease.

She beams, her golden eyes alight. "Nope. Got you one to match."

Then without warning she tosses the garment at me, which I catch easily, before shaking it out and quickly realize is one of my favorite Tom Fords. "Dippy Do, what the hell did you do?"

"That'll be another thousand!" comes from somewhere in the house.

I groan. What the *duck*?

"Ugh, the faucet is acting up again!" Shay hollers from the kitchen.

I roll my eyes. "Maybe if Delia would let one of the contractors I've called come take a peek—"

"Don't need your help, douche-wazzle," Medusa interrupts.

"That's not even a word."

"I had to make up one that encompasses all aspects of your douche-waddery."

"Also not a word. Hire a contractor, Medusa. This place won't fix itself."

Her only response is a death stare, so with that, I spin and head toward the front door.

Outside, propped against the Limo, Charlie's wearing an amused expression as the moms and kids shuffle out one by one.

"Can we drop you off somewhere?" he asks Dylan.

"No thanks, Charlie. We're being one with the universe today, right, boys?"

Kai, who's clinging to her hand on the side farthest from the road, wears a shy smile. On her other side, Finn hollers "Yup!" as he holds tight to her hand and Liam's and swings between them. With his free hand, Liam pushes Addie's stroller down the sidewalk.

Medusa herds Winnie and the Shining Twins into her minivan. Apparently, she sold her Beamer and bought the thing as a big F-you to the world. She still carries the expensive purse and is dressed like every other spineless lawyer, but I keep my comments to myself.

Shayla waves from the house, probably secretly giddy to have a peaceful morning working from home.

Charlie holds the door for Liv. Once she slides in, I follow and take her hand.

"Did Addie sleep okay at your brother's house this weekend?"

Liv looks up, blinking silently.

"Should I not hold your hand?" I ask, loosening my grip. "The windows are tinted, and they were already on their way, I don't think anyone noticed."

Her eyes soften and she leans into me. "It's fine. It's just the first time you've called her Addie and not Little One."

Oh fuck, I did. I'm learning their damn names, and worse yet, their preferences. I'm so in over my fucking head.

Ignoring whatever the hell that means, I prod, "Well? Did she?"

Liv drops her temple to my shoulder. "She sleeps better in her own space."

That's what I thought.

Unable to help myself, I lift her hand to my lips and kiss her knuckles. Then I let out a sigh. "I don't like that you're tired because of me."

She lets out a light laugh and sits up again. "With your ego, I figured you liked keeping women up all night."

I growl and nip at her hand. "If you were in my bed, that'd definitely be the case. But I'm being serious, Livy. I can check into a hotel. Then you can move Addie back into the nursery."

She shakes her head. "The press would catch wind, and then it'd be all over the news. I can see the headline now. *Trouble in paradise already.*"

I groan at just how accurate she is.

"It's fine," she murmurs over a yawn.

It's not, but I'm selfish enough to go along with her, because if I only have a few months as her husband, then the last place I want to spend my nights is in a hotel without her.

When we pull up in front of the office, I begrudgingly release her hand, already trying to think of ways to get her alone in the office. She's got a meeting with Sara though so I'm left staring at my computer screen in complete silence. This is the first moment of quiet I've had in days. I *should* be relishing it. Instead, I find myself craving the noise.

Fearing that I'm losing my mind, I text the family group chat. I need a boys' night.

> Who's around for drinks this week?

> Aiden: Me!

> Gavin: You have a fucking game. You are not around.

> Aiden: <sad face emoji> Okay, Dad.

> Gavin: Nah, that's Beckett's job. He's the dad of the group now.

> Duck you

> Shit. Stupid autocorrect.

> Gavin: See? He doesn't even say duck anymore. Told ya he's a dad.

> Gavin: Shit, I meant duck.

> Gavin: Duck.

> Gavin: Dammit FUCK!

> You were saying?

> Brooks: Everything okay?

> Just need a break.

Gavin: Worried you're getting too attached to your wife?

Dropping my head back, I groan. "Fucking Gavin."

The loud laugh echoing inside my office startles me. I bolt up again, causing my chair to roll back from my desk. As if I spoke him into existence, the asshole leans against the doorway, his arms crossed and a smug look on his face. "You summoned?"

"Come in and shut the fucking door."

Gavin's eyes widen in shock, but he covers it with a smile. "Not the *ducking* door?"

"*Duck* you." I huff, but I smile, which was his intention, I'm sure.

Attention locked on me, he drops into a chair on the other side of my desk. "Weekend went that badly?"

I rough both hands down my face. "No. It went that well."

"Then why the hell do you look like someone ran over your dog? Shit, did you hit another dog on your way to work?"

"I see you've got comedian covered today."

He smirks. "Talk to me. What's really going on?"

"I'm so in over my head, Gav." Dropping my elbows to my desk, I hang my head. "Her kids... Livy." I sigh out her name.

He smiles. "Livy?"

"See?" I blow out a breath. "In over my fucking head."

"Why is that a problem, though?"

"She lives with three other women. In a house that's falling down. There are seven kids and no fathers. It's what nightmares are made of."

"Then why are you smiling?"

Pressing a hand over my mouth, I realize he's right. "Because I'm ducking crazy about her."

"Right," he says with a sage nod.

"Gavin, I can't fall for her."

As if he's settling in, he pulls one leg up and rests his ankle on his opposite knee. "Little too late, no?"

Maybe. "What the hell am I gonna do?"

With a smirk, he licks his lips. "Enjoy it. You don't have to have an answer for everything. Your entire life doesn't have to be planned out before you. Live. See what happens."

"And what if it doesn't work out? What if I hurt her kids? *Hurt her.*"

The words burn like acid coming out of my mouth.

"Keep it casual. Sure, she's your wife." A grin splits his face. Dammit. The jig is so up. "But just enjoy it until you do figure it out."

"That's your great advice? Keep it casual? With my *wife*?"

"Yup." He claps his hands and stands. "Now, I have a hockey team to run, and I'm pretty sure there's a sport you're supposed to be paying attention to."

He's halfway to the door when our phones chime in unison.

> Brooks: We'll all be in Vegas for games this weekend, right? How about we get a drink Saturday?

My chest tightens. *Vegas.* Liv and I will be returning to Vegas for the first time since we got married. Damn if that doesn't ignite a feeling inside me that's half hope and half trepidation.

> Gavin: Pretty sure Beckett will be busy with his wife, reliving their wedding night.

With that, my brother shoots me a wink and strides out the door.

And then I smile as an idea forms in my head. Because yeah, that's exactly what I intend to do.

Liv
25

Shayla: There's a wire hanging in the living room, and I have no idea what it goes to... I'm afraid to turn anything on. If I do, and I get electrocuted, then Kai would have no parents.

Dylan: red you're dead

Dylan!

Dylan: what? gotta have street smarts don't cut the red wire Shay

Delia: Oh my God. Beckett probably cut it.

Why would Beckett cut the wire?

Delia: Because he's a menace. Shay, you are not going to die. Dylan, shut up. Liv, tell your husband to fix this.

Shayla: I can't find the red one!

That's only in cars. Ignore her!

> Dylan: I wouldn't take that chance

I'll have Beckett send someone this afternoon.

> Delia: I need to vet whoever it is.

> Shayla: Oh god, I'm going to die before that happens.

I'm shaking my head at my friends' insanity when Sara walks in the door.

"Damiano came in today. He's not happy." She doesn't even say hello before she gets down to business. I like it like that, though. As a mom, every minute of my day counts, and I appreciate that she doesn't waste my time.

"He'll just have to deal. Clayton isn't going anywhere. We don't have room in the cap."

With a sigh, she studies her iPad. "Maybe you could set up a team-building activity for them in Vegas or something."

That word—*Vegas*—sends a jolt through my system.

I cannot go back there with Beckett.

With a shake of my head, I push thoughts of my husband away for the moment.

"Yes, put together a list of ideas. And make sure Clayton and Damiano are paired up. You can handle the trip, right?"

"Well, no. The hockey team is also in Vegas, so I'm slated to go with them."

I bite my lip. "I can do that. You go with the baseball team."

Sara blinks at me. "Beckett only wants you."

"He doesn't care who travels with him."

Sara cackles but quickly slaps a hand over her mouth.

"What?"

Twisting her lips to hide her true feelings, she squirms beneath my gaze.

I heave a sigh. "Just say it."

"Olivia, Beckett hasn't allowed anyone but you to accompany him on away games since I started working for you."

That can't be true. Sure, the man is demanding and I'm at his beck and call more often than not, but I thought that was just my annoyance with him on the matter.

"Well, he'll have to deal. Plan the activity."

As soon as she's gone, I get out the calendar and look up the dates of Beckett's last few trips. Then I spend the next hour reviewing his calendar for the last five years.

My stomach sinks when I realize our calendars match. When I didn't travel, Beckett didn't travel. When he had to travel and I couldn't, then he went on his own.

My mind is a jumble of confusion. Has my fake husband been telling the truth? Has he really been looking at me all this time?

Hours later, I'm in a meeting with Sara, Hannah—another one of the women who works in my office—and the Revs' general manager, Benny Riordan. Earlier, I filled Beckett in on the issue with Damiano and his catcher so when he peeks into the meeting, I assume he's going to join us. As far as owners go, Beckett is as hands-on as they get. While he trusts the opinions of his inner circle and gives thought to what we have to say before he makes decisions, he's still a control freak who gets the final say.

In all fairness, he works hard to grow this team, and I don't miss the quiet grumbles of admiration from others in the league. So while he may be a controlling ass, he's a smart one.

We all look up expectantly, waiting for him to sit before we continue our discussions.

With a nod at Riordan, he stalks toward me, but it isn't until he's leaning over my chair, his big frame crowding me and his rich scent encircling me, that I see what's in his hand. He slides a Diet Coke in front of me, and while his arms surround me, he flips the top open. Then his lips ghost my ear. "Can't wait for this weekend, Livy."

When I turn to him, our lips dangerously close, he smirks. My tongue sweeps out, sliding across my lips, and in response, Beckett's green eyes practically glow.

A throat clears and I rear back, making my chair swivel and the arm hit the table. I totally forgot we weren't alone.

"Joining us, boss?" Sara asks as she gets up and holds a hand out to her now vacant chair like she's offering her seat to him.

He shakes his head. "No, Livy has it covered."

My eyebrows knit together in confusion. "You just came to drop off the soda?"

"My wife needs her afternoon caffeine. And what wifey wants..." His eyes are still dancing when he turns from me to Sara. "Gavin needs you this weekend. Livy will join me."

Sara sucks in her lips to hold back her smile. "Of course, Mr. Langfield."

I knock my foot into hers, and she dips her head to hide her laughter.

"Riordan, see me when you're done." With that, Beckett disappears.

What the hell just happened?

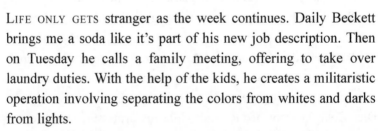

LIFE ONLY GETS stranger as the week continues. Daily Beckett brings me a soda like it's part of his new job description. Then on Tuesday he calls a family meeting, offering to take over laundry duties. With the help of the kids, he creates a militaristic operation involving separating the colors from whites and darks from lights.

And the folding? Don't even get me started on that. I never

thought I'd see the day that Liam would fold laundry beside Beckett Langfield at our dining room table.

On Wednesday night, while we're eating dinner, a rumble of thunder rattles the house so hard pieces of the ceiling fall into Beckett's pasta. When he locks his jaw, I ready myself for his growl. He shocks me, though, when he finally opens his mouth.

"That's it. I'm not risking the kids getting lead poisoning. Give me the name of the contractor you're dealing with, Delia. I'll make some calls and get them to speed up the process."

Not because he's annoyed that the ceiling is literally falling into his food, but because he's concerned for our kids.

Delia stares him down, her nostrils flaring. "You think I don't care about our kids?"

Beckett takes a deep breath, and right before my eyes, he morphs into the CEO who can woo even the toughest critics. Tough doesn't begin to describe Delia, though, so I hold my breath and watch, hoping he can get through to her, because seriously, we need the roof fixed. And the stairs. And the walls. Two walls in Dylan's room are still nothing but studs.

"I know you care about everyone here. And that you work long hours. I know you want a contractor who will preserve your aunt's legacy. I also know that the motto in this house is that everyone helps out. So let me help."

Every eye in the room is on Delia, and I swear even the younger kids are holding their breath while we wait for her reaction. Will she take his head off? And really, how much longer will he stay in a place that's falling down around him?

How much longer can any of us live like this?

Delia takes a bite of her pasta and keeps her attention averted as she nods. "Fine," she grumbles. "I'll send you the contractor's information tomorrow. But no one does a thing without clearing it with me first."

Shay, Dylan, and I exchange surprised smiles. Even Liam looks at Beckett with begrudging respect.

Score one for Beckett.

But also, why the hell is he trying so hard?

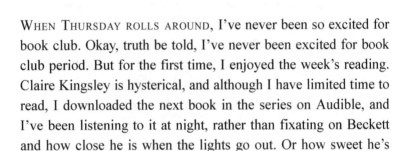

WHEN THURSDAY ROLLS AROUND, I've never been so excited for book club. Okay, truth be told, I've never been excited for book club period. But for the first time, I enjoyed the week's reading. Claire Kingsley is hysterical, and although I have limited time to read, I downloaded the next book in the series on Audible, and I've been listening to it at night, rather than fixating on Beckett and how close he is when the lights go out. Or how sweet he's being and the kisses he gifts me with when no one else is looking.

It's like a game to him, finding places to hide—in the office and around this house. And when he does, he stalks to me, pushes me against the wall, or the door, or the freaking copy machine, and kisses the life out of me.

When he walks off, still looking just as polished and in control as ever, I have to run to the bathroom to splash water on my face to cool my flaming cheeks. And my hair? Don't even get me started on the way he grips it while he devours my mouth. Without fail, he leaves me looking like we've just finished hours of uninhibited sex.

Just before book club tonight, I caught him with a wrench in his hand and before I could even ask what he was doing walking around with it, he pushed me into the coat closet, and all thoughts were lost to his mouth.

Though this book is easily a favorite of mine, I'm mostly excited for a few hours with my besties to discuss the changes in my relationship with Beckett—*and this trip to Vegas*—because for the first time since we started kissing, the kids won't be around. There will be no excuses. We'll be staying in a hotel, in the place where we got married, and he'll probably want sex.

It's not that I don't want to have sex with him—come on, this is Beckett Langfield. The man is like porn in a suit with a god complex. The sex will be incredible.

But I'm *not* porn in a suit; I'm more like cheesecake—and not a delicate slice. I'm the round kind with lots of filling.

God, why do I always compare myself to food?

Although, cheesecake does sound delicious.

"Liv?" Del swings the wine bottle back and forth in front of me, and by her expression, it looks like it's not the first time she's said my name. "Want some?"

"God, yes." I hold out my glass and watch as she fills it.

"Wait!" Dylan screeches. "I got presents for us!"

Shay rears back against the couch cushions and presses a finger to her ear. "I think you burst my eardrum."

With an exaggerated eye roll, Dylan hops up from the couch and picks up the bags sitting on the floor beside her. Each one is a different color. Mine is teal, with pink paper in it, and inside is a wine tumbler with *Fueled by wine and smut* scrawled across it.

Dylan bounces in her seat. "For our book club nights."

Delia pulls hers out of a purple bag with teal paper and grins. Dylan really went all out. "I love it." Immediately, she transfers the wine from her glass into it.

Shayla heaves a heavy sigh. "You should clean that before you drink from it." She grabs it and pours the wine back into the glass. Then reaches for mine and Dylan's before disappearing into the attached bathroom. From there, she lectures. "The chemicals they use to create this…" Her voice is drowned out by the sound of the water.

My heart sinks then, and I look from Dylan to Delia. Their sober expressions match the way I feel. Ajay's cancer diagnosis really did a number on her. I'm not sure any of us knows how to get through to her, or if we even can. Life throws us all curve balls. It takes time to adjust and learn how to hit the ball a different way. But when it hits you square in the chest and you forget how to breathe, it's hard to get back into the game. It's hard to keep swinging.

Since losing her husband, the woman who used to be the most daring of us has been sitting on the sidelines.

And I wasn't far from it either. Before Dylan forced us to admit how much we were spiraling, I was dangerously close to becoming bitter and closed off. With the support of these women, I dusted myself off and got back in the game rather than letting my husband's affair take me out completely.

Is that what I'm doing with Beckett? Getting back in the game? Is any of what we're doing real?

Beckett

26

"Your wife didn't want to sit with us?" Gavin teases, bringing his coffee cup to his lips at the table across from me. Both our teams are playing in the same city this weekend, so we're sharing the company jet. While Sara is traveling with the team, I've always forced Liv to travel with me.

"It was a long night," I say, fighting back a yawn. "Addie kept us up for hours. She's working on a new tooth."

Liv is sitting a few feet away, headphones in, eyes closed, looking completely relaxed. Thank God.

We aren't supposed to be doing the whole married thing in front of the kids, but last night while Addie whined and Liv pleaded with her, tears in her voice, to go back to sleep, I couldn't help myself. My wife hasn't slept all week because her baby girl has been up tossing and turning. The woman needed sleep, and I couldn't bear to hear both of them breaking down. So, I got up, took Addie in my arms, and ordered Liv to go back to bed.

She didn't, but she also didn't fight me. Eventually, Addie

fell asleep on my chest, and I fell asleep beside Liv. My neck hurts this morning, and we're both tired, but waking up with my cheeks smooshed between Addie's chubby hands while she said "Bossy"—her version of Bossman, I guess—over and over again? Let's just say I'd trade sleep for that any day of the week.

We both woke up before her pretty mama, so for a few moments, I got to witness Liv in a completely unguarded state. Relaxed, without filters, and in my bed. My chest aches at just the thought of her like that.

"So, Clayton," Gavin prods, changing the subject.

I groan. My star catcher is driving me nuts. It's a well-kept secret, though, since the guys know enough to keep their shit locked up in public, but whatever is going on with Clayton and Damiano—a pitcher I have a shit ton riding on—is seriously starting to piss me off.

Gavin chuckles. "Too bad Miller is happy with the Metros."

"Tell me about it." Cortney Miller is arguably the best catcher in the MLB. He's also the younger brother of one of my best friends. Miller has been with New York since he was a rookie, and although he's at the tail end of his career, the cost to bring him to the Revs would be outrageous. "We play them next week. Jamie is coming up for a game. You around?"

Gavin picks his phone up off the table and taps the screen a couple of times. "Appears so." He locks the device and pockets it with a long sigh.

"What's wrong with you?"

The crease between his brows is deeper than usual. He's the brother who's always smiling, but right now, he looks exhausted. "Just saw a date in my calendar for this weekend. A woman I met during our series here last year. We meet up when I'm in the city."

I raise my brow, waiting for him to elaborate. So far, it sounds like a typical weekend for Gavin, but the weariness in his tone is new.

"You ever get tired of it?" he asks. "The women? The travel?"

"Yeah. Hence the reason I got married."

Gavin levels me with a stare, and I hold up my hands.

"I've never been like you. I like monogamy, one woman."

"The wrong woman," Gavin grumbles.

Those three words instantly make my blood boil. I sit up straight, ready to unleash hell on him.

Before I can formulate a coherent response, though, he goes on. "Until now. I meant, you were with the wrong woman *until now*."

Deflating, I settle back in my seat. "Yeah. And if you don't like the game anymore, get out of it."

Gavin rolls his eyes. "And do what? Get married like you, Ford, and Jay? That's not in the cards for me."

Hmm, I hadn't realized that all of our friends had gotten married in the past year. First it was Jay, and his wife came with the package deal of their daughter. Then Ford, who's older than both of us, shocked the entire world and started dating his son's ex. Although I guess the real shocker was the destination wedding we all attended only two months later. They weren't wasting any time. Come to think of it, Gavin hasn't been the same since that trip. Was it the wedding that freaked him out? Or is it something else?

"Why?" I know why I believed marriage wasn't in the cards for me. Is my brother's reasoning the same? I almost hope it is so I can be forced to talk him out of it. I want to tell him how good he'd be, how well he could juggle work life and family life. Because I want to say that to myself. I want to believe I can do it all.

Gavin shrugs. "Just never interested me. Or maybe I've never met a woman who made me want to spend the night."

"Thought you've gone out with this woman before?"

One side of Gavin's mouth quirks up. "Never said anything about spending the night, big brother."

At my loud laugh, Liv opens her eyes and settles them on me, her face warming in a smile.

Nope, don't miss the days before her at all. But if I don't figure out how to hold on to this woman, I'm going to miss these.

"WHAT DO you mean you don't have a room for me?" Liv practically growls at the receptionist during check-in.

I rest my palm against the small of her back and bring my lips to her ear. "Livy, you're checking in under the wrong name."

My wife's breath hitches, and tiny goose bumps spread across the pale skin on her arm. Liv is always wearing sleeves, but when we landed in Vegas, she hissed about how it felt like we'd stepped into the third circle of hell and finally took off the damn cardigan that was covering her delicious curves. Just the suggestion of her tits hiding beneath her camisole has me excited to get her alone.

"Can you check under Olivia Langfield?" I ask the receptionist.

Obediently, she types away. "Oh." As she hits Enter on her keyboard, her face splits into a smile. "Mr. and Mrs. Langfield. We have you in the honeymoon suite. Special occasion?"

"Isn't every day with my wife a special occasion?" I tease.

Beside me, Liv is starting to squirm, so I run my hand up and down her back, hoping to soothe her. The last thing I want is for my wife to be uncomfortable and though I wish I'd thought of upgrading us to the honeymoon suite, I didn't do this. It doesn't take a rocket scientist to figure out who did though. Gavin's eyes dance as he watches us.

As I slide my company credit card across the desk, I lean in close to Liv. "It doesn't mean anything, Livy, we can just sleep," I whisper in her ear. Then, unable to help myself, I nip at her lobe and add, "Or not."

Those damn goose bumps skitter down her neck. Shit, now all I can think about is whether they're dusting her entire body, the parts I've yet to see, the spots I've yet to kiss.

Once I've returned my credit card to my wallet, I slide my hand in hers. With key in hand, we leave Gavin to check in.

"Meet at seven?" Gavin calls after us.

Neither team plays tonight. While Aiden and Brooks have a game tomorrow and can't go too crazy, we can grab dinner, and then I intend to spend time with Liv. Alone. Without a child in the bedroom. Without ten other people within listening distance, without her brother glaring at us, or her best friends and my brothers interfering. Just Liv and me and the plush hotel bed.

I nod and then hold tight to Liv's hand, refusing to let go until we reach the door and she pulls aways so I can open it. Immediately, I miss the warmth and softness of her palm against mine.

She clears her throat as she walks in ahead of me, her gaze sweeping across the room, which I'm stupidly excited my brother arranged. When I'm in Vegas, I always stay in the penthouse. It has two bedrooms and would have been fine for us. And it's what my secretary booked for this trip.

But this room, though smaller than the penthouse, has an incredible view of the Strip. Liv walks straight to the window and sucks in a breath as she takes it all in. I head for the bar and spot the bottle of champagne chilling in an ice bucket along with two champagne flutes. Beside it is a note that says, *Congratulations, Mr. and Mrs. Langfield.*

No matter how many times I've heard that name, *my name,* it's never sounded better than with Liv's name in front of it.

Olivia Langfield. Fuck, it gets me every time.

The pop of the cork startles Liv, and she spins in my direction, her eyes wide and her mouth in an O.

"Champagne, Mrs. Langfield?" I hold up the bottle.

She lets out a light laugh as she shakes her head. "It's like stealing, Beckett. We're not really married."

My heart sinks in my chest at the words and the conviction behind them. I nod at her hand, gaze narrowed. "Is that a wedding band on your finger?"

Liv shrugs and rolls her eyes.

"And did we or did we not stand in front of God and Elvis and pledge to honor one another for all the days of our lives?"

A loud laugh slips through her perfect lips. "Pretty sure all your employees make that pledge to you when they meet with HR on day one."

I stalk to her, and she retreats, step by step, until her back hits the window. With the bottle still in hand, I cage her in so she's forced to hear my every word. "Do all my employees know how I sound when I come?"

"Beckett."

Her soft whimper urges me closer. I want nothing more than to feel the way those lips taste when she says my name like that.

"I'm dying to know how you look when you come, Livy. *Dying.*"

Her brows knit, and she searches my face. "We didn't when —" She drops her gaze for a moment before dragging it back up and locking eyes with me. "I woke up naked beside you."

I smirk. "You mean the morning you snuck out on me?"

A flush creeps up her cheeks. "Yeah, did we... um—" She dances around the topic.

"Fuck?" I offer. "That the word you're looking for, Livy? You think you wouldn't *remember* the first time I fucked you?" I press closer so our hips are aligned and buck my pelvis against her. "That you wouldn't feel me between these thighs the next day?" My knee presses between her thighs and I push in, pulling her legs apart. I drop my mouth right next to hers, my cheek against her cheek. "Open," I rasp.

Liv obeys, parting those gorgeous lips. I bring the champagne bottle to her mouth and slide just the rim of it in. Her tongue darts out and licks the interior rim, making us both moan.

"Fuck," I mutter. I tip the bottle and let the cool liquid run into her mouth. Watching the way her throat works as she drinks, my thoughts grow dirtier. My mind can't help but fixate on how good she'd look swallowing down something else. With her lips wrapped around something else. *Choking* on something else.

I pull the bottle back and take a swig myself. With the champagne bubbles still dancing on my tongue, I tug on her bottom lip, lean close, and spit the champagne into her mouth. Her eyes fly open, but I don't give her time to react. My lips collide with hers and our tongues tangle together. Just the sight of her taking what I've given her makes me ravenous. I swallow her moan along with the champagne, and Liv does the same.

She pushes against me. "Beckett, wait—" Her eyes are wild as she studies me. "We should—"

"Talk? Yeah, I'm all set with talking, Livy. Work? *Fuck no.*" After a second swig of the champagne, I lean in and bite her bottom lip, then lick it before kissing her again.

"Holy shit," she whispers tugging me closer.

Dropping my forehead to hers, I sigh, my breath ragged. "Go rest for a bit, Livy. I've got big plans for you tonight."

Liv

27

"There's only one bed," I whisper into the phone.

"One what?" Dylan asks.

"One. Bed," I hiss.

"Oh!" Dylan sounds far too happy on the other end of the line. "Where is he right now?"

"Taking a shower. He told me to rest. That he had, and I quote, big plans for me tonight."

"Oh my God. You are so getting laid."

I lick my lips. I'm pretty sure whatever Beckett has planned cannot be categorized as "getting laid." The man spit in my fucking mouth, and I liked it.

I always thought if a man did something like that, I'd knee him in the balls. But when Beckett Langfield spit champagne onto my tongue, I went feral. I almost begged him to do it again.

God. Beckett fucking Langfield is a beast, and I am here for it.

"Well, you heard the man. Get off the phone and go rest up."

Setting my phone on the nightstand, I blow out a breath. I'm so damn wired. I can't possibly rest right now. Besides, what if I do nod off and he finds me like that? I don't know how I look when I'm sleeping, but when a man who looks like a fucking god is taking a shower, potentially preparing to ravage me, well... I don't want to be lounging in bed looking like a pig. And I mean like a literal pig. When I'm overheated, my arms turn pink, and I can't possibly put a sweater back on to cover them. It's too freaking hot in this city.

Stop, Liv. Beckett obviously likes what he sees.

"I was always looking. And I always liked what I saw." Beckett's words leave me squirming once again, dying for relief.

Maybe I'll listen to an audiobook for a bit. Get out of my head. Focus on this fictional couple I've been reading about who can't get out of their own way. Yeah, that's exactly what I need.

"Do you want me to fuck you until you know you're mine?" Joe Arden's voice startles me into consciousness. God, that man could read the phone book and it would sound sexy. I must have dozed off for a few. I blink a few times only to find my husband's gaze focused solely on me.

Shit, the damn audiobook is still playing. Loudly. I scramble for it and have to tap the pause icon on the screen half a dozen times before it stops.

In the ensuing silence, I peek up at Beckett. *Damn.* He was insanely hot stroking himself last week, but I didn't get a long enough look. Now he stands before me, towel slung dangerously low on his hips, brown hair tousled and wet, his green eyes more intense than I've ever seen them.

"Who the hell is talking to you?" he growls, grabbing for my phone.

I squeal and clasp it to my chest. "It's no one."

Jaw hardened and face turning redder by the moment, he balls his fists and looms over me on the bed. "I thought I was clear. So long as we're married, it's just you and me."

"Huh?" I'm too stunned and turned on by this growly man to

understand what the hell he's going on about. Then his scent hits me—clean, fresh, manly—and all coherent thought leaves me.

He closes his eyes and works his jaw from side to side. When he focuses on me again, he sighs. "I thought—" He swallows thickly, his Adam's apple bobbing. "I don't share, Livy. If you're seeing someone else, we should end this now."

Oh. Oh my God, he thinks there was a man on the phone. Not Joe Arden, my favorite narrator, but a man... who was going to fuck me until he proved I was his? I almost giggle at the sentiment. It's ridiculous, like completely absurd. Men don't talk like that in real life. That's the kind of book boyfriend stuff that Dylan is always going on about.

"Beckett." My voice is breathy as I laugh through the word.

His eyes turn to slits.

"No, baby, I... I would *never* cheat on you."

Who in their right mind would cheat on a man who looks like the one hovering above me? A man with a jawline like *that*. With the most sexy, sinewy muscles and eyes that are, at this moment, glistening at the mere thought of me talking to someone else.

A man who rocks toddlers to sleep and loves spending time with precocious four-year-olds and makes bracelets with eight-year-old girls to cheer them up. Yeah, only an idiot would cheat on him.

Beckett scrutinizes me, his head bent over me, but he says nothing.

"It's an audiobook. See?" I hold up the phone and show him the cover displayed on the lock screen. Then, just to be sure he understands, I press play, and suddenly, we're taken into a scene where my man Joe is threatening to bend his love interest over her desk if she doesn't admit she's his.

Beckett crouches beside the bed and drops his forehead to my chest. Fully engulfed in embarrassment now, I suck on my bottom lip to keep it from trembling. When he starts to shake, I push at his shoulder, forcing him up, and find tears streaming down his face. He's laughing so hard he's crying.

"Holy shit. What are you listening to?"

With a huff, I push against his chest. "Shut it."

He wipes his eyes and reaches for my hand. "Workplace romance?"

I groan. "You are going to be so annoying about this, aren't you?"

The way one side of his lips quirks up is all the answer I need. "Not at all. But maybe we could listen to it together later. Get some ideas?"

"No," I hiss, tugging but unable to free my wrist from his grasp.

With a chuckle, he nods toward the bathroom. "I ran a bath for you. Go relax... or listen to your audiobook. I've got some work to do before we head out."

My heart sinks just a little. I kind of wish we weren't going out. Now that Joe has gotten me all worked up and Beckett is standing before me looking like *that*, how could I not want to stay in? But I paste on a small smile and let him help me. Once I'm on my feet, he loops an arm around my waist and pulls me against his chest. Hand to my jaw, he lifts it and kisses me. It's soft and gentle at first, but it quickly turns hungry. Fueled by lust, our tongues tangle together. With one final nip at my lip, he pulls back. "If you fuck like you kiss, I'm never giving you up."

Damn. My knees wobble and my stomach flips. *What was I saying about book boyfriends again?*

THE WATER in the jacuzzi is steaming, and the only light comes from the one in the shower, creating a dim, peaceful aura.

Exhaling all my stress, I turn away from the mirror and undress. Why do hotel bathrooms always have mirrors in every direction? Who needs to see themselves while in the shower? Or while they're on the freaking toilet?

I swear, this generation just likes looking at themselves.

Not me. I'd prefer no mirrors, especially while I'm undressing. Sometimes I still feel like a twenty-year-old with perky boobs, but one quick look down affirms that isn't true. I've never been slim, but I haven't always been so flabby.

With a pinch of the extra skin on my stomach, I let out another long sigh.

Then I snort when I think about the look on Beckett's face when he walked in on me listening to my audiobook. The man was legitimately jealous. It's barely believable that I landed one hot man. Does he really think I'm the kind of woman men like him would fight over?

God, he's delusional.

Exhaling, I step into the tub and sink beneath the warm water. Toeing the faucet knob, I twist it to add just a little more, then I turn on the jets and close my eyes.

"Holy shit, Livy. Corey Matthews is about to pitch a no-hitter." Beckett flies into the bathroom, holding up his phone. "And Miller hit a grand slam."

"Really? God, that man is good. Too bad he's so happy in New York."

Cortney Miller is one of the best catchers in the MLB, and he's known for his ability to calm even the rowdiest of pitchers. Unlike Clayton, our current catcher, who keeps getting into pissing matches with Damiano. Don't get me wrong, the guy can be a pain in the ass, but it's the catcher's job to settle him. Clayton tends to throw fuel on the fire instead.

"Fucking tell me about it," Beckett grumbles, settling himself on the edge of the tub. He turns and holds his phone so we can both watch as Matthews winds up the pitch again, and... "Strike!" Beckett hollers.

He turns to me, wearing one of those big smiles I see more and more every day. When our eyes connect, it's like a lightbulb goes on, and in the same instant, we both realize I'm naked under the bubbles created by the jets.

He scans the surface of the water and licks his lips. "Sorry I interrupted your bath." His voice comes out almost hoarse.

I can't help but examine his chest, which is still bare, though he's pulled on a pair of navy athletic shorts. The smattering of dark hair across his pecs ignites a low flame in my belly. Because I'm a glutton for punishment, I follow its trail down, wishing he was naked too.

"It's okay." Nibbling on my bottom lip, I shrug.

The movement catches his attention, and his gaze lowers to the surface of the water, where I unintentionally flashed just a peek at my breasts. His phone clatters to the tile floor, and an instant later, his hand is in my hair and his mouth is crashing against mine. Somehow he pulls me close while managing to hold himself above the water.

The kiss goes on and on, desperate and filled with promises. Every swipe of his tongue fans the flames burning inside me. God, if this man doesn't make me come tonight, I'm going to cry.

"Beckett," I pant, overheated. Maybe from the hot water and the steam rising around us, but mostly because of his rough kisses.

With his thumb, he pulls on my bottom lip and smiles. "Yes, Livy?"

"What are we doing?" I whisper, delirious.

"Do you want me to narrate it for you?" He presses closer, his lips ghosting my ear. "If you don't want me to touch you, tell me to stop."

There is no world in which I'd tell him to stop. "I want you to touch me."

He smiles against my cheek. "Where?"

My mind goes completely blank. I'm not a dirty talking person; I don't even know how.

"Use your words, Livy," he says in that smooth voice I'm starting to believe is doused in whiskey. "Or should I use mine?"

"Yours," I husk out.

Beckett's responding chuckle vibrates against me, sending goose bumps skittering across my skin. "*Beg*, Livy. I love it when you beg."

My voice wobbles as I plead with him. "Please, Beckett."

He drags his lips down my neck and nips at my shoulder. "You taste so fucking good. I can't wait to lick you clean. Would you like that, Livy? You want my tongue between those thighs?" His fingers trail down my arm until he dips his hand beneath the water. When he palms my upper thigh and lets out a moan, I almost die. "You feel so fucking good." He pulls back and studies me, as if he needs to see my reaction to his every dirty word. "I want these thighs squeezing my head. Will you do that for me?"

His green eyes are full of nothing but honesty.

Want. Need. Desire.

I bite my lip in response, pulling a curse from him.

"Fuck." His lips are on mine again, taking me in another rough kiss while he slides a hand between my thighs and presses two fingers against my slit.

With the jets on high, it's impossible to watch what he's doing, but the way he narrates his actions is hotter than any visual I could imagine.

"So fucking perfect. You gonna let me fuck this soft pussy with my fingers, Livy? Gonna milk them for me? Come all over them and then let me lick you clean?"

My God, this man could make me come with his words alone. My eyes roll back as he slides one finger between my lips.

"So fucking warm." He groans. "So fucking perfect."

With his thumb on my clit, he circles gently before adding a second finger. "Gotta get you ready for me. You're too tight right now. My cock needs room to breathe in there."

I can't help the breathy laugh that escapes as I arch my back. "Such an ego."

He bites my shoulder again. "Confidence, Livy. Now, be a good girl and fucking come on my hand so I can finally eat what I've spent years hungry for."

The circles don't stop as he fucks me with his fingers and slides his tongue into my mouth. His movements only get more quick, more frantic, until I'm biting down on his lip and writhing against his hand, the heat in my belly exploding through my limbs.

"Fuck, baby, yes," I murmur.

When I come down and focus on him again, Beckett licks my lips and holds his hand still, his eyes laser-focused on me. "That's the second time you've called me that."

Breathless, I blink at him. "What?"

"Baby. You called me baby, Livy. You falling for your husband?"

Pressing my lips together and looking away, I push against him, but he refuses to let go.

He holds me right there, with his fingers inside me, and uses his free hand to tilt my chin so I'm forced to look at him. "Tell me you're falling for your husband... please?"

His expression is so earnest. The desire to be desired is a concept I understand well. But even if I didn't, I'm no liar. All I can tell him is the truth. "Yeah... my husband is definitely growing on me."

His smile widens, then his lips are pressed to mine, almost

like he can't not kiss me. "Oh yeah?" he murmurs against my lips. "That's good, because I'm beyond obsessed with my wife."

We stare at each other for a long moment then. I don't know what game we're playing, and I'm not sure how we got here, but I can't summon the energy to worry about it right now. The orgasm only made me more ravenous for him.

"I need you," I whisper. "If you're so obsessed with your wife, then show me."

Beckett

28

The fucking things I want to do to this woman. She wants me to show her how obsessed I am? I'm not sure she's ready for that. But my cock is so hard it's weeping for her, and if she's asking for proof of how attracted I am to her, then I won't waste this opportunity.

"Dry off. I want you on all fours on the bed. Ass up in the air, Livy, waiting for me."

With her pupils blown out, she licks her lips. "Okay."

Holding out a hand, I help her stand, and when she immediately curls in on herself like she's trying to hide from me, I huff and snatch a towel from the stack under the sink. I wrap her in it and pull her close so she can feel the length of my cock against her, the hardness.

"This is what your body does to me," I whisper, taking handfuls of her ass and pulling her tighter against me. "I never lose my mind. I'm controlled in everything I do. My day—hell, my life—is planned meticulously." I squeeze her flesh. "But you... you make it so I can't think straight. This ass, this body, every fucking glorious inch of you makes me ache. Makes me insane with possession. I almost beat up some man with a smooth voice on your phone because I thought he was interested in you."

She giggles. "His name is Joe Arden, and you should be jealous. He's *very* swoony."

Angling back, I arch a brow and press my lips together.

She grabs my ass and tugs me closer. "But you're swoonier."

I growl and nip at her shoulder. I can't stop biting her, marking her. Like I'm an animal and my need for her can't be quelled. *More. More. More.* That's all that keeps beating through my chest.

Grasping her wrist, I bring her hand to my chest, allowing her to feel the rhythm. "That's not all you do to me," I murmur, grinding my hips against her. "My heart beats for you, Livy. I'm fucking crazy about you."

Her expression softening, she fixates on the way my hand is splayed over hers, at the evidence of the truth of my words.

I'm on the cusp of saying something I can't take back when she offers me a devilish grin. "Don't take too long, baby." With that, she pecks my lips and rushes out of the bathroom.

I don't allow my mind to focus on the fact that she's running from our true feelings, because my wife is about to get on all fours, and I have waited *years* to see that bare ass.

The late afternoon sun casts my beautiful wife in a soft light as she perches on the bed, waiting for me. I bring my fist to my mouth and bite down. "Goddamn... that ass is perfection," I mutter. So fucking big and round I don't know where to begin. I want to run my tongue down the expanse of it. Knead it and squeeze it. Spank her for allowing anyone else near her. I want to own this ass. And one day, let's be honest, I want to fuck it.

Liv wiggles back and forth, making my decision for me. Damn, my need for her is insatiable. Sauntering up behind her, I grasp one hip and run my free hand in a circle over her right cheek. After giving it a good caress, I pull back and give it a light tap. When she whimpers, my already heated blood simmers and my dick throbs.

"You like that, Livy?" I ask, emboldened by her response. "You like being on display for your husband?"

With her face buried in the sheets, she lets out a muffled "no… yes… maybe."

I smack her again, a little harder this time.

She moans. "Please."

Lowering until my face is between her legs, I lick a line between her lips. Holy fuck, she's delicious. She writhes beneath my tongue, but I hold her hips steady and dive in again, then out, fucking her with my tongue.

Panting, she breathes out, "Yes, baby, right there." *Fuck*. The pet name does me in. Never in my life have I wanted to be someone's baby, but God, on Liv's lips, when she's begging and panting and pleading for me, there is no better sound. There's no limit to what I'd do to be this woman's baby.

"Please, Beckett, fuck me." She bucks against me again.

But I hold her still and stand up straight. "I've waited years to eat this pussy, years to taste you. I'm gonna do this until you're ready to pass out. How many orgasms do you think you can take before that happens?"

She pushes herself up on her elbows and glares at me over her shoulder. "Cock tease."

With a dark chuckle, I rub myself against her. "This what you want?"

She bites her lip and nods.

"Don't move," I grit out. Quickly, I shuck my shorts. Once it's free, my cock bobs between us, hard and heavy. I give it a good tug while she watches, licking her lips like she can't control the reaction. With her eyes still on me, I grip the base and slap her pussy hard with it.

She gasps and coats me in wetness, gushing for me. "Good

girl." Crouching again, I take a deep inhale and lick up every delicious drop. "Can I do it again?"

"Yes, please." Her words are hoarse, almost pained, she's so needy.

I give her ass a good caress, then bring my hand down swiftly. The crack echoes in the quiet room, and her skin turns red almost instantly.

"Holy fuck," she murmurs.

The words are barely out of her mouth before I'm spanking her pussy with my cock again and then licking up her desire.

We continue this spanking and slapping, alternating between her ass and her pussy. I haven't even touched her clit, and she's already crying out and shuddering at the lightest touches. Like she's been waiting for this her entire life.

"Please, please, please," she chants as she spasms the next time my cock makes contact with her lips.

So fucking hot and desperate for her taste, I slide my tongue inside her. God damn. I nearly pass out when her pussy pulses around it. But it's not enough for her. She needs more.

Rubbing her ass with one hand, I slide my fingers between her lips, splaying her open for me. Then I slide one finger in and curl it so I can massage her G-spot. "I want you to squirt for me, Livy. I want your cum all over my face. Then and only then will I give you this cock. Can you do that for me? Can you drench me?"

Her ass writhes in the air as she fucks my hand and my face. I love every fucking second of it. My cock is crying at this point, begging for her warm cunt. I work her harder, faster, and when she screams through her third orgasm, my cock spasms in anticipation. Pulse pounding in my ears, I slide beneath her, holding her thighs so she can't squirm away. When I'm in position, I suck her clit hard, forcing her to ride my face. Lost to her orgasm, Liv doesn't try to pull away. She does nothing but soak my face and thrash above me, giving me exactly what I begged her for.

"Oh my God, oh my God," she chants.

I lick her clean as promised and squeeze her thighs.

With a huff, she throws herself to one side so she's flat on her back, her arms and legs splayed. I crawl up her body, one hand on the mattress on either side of her, and take her mouth in a searing kiss. Even though I taste like her, she doesn't pull back. No, she fucking moans into the kiss.

"That was…" she murmurs against my lips.

"You did amazing, Livy." I hover above her, taking in how gorgeous she looks, her skin flushed and her eyes glassy with desire. "I'm so proud of you."

She bites her lip. "I want to return the favor."

"It wasn't a favor," I growl. "It was a delicacy. I could eat you all day and not get tired." I nip her lips, then peruse her naked body, taking in her large breasts, which I've yet to focus my attention on. "Fuck, these are amazing." I drop down and lathe one nipple while rubbing circles around the other. "Do you have any idea how amazing your tits are?" I squeeze both and peer up at her.

She drops her head to one side so I can't see her expression.

Grazing over one nipple with my thumb, I pull back just a little. "Look at me, Livy. Look at how obsessed I am with you."

Her brown eyes find mine, and she smiles softly. "I'm just…"

"Perfect," I finish for her, dropping my hips until I'm cradled between hers. "Beautiful. Delicious. I could go on and on."

She laughs lightly, but the sound is a little hesitant. "You don't have to keep saying those things. I'm going to fuck you either way."

Her comment makes my lungs seize. How the fuck doesn't she see what she's doing to me?

"I do have to say them. You're my wife." I squeeze her tit a little too forcefully, and she whimpers. "You deserve to be worshipped, Livy." I back off and caress her flesh. "I'm just the lucky bastard who gets the honor of doing it. I actually can't *not* say these things, because it's how I feel. I look at you, and God, Liv, I turn into a goddamn animal. I have to have you."

"Beckett," she pants, already rubbing her warm, drenched pussy against my cock. So needy again.

"Yes, wife? Is there something I can do for you?"

"Your cock. I need your cock."

The sound of those dirty words on her lips... Fuck, it's perfect.

"Condom," I grit out, rapt in the way her heat envelops me as I slide my cock between her lips.

She rubs against me again. "On the pill, and I've been checked. You?" Her words come out breathy, making me wonder if this is just the lust talking.

"Open your eyes, Livy. Look at me."

She obeys, stilling beneath me.

"I've never been bare inside anyone... But with you, that's what I want... but *only* if you want it."

I've never trusted another woman like this. I've never given another woman the opportunity to trap me—never risked the chance of a kid with anyone. But with Liv? Fuck, I'd probably be the one doing the trapping if given the opportunity.

Pressing her warm palm to my cheek, she rubs her thumb against my lips. "Fuck me bare, Beckett. Take whatever you want. I'm yours."

The last semblance of my control snaps at those words. I reach between us and guide my cock to her entrance. With an even thrust, I push into her, taking her one fucking inch at a time. I don't watch her pussy suck my cock in; no, my focus is locked on her face. The way her eyes go hazy. How her teeth sink into her plump bottom lip. The soft moan that vibrates between us and the way she gasps my name like it's a prayer. "Beckett." Nothing but a whisper between us.

Unable to stop myself, I dip down and take her lips, all while her hot pussy squeezes me, holding steady when I reach the depths of her, reveling in the feel of her wrapped around me so tightly. Her lips, her fucking pussy, but more than any of that, her heart. I feel it, feel every ounce of this moment between us, my heart pounding in rhythm with hers.

And then, before I go and say the words that have been on the tip of my tongue for far too long, I move. Propping myself up on my forearms, I pull out and slam back in. Her tiny gasps get lost in my kisses.

She snakes her arms around my neck and pulls me closer, until we're chest to chest, her tits bouncing beneath me every time I pound into her.

"So perfect. So fucking good," I murmur in time with our movements.

Our words are lost between grunts and breaths. In no time, the telltale tug in my balls signals my impending release. "I'm going to come. Let me get you off one more time." With one of her hands grasped in mine, I drag it between us, but she pulls away, gripping my ass and forcing me closer.

"I just want to feel you against me. Please," she begs.

"Anything for you." I don't stop, but I limit my movements. My thrusts now are short. She wants me close, so that's the way I stay. "Where do you want it, Livy?"

She bites her lip, her eyes wide and filled with desire, but she doesn't answer.

With a press of my lips, I kiss her deep. "Don't hesitate. Just tell me where you want my cum. On your face?"

She scrunches her nose, and I can't help but laugh. That's a no.

"Your mouth?" I lick at her lips.

She sighs against me, then finally, she whispers, "On my pussy."

My cock swells at the thought. Fuck. I pull out and strangle my dick for a second, holding back my orgasm so I can memorize the way she looks right now.

Liv's full focus is set on me. Her expression so patient, so trusting, while she waits for me to paint her skin. She's glowing, her lips puffy, her cheeks pink.

"So fucking pretty," I whisper as I slap my cock against her pussy. Her responding gasp spurs me on, so I slap it again. That's all it takes to send her hurtling over the edge again, her body thrashing and taking me along with her. My orgasm takes over, and I come in long spurts, coating her swollen clit.

Because I can't resist, I rub it in, sliding two fingers inside her, angling until she's squeezing my fingers and coming a final time.

"Holy shit," she mutters as she comes down from her high.

"Just getting started, Livy," I murmur as I kiss her softly. "Just getting started."

Liv
29

"**F**uckers."

"What's wrong, baby?" There's no stopping the way the endearment rolls off my tongue.

Beckett tosses his phone onto the bed and pulls me to him, dropping his head to the crook of my neck.

"I fucking love when you call me that." He nips at my sensitive flesh. The man seems to like marking me. And he can't get enough of my breasts. "I love these." With a grunt, he squeezes and kneads, already in tune with what turns me on.

It's impossible to stop the moan that slips out, but I'm not sure I can take much more. After what was inarguably the best sex of my life, Beckett dragged me into the shower and washed me down, then administered a fifth orgasm. Afterward, he washed my hair, wrapped me in a towel, dried me off, and ushered me back to bed, where we've been lying for the last hour. The sun has disappeared from the sky. We're going to be late for dinner if he doesn't stop touching me. Not that I'm all that concerned. Although, I am starving…

"Beckett."

"Yes, wife?" he murmurs, sliding his hand lower until he brushes over my stomach.

I suck in with hopes he somehow doesn't feel the way my stomach juts out. The man seems determined to touch me in other places, though, and doesn't stop. He reaches between my legs and cups me, groaning about how it's his new favorite addiction, and I forget all about my insecurities.

"What was the text message that had you upset?" I ask, breathless. If I don't distract him from his mission, we'll never leave the room.

Beckett chuckles against my neck. "Feel free to look."

"You want me to look at your phone?"

Dipping a finger inside me, he groans. "What's mine is yours."

"Beckett," I huff.

Drake would *never* let me look at his phone—probably should have been a sign—but I'm not going to take advantage of Beckett's distraction right now.

"Livy, when I say there isn't a thing I'm hiding from you, I mean it. You probably know more about me than anyone. Including my brothers. There isn't a thing you could find that I'd be concerned about."

Giving in, I grab for his phone and can't hold back my laugh as I read his latest annoyance.

> Aiden: What time is dinner again?
>
> Gavin: 7.
>
> Aiden: Cool, so I have time for a snack.
>
> Brooks: It's 6. You really can't wait for dinner?
>
> Gavin: Your idea of a snack is a fucking cheeseburger. Don't eat a cheeseburger right now, Aiden.

Aiden: Fuck you, I'm a growing boy. Not all of us can work in the front office. Some of us have to keep this family business thriving by selling out arenas.

Brooks: LOL

Gavin: Asshole. Speaking of assholes, Beckett, you there?

Aiden: Nah, he's enjoying time with his wife.

Brooks: Good for you, Beckett. Tell Liv we said hi.

Gavin: Enjoying the honeymoon suite?

Aiden: Wait, you're in the honeymoon suite? Thought he was staying in the penthouse? Gavin, if you're in the penthouse, then why the fuck am I sharing a room with Rivers?

Gavin: Brooks is using the other bedroom. Weren't you planning on getting a snack?

Aiden: Fuck you. How come Brooks gets a room to himself?

Gavin: I like him more.

Brooks: LOL.

Aiden: I'll remember that when I'm scoring points tomorrow that line YOUR pockets.

Gavin: They line your pockets, too, asshole.

We're not coming to dinner. Have a good night.

BECKETT HAS LEFT THE CHAT.

AIDEN ADDED BECKETT TO THE CHAT.

Aiden: WTF man?! You get a wife, and now you're too good for us?

Brooks: He was always too good for you.

> Gavin: LOL

> Aiden: Fuck you. I'm going to dinner with Rivers.

LAUGHING, I toss Beckett's phone onto the mattress and face him. "Your brothers are insane. Are they always like this?" Sure, I've known them for years, but around me, they're far more calm. Their personalities really shine when they're talking to one another.

Beckett grumps. "Yup."

"Why aren't we going to dinner?" My stomach chooses that moment to growl. I was looking forward to that steakhouse.

Beckett palms my ass and squeezes. "Because I'm tired of sharing you. Tonight is about you and me. It's Friday. We have *rules*, Mrs. Langfield."

I smile. "Yes, like no PDA, no kissing, no crossing lines."

He pulls my lip between his teeth and tugs. "Fuck your rules. Mine are better. You must always be naked in my bed on Friday nights. Dinner consists of just the two of us and is always followed by multiple orgasms."

I moan as he licks down my neck and heads toward my breasts. "I mean, those aren't terrible rules..." I say, breathless. "But I'll need my lawyer to look over the revisions."

"Fuck Medusa. She'll cockblock me."

I bark out a laugh. "Fine, but after you eat, you're feeding me."

Beckett smirks. "We Langfields do like our snacks."

WHEN ROOM SERVICE ARRIVES, we enjoy cheeseburgers, fancy champagne, and hours of sitting on the couch, talking. He's got one hand on my thigh, which he's strategically placed across his lap, and he's resting his head against the cushion, watching me.

"Tell me more about growing up with your brothers. You're the only one who went into baseball, why?"

Beckett sighs. "Don't get me wrong—I love hockey. But I don't know." He looks past me, like he's gone somewhere far away. "There's just something about baseball, ya know? The stadium, the smell."

I scrunch my nose. "I guess if you like hot dogs."

He squeezes my thigh. "Lang Field does not smell like hotdogs."

Yes, that really is the name of the stadium where the Boston Revolutionaries play. Despite how wonderful the family is, the Langfields are just a *little* egotistical.

I shrug. "Whatever you say. Keep going."

"The crack of the bat when it connects with the ball. The silence when the whole stadium is waiting to see whether it'll be caught or…" Beckett holds up his hand and pushes across the air, his voice going whispery soft, like he's mimicking a ball whizzing through the air, "be a grand slam."

I can't help the smile that consumes my face. "I like you like this."

Dropping his hand to my leg again, he shoots me a wink.

"Did you play in college?"

He shakes his head. "I've always been more involved with the business end of things. My brothers all played hockey. Gavin didn't make it professionally, but like me, he loved the business side. But he also studied the game. He could coach if he wanted; he knows more than most of the guys we hire."

"Interesting."

"But Brooks? Watching him on his skates?" He shakes his head in quiet awe. "I knew from day one he'd be amazing. And since he and Aiden are so close in age, and Aiden wanted to do whatever Brooks did, it was no surprise when he followed him on skates."

"God, your mom must have spent every waking moment at one of the boys' games." Just thinking about it makes my head spin. I really hope my kids don't get into sports; I'm not sure I can juggle work and that commitment on top of homework and the Zumba class I should apparently be enrolled in.

Beckett lets out a heavy breath. "Honestly, they didn't go to many games. She was so busy entertaining clients for my dad or traveling with him." He shrugs. "But Gavin and I made sure we were there. Between the two of us, the boys always had someone rooting for them."

The thought makes my chest go tight. "You're a really good brother."

He lifts his chin and laughs. "Tell that to Aiden. He's still blowing up my phone with complaints about me not coming to dinner."

A little knot of guilt forms in my stomach. Wringing my hands in my lap, I study him. "You can go meet them. You don't need to sit with me. I know we're just—" I don't finish the sentence because I have no freaking idea what we are. Coworkers? Friends? Fake husband and wife? It was a lot easier to categorize this thing before we slept together.

No, that's not entirely true. Things have been slowly changing since the first time he kissed me. Maybe even before that. But after tonight, I have no freaking idea what we are. I just know I'm already dreading the day it ends.

"We're not *just* anything," Beckett says, his tone fierce. With his eyes locked on me, he stops himself and takes a deep breath in. When he speaks again, his tone is softer. "I'll see them Tuesday. Jay is coming in from Paris, and we're going to the game. We're playing the Metros, so Jamie is coming into town too."

"Oh yeah, I forgot about that. This is a big series."

Beckett works his jaw from side to side. "Yeah, and if Clayton doesn't work his shit out, I don't care if he can hit the ball better than the rest of the guys on the team, I'm benching him."

"You can't bench him." I have to hold back a laugh. "You aren't the coach."

Brows furrowed, he eyes me. "Watch me."

I give him an exaggerated roll of my eyes, which leads him to tickle me. The next thing I know, I'm straddling him, and he has a hand pressed to my cheek. "What about you, Livy? Tell me what you were like growing up."

"Not much to tell." I shrug. "I was your typical girl, I guess. My brother was my hero, my mother worked herself to the bone, and our father wasn't in the picture."

Beckett strokes a thumb over my cheekbone, his expression warm. "That must have been hard."

"Wasn't easy," I admit. "But we made do. My mom always went above and beyond. My brother too. I know he was an ass to you when you showed up at his house, but he's spent his life protecting me. And he's taken on that same role with my kids. He never liked Drake." I let out a bitter laugh. "Shoulda listened to him."

"But then you wouldn't have your kids," Beckett points out.

"True." I drop my chin, my chest aching just a little with pride and longing at the thought of them. "And as much work as they are, they're my everything."

"They're amazing, Livy. You've done a great job with them."

I've always struggled to accept compliments, but when it comes to my babies, it's easier. "Thank you. I know they're a lot more than you bargained for—"

Pressing a finger to my lips, he shushes me. "Package deal. And I happen to like the package. It's like a two for one sale."

I laugh. "More like eleven for one. You must be dying to get back to your penthouse."

Beckett grasps my shoulders, his green eyes holding mine, and pulls me down until our lips are a breath away from one another. "I don't miss it even a little."

Closing that last bit of space, I kiss him. Long and slow and languid. Every aspect of this night, every word he's spoken, every one of his actions, is too perfect. Just for tonight, I don't want to think about what the future holds. I just want to enjoy it.

Liv
30

Dylan: Cable stopped working

Shayla: That's what that wire was…

Dylan: I told you not to cut the red one

Delia: Can't blame this one on the house.

Shayla: Liv, when will you be back? We need Beckett.

Delia: We absolutely DO NOT!

Dylan: I wanted to watch hgtv. I had plans

Shayla: LOL. Delia probably cut the cord because the idea of you DIYing anything in this house scares the living shit out of her.

We'll be back tomorrow. He says we can pick up a new wire on the way home.

Delia: There will be no DIY anything!! Ladies, we do not NEED a man to fix things. I'll go buy a damn wire.

S haking my head, I drop my phone to the floor beside me and go back to the task at hand: finding a damn matching pair of heels.

You have got to be kidding me. I chuck a shoe over my shoulder. Then another, and another. Is one matching pair really too much to ask for? From the looks of it, the leather boots I wore on the plane are the only complete set I have. Leather boots that would look ridiculous at an afternoon baseball game in Vegas.

With a groan, I collapse to the floor in front of my suitcase.

"What the duck is going on in here?" Beckett wanders out of the bathroom wearing the fuck out of a pair of dark blue jeans and a Revs jersey, his brown hair perfectly tousled.

I cannot go to the game with him today. He's too pretty.

Pointing to the heap of clothes and shoes on the floor, I sigh. "I don't have any matching shoes. You're going to have to go to the game yourself. I'll stay here and keep my phone close if you need me to work any emergencies."

Beckett hovers over me, wearing a bewildered frown. "What?"

I blow out a breath and peer up at him. "I can do my job from here. You don't need me there anyway. I don't want to point out the obvious, because job security and all, but I can do the majority of my job from my phone. There's really no need for me to be here."

Swallowing audibly, he tilts his face to the ceiling and lets out a long breath, as if he's exasperated by me. Right now I'm not sure I blame him. I'm lying in the middle of my own mess, my hair stuck to my face because I broke into a sweat while searching for my shoes, and I still haven't changed for the game because I planned to wear a dress and I didn't want it to wrinkle before we left. All I'm wearing is a waffle-knit robe supplied by the hotel that doesn't quite fit me. One size fits all, my ass.

He crouches before me, elbows resting on his legs and his hands clasped in front of him. "You still don't get it, do you?" He lets out a gruff sigh. "I don't *need* you at the games; I *want* you there."

I frown, a hint of unease lodged in my chest. "Right, because you like to be at every game. You have control issues."

Laughing, he falls back on his ass. "No, Livy, I didn't invite you to the game this weekend because I need you to work. I want you at the game as my wife. You'll be there as the *owner's wife*."

Oh shit. Right. My part of the deal. Pictures as husband and wife.

"I don't have shoes," I mutter, dropping my focus to the floor between us.

Beckett pushes to a stand and holds his hands out to me so he can pull me to my feet. "I grabbed the ones you keep under your desk; they're in my carry-on. Give me a second." He disappears into the closet, and when he reappears, my black heels dangle from his fingers.

"Huh?"

Holding them out to me, he lifts one shoulder. "There isn't a single matching pair in your closet. I'm not sure what Devil Spawn or the Shining Twins are up to, but I figured I'd bring these in case they got into your suitcase too."

"You grabbed my shoes from beneath my desk?"

He frowns at me like he doesn't get my confusion. But seriously, how does a man with a hectic schedule like his remember to grab an extra pair of shoes for me? A guy who, by all accounts, cares only about himself. At least, that's what I always thought. But every day, I realize a little more that he cares more than most. And that when it comes to me, he sees more than anyone ever has.

He nods toward the bathroom. "I left you a matching jersey in there."

When I frown, he rolls his eyes.

"I know you'll probably wear a dress. I don't think I've ever seen you wear jeans. But maybe you could wear the jersey over it?"

"A jersey over my dress?"

He shoots me a grin that's damn near irresistible. "Please? For me. We'll look good together."

Right. In pictures. We've got to sell this marriage to the world. Dropping my shoulders, I sigh in resignation. I made a promise, and I never break my promises. I just wish I could do it in a dress instead of a jersey. For a woman like me, with big breasts and a tummy, there isn't anything less flattering.

Resigned to keeping up my end of the bargain, I grab the Spanx from my suitcase, along with my black dress, and head to the bathroom to change.

Several jerseys hang on the hook next to the shower. On closer inspection, their designs are identical. The only difference is the size. My heart rate spikes, and my eyes well with tears.

Why is this man so thoughtful? He literally thinks of everything.

Once I change into my dress, I pick the jersey that will likely fit best. Turning so I can check myself out in the mirror from every angle, I can't help but smile. The outfit may not be what I would pick to wear while standing beside Beckett at a game, but tying it at the bottom rather than buttoning it makes it look less boxy, and surprisingly, it highlights my curves well.

When Beckett knocks, I quickly open the door.

"Almost ready?"

Embracing the confidence the outfit and my husband's thoughtfulness have imbued me with, I smile. "Thank you for getting different sizes. I appreciate it."

His eyes go hungry as he gives me a thorough once-over. "Okay, wife, I'm not going to lie. The sight of you in my team's jersey is doing something to me. We better leave before I bend you over that counter and fuck you."

My stomach dips at the thought. No one has ever made me feel so desired. Taking his outstretched hand, I pop up on my toes and kiss him on the cheek. And when I follow him out of the room a minute later, I feel like the luckiest woman in existence.

HOURS OF SMILING and cheering and dealing with the media after the game are followed by a limo ride to the rink to watch the other Langfield boys take on Las Vegas—a game they win in overtime thanks to Aiden Langfield and the right winger, Tyler Warren.

But all that means is that for the last twelve hours, I've been stuffed into a pair of Spanx, and after being on my feet all day, I feel like a balloon ready to pop.

The moment we step into the bedroom of our suite, Beckett is on me. "Fuck, today was long." His lips are already on mine as he guides me to the wall and presses the length of himself against me, his hands traveling up and down my hips.

As tired as I am, I want to soak up every moment with him before we head back to reality tomorrow. Before we return to life in the brownstone with seven children and three judgy roommates.

Okay, Dylan and Shay aren't judgy, but Delia's constant commentary is enough for the three of them. And even if the other girls are supportive, they still watch us like we're a circus act: Dylan waiting for vindication because she called this from day one and Shay studying us with silent scrutiny, like she just can't quite figure out what we're doing.

Or maybe that's just my insecurities.

So, I allow Beckett to touch me. To work me into a frenzy alongside him. To kiss me so stupid I forget about my undergarments until the moment he slides his hands up my legs and reaches the sexiest panties ever known to man.

Spanx.

"What the fuck are these?" The timbre of his voice is low and harsh and sends a mixture of nerves and desire skittering down my spine.

Releasing my hold on his neck, I tug at the hem of my dress, mortified. Naturally, he'll have none of it. Instead, he drops to his knees, bats my hands away, and pushes my dress up.

"Please, Beckett," I beg, pressing my knees together in a vain attempt to hide the embarrassing undergarment. "How about you get undressed and get in bed? Give me a minute to get comfortable. I promise I'll make it worth your while." I waggle my brows, though with the panic rising up in me, I can't imagine the move is a sexy one.

He growls, "What is this?"

With a huff, I give up my fight and allow him to lift my dress so he can stand witness to my complete and utter humiliation. All the allure and confidence I garnered last night is long gone.

The black Spanx dig into my ribs and my thighs, making me look like a sausage.

So fucking sexy.

Beckett hooks his fingers under the black fabric, pressing into one thigh and tugs. "Fuck."

I drop my head back against the wall and close my eyes, fighting off the sting of tears. "Just let me go."

With a growl, he pushes my dress up to my abdomen. Once there, he yanks on the fabric, trying to pull it over my thick hips. "What is this? How the hell do you get this thing off?"

I groan. "It's Spanx. It's meant to keep in all my wobbly bits."

"Your wobbly what?" He tugs again, eyes crazed. "We need scissors!" The pitch of his voice is high, panicked, like he's seriously concerned, and for some reason, that makes me giggle.

"Beckett, it's okay."

"It's not okay. Your body's being strangled inside this contraption. And you've been wearing this all day? You could have lost blood flow." He pulls at it again.

At the seriousness of his expression and the urgency in his voice, I lose it. Shaking with laughter, I keel over, taking Beckett with me with a loud *thump* to the floor.

"Are you okay?" he asks manically, his eyes impossibly wide.

I'm laughing so hard I can barely breathe. He's so worried, so concerned—*about my Spanx*—it's ridiculous. A snort is the only response I can manage.

He pushes me off him and onto my back, prepared to what? Give me mouth to mouth? Perform surgery to save my wobbly bits? That thought sends me into another bout of laughter.

Wearing a look of pure terror, Beckett scans my face. "What is happening?"

"Baby, I'm fine," I say, gulping in air. "It's just underwear."

"That is *not* underwear." He digs a finger under the fabric at my thigh again, sounding affronted. "That's a torture chamber."

We both burst out laughing. This time, he's the one to fall over. On our backs, side by side, we shake and sputter and wheeze. When we finally catch our breath, Beckett turns onto his side and props himself up on his elbow. "Why the hell would you wear that?" He reaches for my hand and twines our fingers together, waiting for an answer.

My exhale is long and loud as defeat creeps in. "I'm not like the women at the stadium or the rink today."

He frowns, his brows set low. "What does that even mean?"

"The players' wives, your brother's girlfriend—they're all

young and gorgeous. They look good in a jersey. Adorable little things wearing their boyfriend's names on their backs."

"So… you want my name on your back?"

"No." I tip my head back and groan at the ceiling. "My point is… I'm not a young little thing. This jersey? If I'd buttoned it up, it would look like a tent. And this dress? If I don't wear Spanx," I pull my hand from his and motion to my stomach area, "*this* would all be on display."

With his hands gripping my waist, he lets out a feral growl. "Take this off."

I huff out a sigh, but seriously, I'm so over wearing this girdle. It's pulled down now anyway, leaving my stomach on display, no longer serving its intended purpose.

I head into the bathroom and turn on the shower, not bothering to shut the door. After twelve hours in and out of the Vegas sun, I'm done.

I've just settled under the spray, tilting my face to the hot water, when the glass door opens and Beckett steps inside. "C'mere," he murmurs, holding out his hands.

"But you'll see all my wobbly bits," I whine half-heartedly.

He doesn't allow me to hold back, though. He pulls me to his chest and hugs me tightly, pressing his lips against my forehead. "You don't need to hide your wobbly bits from me. You're beautiful."

"That doesn't change how I feel," I murmur against his chest.

"I understand that, but can I tell you what I see? Can I tell you what *I* feel?" He spins me so my back is to his front and drops his face to my shoulder, trailing his hands down my arms. "You're the first woman I've ever wanted to spend hours with alone. The first woman whose body I can't get enough of."

Warm lips press against my neck, and his hands snake around my waist, caressing the part of my stomach I hate the most. "This right here? Fuck. It's so soft. I love it."

My chest tightens, and I have to fight the urge not to push his hand away. It's the flappy skin left over from my pregnancies. It's soft because it's loose and never sees the light of day. "Please."

It isn't until this moment that I realize he's turned me toward the mirror. It's foggy from the heat, but I can make out his features and see the way he studies our reflection under the spray of water.

"You don't like it when I tell you how to feel, so don't tell me how I feel. This"—he smooths his hand across my stomach again and licks his lips in a way that isn't forced; it's innate, like he's truly hungry for me—"feels so fucking good against my hands. Like you were made for me, Livy. I love how soft you are, the soft to my hardness. I love how the outside world sees one version of you, but you let me see another one, the more vulnerable one. That I get this part of you." With another squeeze, he rubs his hard cock against me. "I love this part." His voice is low, guttural. "Now, can I keep going?"

Entranced and a bit stupid with lust, I nod.

"These thighs? Fuck, I love when they're wrapped around my neck and you're riding my face. These tits? Don't even get me started on how much I love them." He squeezes one roughly and runs his thumb over my nipple. The sensation nearly makes my knees give out. "I've tried not to stare at these tits for years, Livy, *years*, but you're my goddamn kryptonite. The only woman I've ever wanted as my wife, and now you're mine."

Whimpering at his rough touches mixed with his soft words, at the love dripping from every syllable, I spin around and reach for him. "I'm yours."

"Good girl. Now tell me, wife, where do you want me to fuck you first?"

"I need your cock in my mouth." Never in my life did I think I'd utter the words that rush out of me, but after all he's given me over the last twenty-four hours, my body aches to give back to him.

Beckett pinches a nipple and lets out a ragged breath. "Such a fucking needy wife." He bites down on my neck and then licks at it. "But I want you to watch me fuck you first. Can we do that? Can I hold you like this? I want you to keep your eyes on the mirror while I take you from behind. Can I show you how beautiful we look together? I want you to see us the way I see us."

Studying his face, looking for any sign of untruth, I swallow thickly.

He brings the hand still cupping my breast to my neck. "Do that again," he whispers in my ear. I obey, swallowing again, and he groans against me. "Fuck, I'm going to hold your neck like this later so I can feel it when I come down your throat."

Oh my God. Liquid heat warms my core, and a shudder rushes through me.

He leaves his fingers where they are, squeezing a bit more. "Hands on the glass. Stick that gorgeous ass out so I can fuck you like you deserve."

"And how is that?" I ask, emboldened by the obvious desire in his voice.

"Like you're mine."

Heat pools between my legs.

"Now grab my cock and line us up, my beautiful wife."

He doesn't move his hands. Still holding me by the neck and stomach, he forces me to feel every second from when we're two separate people to when he pushes inside me in one hard thrust and makes us one.

With his fingers digging into the flesh of my stomach, he sighs. "So fucking good. My perfect wife. Made just for me."

My eyes fall shut at the intense pressure, at the euphoria he's bringing forth and the completeness I feel when he's inside me. Never in my life have I felt this cherished, respected, and loved, all in the same breath.

Thrust. "Eyes." *Thrust.* "On." *Thrust.* "Us."

Pulling in a sharp inhale, I watch our reflection in the mirror, locked into his haunted gaze. Every ounce of him is pure hunger and lust as he watches the pounding he's giving me. He squeezes my neck a little tighter and bites down so hard on my shoulder I yelp. He doesn't apologize, though. Without slowing, he drops his hand to clutch me between the legs, putting pressure exactly where I need it most.

"That's it, wife. Ride my hand while I fuck you. Show us both how wild you can be, how beautiful you are with your husband's cock inside you. How fucking greedy you are. Demand it all. There isn't a thing in this world I won't give you."

Stars. I'm seeing fucking stars. The way he drills into me so deep. The pressure of his palm against my clit. The power he gives me with his words. The confidence he elicits with the hunger he has that only I can seem to feed.

"Now fucking come all over my cock, Mrs. Langfield. Soak me with your cum so I can paint you with mine."

That's all it takes to send me over the edge. I shatter in his arms with his name on my lips. My knees give out, but he holds me up. Pulling out, he spins me and slams his mouth against mine.

He strokes my cheek as water rains down between our mouths. "Do you see now?" he whispers, his green eyes cataloging my every feature.

"See what?" I'm breathless.

"How beautiful we are together. It's how I've seen you every damn day since I first laid eyes on you."

Still too raw to fully accept the praise, I avoid the question by giving him a flirty smile and a peck on his lips. Then I drop to my knees. "Eyes on the mirror, baby. Watch me make you come."

He groans as I take him down my throat, but I should have known he'd never let me get off that easy.

"Nuh-uh," he murmurs, wrapping his hand around my throat.

"The only one I watch when I come is you, beautiful." With that, he lets loose, squeezing my throat and fucking my mouth until I swallow every last drop.

An hour later, we're curled up together in bed. There isn't a place in the world I'd rather be, and I'm starting to dread returning to reality tomorrow. Swirling fingers dance against my bare back, and he kisses my forehead. "Thank you for coming with me today. I know it was a lot."

I blush under his praise, nuzzling against his chest. "Of course. It's part of the deal. I hope I'm holding up my part of it."

"What are you talking about?"

My throat tightens, and my heart aches, but I force myself to look at him. To pretend all is well. "How you wanted me to act like your wife today rather than your employee. Take pictures, ya know, for the PR stunt. So the public views you as a family guy. Hopefully it's enough to help with ticket sales."

Beckett is silent for a moment. He's frowning, examining every inch of my face.

Worried I've said something wrong, I go on. "That's why you wanted me to come today, right? You said I was there as the owner's wife, not for work."

Shit. Did I screw up? Should I have worked during the game, when all eyes were trained elsewhere? Did I act too much like his wife?

"I meant," he grinds his teeth, "I wanted you there as my wife. Not for some PR stunt, but as the woman I want to show off because I'm crazy about you."

My heart leaps into my throat, and my mouth falls open. "Oh."

He uses two fingers to lift my chin and presses his lips to mine. "Yeah, oh. So, like I was saying, thank you for today. I enjoy spending time with you, Livy—maybe a bit too much. I know it was crazy, but unfortunately, that's my life, running from one event to another, never quite getting to spend as much time with the people I want to." He blows out a breath and looks out toward the Vegas skyline. "But it was nice that, just for today, I had you by my side as my wife. That I got to experience what that was like."

He manhandles me until I'm sprawled across his chest, and just for tonight, I experience what it's like to be truly happy, truly treasured, in this man's arms.

Beckett

31

One weekend with Liv all to myself didn't even touch the surface of feeding my obsession. If anything, it fueled the fire. Monday morning, my back hurts, and it's not just because I'm sleeping in the damn twin-size bed in what should be Addie's nursery. It's because I didn't spend the night wrapped around Liv's body.

But that's only the start of a long list of things that go wrong on our first day back.

"Another shoe!" Liv screeches from her closet.

That's it. I'm calling a family meeting tonight. I've had enough of these kids playing tricks on her.

The contractors Medusa approved are meeting me at the house this morning after everyone leaves for the day—I made sure Gavin asked Liv to come to the arena so she isn't here for this meeting.

Still in my boxers, I head to the closet to help Liv look for her shoe. Halfway there, a brown ball of fur rushes past me. I'm not proud of the loud scream that rips from my throat as I jump so fucking high even Aiden would be proud. "What the fuck is *that*?"

Liv pops up and rushes to the closet door, but I block her exit as an animal bigger than a cat scurries to the other side of the room.

"That's another thousand!" one of the twins hollers from the hallway.

Without taking my eyes off the creature, I whisper, "Go get me a bat."

"What is it?" She grips my bicep hard but releases it quickly and backs into the closet again.

"No fucking idea."

My voice is low, but the damn Shining Twins are apparently equipped with superior hearing, along with those damn big brains that make me squirm.

"We are going to be so rich," one of them squeals.

The animal bolts to the corner, and just as Liv slips a bat into my hand, Huck throws the door open and bellows, "Don't hurt Junior!"

Startled, the beast freezes and turns its black-ringed eyes on me.

A raccoon.

With a shoe wedged between its teeth, it rears back on its haunches and holds up its paws, almost like it's surrendering. But then those beady little eyes narrow, and the shoe clatters to the floor as the thing fucking hisses.

Game on, motherfucker.

Striding toward it, I brandish the bat, swinging it back and forth like a gladiator. For good measure, I let out a roar. The kind the people in this house have told me I'm exceptionally good at uttering.

This raccoon is going *down*.

"Bossman!" Huck cries, suddenly appearing beside me.

Before he can get too close to the likely rabies-infected animal, I drop the bat and snatch him off the hardwood floor. He kicks his legs and pushes against me and the raccoon takes this as his opportunity to escape. It snaps up the shoe again and dashes into an air vent. The grate that had been pushed aside clatters to the floor as it darts past.

Smart little fucker.

"What the hell is going on in here?" Medusa barks.

With Huck still in my arms, I turn to face the music—otherwise known as the very angry moms. They're all staring at me like I'm the one who fucking crawled into the vent after stealing Liv's shoe.

I hold Finn in front of me since I'm dressed in nothing but boxers and every eye in this house is trained on me like I'm the problem here. "We have rodents."

Medusa narrows her eyes. "That's why we keep you in here. You're not house trained yet."

Liv nudges her. "Real rodents, Delia. Play nice."

Medusa folds her arms over her chest. "That's why he's screaming? A little mouse scare you?"

"It's not a mouse, Auntie Delia," Huck sings. "It's my pet."

All attention immediately diverts to the three-foot-tall kid in my arms.

"Your what?" I ask, turning him so he's forced to look at me.

Liv moves closer. "Finn, what did you do?"

Huck breaks out in a toothy grin. "Don't worrys. I feed him just like Auntie Shayla showed me."

We all whirl on Shayla.

She looks just as confused as the rest of us. "I never told him to feed a rat."

"It's not a rat," Liv and I say at the same time.

"It's my pet raccoon. Junior." Finn beams, wrapping one arm around my neck.

Holy fuck. My stomach bottoms out. He has a pet raccoon. In the house.

"A raccoon!" Shayla shrieks, snatching Kai from her side and pushing him behind her. "We all need to get checked. Do you know what kind of diseases those things could carry?"

"My raccoons does not have dismiseas." Finn scowls at Shayla, then turns to face me, grabbing my cheeks in his pudgy hands. "You won't hurts him, right, Bossman? We take care of everyone. We don't hurts them."

I resist the urge to hang my head. Shit. The boy went and fell in love with a raccoon. "We won't hurt him, Huck."

"Um, yes, we will," Medusa counters. "I'm calling the exterminator right now."

Finn tenses in my arms, his eyes rimming red.

At his reaction, I can't help but growl. "Nothing is happening to the damn raccoon, Medusa."

"Should we just call it a clean five thousand?" Twin A asks. "It's looking like today is going to be an expensive day for you, so I think I'm offering you a deal."

When Liam appears in the hallway, Finn squirms out of my hold and runs toward him. "Tell them, Liam! Tell them we feeds Junior good. Tell them I'm a good daddy to him."

Liam has the good sense to drop his gaze to the floor when every one of us turns to him. "Shit," he mutters, redness creeping up his face.

Dylan smacks him on the back of the head. "A raccoon, Liam?"

He winces and peeks up at her. "The universe brought him to us, Ma. What did you want me to do?"

"That'll be a dollar." Twin B holds out her hand.

Without hesitation, Liam pulls his wallet out of his pocket and slips a crisp one-dollar bill into her hand.

"Wait a second. I thought it was a thousand." I glower at the two scam artists.

They shrug in unison. "We like him better."

Liv sighs and drags a hand down her face. "This has gotten

out of hand. Everyone out so I can talk to Finn. You're going to be late for school if you don't get moving."

Finn pulls on Liam's arm, jostling the headphones hanging around the kid's neck. "Don't let them call the experimenter."

Liam's face scrunches in confusion.

"Exterminator," I correct, then I get down to Finn's level. "No one is going to hurt your pet. But we can't have him running around the house either. We have to get him checked for rabies."

"He's not a rabbit, silly Bossman." Finn boops my nose.

God, this kid. How can I not chuckle at that? "Not a rabbit, right. But can I get him checked anyway?"

"Only if I get to stay while the doctors is here." He crosses his arms over his chest and pulls his shoulders back. "Mommy always holds my hands when I'm at the doctors so I don't gets scared."

"This is ridiculous," Medusa groans. "Come on, girls. You've witnessed enough stupidity this morning."

When Liv and Finn are the only ones left in the room, I go in search of tools so I can close up the vent.

A fucking raccoon for a pet. What the hell have I gotten myself into?

IT'S NOT until after dinner that we understand what Finn meant when he said he feeds Junior as good as Shay. It's Dylan's night to cook, but the side dish Shay insisted on making—the one we all push around with our forks to make it look like we've eaten it —is Junior's favorite, according to Finn.

"Follows me," he says.

Like he's the damn Pied Piper, the whole group obeys. We follow Finn to the fireplace, where he puts the food on a plate.

Nothing happens. Sure he's playing make believe, I ruffle his hair and give him an indulgent smile. It isn't until we're all watching *Thor* a little while later that the damn raccoon appears. He snags the food, then scurries back up the chimney.

I type out a quick message to the contractors I met with today, demanding they board up the fireplace first thing tomorrow. They have a long list already. Addie's room and the roof are at the top of it, and now, apparently, so is a room for the damn raccoon.

"I love him," Dylan coos, settling on the arm of the couch beside Liam.

"The raccoon?" I ask, rearing back.

She rolls her eyes and laughs. "No, Thor."

"We *know*, Ma, you say it every time we watch this. If only Chris Hemsworth was a baseball player," Liam mutters.

"Not Chris Hemsworth. *Thor.* He's one with the universe with that head of hair."

"Oh my God. I feel like absolute death," Medusa mutters, throwing herself onto the chair in the corner.

"Same," Shay murmurs, pulling Kai against her side and covering his eyes when Thor is on the screen.

"Mom," Kai whines. "I've seen this movie like five times."

She grumbles under her breath. Probably something about what a bad influence these movies are.

Dylan pipes up. "Should I get out my crystals? It will help with your cramps. Mine are so much less painful because of them."

Cramps? Oh shit. My stomach sinks as I look from one woman to another and another.

Liv snorts and bumps me with her shoulder. "Sorry," she mouths.

The evil grin on Medusa's face makes my skin crawl. "Aren't you so glad you took over laundry duty, Bossman?"

"Huh?"

"Two words," she whispers. "Period panties."

"That's it!" I launch myself off the couch and head for the foyer. "I'm going to get some fresh air."

As I'm slipping my shoes on, Liv chides, "Will you leave the poor man alone?"

Ducking period panties. Raccoons for pets. Too many ducking women. I need someone to talk me off the ledge.

Gavin: I'm afraid to ask.

Gavin: Period panties?

Aiden: That's disgusting. I'm removing your texting privileges in this chat.

AIDEN HAS REMOVED BECKETT FROM THE CHAT.

BLOWING OUT A LONG BREATH, I head down the street, phone in hand. Not a minute later, it lights up again.

Gavin has created a new chat.

Gavin: You okay?

Brooks: Aiden is an asshole.

I am anything but okay.

Aiden has added Beckett to the chat.

Aiden: Did you start a chat without me?

Aiden: Hello?

Aiden: I'm calling Mom.

I DON'T EVEN LAUGH at the idiot. My head is still spinning. It has been a *day*.

Brooks: I say none of us respond to him until tomorrow.

Gavin: Deal.

I need a poker night.

Gavin: Want to come over?

Brooks: I can be there in fifteen.

JUST AS I pull up the Uber app, my phone buzzes, and a notification appears at the top of the screen.

Livy: Sorry about today.

I SIGH and shoot my brothers a text.

Aiden, grow up. I need all three of you at the game tomorrow. I'm in over my head.

Gavin: We'll be there.

Brooks: Whatever you need.

Aiden: Want to go out? Jill is taking selfies, so she won't even notice I'm gone.

Nah. I'm going home to my wife. Night, guys.

Beckett

32

As luck would have it, all four women in the brownstone are on their period. At the same time. Something about the moon, according to Dylan.

Regardless of the reason, emotions were running high, and I couldn't, in good conscience, leave my wife, who was clearly in pain, to look after all three kids while I went to a baseball game with the boys. Well, at least I couldn't leave her with *all* the kids. So I offered to take Huck and Bear—though Bear said she'd rather stay home and work on an art project she was close to finishing—and because I'm not a complete dickhead, I also invited Kai and Liam.

Liam tried to play it cool, but he lived in New York until recently and was a huge Metros fan. Saying no to box seats to watch his favorite team play just to spite me *and* stay home with four whiney women? He may not be my biggest fan, but he's got a healthy sense of self-preservation.

Shay was against the idea at first, but in the end, Dylan reminded her that it would be good for Kai to have some male bonding time. Although that didn't stop Shay from providing me a long list of food he was not allowed to have. Not a single item on the list of suggested foods was available at the stadium, but I'll keep that to myself.

With a mouthful of hotdog—definitely not on the approved list—he grins at me.

Yeah, I gave the kid a hot dog, so sue me.

While Liam is seated at the front of the box, watching with fierce attention, my focus is on the little guy on my lap, who is, of course, wearing a navy-blue tutu with his Boston Revs jersey.

"How's the raccoon?" Gavin asks between bites of his hot dog.

Finn's smile is blinding. "Junior is great! Bossman had the mens with the hats make him a room, and now he watches me from inside and smiles all day."

That's not quite how it happened. First, the vet came and informed us that Junior is, in fact, female. Then he told us she's pregnant.

There was a lot of screaming from Medusa and concerned rambling from Shay, but Dylan and Liv reminded them that this is what they do—they take care of mothers. I'm not sure what the hell they were talking about. All I know is that, somehow, that meant we needed to find a safe space for Junior to gestate. Since she's a fan of the chimney, the vet suggested putting a metal gate up so we can still feed and monitor her, but so she doesn't come out. He then gave Junior her rabies shots while Finn told her how brave she was for not crying.

It was all a big to do, and in the end, it means that in a few short weeks, more little raccoons will be living within our walls.

Fucking fantastic.

Gavin tries to bite back his grin but fails. "Oh yeah? It's getting awfully crowded in that house, hmm?"

Huck shakes his head. "No, we loves having Bossman, and he loves us, right?" The kid looks up at me with his mom's brown eyes, and I fucking melt.

I ruffle his hair. "Sure do, Huck. The guys are getting outnumbered, though. We gotta stick together."

"Holy shit!" Liam yells.

We all shoot up and crane our necks just as Cortney Miller from the New York Metros hits a grand slam in my fucking stadium.

"God dammit."

Beside me, Miller's brother, Jamie, hoots and claps.

"Ooh, good thing the twins are nots here," Finn says, scrunching his nose. "That'd be too many dollars, Bossman."

I sigh and drop back into my seat. "Don't tell the moms."

With a bobblehead nod, Finn jumps off my lap and dashes for Liam. "Heys, it's Thor!" he yells, pulling on Liam's arm and pointing to Miller, who's running the bases.

Liam is unamused, but those words instantly have my brain firing on all cylinders.

A baseball player who looks like Thor.

A catcher who knows how to calm his pitcher down.

A player who can hit the goddamn ball.

Fuck, I'm a genius.

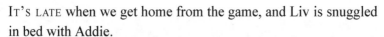

IT'S LATE when we get home from the game, and Liv is snuggled in bed with Addie.

"Hey, how'd it go?" she asks, pushing up on one arm.

I lift Addie from the mattress and kiss her head, taking a moment to soak her in before placing her in the crib. My next kiss belongs to the woman who is not so slowly unraveling my entire life.

Not a single thing about my new life is familiar or comfortable, and I can't say I miss a thing about my old lifestyle.

"Game was great. We won, even after Miller's grand slam."

Liv yawns. "I saw. Boys good for you?"

Unbuttoning my jersey, I shuffle to the closet, keeping my voice low so as not to wake Addie. "They were great. Don't tell Shay, but Kai had two hot dogs. He declared it the best day ever when Brooks and Aiden showed up to hang out with us."

I toss my jeans and jersey into the hamper we share and snag a pair of mesh shorts to wear to bed. After *Raccoongate,* Liv insisted I stay in her room. Just in case the raccoon finds her way into the closet again.

It's not fucking happening, since I paid the contractors an extra ten grand to raccoon-proof this house, but I took her up on her offer anyway. The opportunity to hold Liv all night is too great to pass up.

I can pretend to be scared if it keeps me in her bed. Hell, I'll run around the house in my boxers, screeching like a girl again just to sell it.

"How are you feeling?" The bed dips as I slide in beside her and pull her into my arms.

She nuzzles me like she needs me as much as I need her, and it makes my dick harden. Not that he's getting any attention tonight. Even without Little One in the room, we've got her damn period to contend with.

"Better now." She sighs, brushing her lips against my chest.

I couldn't agree more. Everything's better when we're together.

LIFE inside the brownstone was looking up. The contractor closed off Addie's room and added a door. I'd given Liv strict instructions not to snoop since I wanted to be there when she saw the finished product. I made the fucking trade of a lifetime—one that would improve both my professional and personal life if I had anything to say about it. And I was one day away from date night with my favorite person.

First, though, I had to survive my regular Thursday night gig.

"What day are we going to the hockey game?" Kai asks for the tenth time since he saw my brothers on Tuesday. They made the mistake of offering to get him on the ice if we came to a game.

A mistake only because there is no way in hell Shayla will say yes. I've asked her three times, and she keeps saying she'll look at her schedule and get back to me. Problem is, the season is coming to a close—unless they keep winning. No one in Boston would be sad about that.

Blowing out a breath, I give the kid the honest truth. "I'm trying, Iceman."

He sighs and frowns at the door the moms disappeared through for their weekly evening in. I'm not sure what the hell they do in the basement, and I'm just crazy enough about Liv to want to find out.

"Hey," I whisper, motioning for Kai to come closer. "Any idea what they do down there?"

He shrugs and heads for the dining room, where Liam is setting up the pizzas we ordered.

"I've been studying your latest acquisition," Twin A says. I really should learn their names.

"Oh yeah?" I arch a brow.

"Yes. Statistics would say it was the dumbest trade ever made."

"The fuck?" I mutter.

Before either of the twins can get a word out, I hold out my phone. The smaller of the two, Twin B, grabs it, smiles, and makes quick work transferring the funds.

"I was saying," the other one continues, lifting her chin,

"offering up your catcher and four future draft picks is statistically idiotic."

I turn to Liam, who's stepped back into the room carrying two paper plates full of pizza. "Bet you don't think it was dumb."

Liam scowls. "You stole our best player."

"Cortney Miller was not your best player," I scoff. "He's thirty-five; he's got two seasons left at best."

"See, told you it was dumb." Twin A clears her throat. "I've come up with a list of catchers who would be better selections. Perhaps we could go over them?"

Ah fuck, I should just ask. "What's your name again?"

She frowns. "You seriously don't know our names?"

I wave between the two of them. "I know one of you is Collette and one of you is Phoebe. Is there like a mark somewhere I can use to tell you apart? Or, I know, how about we just put a C on one of you, then I'll be able to tell you apart?"

As if they're mirror images, their jaws drop identically.

"I'm kidding." I scoff out a laugh.

I'm not, but the second the words left my mouth, I realized how ridiculous they were. My balls shriveled a little just imagining Medusa's reaction to my suggestion.

Liam hands out the pizza slices, and we go through a round of questions. Tonight's discussion is apparently all about my bad decisions as the owner of the Revs—never mind that we're doing pretty well this season. I allow them to drone on and entertain each question they throw my way until they get bored and ask if they can turn on a movie. I get them all settled, then make a loop around the room, picking up plates and napkins. I'm still cleaning up in the kitchen when Winnie comes in holding a flyer.

Drying my hands off, I turn to her. "Hey, Bear. What's that?"

She sighs and drops her focus to her feet. "Oh, nothing."

"Show me." I take two steps closer and crouch in front of her.

With another deep sigh, she presses the paper into my hands.

"An art show at school?" I take a minute to scan the flyer. "This is exciting. Why don't you seem happy about it?"

"We'll be at Dad's that weekend." Her voice is so small it's hard to hear her. The defeat in it chips away at my heart.

"Maybe your mom and I can still come. Let me check the calendar." I slip out my phone and immediately note that we've got a problem. A big *ducking* problem. Pasting on a smile, I look up at Winnie. "Putting it on the calendar now."

She eyes me from beneath her lashes. "You don't have to come."

"Are you going to be there?"

She rolls her eyes and smiles. "Well, yeah."

"Then I want to come. Just got to move a few things around, but don't you worry, little Bear, I've got this."

I'm so surprised when she throws her arms around me I almost teeter over on my ass. Once she disappears into the living room, I stand and pull up my Messages app. I've got a promise to keep.

I need you to move the premiere to Boston.

Jay: Um, I'm going to need more information than that.

My kid has an art show.

Jay: Your kid?

I SQUEEZE the phone tight to keep myself from throwing it across the room.

Liv's daughter. Her dad is a complete waste who never shows up for anything. I don't want to let her down, but I want to be there for Sienna too.

Jay: Shoulda led with that. I'll talk to Cat and Sienna. Consider it done.

Thanks, man.

WITH A FIRM NOD TO MYSELF, I slide my phone into my pocket again. I'm so in over my goddamn head I can't see what's up or down anymore.

"Oh shit!"

I laugh at the curse echoing from the other room, suddenly reenergized. "That'll be a thousand dollars." Sauntering into the living room, I hold out my phone. My smile falls and my stomach drops the moment I clock the scissors in Twin A's—okay, I seriously have no idea how to tell them apart—hand.

"What the duck did you do?" I grip my neck with both hands and run them over my head as if, somehow, I can hide from this.

Liv is going to kill me.

Liv
33

"So next week's book…" The humor dancing in Dylan's eyes can only mean one thing. She's up to something.

"Oh shit!" The scream from upstairs has us all gaping up at the ceiling.

"Was that… Phoebe?" Delia asks, a hand to her chest like she can't believe one of her sweet twins would curse like that.

It was so obviously Phoebe, but I keep my mouth shut to avoid being on the receiving end of her snark.

She's on her feet in a heartbeat and rushing for the stairs. "I told you he was a bad influence," she mutters.

She's talking about Beckett, of course. "We have no idea what happened. Let's remain calm until we sort this out."

We trail behind her up the steps and follow the loud voices to the living room. Delia stops short, and one by one, the rest of us bump into one another. With a gasp, she slaps a hand to her mouth. "Oh!" Only instead of sounding affronted, I swear she's stifling a laugh.

When I finally peek around her, I find Beckett standing next to the couch with a pair of scissors in his hand. Before him, Finn

has his head tipped back, and the look on his face is one of pure
terror.

"What the hell, Beckett?" My tone is sharper than I intend.

No one turns my way. Not even the twins. Like they're too
terrified to make any sudden movements.

It takes a moment, but Beckett finally looks from Finn to me,
his green eyes swimming with guilt and his shoulders sagging.
"I'm so sorry."

"I don't get it." I rush to Finn and lift him into my arms. His
panicked expression quickly morphs into a smile, like he's proud
of how ridiculous he looks. His hair—the beautiful little boy hair
I've yet to cut—has been sliced across the front so he has inch-
long bangs brushing his forehead. I run my hand through it and
gape at Beckett. "Why?"

The room is silent and every eye is locked on us.

Cringing, Beckett points at the television, where *Dumb and
Dumber* is playing. "He wanted to look like Harry."

Delia chortles behind us, but when I whip around, she
recovers quickly and grabs the twins. "It's time for bed, girls."

In unison, they blink up at their mom, then silently look at
Beckett. Then, in the strangest move I've ever seen, Phoebe
shuffles over and loops her arms around his waist in a… hug?

He sighs and swallows audibly. Lowering, he mumbles
something I can't make out from here and hugs her in return.

One by one, the rest of the kids follow suit. Even Liam nods
at him, almost in solidarity. Apparently, it's obvious that he's
living his last few moments on earth because I'm going to
kill him.

Finn flattens his palms against my cheeks and turns my face
until I'm looking at him. "Don't be mad, Mommy. Bossman is
the bestest."

Dragging my focus to the ceiling, I breathe in for four, then
let it out for four. "Head up to the bathroom, kiddo. We're going
to have to do something about this hair."

Beckett grumbles, "I'll go get my shaving kit."

"You're not shaving my kid's head," I growl, pulling Finn into my chest. Oh yeah, mama mode is activated.

Beckett works his jaw from side to side. "Liv, we can't leave his hair like that."

With a scoff, I lift my chin. "Obviously."

My indignation quickly turns to distress when I replay his words.

Liv.

He called me Liv, not Livy. My stomach sours. Things were so good only a few hours ago.

I'm pulled from my pondering when a hand grasps my shoulder.

Dylan steps up beside me and squeezes my shoulder, pulling me from my downward spiral. "How 'bout you and I go finish our wine and let Becks take care of this?"

I stare at her, dumbfounded.

With a nod, she leans in and whispers, "Finn is watching you. Little eyes, little ears… they see more than we realize."

Beckett holds out his arms for Finn, and my son jumps for him. He's getting so attached. What the hell are we doing? I need concrete answers. I'm never this reckless.

"Trust me?" Beckett asks.

Those two simple words carry so much weight. Do I trust him? If I were smart, I wouldn't trust any man. Not after the way I've been burned. But Beckett isn't Drake. This was obviously a mistake. A big, stupid one, but an innocent mistake all the same. Finn is smiling at him. My son is happy, not crying.

Beckett cares.

And he encourages Finn to be himself. He didn't flinch when my little boy came down the steps wearing a tutu with his jersey the other night. Without batting an eye, he scooped him up and took him to the game. I'm sure people were staring—maybe even his brothers—yet Beckett didn't say a word.

He's not Drake.

I bite my lip and acquiesce. "Okay. I'll be up in a bit." Tilting closer, I drop a kiss to Finn's head and run my hands across his soft hair. It will all be gone when I go upstairs. I definitely can't watch it happen.

Dylan loops her arm through mine and pulls me into the kitchen. "Deep breaths," she murmurs.

I grab the bottle of wine and pour it into the glass that reads *Fueled by wine and smut.* Then I down the contents and wince when the alcohol burns my throat.

My other friends appear in the kitchen shortly after. Delia's lips are pressed in a firm line and her arms are crossed over her chest. I don't have it in me to deal with her ranting tonight. I hold up my hands. "Before you say you told me—"

She clears her throat and shakes her head. "It was Phoebe."

I frown. "Huh?"

"Phoebe cut Finn's hair."

"Then why did Beckett take the blame?"

Beside me, Dylan smiles that damn knowing smile of hers.

"Fuck," I mutter. I am so in over my head. He isn't just trying to win over me and my kids. He's a genuinely good guy. And that is so much more dangerous for my heart.

UPSTAIRS, Finn is grinning adoringly at his buzz cut in the mirror. Honestly, the new look is adorable, but my eyes well at the sight. Gone is his baby face. He appears so much older now.

"You going to shave yours to match, Bossman?" he asks, dropping his head back.

"No!" The protest slips out of my mouth before I can stop it.

Beckett locks eyes with me in the mirror and smirks. "Attached to my hair, Livy?"

Images of me pulling on that full head of hair while he's between my thighs float through my mind. I have to bite my lip to dampen the desire threatening to flood me. "Just don't think you have the kind of face that can handle a shaved head."

Dropping his head, he chuckles.

Finn clutches his arm and frowns. "What's funny?"

Beckett runs his hands over my little guy's head and tries, in vain, to school his expression. "Nothing. Your mom is just a silly lady. Okay, bed. Now."

Finn gives him a succinct nod and clambers out of the room. Once again, I'm left dumbstruck at how normal this all is. How easy it is having this man here with us during our bedtime routine.

But he doesn't want kids, I remind myself. No matter how easy this feels, this isn't what he wants.

After tucking Finn in, I head to my room and find Beckett lying in bed with his phone in his hand, furiously texting.

"Hey," I whisper, not wanting to wake up Addie.

He gives me a soft smile and sets his phone on the mattress beside him. "Hi."

"I'm sorry about earlier," I hedge, sitting beside him. I still need to wash my face and change, but I didn't want to do it now, only to find him already asleep when I finished. Not that he would be; he's normally up later than me, reading or going through emails.

"You have nothing to apologize for." He squeezes my arm gently.

"Beckett," I say, my heart heavy. "I was awful to you. I jumped to conclusions."

Frowning, he tilts his head on his pillow. "Livy, we're going to have disagreements. I'm going to fuck up. This is marriage.

But I'll always put you and your kids first. I'm sorry I let you down tonight."

What? My heart pounds out a furious rhythm against my ribs. *This is marriage?*

"A fake marriage," I whisper, almost like it's a question.

He tips his chin up, his jaw locked tight. "Has any of this felt fake to you?"

A whoosh of air slips past my lips, and my hands tremble just a little. "The rules…"

"Were broken the moment our lips touched." He turns his body so that he's looking at me. "Livy, I don't know what the future holds, but I know that this," he motions between us, "is the most real thing I've ever experienced. I swear I'll do better by your kids. I should have been watching them."

"Phoebe cut Finn's hair," I interject.

Under his breath, I'm pretty sure he mutters, "So that's her name."

I laugh. "*Beckett.*"

He shrugs and drops his gaze to the sheet beneath him. "I'm not good at this, Livy. I'm trying." His eyes swim with true heartache when he looks up at me again. "But I'm *really* not good at this."

Instinctively, my fingers go to his hair, and I push it back from his face. "You're a hell of a lot better than you give yourself credit for."

His phone buzzes on the bed, and he groans. "Sorry, it's my brothers." He picks it up, smirks, hammers out a message, then tosses it back down. "They're giving me shit over Paris."

Paris. I forgot all about it. It's only a couple of weeks away, and he hasn't mentioned it again. Maybe he plans to go by himself.

"Why?"

He hands me his phone, and I scroll up through the messages.

. . .

> Gavin: You are so whipped.

Screw you.

> Brooks: Why's Beckett whipped?

> Aiden: <Rubs hands together emoji> Yes, spill.

Shut up.

> Gavin: He had Hanson move Sienna's premiere from Paris to Boston so he wouldn't miss Winnie's art show.

MY HEART STOPS for half a second, and I suck in a breath. "You did *what?*"

Beckett peeks around my arm to see what I'm reading and shakes his head with a smile. "It's not a big deal. Winnie's art show is the same weekend. Obviously, you can't miss it."

"But you can." I don't mean to sound so accusatory, but I'm too shocked to control my reaction.

He frowns. "No. I refuse to be another man who lets her down."

"She's eight. This wouldn't be the last time someone let her down. It's life."

His jaw clenches. "Not. Me."

"What?"

"I spent years watching my siblings be disappointed because my parents didn't show up for things."

Warmth spreads through me as I realize what he meant earlier. He's not good at this, but he's trying. He's trying for me and my kids. Trying to be better to us than his father was when they were kids. Trying to be more present than Drake has ever been.

"So you convinced Jay Hanson to move your sister's television premiere to Boston," I say slowly.

He nods, and when a shy grin replaces his normal smirk, I know I've officially lost the battle. I'm falling for Beckett Langfield. I broke all the rules and fell in love with my fake husband.

Liv

34

M ay 25th

> Shayla: I'm dying. <laughing emoji> Beckett just fell through the loose step.

Me: OMG! Is he okay?

> Shayla: He's fine, but guess who has a new step? So long Trippy. We'll miss you!

> Delia: I'll kill him if he destroyed the original oak.

> Dylan: It looks good actually and Shayla is right we found Becks with his leg stuck in Trippy. It was hysterical.

> Shayla: Dylan has literal tears streaming down her face.

JUNE 8TH

Cannot believe you did that.

Beckett: What? Brought my wife a soda?

Benny was not hitting on me, you insane person! There was no need to growl at him to back up.

Beckett: You look too gorgeous today.

You can't growl at every person I talk to.

Beckett: Can't wait for date night tonight.

Beckett!

Beckett: Livy!

<Eye roll emoji> You're insane.

But I can't wait, either, baby.

JUNE 10TH

Dylan: pretty sure junior is nesting

Beckett: What the duck does that mean?

Delia: Means it's time to call the damn exterminator.

Me: DELIA!

Beckett: Does she need a midwife? Do baby raccoons need a special kind of milk?

Beckett: Can one of you care about this, please?

Shayla: I'm not going anywhere near that animal.

Dylan: OMG I just googled baby raccoons they are the cutest! <Picture of baby raccoon attached>

Shayla: Okay, well, that is cute.

Finn is gonna lose it! They're adorable.

Beckett: Anyone? Does anyone care that we need to figure out how to BIRTH those things?

Delia: LOL. A man concerned about birth. That's a first. Don't worry, Beckett, the women will handle everything, like always.

JUNE 10TH

I'm sorry.

Beckett: I can think of a few ways you can make it up to me.

Me: LOL I'm sure you can.

CLICKING OFF THE BLOW DRYER, I glance at Dylan's phone. "How much longer do we have?"

We're getting ready for Winnie's art show in her bathroom. Beckett insists the entire family go. He even arranged for a limo to bring us. He's ridiculous, but Winnie is over-the-moon excited, so I didn't tease him too much. Unsurprisingly, when I told Drake that the art show fell on his weekend, he said he wouldn't mind switching. I don't imagine he'll show up tonight.

"Shit, the limo is going to be here in twenty minutes. I better go check on the kids."

As I hand the blow dryer over to Dylan and she turns it on, the fuse makes a buzzing sound and everything goes dark.

"Dammit!" Shayla screams from the other room. "I was so close!"

Dylan and I burst into giggles. Shayla needs to find a man. Her obsession with her battery-operated toys has gone a bit too far.

"You girls okay down there?" Beckett hollers. I peek out of the bathroom and find him standing at the top of the stairs. There's just enough light that I can make out what he's wearing. Damn, he fills out a pair of jeans perfectly. He's got on a light pink shirt that I believe used to be white and a navy blazer. He looks hot.

I sigh. "Yeah, I think we blew a fuse."

"I'll take care of it," he offers, jogging down the steps. "Just tell me where the fuse box is."

Dylan nudges me, and I inwardly groan. Why is nothing in this house simple?

Behind Beckett, Finn clambers down the stairs holding a flashlight. Both of my boys stop in the hall and look at me expectantly.

"The fuse box, Livy. Where is it?"

Dylan smiles. "Over there."

"As in through that door?" Beckett points the flashlight on his phone toward the opening at the end of the hall. It's like a half door meant for a dog, or maybe an elf. We discovered it the first weekend we moved in and forced Liam to reset the circuit. Since then, we've been pretty good about getting ready in shifts so as not to trip it again. Old houses, old electric.

Although Beckett's been slowly getting things fixed around the house, the electric is absolutely a huge project. We're nowhere near ready to tackle that nightmare yet.

He eyes the door, then frowns back at us. "We'll go to a hotel until I can get someone out here."

My lips quirk. "You want to stay in a hotel rather than reset the circuit?"

He rubs a hand over his jaw. "Livy, do you see that room?" He aims the flashlight at the cobwebs in the crawl space.

I bite my lip to try to keep from laughing. "I'll handle it."

Finn grabs my wrist. "Bossman, what do you always says?"

"We men take care of the girls," he grumbles.

Finn smiles at Beckett like he's a proud parent. "I'll holds the flashlight, and you do the crawling."

Five minutes, one girly scream, and a slew of curse words later, power is restored. As Beckett crawls back out, his face ashen, I try hard to hold back my laughter. He swipes at his jeans, which are covered in dust. "Better call the exterminator, unless we want Finn to have snakes for pets."

I blanch. Absolutely not.

As Beckett takes my hand to lead me up the steps, Shayla appears in the door with a wand in her hand. "Thanks, Beckett!"

Under his breath, he murmurs, "Please tell me that was a curling iron."

WINNIE GUIDES us through the throng of students. To no one's surprise, Drake couldn't be bothered to show up. But that's okay, because Winnie has quite the entourage, and Beckett is the loudest of us all.

"This is amazing, Bear. Livy, we gotta bring this girl to Paris."

Winnie's cheeks pink under his praise. She drew the exterior of the brownstone. In the foreground, she added her "Four moms." We're all facing the house so all onlookers can see is our backs. I don't think it'll be hanging at the Louvre anytime soon, but it's adorable.

When her art teacher walks by, clipboard in hand, Beckett waves her down. "How much for this piece?"

The woman is short, with black hair tied in the back with two chopsticks. She tilts her head, her brows pinched together. "Excuse me?"

"I want to make an offer before the bidding starts," Beckett explains.

Delia snorts, and the art teacher shakes her head. "Sir, it's not for sale."

"Oh, I know how this works. Fine, you want to play hard-ball." He smirks. "Fifty thousand."

A shocked gasp escapes me, and my friends all snicker behind me.

The teacher frowns and hugs her clipboard to her chest. "No, seriously, we don't sell it."

"I'm not playing games. I need this painting." Beckett pulls out his checkbook. "One hundred thousand. Should I make it out to the school?"

Nerves skitter down my spine and sweat begins to bead at my hairline when I realize that we've drawn a crowd.

"Sir, seriously," the teacher tries, but she's cut off by the principal.

"Oh yes," she says, hurrying to stand beside the art teacher, "we could use it for the new—"

"No," Beckett says, sliding the check into her hand. "My only stipulation is that it's used to fund the arts program exclusively."

She nods, inspecting the check, and then looks back up at Beckett as if he's an apparition. We all are. What the hell has gotten into him?

Winnie pulls on his arm. "You know the artwork is free,

right?" She points across the room, where several kids are taking their artwork off stands and handing them to their parents.

Beckett crouches so they're eye to eye. "I know that, Bear. But now there's funding for the program you love."

With tears in her eyes, my daughter throws her arms around Beckett and he squeezes her right back. When he stands and his eyes meet mine, shining with emotion, I know I'm done for. My heart never stood a chance against this man.

AFTER THE SHOW, the limo takes us to an ice cream shop. Our family takes up three booths. Winnie and the twins have claimed a booth for girls only. Beckett's fan club—Finn and Kai—beg him to sit with them, and to everyone's surprise, Liam drops into the seat across from Beckett. They talk baseball, which gives me time to freak out to my friends in our own booth.

"He bought her artwork," I hiss, leaning across the table to avoid being overheard.

Delia hums as she spoons her sundae. "The idiot is growing on me."

My mouth falls open, but it's Shayla who speaks first. "Cordelia Masters actually found a man she likes?"

Delia's response is a glower. "I didn't say I *liked* him. I said he's growing on me. Fungus also grows on people. Let's not get crazy here."

Dylan laughs and licks at her soft serve cone. "She so likes him. Hey, Becks," she hollers across the shop.

Beckett rolls his eyes, even as he smiles at her. "Yes, Dippy Do?"

She sits up straight and bounces on the bench seat. "Delia just said she likes you."

He shakes his head, all charm. "Sorry to break your heart, Medusa, but mine is taken." He winks at me, then turns back to his conversation, like everything that's happening is normal.

Is it normal? Is this how it feels to be comfortable in a relationship? Secure? To be cherished? Surely, it'll get old eventually. He'll tire of me. This *can't* last. But God, do I want it too. And part of me believes that if there was ever a man who could make it happen, it's Beckett.

He'll will forever into existence.

Back at the house, the group disperses. Bedtime routines must be followed, even on special nights like this.

Beckett and I climb the steps to our floor, and he offers to get Finn ready while I take care of Addie.

"Oh, Livy," he says from my doorway once I've stepped inside. He's holding a giggling Finn out like he's Superman. "Could you grab a T-shirt for me from my room? Don't want my shirt to get wet while this one takes his bath."

With a nod, I set Addie on her feet. Immediately, she babbles and toddles toward Beckett. He's her new favorite person, and he's becoming mine too.

At the back of the closet, I push open the door Beckett had installed. I haven't been in his room since the work was finished. When I cross the threshold and take it in, I can't hold back my gasp.

Purple walls and ballerinas galore. A white toddler bed with the railing still up for protection. Stars glitter on the ceiling, and above the dresser, stenciled in white, are the words *Little One*.

My heart swells and tears fill my eyes. I blink them back, but the effort is futile. They're coming too quickly. When I spin, Beckett stands behind me, holding Finn in one arm and Addie in the other.

"Why's Mommy crying?" Finn asks. Wearing a frown, he reaches for me. My sweet boy is instantly prepared to comfort me.

I pull him into my chest and nuzzle his neck. He giggles. "Mommy, that tickles."

When I look up, Beckett is closer, and then he's stretching out his free arm and swiping away my tears. "Like it?"

I press into his chest, and with Finn on one side and Addie on the other, I fall apart. "Love it."

Beckett sets Addie down. "What do you think, Little One? Want to stay in your room tonight?"

Finn's brows knit together adorably. "But where will you stay?"

Holding back a smile, Beckett taps on his chin. "Hmm, maybe the roof?"

"That's crazy!" Finn shouts, throwing his head back.

Beckett has to brace himself to keep Finn from tumbling to the floor. When he rights my little guy, he shrugs. "Your room?"

"I only have a tiny bed." Finn shakes his head furiously. "You won'ts fit."

"Fine. What do you say, Livy? Can I have a sleepover in your room?"

"I mean, I guess, since you went to all this trouble, we can put a pillow on the floor for you," I tease.

"I gots a sleeping bag. It even has Spidey on it!"

Beckett barks out a laugh so big he jostles Finn. "Deal, Huckleberry. Now let's go get that bath started."

As he turns for the door, I grab his hand and squeeze.

Eying me, brows raised, he mouths, "No cockblock tonight."

I laugh and mouth back, "Yes, baby. You are so getting laid."

Beckett
35

"There's an actual door," Liv whispers, her attention fixed solely on me.

We're lying side by side, hip to hip, enjoying this moment of peace and quiet.

"Beckett, that room…" She shakes her head and blinks, her eyes glassy again. "It really is incredible."

"It's nothing."

"*No.*" She pushes closer so our bodies are flush. "It's *everything.*"

Unlike when we were in Vegas, I take my time pulling her closer and kissing her softly, then linger far too long. Or maybe the perfect amount of time, because each caress only gets Liv more worked up. Soon, she's rubbing against me, whimpering softly, and pleading for more.

"Can you stay quiet, Livy? We both know how loud you can be. How you scream for me." I lick a trail down her neck and give her a sharp nip to test her ability. When she moans too loudly, I pull back. "If you make a sound louder than a whimper, I stop."

She sinks her teeth into the flesh of her bottom lip and nods.

Damn. I can't help but give her a quick peck. "Now be a good girl and take out my cock."

Before she even wraps her fingers around my shaft, I'm rock hard and eager. I have to bite down on her shoulder to not break my own damn rule when she tugs.

She lets out a breathy laugh but doesn't release me. "Not so easy, is it, big guy?"

"Please," I grit out. "I could beat you in this game any day of the week."

With a wicked grin, she slips down the mattress. The instant her lips make contact with my shaft, I have to press my tongue to the roof of my mouth to keep from groaning.

"We'll see about that," she murmurs. She circles the head of my cock and then sucks, long and hard.

"Fuck," I mutter. It's guttural. Being enveloped in the wet heat of her mouth as she's deep-throating me has me losing my damn mind. "Look at me."

Obediently, she drags her attention to my face, but she doesn't slow.

I grasp her neck just tight enough that I can feel every time she swallows. "Good girl. Now, keep going."

She moans around my dick, then hollows her cheeks and sucks again. With every lick, she rubs her greedy pussy against my thigh, making me grow impossibly hard.

"That's my girl. Ride my leg. I want you to come while I spill down your throat."

My commands spur her on. Soon, she's writhing against me with abandon, and I'm pistoning into her mouth as I hold her neck in place, fucking her at the exact speed I need. Her moans are muffled, but they grow more fervent, signaling her impending orgasm. I squeeze her throat just a little tighter, and then we shatter in unison, the feel of her swallowing around me, of her throat bobbing as she takes everything I give her, plunges me into blackness.

"Holy fuck," she whispers when I release her.

"Come up here and sit on my face, Livy. Then I'm going to fuck you into tomorrow."

TOSSING A PILLOW ONTO THE DUVET, I stare at my wife like she's got two heads. I try to arrange them the way she likes as we make the bed together. "You have to leave tomorrow? Why?"

"I *do* work for both teams. The Bolts are in the playoffs. I need to be there."

"No. You work for Langfield Corp. You need to be *here*."

She laughs and fluffs a pillow on her side of the bed. "I travel with you all the time. Gavin needs me sometimes too."

"I need you." I'm not the least bit reluctant to admit it. But what I should really say is *I want you*. Need sounds like it's work-based, and this? This is so beyond that.

She rolls her eyes. "Yes, I'm aware. You have always been my biggest pain in the ass."

"Hire someone."

"What?"

"Don't you have an intern or something who can handle the hockey team?"

Dropping her chin, she sighs and smooths out the duvet. "Yeah, I have an entire support team under me. They're supposed to handle each team, but you don't let me do that. You're the one who insists I attend every baseball game."

"Right, and since when are you needed at the hockey ones?"

She shrugs. "Gavin doesn't usually need me to travel with

him. He's not as needy as you." She peeks up at me from under her lashes. "But he told me he'll need me more often now."

My ducking brother. He's trying to torture me. He thinks I won't admit that I'll miss Liv.

"Pick someone," I demand.

Liv stands ramrod straight, her face blanching. "*Pick someone*? Nothing is going on between me and your brother."

I laugh. "Obviously. There's no competition. I'm clearly the better-looking, more fun brother."

"No, you definitely are not." She belts out a laugh when she gets a look at my face. I'm not amused. "Fine, you're the better-looking one, but you can't make me agree that you're more fun."

There's a teasing in her tone, a lightness I rarely see. And I fucking love it. She can tell me I'm a boring grump all the time if it makes her smile like this. If it means she'll flirt with me like she is right now.

My pants grow tighter, and I itch to grab her thick thighs and pull her closer to me. To toss her back on the bed and spend the day here, lost in her. I settle for rounding the end of the bed and pulling her toward me so I'm at least touching her.

"Pick someone to head up PR for the hockey team." I take a deep breath. "And the baseball team." I can't believe I'm doing this, but the truth is, her kids need her around more. I shouldn't be forcing her to come to games with me. One of our employees without kids should be handling these jobs.

She drops her gaze to the bed again, and the lightness I felt only seconds earlier dissipates. "You don't want me to come with you anymore?"

This time I don't hold back. I dig my fingers into her hips and pull her close, then I tip her chin up so she's forced to look at me. "As my wife, yes. I always want you with me. But the kids need you here. It was selfish of me to force you to come to away games." I lick my lips. "I'm trying to be better."

Coyly, Liv bites her lip, her eyes sparkling once more. "You trying to tell me you want me all to yourself, Mr. Langfield?"

I crash my mouth against hers. No words necessary. I don't want her all to myself. I need her.

EVERYWHERE I LOOK, the press is hovering. Jay and his wife are constantly in the news, so it really comes as no surprise. Not only did they come from rival business families, but they recently purchased a media company. The whole world is eager to see what they do with it. My sister's show—a reality show focused on her career and the fashion world—is their first production, and everyone who is anyone is here to witness media history in the making.

"All right, you two. Remember, big smiles. All is happy at home. You're in love, and Beckett is great with the kids," Hannah, one of Liv's assistants, says. She's wearing a painted-on look of excitement.

The scowl on Liv's face at being "handled" makes me laugh. "I don't need you to tell me how to smile," Liv deadpans. "I'm your boss."

Chuckling, I squeeze my wife's hips and bring my lips to her ear. "Not so easy taking direction from a bossy woman, is it?"

The glare she directs at me makes me positively giddy.

"Come on, Mrs. Langfield. Go tell the press how good I am."

Even though she's rolling her eyes, her lips tip up just a fraction as she tries to hide the smile that's just for me.

The first of many handheld recorders gets shoved in our faces a moment later. The wicked smile on the reporter's face says it all. This question is going to be a doozy. "Olivia, we aren't used to seeing you on this side of the camera. You and

Beckett have worked together for years. At what moment did you know things had changed?"

Liv licks her lips and shimmies her shoulders just a little as she prepares to answer. Fuck. She's all sass right now. I can only imagine what she'll say.

"Well, you see, Beckett is a very demanding boss."

The woman nods. "I can imagine."

"And there was this blue stuffed animal—"

I dig my fingers into Liv's hips, silently begging her not to tell the world this story.

She lets out an airy laugh. "I'm just teasing him. Honestly, there's no big story. One day we just..." Her eyes meet mine. The smile on her face is so genuine and so full of adoration. "We just knew. To the world, he's the CEO and the overly involved baseball owner, but at home, he's so good with the kids. He brings me a Diet Coke every afternoon because he pays attention to my routines. He makes sure I don't forget matching shoes—"

"Oh my God. Is Beckett Langfield a softie?" the reporter asks.

With a shake of my head, I kiss my wife's temple. "Only for her. And our kids."

Liv goes rigid in my arms for a second, and the reporter's jaw drops.

"Now, if you'll excuse us, my wife and I have a party to attend."

I steer Liv down the red carpet. When we finally make it inside, I suck in a deep breath and will away the tension crowds like this always bring.

The event is being held on the rooftop of *Jolie*'s headquarters. *Jolie* is the most popular women's magazine in the world, and it's where Jay and his wife reconnected and fell in love again.

As we ride the elevator up, I take a moment to drink in the sight of my wife. "You enjoy that?"

Rounding her shoulders, she giggles. "Immensely."

"If the entire world thinks I'm a softie—"

She presses her fingers to my lips. "One little interview won't fix your reputation. Don't you worry. You've been an ass for most of your life. People will remember that."

I chuckle, once again finding myself wanting to pull her close and tell her exactly how I feel.

Later.

Now is not the time for that conversation. She deserves more than a quick elevator confession.

"Holy shit," Liv mutters as the stainless-steel doors open to the rooftop.

Her reaction is understandable. Every surface is draped in greenery, almost creating a ceiling. Candles of all different heights line the space. At the bar setup in the corner, my brothers are circled together, chatting.

Liv points to my sister, who's mid-conversation with another woman. "Oh, there's Sienna. We should go say hello."

I press my lips to her shoulder. "You go on ahead. I'll grab drinks. Wine?"

Liv gives me a small, almost shy, nod, like she still doesn't know what to do when I dote on her. I push her forward, though. No more overthinking. My wife better get used to being treated like a queen, because I don't intend to stop.

"Heard you're to thank for getting my best friend at all the playoff games," Brooks says as I settle myself beside him at the bar.

Gavin chuckles and claps me on the shoulder. "Sara's going to be accompanying us, since you forbade Liv from traveling with the team."

Pushing his arm away, I sigh. "You're an ass."

"Just trying to get you to come to your senses over your little marriage farce."

Anger burns in my chest at the word *farce.* "My marriage isn't fake."

With his hands in his pockets, Gavin gives me a pointed look. "Anymore."

Because he's got half a brain, unlike Gavin, Brooks covers the grin spreading across his face with his palm.

"Shut it," I growl. I take the whiskey the bartender slides my way, as well as Liv's pinot noir. "Now, if you'll excuse me, I have a wife to spend time with…unlike you two."

Gavin rolls his eyes. "Dates to family events give women the wrong impression."

Brooks tilts his head. "And what impression is that?"

"That I'm interested," Gavin quips.

"One day you'll meet her," I warn him.

He takes a long sip of his whiskey before he responds. "Who?"

"*Her.* The woman you'll do more than invite to family events to prove to her that you're interested." I zero in on Liv, who is standing at a table with my sister, laughing. "The person you'll upend your entire life for."

When I turn back to my brothers, Gavin is wearing an amused smirk, but Brooks's attention is locked on the dance floor. The expression on his face is almost pained. When I follow his line of sight, I see why. Sara is dancing with War, one of his teammates.

Looks like Brooks understands what it feels like to find that person. Even if he doesn't know it yet. Hopefully he doesn't take ten years to make his move like I did.

I squeeze his shoulder to get his attention. When he blinks out of his stupor, he gives me a sheepish smile. He knows he's been busted. "I'm going to take this to Liv. You should go dance."

Gavin snorts. "Two months in a fake marriage, and he's the Dalai Lama of love."

Shooting him a glare, I take off. I'm beginning to hate that F word.

Before I make it to her side, my mother swoops in to steal my wife's attention. I have to fight not to scowl at my own mother as my hands itch to squeeze Liv's hips or hold her hand. I have to keep my hands off her when we're around the kids, so on the rare occasion we're on our own and not at work, I need the physical connection.

I'm so over hiding the way I feel. She's my wife, and I want everyone to know it, including her children.

"This event is amazing," my mother gushes.

My sister blushes under her praise. "Cat gave me a lot of control when it came to the show, but the party? It's all Jay. That man is a bit of a control freak."

A laugh rumbles up my chest. Truer words have never been spoken. The guy loves to plan a party. I spot him at the bar with his arm wrapped around his wife. While Cat chats with another woman, his full attention is on her alone. Like he can't look away. Like she's the most fascinating thing he's ever seen.

It hits me then that I probably look at Liv the same way.

Almost as if she can hear my thoughts, she turns to me and bites her lip.

"Hi, beautiful," I mouth.

Her responding smile is the most gorgeous sight. Her lips are glossy, her hair is down and curled in soft waves, and her cheeks are already flushed. She only holds my gaze for a moment, though, before she dips her chin and shakes her head. The faint flush turns into a full-on blush that creeps up her chest.

I can't wait to trace that blush with my tongue later.

"Beckett, I have good news," my mother says, drawing my attention. "After our talk the other day, I spoke to my contractor. We're two weeks ahead of schedule, so you can be back in your bed by next week."

Liv's eyes collide with mine, and I see the moment she

believes that I'm trying to run from the brownstone. Run from her. In the beginning, we agreed that this "arrangement" would last until my mother's house was finished. But if she thinks for a second that my whole world hasn't been flipped on its head since we made that damn deal, then she hasn't been paying attention.

Or I haven't done enough to show her how I feel.

Jaw tense, I try to navigate my way out of this conversation as quickly as possible. "Thanks, Mom. Livy, I want to say hi to Jay. Come with me."

She purses her lips at my obvious attempt to get her alone, but she doesn't call me on it. "Congratulations again, Sienna. The show is going to be an absolute hit," she says as she squeezes my sister's arm.

I hand the glass of pinot noir to Liv and take her free hand. "I'm not trying to run," I murmur as we head away from the table.

Liv's heavy sigh guts me. "I know the brownstone needs work."

I can't hold back my chuckle. "Livy, it's a hazard, not a brownstone. Your kids could each have their own room at the penthouse. There's a pool. A space we can turn into a playroom. And walls. There are no snakes or pet raccoons. The master bedroom has a private balcony where you can relax and breathe. And there's a hot tub."

She frowns, and her eyes swim with hurt, though she avoids looking at me. "But there's not enough room for the girls and their kids."

I frown. "Well, no. But your situation was temporary. We can't live with them forever. I'll meet my end of the bargain. I'll hand over the check for home repairs. You've obviously done what you're supposed to with the media and our marriage, but we don't have to stay with them."

Pinching the bridge of her nose, she hangs her head. "That's the deal."

"Deal?" I ask, but before she can respond, I spot the only person who could tear my focus from my wife.

Liv's ex.

How the *fuck* did he get an invite to this party?

He's standing only a few feet away from us, sporting a sinister grin. "I fucking knew it," he hisses.

Liv flinches at the sound of his voice, then she spins and glares at him. "What the hell are you doing here?"

The wicked smirk on his face when he gives her a once-over makes me want to punch him square in the face. "My firm works with Bouvier Media."

"For now," I grumble. There's no way this weasel is going to work on anything associated with my sister. My first call tomorrow will be to Jay to ensure he fires this asshole.

Drake clenches his jaw, his hard eyes on me. "Nah. And soon enough, I think you'll be hiring me to represent Langfield Corp as well."

"You're delusional," I spit.

He shrugs like he has all the power in the world. "You wouldn't want our kids finding out that their mother is a whore —trading marriage for money. I never could figure out why you were with my fat ex-wife when you could have any woman in this room. But if she's willing to whore herself out... Makes you wonder what a judge would think—"

His threat is interrupted by the crack of his jaw as my fist connects with it.

"Beckett!"

I can make out the sound of Liv's voice, but it's far away as I straddle the fucker and pound his face, unable to contain the rage tearing through my system.

No one talks to my wife like that.

Liv

36

It only takes a minute for Brooks and Gavin to rip Beckett off Drake.

My ex-husband scrambles to his feet, dazed and bloody. He spits on the floor, and a tooth goes flying.

Shit.

"I will own you," Drake grits between pants, glaring at an equally heavy-breathing Beckett.

"What the fuck?" Gavin hisses while Brooks holds Beckett back.

"He called my wife a whore. He threatened her." Beckett points at him. "I'll fucking murder you."

"You gonna tell your brothers about your little deal with my ex?" Drake taunts. "With the settlement I'll get from this assault, I'll have plenty of cash to throw at an attorney who'll help me get sole custody of my kids."

Gavin looks at me and then back at Drake. "Nah, from where I was standing, it looked like you tripped and fell. Too much alcohol, no doubt. Must have hit your head on the way down."

Drake's eyes bulge, and he puffs out his chest. "You can't be serious. There are cameras everywhere. The media is all over the place."

Gavin nods. "Yup, Bouvier Media. You know who owns that? Jay Hanson. You know who his best friend is?" He points at Beckett. "So let's try this again. You tripped and fell. Isn't that right?"

Drake turns his hardened gaze on me. "You won't get away with this."

My heart pounds and blood whooshes in my ears as Drake's threats run through my brain on repeat.

"You don't speak to her," Beckett growls.

Sara appears by my side and takes my shaking hand. "Let's get you out of here. People are watching."

Numb, I nod and allow her to lead me out of the venue and into a limo.

The ride home is a complete blur. Rewinding every moment from the last twenty-four hours I'm confused how we even got here. Things were so good. Perfect even. After tonight, there's a good chance that all the work we did to turn Beckett's reputation around was erased in a single moment. Swiped away in one spectacular punch.

And what if Drake does go to a judge? Could he really take my kids?

IT DOESN'T TAKE LONG for the story to break.

I'm lying in bed, staring at the ceiling, dress still on, waiting for Beckett to walk through the door, when the alert pops up on my phone.

Premiere for Sienna Langfield's new television show cut short by fight.

I don't click on the link. I can't bear to read in black and white what I had to witness with my own eyes. Every moment is seared into my brain, playing on repeat in the quiet of my bedroom.

My phone chimes again, this time with a text.

> Sara: Don't stress. We've got this under control. You okay?

Yeah. Any word from Beckett?

> Sara: His brothers got him out of there. Put him on the plane early to avoid the press. He's traveling with the team for the next few days. Probably a good thing if he's not here during this shit storm.

MY STOMACH DROPS and tears burn at the backs of my eyes. I forgot Beckett is traveling this coming week. Normally, I'd be right there with him, but since he put his foot down this morning about me staying home with the kids...

I sigh. I just want to see him. Talk to him. And now he's on a damn plane?

> Sara: He said to make sure you don't go into the office tomorrow. Let us get our stories straight first.

RIGHT. I don't even respond to her text. I have no idea what to say.

A knock sounds against the door and Dylan pushes her way in. Behind her, Shayla and Delia follow. At their stricken faces, I offer a weak smile.

"Who do I have to kill?" Delia asks, settling on the bed beside me.

I huff and run a hand down my face. "Drake."

"Never liked that name. Let's come up with one more fitting. Take a line out of Beckett's playbook," Shayla muses as she paces my room. The girl is never not moving. "Douche-wad? Dickface? Tiny dick!"

Dylan curls up on Beckett's side of the bed and studies me, her red hair splaying around her. "You okay?"

My entire being shrugs. "Drake overheard us talking about 'the deal.' He called me a whore, so Beckett punched him. Then he threatened to take the kids…" I fling myself back onto my pillow. "I think that about sums it up."

"Holy shit," Delia mutters. "Score one for Beckett."

"Where is he now?" Dylan's brows pinch together.

I huff out a laugh. "Probably on a plane, far, far away from here." I close my eyes and let out a long sigh. "He asked me to move into the penthouse," I whisper.

Delia sucks in a breath. "You're leaving us?"

"No." I shake my head. "I would never. It's us forever."

Dylan frowns, still resting on Beckett's pillow, but on her side now so she's facing me. "What did Beckett have to say about that?"

I let out a choked laugh. If I don't laugh, I'll most certainly cry. "He doesn't want to be here; he never wanted kids. Now I'm telling him that if he wants me, he not only has to live with my kids, but my three best friends and their kids too? It's too much."

Shayla comes to a stop and hovers over the bed on the other side of Dylan. "We love you, and the last few months have by far been the best I've had since I lost Ajay, but that doesn't mean you have to stay."

Delia squeezes my leg. "If Beckett makes you happy, and it's clear the big idiot does, you should give this a real chance."

I look from Delia to Shay to Dylan, at an absolute loss as to what I should do. I'm not leaving them, I know that. But if Beckett doesn't want to stay, am I willing to say goodbye?

When the phone rings, I startle. I leap for it and accept the FaceTime call from my husband.

"Hey," I whisper, wincing at my image reflected back at me in one corner of the screen. My face is red and my eyes are puffy from crying.

He scrubs a bandaged hand over his face. His eyes are rimmed red, and the scowl he so often wears has been replaced with a frown filled with pain and exhaustion. "I'm so sorry, Livy. Are you okay?"

"I'm okay." I force a smile, but it's not very convincing. "Why are you apologizing? It's my asshole ex who caused all this."

Beckett's jaw tenses and his eyes dart away from the screen. "He won't be a problem."

"How do you know that?"

"We'll figure it out."

A heaviness settles between us. Can we really? There's no stopping the story from spreading now that it's out there. I've avoided reading anything about it, but it's only a matter of time before the truth comes out—before the details of our arrangement are spelled out in black and white. And then what?

"I'll talk to Sara. We'll make a plan."

"No, Livy. Stay away from Langfield Corp for now. I don't want this to affect the kids. Take them to your brother's. Just—" He grunts. "Just worry about the kids; I'll deal with the rest."

"When will you be home?" I bite my lip and scan the room. Why in God's name would he want to come back here if the penthouse is available?

Beckett lets out a sigh full of defeat.

In this moment, I want nothing more than to crawl inside myself.

"We're on the road for the next few days."

I knew that, but I just, I don't know... I wanted him to tell me that he was choosing us—that he'd stay. It's ridiculous, really, because he told me when we started this ruse that this was exactly what he was afraid of. Becoming attached. Being needed like this. Letting his family down.

He didn't want this.

He *doesn't* want this.

"Okay. I'll take the kids to Bristol. Have a safe flight, Beckett."

"Livy, I—" He clamps his mouth shut and swallows, his Adam's apple working. He watches me silently for a moment. Is he thinking all the same things I am? That he doesn't want to let me down, but he can't relinquish his responsibilities. He can't change himself completely and suddenly become a man who's yearned for a family all his life. He tried, he gave it his best, and I won't hold him to his promises when I know that it's hurting him to let me down. "Get some rest," he finally says.

As the screen goes black, I look at each of my friends, who've practically been holding their breath around me, feeling lost, confused and a whole lot sad.

"WE'RE PLAYING BASEBALL, bud. Tutus and cleats don't really go together," my brother says to an unamused Finn.

We spent three days hiding out at Declan's house before I packed the kids back up and headed home. Pulling Winnie out of school for three days was dramatic enough. I needed to start acting like an adult and face the music. My brother wouldn't let me do it alone, though. He followed me back to Boston for the weekend and now we're heading to T-ball for Finn.

For weeks, Beckett had been upset about missing his first game, but I told him not to worry, that in the grand scheme of things, Finn was unlikely to remember it anyway.

Now, after what happened with Drake, the last place Beckett should be is at my son's T-ball game. It's unlikely that Drake will be there, but that's a risk I'm not willing to take.

"Bossman says I can wear whatevers I want." Finn taps his foot as he stares my brother down.

Declan holds up his hands in surrender. "Tutus and baseball cleats it is."

Holding back a laugh, I pat my brother on the back. "Thank you for your help."

He drapes an arm over my shoulders and pulls me close. "Anytime." Then, under his breath, he replies, "Speaking of Bossman, where is the idiot?"

I shrug. He should have landed this morning. They're playing at Lang Field tomorrow, but he hasn't come home.

Or maybe he has. Maybe he went back to his penthouse.

Examining my bare ring finger, I wiggle it. Since I haven't been to the office for the last several days, there's been no need to wear that piece of jewelry, but God, does my finger feel empty.

The T-ball game is far too long, but I snap a few pictures and send them to Beckett, per his request. He replies that Finn looks great, but that's all.

No *When will I see you?* No *I miss you.*

Maybe the week away gave him the clarity he needed. Maybe he realized that this life is just too much—that all his fears were warranted.

My brother offers to take us out to dinner, but this week has taken its toll on me emotionally. All I want is a bath, a couple of glasses of wine, and some space, so I let him take the kids.

Bottle of wine in hand, I pull the tumbler Dylan got me from the cabinet. On second thought, though, I put it back, opting to take the bottle with me. As I'm heading up the stairs, I hear the first giggle, followed by an "Oh shit. He didn't!"

I follow the squeals, bringing the open wine bottle to my lips as I go.

"Wait, rewind! Go back!" Shayla howls, pointing at the computer in front of Dylan.

Delia rolls her eyes. "I knew he was behind the water in my bathroom."

My mind swirls in confusion, and I'm not even drunk yet. "Huh?"

Dylan beams at me, the glow of the computer screen brightening her expression further. "And you thought he didn't want to stay."

I repeat, huh? "What are we talking about?"

Dylan points at a frozen image. "We're watching footage from the camera Delia had installed when Beckett moved in."

"Delia!" My stomach drops. "You promised you wouldn't do that."

Delia pries the bottle of wine from my fingers and takes a swig. "You think I was going to let that man move in and not watch his every move? It's a good thing I did. He's been sabotaging this house. The brownstone isn't nearly as bad as we thought."

Dylan giggles as she takes the bottle from Delia. "Yes, it is. This is all child's play. Look here." She backs up the footage.

When she hits Play again, Beckett is walking into the kitchen. He tilts his head one way, then the other, as if he's checking to make sure he's alone. Then he takes out a wrench and drops to the hideous linoleum, the upper half of his body disappearing under the sink.

I steal the bottle and take another long pull. "That's when we asked him to fix the faucet."

Dylan giggles. "Not quite. Watch, here."

We all obey, rapt, as Liam ambles into the kitchen and turns on the faucet. Water shoots out at him, hitting him straight in the eye and taking him by surprise. He stomps out of range of the camera. A moment later, Dylan appears. She studies the faucet and shakes her head.

"I told Liam I wasn't falling for this trick. I figured he or one of the other kids was pranking me."

Delia grumbles, "Turned out to be the biggest freaking kid of them all, Man-child Beckett."

Shay slaps a hand to her mouth to mute her laughter and shakes her head.

On screen, Dylan drags Beckett into the kitchen. He makes a big deal of looking at the faucet. Then he disappears from view, only to return with the same damn wrench he had before. He drops to the floor, his movements so like the ones from earlier, and disappears under the sink. When he pops back up, he tests the faucet, and voilà, all fixed.

Hmm.

"This doesn't prove anything," I murmur before taking a healthy swig of wine.

Dylan waggles her brows. "Just keep watching."

She jumps to footage from another camera. This time, Beckett is pulling the broken step off the stairs—the one Dylan and Shay watched him fall through. He cuts a cable. One he told me later he found hanging. In another shot from the hallway upstairs, he's jumping just inside the bathroom. He does it over and over. Footage from a camera downstairs that lines up with this one's time stamp shows plaster from the ceiling in the living room raining down all over the furniture. He vacuumed up the mess and spackled it that same evening.

"I don't get it," I mumble.

Dylan tilts her head back and smiles up at me. "He wanted to be needed, Liv."

"Or he wanted her to believe the house was crumbling around us so she'd move out," Delia points out.

Dylan shakes her head, clicking on another video. "Then why would he have worked so hard to decorate Addie's room? Or to fix the stairs? Everything he tampered with was something we were already having problems with. He made them worse so that we were forced to fix them."

"And yet, we still have a leaky roof," Delia grumbles.

My heart skips a beat. "Actually…" I hedge. "I was staring at the ceiling in my bedroom last night—the water spots are gone."

Dylan sighs. "Go take a look at the roof, ladies. Then tell me Beckett was trying to get her to leave."

I tuck the glass bottle in the crook of my arm and practically sprint out of the room, the wine sloshing as I go. With every step I take, I feel more sure of Beckett's feelings. Maybe I'm delusional, but he worked so hard to break things so we were forced to fix them—why else would he do that if he didn't care? Sure, it's slightly unhinged, but isn't that precisely what love is? What it does to a person?

It's not rational; it's leaping and believing with no chance of knowing what the outcome will be. And yeah, it can make a person a little unhinged—a little crazy—but God, I'd prefer that over the robotic life I was living before Beckett asked me to marry him in Vegas like it was the most rational thing in the world.

I fling open the door to the roof, and all the breath whooshes from my lungs. It's beautiful. It's everything I described that first night he moved in.

A place to relax. A place for our family to spend time together. Couches with outdoor cushions in shades of teals, purple, pink, and blue. Twinkling lights and plants. A water table for Addie, a small table for the kids, and a longer teak one for the adults. A small patio table with a fire pit built into its center. Candles, big and small, in all corners of the space.

"Holy shit," Shay mutters from somewhere behind me.

I can practically hear Dylan's smile. "Told you. He loves her. He wants to give her everything. Whether it's with him or without him."

"But what if I want it with him?" I whisper, taking in the space, envisioning our family gathering up here. The kids crowded around their table with coloring books, us girls curled up on the couches with a bottle of wine or two to share. And Beckett, right there in the middle of the mess. Sometimes beside me, holding my hand or kissing my forehead. But more often sitting cross-legged on the floor, having a tea party. Going over stock options with the twins. Making bracelets with Winnie. Discussing baseball with Liam or watching hockey on his phone with Kai.

That's when it hits me.

"I know what I need to do," I whisper to my friends. "But I'm going to need your help."

Beckett

37

Gavin: Are you doing okay?

Beckett: Just miss my wife and kids.

Gavin: Never thought I'd see the day.

Aiden: Can I keep the penthouse? My place isn't nearly as big, and you have better sunsets.

Gavin: Too soon, bro. Too soon.

Beckett: When will we hear back?

Gavin: Might be a few days, why?

Brooks: Thinking what I think you're thinking?

Aiden: No clue what you're thinking, but if it's about selling the penthouse as some grand gesture, sell it to me!

Gavin: Aiden, shut the duck up.

> Gavin: Duck.
>
> Gavin: Duck.
>
> Aiden: Goose!
>
> Brooks: Oh my god, you're an idiot.
>
> Aiden: Uncool, man. Uncool.

BECKETT HAS LEFT THE CHAT.

"You've got an interview with ESPN at eleven and *Sports Illustrated* at eleven thirty. ESPN Kids has also requested an interview slot, but we'll wait and see how quickly you finish with *Sports Illustrated*." Hannah refers to her notes, barely looking at me, then types something into her phone.

From the owner's suite, I appraise the baseball field, the place that's owned my life for the last forty years, and sigh. I miss Liv. Hannah's good at what she does, but she's not my wife, so by default, I dislike her.

"What's *Sports Illustrated* want?"

Phone still in hand, I watch as Aiden adds me to the chat again, then I immediately remove myself. My lips quirk into a smile. As much as I pretend the guys drive me nuts, I'd be lost without my brothers.

"You're their pick for Baseball's Most Popular Bachelor. I'd like to say it was a toss-up between your brothers for hockey, but Brooks won in a landslide." She giggles. "Maybe it's the under-wear campaign. The man can wear the shit out of a pair of tighty-whities."

I don the scowl my staff has come to expect from me in response. No one jokes around with me at work. Well, no one except Liv. Hannah is not Liv. Have I gone soft? Do my employees think I want them to laugh with me? I grip my neck and bite back a curse. "I'm not a bachelor."

Hannah's face falls. "Not technically, no... but now that the press knows the marriage was a mistake... Well, what happens in Vegas—"

"I'd suggest you don't finish that sentence. Nothing about my wedding was a mistake. Nothing about my *marriage* was a mistake. I knew exactly what I was doing. I'll leave it up to my wife to set the record straight. If she wants a divorce, then I'll grant her that and take the blame. But I'm not a ducking piece of cattle that can be put up for auction next week. Put ESPN kids at eleven. I'll meet with ESPN after. Have Damiano fill in for *Sports Illustrated*."

She blanches. "He's got the worst personality in baseball."

Pressing my forefinger and thumb into the bridge of my nose, I shake my head. "He's no worse than me."

"But you're"—she waves a hand up and down—"a Langfield. Baseball royalty. Everyone puts up with your personality because, well, respectfully, you're *you*."

I laugh. Hard. She's not trying to suck up, and despite the turmoil I'm up to my eyeballs in, it's refreshing. Liv trained her well.

There was no sugarcoating. No stroking my ego by telling me I'm a catch or that I'm really a nice person *once people get to know me*. She basically said I'm rich, and that's why people want me. Well played. And the truth is, she's right. For everyone except for the one woman who actually matters. She doesn't care about my bank account, or my penthouse, or what kind of luxury gifts I could shower her with. The woman chooses to stay in a brownstone that's crumbling around her because it's where her family is happiest.

Granted, it's not falling down as much as it used to be—I made sure of that. Ducking Medusa and her insane need to control everything. If I hadn't made things worse in that house, it'd still be a freaking disaster. It's not perfect, but at least she let me do what was necessary to make the place safe.

Dylan still doesn't have walls, though, and that really bothers me. I rub at the ache in my chest. Dammit. I think I miss all of them. Even ducking Dippy Do and Medusa.

Okay, I don't miss Medusa, but I do miss my nightly conversations with the twins about the stock market. I planned to introduce them to my financial planner next week. They keep telling me I'm missing out on high-yield investments, so I figured I'd let the man I pay hundreds of thousands of dollars answer to them.

Hannah drops her chin and scrolls on her phone. Lighting up, she gasps. "What about Cortney Miller? Billionaire hot-shot, New York royalty, best catcher in the MLB, and our newest trade."

I glare at her. "No. I've got plans for him."

She sighs, shoulders slumping. "Damiano it is." She trudges out of the owner's suite, on a mission to locate my surly pitcher. I have no doubt he's going to drive her and *Sports Illustrated* nuts.

It makes me smile.

A moment later, my father appears in the doorway. Without greeting him, I head to the bar. We'll need a whiskey for this conversation.

"So it's true?" he mutters. "It was all fake?"

Gritting my teeth, I focus on the ceiling to rein in my ire. My father's the one who got me into this damn mess. "It was real, Dad. She knows it just like I do."

"But it wasn't always," he deadpans. The man is annoyingly astute.

I rub at my chest again. Saying it wasn't real would be a lie. It was always real to me. There's nothing fake about the feelings

I have for Liv and there never has been. "Maybe for her it wasn't."

Stepping a little closer and sliding his hands into his pockets, my father prods. "But it was real for you?"

Pouring a finger of whiskey into my glass, I sigh. "Yes. It was always real. She was always the one I wanted. Happy?"

The old man beams and takes another step toward where I'm hovering at the bar. "Well, I'll be." Then he furrows his brow and tips his chin at me. "If it's real, then why are we drinking whiskey at ten thirty in the morning?"

With a sigh, I swirl the amber liquid in my lowball glass. "Because I don't know if I'm enough."

"Why don't we take a seat, son?" My father motions to the chairs outside. Like me, his love for this game is all-encompassing. The smell of the grass, watching the staff prepare the field and ready the concession stands, fucking everything about this place... it's always been our heaven. But recently, a broken-down house in Boston knocked the stadium out of the top slot of my favorite places to be. I won't relax in these seats until I know that the woman who lives in that house has chosen me. That her family wants me around. That *I'm* her family.

"I may have pushed you to settle down with a woman with kids."

I snort. "You blackmailed me, Dad. My choices were giving up the team or jumping into a fake marriage."

A heavy sigh leaves his lips as he scrutinizes the field. "You were always so good with your siblings. Attentive. Patient. Protective. You made sure they always knew they came first."

"Someone had to," I mutter. Though the second the words leave my mouth, I dart a wary glance at my father. I don't begrudge him. I am my father, or at least, I thought I was. For my whole adult life, I've believed that the game mattered more than anything. When I was a kid, my father had loads of responsibilities. I've always respected that. At the time, I believed my responsibility was to my siblings. I always knew that would change, evolve, and eventually, I'd be the one who had to put baseball first.

At least, that's what I thought. Until I married Liv.

"Sorry," I grumble.

My father shakes his head. "You have nothing to apologize for. You're right. Someone had to, and I didn't. Your mother and I—" He scrubs at his face. "We were terrible at maintaining balance. You're much better at that than we were."

The ache in my chest flares. This topic is always just a little painful, but add it to the misery I'm currently wallowing in, and it leaves me wishing I had antacids handy. "What?"

My father chuckles. "Beckett, you're running the baseball team smoothly, plus you make it to hockey games pretty regularly. You cheer on your sister from afar, you put Liv and her kids first—"

Dropping my chin to my chest, I squeeze my eyes shut and shake my head. "Not this week. I missed Finn's first T-ball game."

"Who's Finn?"

That brings a smile to my face for the first time in far too long. "Huck. You know, Huckleberry Finn. I thought if I didn't call them by their names, I wouldn't get attached. Turns out that was just another lie I told myself."

My father pats my leg. "You feel too much. You could never not get attached."

"I was never attached to Sabrina."

My father shifts in his seat and considers me for a long moment. "You dated Sabrina for years because you couldn't have who you really wanted. Subconsciously, you didn't think you could have *what* you really wanted—a family *and* this job. That's my fault. I made you think you had to choose. So you chose baseball. That way you'd never let anyone down. You could put up walls, call Liv's kids by different names, groan about the mess they made, but in the end, you will always be the man who takes care of the people in his life. I knew you'd figure it out eventually. When you told us you'd married Liv? Let's just say I was mighty pleased with myself. Figured I'd forced you to really go after what you want."

I laugh. "You made me an offer I couldn't refuse. But if Liv hadn't been the one to sit next to me at that bar, I never would have gone through with it. She made the decision easy. The opportunity to taste what that life was like." I sigh. "She's the only one I've ever wanted to experience those things with."

"I always knew you could balance it all. You've always been good at prioritizing. And your priority will always be family. Everything else"—he sweeps his arm across the baseball field—"is just a game."

"I know that," I reply stupidly, bumping my knee against his when he laughs. "But I'm glad you do too now. And Dad?" He focuses his attention on me, his eyes warm. "Thank you."

"No need to thank me, son. Just be happy. That's all I've ever wanted."

The smile that breaks across my face is a genuine one. I am happy, or at least, I will be. Once my wife and I are finally honest with one another. Because nothing about this was ever fake, for her or for me.

THE GAME HASN'T EVEN STARTED, yet I'm itching for it to end so I can go home and tell Liv how I feel. It's been a week since I last held her, and if I have my way, I'll never go that long again.

"How'd the interview go?" I ask as Brooks settles into a chair outside the owner's suite.

Beside him, Gavin tips his head back and laughs.

"Not sure what you're laughing at." Brooks elbows Gavin. "And as for you," he says to me, "wipe off that smirk. The interview was fine."

Aiden groans. "If I was single, I'd totally be the pick for most eligible bachelor."

Sara smirks. "Sorry, Aiden. Saint Brooks and his tighty-whities will always win."

Brooks blushes, peeking over at Sara. I want to smack him on the back of the head. This is painful to watch. Does she not see how he looks at her? Or is she just not interested?

I consider him for a second longer. Nah, he's a Langfield. Of course she's interested. We're magnificent.

"I hate that nickname," Brooks grumbles, crossing his arms over his chest.

Sara bumps his shoulder and tips her chin up, scanning the field. "Too bad. It's who you are. Own it." She sucks in a breath, prompting us all to follow her line of sight. "Holy crap, that's like a baseball team, Beckett!"

"You've made some questionable trade choices as of late," Gavin mutters, "but maybe recruiting players who are over five foot would help this team win."

I laugh, admiring the way my wife, her three best friends, and all of our kids look standing out on the field.

Yeah, our *kids.*

Every single one of them is wearing a Revs jersey, and when Liv bends down to scold Finn, who squatted, snatched something from the dirt, and put it in his pocket, the name on her back comes into view.

Mrs. Langfield.

My wife is wearing my team's jersey with my name on the back.

When I thought there was nothing hotter than hearing people calling her Mrs. Langfield, I never even considered this possibility.

Sara's phone buzzes in her hand, and she lets out a laugh. "Beckett," she says, holding up her device, "you're being summoned to the field."

I'm already running through the door, though. It's time to get my family back.

Liv
38

"Finn, what do you have?"

My son peers up at me with a sly grin. "Nothing, Mama."

"Tummy hurts," Addie whines. She's sitting on the ground with fistfuls of grass in her hands.

"Please tell me she didn't eat that." Collette hovers over Addie, grimacing.

"Statistically speaking, it's likely." Phoebe shrugs. "She should be fine, though. Civilization used to subsist on a vegetarian diet, which I'm sure consisted of grass."

Shayla scoops Addie into her arms. "Auntie Shay is so proud of you."

"Can we get this over with? I can't wear this jersey for much longer," Liam grumbles, scratching at his neck like the offending piece of fabric is physically irritating him.

Dylan pops him on the back of the head.

"Ma, please."

"Don't be an idiot," she retorts. Then she turns to me and breaks into a sunshine smile. "This is so much fun! I've never been on a baseball field before. Where are the men?"

Liam rounds his shoulders, sinking further into himself. "Please stop."

I laugh. This was probably a horrible idea.

Winnie's got her attention fixed on the doors where Sara said she and Beckett should be entering from. Outside of me, she's taking his absence the hardest. No one has ever shown up for her quite like Beckett. I told myself it was good for her to experience disappointment. To understand that people don't always show up. And maybe that's true to an extent, but for now, I just want her to be eight. I want her to trust men. I want her to know that not everyone will let her down, that sometimes people love us enough to make an effort. Step one of proving that to her is to put my heart on the line and show up for Beckett. Show him that he matters. To all of us.

"He's coming, Win," I whisper, squeezing her hand.

"If he doesn't, I'll cut his balls off," Delia mutters under her breath.

Dylan and I shoot her matching frowns. Shay hides her laughter in Addie's soft hair.

The doors to the field fly open, and Beckett runs out wearing his typical game day attire—a Langfield Boston Revs' jersey, the classic blue baseball cap, and dark jeans. God, he looks good, and slightly out of breath.

Coming to a stop in front of me, he slaps a hand to his chest.

"Are you okay?"

He shakes his head and bends at the waist, planting his hands on his knees. After a few heaving breaths, he straightens. "I am now."

Suddenly nervous, I nibble on my bottom lip and lower my focus to the ground. We had a whole plan, but my brain has short-circuited with his arrival.

"You going to come give me a hug, or do I have to beg?" Beckett's words catch me off guard, and I peer back up at him. The smile splitting his face is so big, so bright that I can't help but to launch myself at him. Wanting to feel that smile against my cheek. Needing to soak in its warmth. He squeezes me close and breathes me in, his breath tickling my neck. "Duck, I missed you."

Pulling back just a little, I peer up at him. "You did?"

He brushes my hair out of my face and presses his palm to my cheek. "Tell me now if you're here for the reason I think you are. Because I really need to kiss you, but I won't do it in front of the kids if you're not ready."

"Kiss me, Beckett. Show them what love looks like. You've been doing it all along, anyway."

He licks his lips, and then he presses them against mine. It's not chaste, but it's not too graphic. I melt into him, like I'm finally at home after a week without the person who completes our family.

When he pulls away, he sighs against my mouth. "Did you say love?"

I shake from my stupor. "Shit, I had a whole plan."

Collette hollers a "hey!" but Delia covers her mouth. "Not right now."

Beckett drops his forehead against mine. Without letting me go, he slips his phone from his pocket and holds it out. "Take my money. She's worth it."

I roll my eyes, but my cheeks hurt from smiling already.

"So, tell me about this plan?" he murmurs.

"First they were all going to tell you they love you."

Beckett pulls back, his brows raised. "They were?"

From my side, Finn yells, "You're the bestest, Bossman. Course we loves you."

Beckett spins me so my back is to his front and we're both facing our family. "I love you too, Huckleberry Finn."

"Wait, we were gonnas tell you why we loves you. Right, Winnie?"

Winnie tucks her chin to her chest, but she shoots Beckett a shy smile. He leans around me just a little and holds out his fist to her. When I spot the bracelets they made together still on his wrist, my heart squeezes.

Winnie beams. "No one has ever been so ridiculous for me."

Beckett releases me so he can crouch down to her level. "People who matter and who care about you will always be ridiculous for you. Remember that, Bear. Now come here and give me a hug."

My daughter flings herself at him, and he falls onto his ass in the orange clay.

Finn follows suit, jumping on them. I grab him quickly before they all ruin their jerseys.

Beckett lifts his chin so he can see the twins and Delia over Winnie's head. "The three of you even wore the jerseys?"

Delia mutters, "I guess, for a man, you aren't the worst. I mean, you are still an idiot, but you're *our* idiot."

He looks up at her, his mouth forming an O. For a second, they just look at each other, and I think an understanding passes between them. My best friend actually approves of my grumpy boss of a husband. Who woulda thought we'd see the day?

"You covered for us when we cut Finn's hair. That was very magnanimous of you," Collette says.

Phoebe nods. "I'm Phoebe, by the way."

Beckett holds out his free arm, and the twins launch themselves at him, joining my kids on his lap.

Liam sighs. "For a Revs fan, you aren't half bad."

Beckett throws his head back and belly laughs. "I'll take it. Also, we're getting a pic of us in matching jerseys."

Liam scowls. "Don't push it."

Shay smiles. "It's nice having someone who actually drinks my smoothies."

Beckett watches Kai, who's shuffling closer, and holds out his fist. "Iceman, thanks for coming to the game."

Kai grins. "Are your brothers here?"

Beckett's loud laugh makes my cheeks hurt. He pulls himself up off the ground and points to the glass above home plate, where the owner's suite is located. "Why don't you guys head up there and let me talk to Livy for a minute?"

Dylan ushers my kids toward the door that'll take them up to where Beckett's brothers are, but when Winnie hits the threshold, she spins and rushes back. Throwing her arms around Beckett, she rests her chin on his abdomen so she's looking up at him and whispers what I swear is "Love you, Bossman."

I'm pretty sure he tells her he loves her too and that she can call him Beckett if she wants.

She shakes her head. "Nah, I'm your Bear, and you're the Bossman." After one more squeeze, she runs to catch up with everyone else.

When Beckett looks at me, his eyes shine with unshed tears. He ducks his head and swipes at them quickly. "God, they're special. Now tell me, Livy, what was all this about?"

I take a deep breath and square my shoulders. "I know we're a lot, and asking you to stay in the brownstone is slightly insane when you could easily afford to buy a new house for the five of us. But I made a pact with the girls. We're a package deal." Licking my lips, I take a moment to gather my courage to continue. My heart pounds in my chest, and my palms are sweaty, but I'm determined to lay it all out here and now.

Beckett doesn't interrupt me. He watches me closely, not giving away what he's thinking.

"You're excellent with the kids—all of them. I hope you see that. And I know this isn't what you ever pictured—I mean, really, who could ever dream up this insanity—but if anyone can figure it out, it's you. You don't have to be your father. And this family comes with four moms—so there's a lot of help. I'm rambling, I know. What I'm trying to say is, please, baby, don't move out."

Beckett smiles and swipes his thumb across my cheek. "I

know, Livy. And I loved everything about the declaration the kids made, but why did you think I was moving out?"

"The penthouse was ready." I lower my gaze and fiddle with a button on his jersey.

With two fingers under my chin, he tips my face up so I'm forced to look at him. "Yeah?"

"And you made the contractors work overtime."

Beckett sighs, his breath tickling the hair at my temples. "Because the house is falling down, and you refuse to leave it."

I nod. "Right, and you wanted it safe before you left."

"You think there is a world where I'd leave my wife and kids behind?" He clamps his hands around my upper arms gently. "Have you not been paying attention? You're mine, Livy. Your kids..." He licks his lips and looks up to the owner's suite, where the kids are likely already driving the staff crazy.

"You don't like kids," I remind him.

"I like your kids, Livy. As I was saying, your kids are my kids. I love *our* kids."

My brain malfunctions, and I blurt out, "Thought you didn't want kids?"

He chuckles. "I don't. Never did. But I want our kids. Our kids are ducking awesome. And all my fears, the reason I didn't want kids... none of it matters because when it comes to choosing between work or you and the kids, there's no contest. I'll always choose you."

Butterflies take flight inside me. "You're really ready for this? If you haven't noticed, we're *a lot*."

He brings a hand to my cheek again. "You know what I did while I was on the road the last few nights?"

I shrug.

"Watched videos of the kids I've recorded over the last few months. Some are nothing but screaming and chaos. I didn't even mute my phone. I scrolled Facebook to see if any of you had posted updates about what was going on at home. Stared at the wall and twiddled my thumbs, trying to figure out what the hell I'd do if you didn't forgive me."

"Forgive you? What could you possibly need forgiveness for?"

Beckett pales. "I punched their father. He may have deserved it, but I made your lives all exponentially harder when I reacted like I did."

My heart aches for this man who did the right thing by standing up for me but still beats himself up over it. "You were defending my honor."

Beckett's jaw tightens. "He won't bother you again."

"You can't promise that. Even if you could, it's not your job. Drake is responsible for his actions."

"Actually, pending your approval, I *can* promise that."

My brows pull together. "Huh?"

"Gavin had our lawyer contact Drake. It's why I've stayed away for the past week. I wasn't sure if he'd agree and I didn't want to make things worse for you." Beckett brushes a hair out of my eyes, and he lets out a tired sigh. "But fuck, I missed you. I can't do it again. So if you agree, when he signs the settlement documents, he won't be a problem anymore."

"Settlement documents? What for?"

"Livy, I assaulted him. Even if he deserved it, he has leverage now. But we can use this to our advantage. If he takes the money, Bouvier Media will continue to use his firm, which is good, because he needs to pay child support. He will have to agree not to bother you again and guarantee that he will not slander your name or mine. I also added one additional stipulation."

I bite my lip, my imagination running wild as to what this man came up with. Drake can't look at me when he picks up the kids? He disappears from our lives forever?

"He needs to show up for all the kids' extracurriculars."

My heart lodges in my throat. "What?"

"He's either in their lives or he's out. I won't have Winnie feeling like she doesn't matter."

"Beckett…" I murmur. "What if the kids find out?"

"Then they'll know their mom and stepdad did everything they could to ensure they have a relationship with their dad. They'll know we set aside our feelings for him and chose them. That's all I ever want them to see. Us putting them first, choosing them. Hopefully Drake won't screw this up. Hopefully he'll take this second chance and run with it. But if he doesn't, they'll always know love, Livy. And so will you."

I swallow heavily, my heart beating out of my chest. "Because you love me," I whisper into the breeze.

Beckett cups my cheek. "Very much. I didn't know what love was until I met you. To me, the definition of love is you. Not this baseball field. Not our jobs. You, me, and those kids, Livy. Our family. That's all that matters. I love you, Olivia Langfield. I love you so ducking much that sometimes I can't think straight."

"I love you too. God, do I love you. But are we really doing this?" I laugh as he licks his lips and edges closer to me.

"Yeah, we're really doing this. Stay married to me? Tell the press the truth with me? That none of this was fake. That you and me, our marriage, we're the real deal."

In answer, I press my lips to his, pulling a moan from him. When he loops his arms around my waist and pulls me closer, it's like coming home. This crazy warm feeling eases through my body, and I sink into him, finally accepting what he's been telling me all along.

I drive him crazy. *I* leave him breathless. *I'm* who he's always wanted.

And he's the man I'll want for the rest of my life.

A throat clears a couple feet away and we break apart, finding Hannah watching us, a flush creeping up her cheeks.

"Uh, Mr. and Mrs. Langfield, the team needs to take the field, if you're uh… done using it."

I hide my face in Beckett's chest and laugh as he presses a kiss to my head.

"It's all yours."

Then we stroll, hand in hand, up to the owner's suite, to spend the day watching baseball with our family.

"FINN, DON'T TOUCH THAT!" I chide as we walk through the family room in the back of the stadium. We won six to one. Now that the guys are all busy with the press, Beckett is giving the kids the tour he promised them while Dylan's head swivels in all directions, not being shy in the least about checking out the players' *assets.*

He waves over a few players who are finished with post-game interviews and introduces us. "These are the moms."

"The moms?" Eddie Martinez, my favorite player, asks.

"Yeah, I live with them in the mom-com."

"Is that a play on rom-com?" Coach asks.

Beckett frowns, incredulous. "What? *No.* A mom commune. You know, like *Fuller House?* Moms living together to help raise each other's kids, because *who needs a man?*"

I smile proudly at my insane husband, fighting back a giggle.

"Dude, he's pranking us, right?" Damiano asks Eddie.

Wrinkling my nose, I shake my head. "No, boys. He's serious."

"Let me find Miller; he's chatting with the press, but I want to introduce you," Beckett says, scanning the room for the younger brother of one of his best friends. The catcher has settled in with the team almost seamlessly if his batting average is anything to go by. The man scored another home run today.

Finn pulls on my shirt. "Mama, Slimy needs to go to the bathroom."

I sigh. "Who's slimy?" A new invisible friend is my guess.

Finn hikes up his tutu and digs around in the pocket of his camo pants. With a grin, he pulls out a snake and holds it high above his head. Shayla screams and scrambles away, and as she turns with Addie in her arms, green goo shoots from my little girl's mouth and covers Damiano.

"Is that kid sick?" Damiano hollers.

The man is a bit of a hypochondriac, among other things, though anyone in their right mind probably wouldn't be thrilled after being barfed on.

"Sorry!" I snatch the snake from Finn's hand before I realize that, holy shit, I'm holding a snake. When it clicks, instinct takes over, and I fling it across the room.

Damiano screams like a girl and bounces on one foot, then the other. In a heartbeat, the entire room spirals into mayhem. Beckett tugs Addie out of Shay's arms and pulls her to his chest. With one hand, he points to Finn, signaling me to get him.

"You sure you're up for this?" I mumble as we rush out the door.

Beckett just smiles and throws his head back in laughter. "It's going to be a ducking disaster."

Epilogue

Two Weeks Later
Beckett

The screeching noise bouncing off the walls of the brownstone as I push open the front door could not possibly be human.

Dylan rushes ahead of us. "Oh my gosh! I think Junior's having her babies!"

"Nope." I shake my head and pull my wife back. "Not doing it. I love you, Livy, but we are not staying in this house tonight."

She laughs. "Because Junior is having her babies?"

Finn pushes off my leg, ready to rush for the living room to check out the situation, no doubt, but I pick him up by his waist and toss him over my shoulder, then begin my descent down the front steps. I know how this will go if we go inside. Finn will cry right along with the damn raccoon. Then he'll convince me that I need to climb into the fireplace to help birth these damn animals. I'm not doing it. Nope. Not going to happen.

"Bossman!" Finn kicks at my stomach

I hold his feet down with one arm and continue on my way. "Finn, here's a life lesson: We don't belong in there. Birthing is for women."

Medusa sucks in a breath as she stomps past me. I swear I can feel the eyes in the back of her head coming out of her skull. Soon they'll pop out and scare the bejesus out of me.

I keep walking.

Winnie chases after me, and Liv is close behind with Addie in her arms.

"You really won't go inside?" Bear whispers as I toss Finn back into the limo and put a finger to my lips, motioning for him to be silent.

My expression must convey how serious I am. The kid doesn't even whine. He just scoots across the seat and folds his arms over his chest, angry at me. Whatever. I'll do just about anything for this family, but birthing a litter of raccoons is a step too far.

"Livy, we'll come back in the morning. I don't ask for much, but please, do not make me go into that house right now."

She folds her lips over like she's fighting a smile, but her dark eyes dance. "All this over a little raccoon?"

"A *pregnant* raccoon, Livy. A ducking pregnant raccoon in *active* labor. I'm not doing it."

She sucks in air, still fighting back laughter, and holds Addie out to me. "Fine, I'm just going to grab a few things for the night."

With Little One propped on one hip, I let out a sigh and lean against the limo.

"All okay, boss?" Charlie asks as he steps out of the driver's door to chat with me.

I nod, pulling my phone from my pocket. "We're going to

spend the night at the penthouse. Just give Liv a few minutes to pack up some stuff."

The door to the brownstone flies open, and Shayla comes out, pulling Kai with her. "Can you give us a ride to a hotel?"

Her short hair is hanging over one eye, and she's practically panting.

Concerned, I push off the car. "What's going on in there?"

Her eyes bulge, and she shakes her head. "It's not pretty."

"You don't have to stay at a hotel. There's plenty of room at the penthouse if you and Kai share a bed."

She nods. "That works."

Medusa is next, flying out the door and pulling the twins behind her. "Not a word, man-child. We're coming with you."

I laugh and roll my eyes. "I take it even a woman doesn't belong where animals are giving birth?"

She glares at me. "I'm all for teaching the girls about the circle of life, but that's not normal."

I hold an arm out toward the open limo door, and she and both girls scramble in.

Liv is next. Her face is flushed, and she has an overflowing bag over one shoulder and a folded-up Pack 'n Play in her other hand. She swipes at a few strands of hair that have come loose from her bun. "Do *not* go in there."

I laugh, feeling better about my decision by the minute, and nod at Charlie so he knows we're about ready to take off.

Dylan appears in the doorway next. "Guys, you're going to miss it!"

Liam slides past her. "Sorry, Ma. You're nuts if you think we're staying here." He grabs her hand, slams the door, and pulls her toward the limo.

"You're all really afraid of a pregnant raccoon? Pregnancy is beautiful."

Liv rolls her eyes. "Says the woman who hasn't been pregnant since the early 2000s. Believe me, Dyl, there's nothing beautiful about what's about to happen in there. We'll come home tomorrow, and you can dote on her babies then."

Dylan frowns and tilts her head. "But what if she needs help?"

"That's precisely why I'm not going in there," I remind her.

She laughs and pushes past me to the open limo door. "True, the last thing Junior needs is to listen to your screaming when she's trying to have a calm birth."

I roll my eyes. *Calm birth.* Is that even a thing?

Once Dylan's inside, Charlie points at the car. "You getting in?"

I shake my head and shut the door. "Nah, I'm riding up front with you. My head needs the quiet for a few minutes before I welcome this insanity into my penthouse."

Charlie laughs and rounds the hood. I take a second to run up the steps and lock the door. Back at the limo, I spin and look up at the brownstone. The holiday decorations, the *Happy V l Day* sign that's lost another letter or two, the gutter hanging precariously from the edge of the roof. It's still not perfect, but it is home.

I take Medusa and Liv and our three kids up to the penthouse first, then Finn and I ride the elevator down again for the rest of the crew since we couldn't all fit at once. When the elevator opens into the foyer, the kids explode out of the stainless-steel box. I have to hold my breath as they run wild around the open concept living and dining area, hollering and bouncing all over. It's not childproofed, and it's definitely not mom-com proofed but the women make themselves comfortable, grabbing wineglasses and pulling open the fridge in search of dinner. Before things get out of control, I head to the drawer where I keep the takeout menus and motion to Liv.

"Sorry, baby. I know this wasn't what you had in mind," she says as she sidles up next to me and snakes her arm around my waist.

Pulling her closer, I brush my lips against hers and smile. "Just tell me you love me. That always makes me feel better."

She melts against me, her smile consuming her face. "I do love you, Bossman. So much."

Soaking in the meaning behind those words, I relax with her in my arms. The chaos around us continues, but I tune it out. I don't care who has crayons near my marble counters or who's jumping on my ten-thousand-dollar couches. Vases may be broken, bottles of wine worth more than the average person's annual salary may be consumed, and I legitimately couldn't care less.

We order takeout—each family choosing food from different restaurants, and some ordering stuff from multiple places and then we all sit around the big table and argue over Delia's assigned topic for dinner.

We split the kids into two rooms for a giant sleepover. Dippy Do, Medusa and Pip share the guest room. I don't know how they all plan to fit in the king-size bed, and I really don't care.

It's after ten when I finally have my wife alone, in my room, in the quiet.

"You think Junior is okay?" Liv asks from the master bathroom.

I lean against the counter, legs crossed, and stare at my wife as she washes her face. I'm already smiling. "I'm sure she's enjoying her time alone with her babies."

Liv hums. "Probably."

"I like seeing you in my bathroom."

She smiles. "Beckett, you can't sweet talk me into moving into your penthouse. I told you—the girls and I are a package deal."

"I know. We're living with them until they find their perfect men."

She laughs and pats her face dry. "Ha. You think Delia is ever going to settle down and live with a man?"

I shrug. "Stranger things have happened."

Liv's eyes dance. "Yeah, like me marrying my boss."

Grasping her by the hips, I pull her close and drop my lips to my favorite spot on her neck. I bite down, eliciting a moan from her. "That was fate, Livy."

She sighs as she plays with the hair just above my nape, her fingers raking through it and making me want to stay in this position for hours.

"This place is nice, though," she says quietly. "If Drake keeps his word and takes the kids every other weekend, maybe we could come here when the kids are gone. You know, get away from the chaos."

My heart jumps. The idea of forty-eight hours alone with my wife is too good to be true. "Really?" I ask, giving away just how hopeful I am when I look up at her.

Liv bites her lip and nods. "Maybe we could bring the kids here every once in a while? You did say you have a swimming pool."

I squeeze her to me. "God, I love you."

"We can have it all, Beckett. The crazy chaos of the brownstone and the quiet moments just for us. I want to give you everything you deserve."

She still doesn't get it. She's all I need. I'm not sure she'll ever really understand the depth of my obsession, but that's okay. I'll allow her to "make it up" to me if it means more nights alone with her like this.

"You going to give me what I deserve right now?" I tease, tugging her into the bedroom.

"Only if you can be quiet. After the incident with the snake in the basement, we both know how loud you can shriek."

I lunge, gently pushing her onto the bed and pinning her to the mattress. "The question is, can you be quiet, Livy? Because we both know how loud you were last time I had you in this position. I had to gag you to keep you quiet."

I grind against her, pulling a moan from deep within her. It takes no time at all for her to pull my pants down and for me to strip her bare. Then I'm sliding inside her, finally returning to the only home that matters to me. It's not about the location or the money or the disasters that surround us. It's about this right here. The quiet moments with my wife when we become one. When I get to see the woman no one else sees. When she's all mine.

"God, that feels good," she murmurs.

"It always feels good when my cock is inside you," I say, thrusting into her slowly, taking my time.

"Harder," she begs.

With a wicked smile, I grip the headboard and quicken my pace, pistoning my hips.

The bed squeaks beneath us. "You said you'd be quiet," she teases.

"Can't help that my massive cock makes this much noise."

We both laugh, and I drop to my forearms and kiss her slowly, smiling as we make love. No, it may not be the roughest sex we've ever had, and definitely not the kinkiest, but laughing with her, while inside her... Fuck, it's the best sex of my life.

Because it's her.

The End

Extended Epilogue
A few months ago in Vegas
Beckett

"THIS IS INSANE. You know that, right?" Liv teases, her voice lighter than I've ever heard it, her smile unbidden.

I stare up at the tiny white chapel and then look down at my bride-to-be. Cheeks rosy, hair having been taken out of her standard bun hours ago when we finished our first bottle of wine. I made sure to ask the manager to send me a case of it before we left. Fuck, I probably should have ordered six. Hope I remember to do that tomorrow.

"You're beautiful."

"Beckett," she chides. It makes my cock stir to life. The number of times I've jacked off to the idea of how this woman would sound saying my name just like that is embarrassing.

Well, it was embarrassing before this moment, because now she'll be my wife, and I should definitely be allowed to jack off to my wife's voice, right?

"Do you like your ring?" I lift her hand, and we both study it. Vegas really is a magical place. It's one a.m., and we're getting married in a few minutes with very little planning, yet I was able to tell the hotel precisely what I wanted—carat size, band size, and her yellow gold preference—only to have ten options delivered to us at the bar.

Liv pretended not to care, but I saw the way her eyes immediately went to the one on the right. It's three and a half carats, certainly not the biggest diamond in the selection—if Liv wanted the six-carat diamond, she'd be wearing it right now. The emerald-shaped diamond sits in a thin gold band braided with diamonds.

It's classic, just like my bride.

"It's beautiful, Beckett." The soft smile she offers me has my chest swelling with pride. For a moment, I'm transported back to the first time I met her.

"Hold the elevator, please!"

I press the button to keep it open at the sound of the stressed female voice coming down the corridor.

A man grumbles beside me. "I'm going to be late for my meeting."

I glare at him. Kindness costs so little. It's five fucking extra seconds. The moment the woman comes into view, my scowl morphs into a grin. She's fucking gorgeous, all curves and red lipstick, her hair tied back loosely at her nape in a bow. She lets out a sigh of relief and looks me right in the eye. "Thank you so much."

I step back, making room for her. "Not a problem. What floor?"

Her face transforms from relief to panic in an instant. "Shit, I forgot to ask the front desk."

The grumpy man behind us snickers, and I glare at him again. He hasn't even looked up from his phone yet.

"Where are you going?"

"I have a job interview. It's with—" She glances down at her phone. "Langfield corp. Ever heard of it?"

The man grumbles behind us. "Who hasn't?"

Once again, I pay him little attention. "It's on the thirtieth floor." I choose not to answer the question because I now know this woman is interviewing with my father, and for a few more minutes, I want to just be Beckett, not Beckett Langfield. She'll find out who I am soon enough.

Her soft fingers wrap around my wrist, forcing me to really look at her as she says, "Thank you so much."

God, I like the sound of her voice. And I can't stop staring at her lips. Then her eyes again. Her cheeks turn rosy as we stand frozen, smiling at one another. She is absolutely stunning. Instantly, I feel at ease with her, which is a strange thing.

"What's your name?"

"Olivia, but my friends call me Liv."

"Liv. I like that."

"Oh, we're going to be friends?" Her tone is teasing, and fuck, I like that too.

"Yeah, Liv, I think we are."

"Then you should probably tell me your name."

"Beckett."

"Beckett." She tests my name on her tongue, and I like that even more.

"I'm Drake," the rude man behind us says.

Liv jumps like she's just now realizing we're not alone. And for the first time since she got on the elevator, Drake looks up as she spins in his direction. I watch in horror as the man smirks and pockets his phone.

"Drake Maxwell." He holds out his hand, and Liv smiles.

My mood grates as I realize she's smiling at him just like she smiled at me. Does she always smile like that? And why do I feel irrationally possessive over a damn smile?

"Nice to meet you."

She turns back to me, but the man continues talking. *"What type of job are you interviewing for?"*

"Oh, it's just an internship. It's in the PR division, though."

"That's amazing. I'm in marketing." He reaches into his pocket and takes out his wallet, then hands her a card. *"We should get a drink. I would be happy to discuss your career and maybe help you find a job when you're done with your internship."*

"Oh my gosh, that's amazing. It's so hard meeting people in this industry, right? Everyone is so cutthroat."

Drake laughs. It's smarmy, and I want to push him off the elevator so that Liv will pay attention to me, but we're reaching the twenty-ninth floor and I have to get off. I have a meeting with a liquor company. The young billionaire who just inherited it *wants to discuss getting his brand in our stadiums. We currently carry James Whiskey, but I met Jay Hanson at an event recently and I liked him enough, so I agreed to hear him out. Besides, his story is kind of tragic. His father died in a burglary gone wrong, and Jay spent months in a coma. I figure the least I can do is give him a meeting. As the elevator stops at my floor, I turn to say goodbye to Liv.*

"This is me."

"Thank you again for holding the elevator. Maybe if I get the internship, I'll see you again?" There's a part of me that thinks her voice has a bit of hope in it.

"Maybe. Good luck on your interview."

I step off, but before the doors close, I look back, only to find Drake moving infinitely closer to the woman I felt this strange pull to. As the doors shut, I hear the echoes of her laughter.

Next week. I'll make sure my father hires her and assigns her to me. Drake will be gone, and I can ask her out.

Yes, that's the plan.

I straighten my jacket, convinced that like everything else in my life, I've got this under control, and head into my meeting.

But Liv's smile stays with me all day.

"Langfield!" the woman calls from inside the chapel. "You're up!"

I look down at Liv. "Ready?"

With her lip caught between her teeth, she shrugs. "Are you?"

"Fuck yeah."

Liv's face morphs into the most glorious smile, and she lets out one of her rare laughs. I catch them here and there when I'm lucky, but this one is by far the most beautiful, because it's directed at me. It's *because* of me. And fuck, I want all her laughs. All her smiles.

"All right, Mr. Langfield," she teases, "let's go get married."

I practically drag her into the church, and when the woman

asks if I want to stand at the altar and wait for Liv, I contemplate it, but then I shake my head. The last time I walked away from this smile, I turned around and she was aiming it at someone else. And by the time I saw her again, she'd already gone on a date with the asshole.

I hesitated, and it cost me years without her. Years of watching someone else get these smiles. Years of watching that man cause her tears.

Fuck. That. Shit.

With her hand held firmly in mine, I turn to her. "I don't want to wait for you anymore, Liv. I'm not letting go this time."

She swallows heavily as she studies me, but it almost feels like she knows what I mean when her brown eyes soften. "What do you suggest, Mr. Langfield?"

I shake my head and laugh at her use of that goddamn name. But this one time, I don't correct her. "If it's okay with you, Olivia, I'd like us to walk down the aisle together."

Moments later, when Elvis is pronouncing us husband and wife, and I'm finally given the okay to kiss her, I don't hesitate. "Fuck, I can't tell you how long I've wanted to do this," I murmur right before our lips touch.

Her soft moans stir me to life, and my heart beats wildly. Though that's not a surprise. I've known for years that my heart would only beat like this for her.

I tilt her head and deepen the kiss, devouring this moment. *Living for this moment.* When she pulls back, a surprised but pleased look on her face, I don't give her time to overthink it. I take her hand in mine and rush us out the door.

Olivia Langfield is mine, and I don't intend to ever let her go.

MOTHER MAKER SNEAK PEEK

BY: JENNI BARA

Cortney

A mid-season initiation. That was the only explanation for this.

I narrowed my eyes, taking in the four-story...let's call it a house. *Dilapidated money pit* was a mouthful.

I chuckled. Did the idiots I played with every day really think I'd be dumb enough to believe Beckett Langfield lived in this dump? No freaking way the grouchy asshole who owned the team would be caught dead in here.

The large front window announced *Happy... Day*. A word was obviously missing between *Happy* and *Day*, but maybe it was fitting for the brownstone which seemed to have a mixed holiday vibe. A Christmas wreath hung on the blue front door, while a huge Easter bunny sat off to the right of the brick steps. The railings were adorned with white ghosts and part of a skeleton. None of it would be that weird if it weren't almost July. At least the red, white, and blue stars on each one of the zillion windows actually made sense.

Chalk drawings and tic-tac-toe games covered the sidewalk

and steps like a preschool stopped to have recess in front of the house.

I pulled out my phone to snap a picture, because, fuck, they went all in for this prank. Life was too short to not laugh.

My finger hadn't even left the little red button before the shower started. A zipping sound and a ping, then rubber balls smacked against my chest. Then my ear and my cheek and my forehead. Jeez, a true Nerf sharpshooter. Something I'd appreciate more if I wasn't the target.

I zeroed in on the screenless window, where a small kid with a shaved head stuck the upper half of his body out. His tutu was navy; the gun was orange and white.

"Gets off my sidewalk."

Squinting at the kid, I grunted. I was pretty damn sure that sidewalks were public property. But did I really want to argue with a child? Drunk? Maybe. But sober? Less appealing.

The kid climbed through the window, and like a monkey, he flung himself through the air and landed on his feet on the porch a foot and a half below. Holy shit. He's lucky he didn't break his neck.

"Bossman says it's up to us guys to potect this house and the one *zillion* annoying girls in it."

I smirked at the kid. Between the shaved head, the camo pants, and the navy ballet tutu, he stood out. Had to appreciate that this kid's parents let him *do him*.

Before I could tell him why I was here, he fired again, and the neon orange ball bounced off my forehead.

"Ouch, what the hell?" Rubbing the spot, I shot him a glare.

The kid, who couldn't have been more than five, might be a good shot, but shit, didn't his parents teach him rule number one in Nerf battle? *Don't aim for the face.* He could leave someone blind, and I, for one, needed to see.

"Hey, Huck, you better not be shooting the mailman again."

The front door opened, but it was too dark in the foyer to see who finally came for this kid.

"No, it's an invasion of tall guys with weird ponytails." The kid stomped his Timberland boot on the landing of the brownstone and aimed again.

I threw my hands into the air in surrender. "I'm just here for my socks." Ridiculous but true. According to my teammates, the punk-ass teenager who'd stolen my lucky socks lived here.

But with every minute that passed, it became more obvious that this was a setup.

"Miller?"

Holy shit. Beckett Langfield.

My broody, dark-haired boss stepped out of the shadows and onto the top step.

How the hell had the team gotten *him* to go along with this prank? Beckett *had* brought a bunch of kids to the game earlier in the day—some kind of publicity stunt that helped smooth things over after all the crazy press lately—but to get in on a team prank was on a whole other level.

"Don't shoot." Beckett held one arm out to the kid. "If you hurt him, my team's going straight back into the toilet."

Hell yeah, they were. Beckett might not like me, but since my arrival a few weeks ago, his team was winning. He and I both knew he needed me calling the pitches. But to do that effectively, I needed my lucky socks.

"Why are you here?" Beckett still held his hand out to the young boy to his left, but his attention was trained on me. The cocked head and pursed lips implied that he wasn't expecting me, so either he was a good actor, or this wasn't a joke.

"Good to see you too, Bossman." I smirked, falling into my role as the shithead Beckett would expect.

His father and mine had been friends for a long time. The Langfields focused on baseball and hockey empires, while the Millers dominated the real estate and racing worlds. Both families were respected and liked across the board. None of that meant Beckett and I got along.

"Don't be a d—" The curse died on his tongue. Swallowing it back, he cut a glance at the kid still training his Nerf gun on me.

I surveyed the brownstone again. Although the foyer lights were off, all the windows of the second floor and the basement were lit up like the Fourth of July night sky. The noise coming from inside the open front door spilled out into the quiet summer day.

"Is this your house?" I couldn't not ask the question. Just like I couldn't hold back the shit-eating grin that overtook my face. If Beckett Langfield lived here, then the world needed to know.

Beckett rolled his eyes. "It's complicated."

"No, it's not," the kid said. "You love Mom, and Mom lives here, so that means we get you."

Beckett smiled down and rubbed the little guy's head. "You're right, Finn."

Ah. That's right. Beckett had recently married the head of the team's PR division, Olivia Maxwell. I still couldn't believe it was true. Beckett hated everyone. He and love didn't mix in my brain. Yet he'd fallen for a single mom with a couple of kids? Mindboggling.

My team's owner sighed. "What do you want, Cortney?"

"Some punk-ass kid stole my socks." I shrugged, going for chill, like I wasn't freaking out over the possible loss of luck.

Being rational didn't matter to me, but playing ball did. I wasn't twenty-five anymore, and I wasn't ready to lose my spot on the team I had only just been traded to. My unexpected trade had rocked the baseball world. I had been with the New York Metros for almost ten years, and there hadn't been even a whisper before I was called into the office and informed of my new status as a Boston Revs.

As much as billionaire Beckett grated on my nerves, the last thing I wanted was another trade. Bonding with a team took time and work, and I was too old to start again next year. Hell, according to some, I was too old to be playing, period. During every game, I had to prove I still had what it took to crouch behind the plate. Sure, I was known for being one of the smartest catchers in the league and for getting the pitchers winning games, but my hips and knees felt older than my thirty-five years.

Beckett's ever-present scowl was still in place when I pulled myself out of my thoughts, so I cleared my throat, ready to explain and get the hell out of here.

"Heard I could find the sock thief here. Damiano said the redheaded kid you brought to the game swiped them from my locker."

"Demon Spawn," he muttered.

"Don't worry, I won't tell the moms," the kid warned. "Auntie Dylan hates when you call him that."

Beckett looked at me for a long minute before he blew a long breath out of his nose. "Come in. We'll find the ducking socks."

Ducking?

"Use the door. Medusa gets mad when you climb in through the window." Beckett headed back into the brownstone.

I ran up the steps behind him, equally curious about how this would play out and desperate to get my hands on my lucky socks. If I didn't get them back before the long road stretch the team was about to leave on, I'd be fucked.

Inside the foyer, I stopped to let my eyes adjust to the darkness. Once they did, I scanned the space, catching sight of a hole in the ceiling—two, actually—and wires that stuck out in place of a light fixture. Part of the floor was nothing but plywood. Damn. The inside of the house looked worse than the outside.

"*Don't* ask." Beckett gritted out, his jaw clenched. "If you want the socks, keep your mouth shut and look pretty, Man Bun."

Without thinking, I ran my hand over my hair and the bump of my bun. These days, I was known for my hair as much as my ability to call pitches. It was my trademark and the reason my agent received constant endorsement calls.

Beckett shot me the side-eye, confirming that I wouldn't open my big mouth. I was tempted, but I wanted to keep my job and leave with the damn socks, and I still wasn't 100 percent sure this wasn't a prank.

He tilted his head and strode off, so I followed him into a large family room. This space was somewhat finished, with lights, a full ceiling, and finished floors. It could have used an update, but it wasn't a construction zone. The only aspect that jumped out as odd here was the large brick fireplace. The handles of the screen were linked together with what looked like wire. Or maybe it wasn't a fireplace screen. Could that be a wired-shut gate? Almost like they were trying to lock something inside.

A dark-haired kid on the sofa peeked back quickly, then did a double take. "Oh, wow." It was almost a whisper. His brown eyes were wide as he looked from me to Beckett. "He's going to teach me to play baseball?"

Beckett crossed his arms. "I thought you wanted to play hockey, Iceman."

"I'm not picky." The kid spun until his knees were planted on the cushion and his elbows were propped on the back of the sectional.

"I'm working on the hockey thing." Beside me, Beckett uncrossed his arms and pounded a fist against the wall twice. A sprinkle of plaster dust from a crack above him fluttered down and coated his brown hair. With his jaw clenched, he banged again and yelled into the air conditioning vent. "Team meeting. Let's go, crew."

The house erupted before Beckett had even finished his directive. What sounded like a stampede of horses echoed above us, and a moment later, a horde of kids made their way into the room. Twin girls with matching blond French braids appeared, along with another girl who looked to be about the same age as the dark-haired kid on the sofa. The kid in the navy tutu reappeared as well. Just as I began to think this house was like a clown car and people would keep popping up until the place was bursting at the seams, a tiny girl toddled in. Her hands were covered in a slimy yellowish substance.

She wobbled over to Beckett on her chubby legs and yanked on his pants. Without hesitating, Beckett lifted the kid and propped her on his hip.

Grinning, she opened her hand and offered Beckett what looked like mashed banana.

"I'm good, Little One." Beckett shook his head, wearing a surprisingly chill expression even as the little girl shoved the mashed food into her mouth, then wiped her dimpled hand on Beckett's Revs jersey. "Livy, we need a wet paper towel."

"Got it," came a familiar voice. A moment later, the team's head of PR rounded the corner and stepped into the room. At the stadium, Liv was always the picture of perfection, so this woman, the one sporting a messy bun and a handprint on her leggings, was almost unrecognizable.

I opened my mouth to greet her, but truthfully, I didn't know what to say.

What the hell was going on right now? I wasn't sure whether the house itself was the most whacked-out part of this moment or if it was the sight of Beckett and Liv—two of the most puttogether people I knew—inside it. Either way, I was getting major *what the fuck?* vibes.

Liv went straight for Beckett's jersey with the paper towel, but he held up a hand.

"I'm not worried about me," he said, holding the little girl's hand out. "Get this wiped off. We don't need Junior gnawing through wire for a taste of mashed banana *again*."

"It only happened once," Liv said, chuckling. "But Raccoongate and watching you jump around in your boxers to escape her was definitely the highlight of my year."

"The stuff I put up with for you." Beckett shook his head.

I was floored, because the expression on his face didn't scream anger or annoyance. No, when he looked at Liv, he wore a goofy expression that was reserved only for men who had been flat-out knocked over by love.

I shook my head. *Poor schmuck.*

"Where are the rest of them?"

"The rest?" I sputtered.

Beckett's only response was a frown.

"Bro, this is enough."

I knew Liv had kids, but not an army of them.

Beckett's frown deepened, and his face turned a darker shade, but before he could respond, the reason I was distracted enough after the game to let my socks go missing stepped into the room.

Willowy, porcelain skin, auburn hair, and eyes that sparkled like gold. Just like when I spotted her across the team room after the game, her presence alone knocked the air out of my lungs. And I almost fell to my knees when her full pink lips lifted into a smirk that said *I've got your number.*

And damn if I didn't want her to have it.

MOM COMS
Mother Faker - Brittanée Nicole
Mother Maker - Jenni Bare
Mother Pucker - Swati M.H.
Mother Hater - Daphne Elliot

ACKNOWLEDGMENTS

You know the saying, if we don't laugh about it, we'll cry? That's kind of how this series came to be. Four women sitting around commiserating about how hard motherhood, marriage and writing is and laughing over glasses of wine about the ridiculous things that happen to us on the daily.

Truth be told, my husband is sprinkled through each of my book boyfriends because we all write from some type of general experience. Beckett and Jay Hanson may be the closest to my husband I've written. Good dads who say ridiculous things that leave us shaking our heads and laughing quite often.

But I wouldn't get through my day to day life without my girlfriends and that is what this series is about. Friendship. Love. And figuring out how to laugh through the crazy.

So first and foremost, thank you to my co-writers Jenni Bara, Daphne Elliot and Swati M.H. for dealing with my many messages about something funny I think we needed to have Beckett do, or something ridiculous that could occur in the house. Thank you for taking this idea and turning it into four wonderful books that I know readers will be able to feel seen in.

And to the two people who literally listen to my every inner thought on the daily, who share my day to day and help me deal with the crazy—Jenni and Sara, if not for you, I'd be certifiable. We are in our Bestie Era and I'm so thankful I have the two of you in my lives.

Sara also does the formatting, graphics, marketing and general Brittanee herding for every one of my books. Without her, I'd be lost. I love you. You're a good girl and I'm so proud of the continuous growth and leaps you make in your career.

A special thank you to the editors who helped make this series what it is, Beth and Sylvia. You are so appreciated. Beth, the way you just pivot whenever I ask *can I sneak in a book tomorrow* makes it so this crazy train keeps moving.

And to Kristie who not only helped all of us with the general series plotting but who helped me write the beautiful story of Liv and Beckett, I appreciate you. It was so important to me to write a relatable heroine, someone who isn't perfect but doesn't need a man to make her perfect either. She's accepting of herself, sometimes annoyed by things she can't change, and also just because she accepts herself doesn't mean she can't also have weak moments. I saw myself in Liv and I hope some of you did too.

An extra special thank you to Brittanee's Book Babes, my street team and the Momcom Street team. We couldn't do this without your support.

Thank you to my wonderful beta readers, Becca and Rachel, your love for these characters and your insight is so appreciated. And to Amy who is always there to read, listen and highlight all the pages so that everyone can hear these beautiful words in audio. And to the Author Agency and KU Steamy Romance Reads, thank you for your help in promoting this book.

To Madi, thank you for taking our idea of a falling down brownstone and turning it into five absolutely adorable covers.

Last, but never least, to my family and friends who love me in spite of this world that has taken over my life. I love you all.

Now, who is ready to fully immerse themselves in our HOCKEY ERA and to spend more time with the Langfield brothers? Make sure to follow me on Instagram and join my reader group on Facebook.

https://www.facebook.com/groups/brittsboozybookbabes

And don't forget to subscribe to my newsletter!

Lots of love!

ALSO BY BRITTANEE NICOLE

Bristol Bay Rom Coms

She Likes Piña Coladas

Kisses Sweet Like Wine

Over the Rainbow

Bristol Bay Romance

Love and Tequila Make Her Crazy

A Very Merry Margarita Mix-Up

Boston Billionaires

Whiskey Lies

Loving Whiskey

Wishing for Champagne Kisses

Dirty Truths

Extra Dirty

Revenge Games

Revenge Era

Standalone Romantic Suspense

Deadly Gossip

Irish